Charles Martin Newell

Kalani of Oahu

An Historical Romance of Hawaii

Charles Martin Newell

Kalani of Oahu
An Historical Romance of Hawaii

ISBN/EAN: 9783337348540

Printed in Europe, USA, Canada, Australia, Japan

Cover: Foto ©Andreas Hilbeck / pixelio.de

More available books at **www.hansebooks.com**

KALANI OF OAHU.

AN

HISTORICAL ROMANCE OF HAWAII.

By C. M. NEWELL,

AUTHOR OF "PEHE NU-E, THE TIGER WHALE," ETC.

As ductile marble, poetized in dreams,
 Reflects its Alcazar in Guadalquiver;
And famed Alhambra in ardent sunlight gleams
 Along the yellow sheen of Darro river:

So drifts Oahu's Queen, in lithe canoe,
 Where coral fanes like marble cities rise;
· Where gnomes and mermaids sport in ocean's blue,
 And crimson madrepores entrance the human eyes.

BOSTON:
PUBLISHED BY THE AUTHOR.
1881.

Stereotyped at the Boston Stereotype Foundry,
No. 4 Pearl Street.

TO

HIS MAJESTY,

DAVID KALAKAUA,

KAMEHAMEHA, THE VII. KING OF THE "EIGHT ISLES,"

𝕿𝖍𝖎𝖘 𝕽𝖔𝖒𝖆𝖓𝖈𝖊

IS RESPECTFULLY INSCRIBED

BY THE AUTHOR.

PREFACE.

THE myths and religious superstitions of the indigenes of a barbaric nation present as enticing subjects for the romancist, and as interesting researches for the anthropologist, as their countless shells and exquisite madrepores may do to the zoötomyst.

Bereft of such knowledge, the prehistoric past of a people of Polynesia becomes a period of darkness to the physicist, unrayed by sufficient glimmer of light by which to judge of the remote anterior conditions of their religious or social history, not to mention the ever-disputed point of their anthropophagy.

While, aided by a well-digested system of their mythology, we may follow as easily down the circuitous stair of their dim, uncertain past, as the burrowing geologist delves into the nether world, and evolves his system from the dislocated ribs and broken spinalia of mother earth.

Lest we be accused of an anamorphosis in materializing some of the invisible gods of the Hawaiian mythology, permit a word in extenuation. Among an isolate people mythology always takes its rise

5

from visible events, or is born of the most impressive local aspects of nature. The earliest awakening of mythological religion in the savage mind is shown in the individual worship of some crude personal conception, like that of the Easter Islanders and other isolate amphiscii — each man constructing his own god — made simple or ingenious according to the degree of mental acumen of the worshipper.

In a more advanced stage idolaters will gather into communities, having agreed upon a generally accepted method, or object of worship, to the exclusion of their previous multiform inchoate inceptions; while, in a yet more enlightened condition, priests are suffered to not only select the deity for general worship, but also to become the sole intermediate between the chosen god and man, in all times of national exigency.

A yet still further advance had been made by the Hawaiians when rediscovered by Cook, for they had become the most perfect heathen theocracy known. Their religio-secular system of Tabu was without parallel in the history of nations. The Kapu Kane (human sacrifice) being the most fiendish rite of ecclesiastical cunning ever devised, by which to exalt the rights of the chiefs over the peasants, and by which to legalize public murder of one's enemies, and sanction wholesale thievery.

The quality of viability in Moa-alii, — the terrible sea-god, — ravenous to capsize canoes and devour their human contents, inspired no greater certitude

of his existence than did the invisibility of Pele —
the dread goddess of Kilauea — conduce to the
universal belief of her material existence, and of
her dual power of supreme dominion over volcanic action and the destinies of men.

Pele's frequently reputed interviews with the
priests and kings were unquestioned. And the
supposed something sometimes seen dancing on
the crest of a fiery eruption acquired credence,
somewhat authenticated by the numerous locks of
amber " Pele's hair " thrown broadcast over the
land after every eruption, and even falling upon
vessels hundreds of miles from shore, all of which
were deemed proofs positive of the material existence of the terrible Ignipotent of Mauna Loa.

The impunity with which Princess Kapiolani
subsequently descended into Kilauea crater, and
defied Pele in her own stronghold, without being
consumed on the instant, was an act of sublime
heroism few women are equal to. That she could
do it and live, was attributed to the visible superiority of her new God over Pele.

THE AUTHOR.

CONTENTS.

9

CHAPTER XIV.

CHAPTER XV.

CHAPTER XVI.

CHAPTER XVII.

CHAPTER XVIII.

CHAPTER XIX.

CHAPTER XX.

They steal like ghosts from the moonlit grove,
From the "Tabued Grove," where the goblins rove;
For the awful Pele, in pride and power,
From the "Kiowai" rose at that midnight hour!

From the fountain sprang, being wrought with ire;
Flamed her azure eyes and her locks of fire!
While she sat 'neath the spray full of wondrous grace,
With her goddess' form and her godlike face.

Then the fountain stilled its falling spray,
And the moonbeams chill o'er Nuuanu lay;
While the leaves in the grove seemed to hold their breath,
Hanging limp, as with fear, at the hush of death!

KALANI OF OAHU.

CHAPTER I.

OME with us down the dark ages. Back even into the benighted past, when the heroic kings of Hawaii and Oahu were contending for supremacy over the "Eight Isles." Fiercer warfare, and deeds of greater daring never cast their lurid halo over the Homeric age, than were witnessed in the sanguinary battles between the Giant Kamehameha on the one hand, and Kalanikupule — the Boy King of Oahu — on the other.

It was the land of Pele! Pele, the most sublime and terrible goddess in the mythology of nations. Though this fearful ignipotent comprised in herself all that was grand and adorable in her sex in placid moments, she was at times coquettish, and cruel, and unrelenting in her demands for human worship and human sacrifice.

Unique and lofty was the dwelling-place of this

13

Juno of the mountain land of Hawaii Nei, whether she sported in the *Hale-mau-mau* — the boiling lava-lake of Kilauea — or flung devastation over the land from high *Mokuaweoweo*, among the stars — her palace crater on snow-clad Mauna Loa's brow.

While she dwelt in Kilauea in times of peace, and there received the first-fruits of the land, and the first catch of the sea from the trembling hands of her worshippers, in the dread times of war her throne was Mauna Loa. There she presided over the heavens and the earth, dictating the music of the spheres and the motions of the stellar worlds; while she goaded her human subjects to war and rapine, and instigated the terrible Tabus, till there hung over the land a hideous pall of blackness, reeking with the gore of human sacrifice in the cloistered walls of every *heiau* among the Isles.

While dispensing the amenities of life to her human subjects from Kilauea, it was the frequent pastime of herself and her god-people to dance joyously in the fountain-jets of red lava that leaped up from the awful abyss, or swim playfully in the fiery surf of the volcanic sea, that rolled in great breakers, like an aqueous ocean, against the black walls of the seething crater, twelve hundred feet below.

Leaving the wide sea, and all therein, to the ruling of *Moa-alii* — the fierce god of the sea — Pele ruled in person over the Hawaiian world, and often condescended to dabble, with womanly instincts, in the destinies of heroic men. Being a goddess, she assumed the most essential preroga- tive of her sex, the inherent right to prompt an ever continued rivalry for her favors among the kings of the Isles.

To retain the affection of such a female deity, and to acquire the worldly benefits consequent thereon, a warrior must not fail either in battle- deeds with his fellows, or in humble obeisance to her godship; nor a priest lessen the enormity of his sacrifices in the *Wahi kapu* — the sacred places — of the land.

Though the divine Pele was captivated by the warlike deeds of Kamehameha — the hideous Her- cules of the Polynesian world — she was also daz- zled by the godlike spirit and manly beauty of the Boy King of Oahu. And as the last object of adoration ever takes precedence with her sex for the time, the ardent Pele breathed a fiery valor into the soul of Kalanikupule, and taught him the cunning use of arms, with something more than woman's fondness.

Thus fostered, the courage of the young king rose to the supremest height, acquiring at length a sense of invincibility from the frequent prompt- ings of his imperial patroness, until he sought for a personal encounter with his gigantic rival of Hawaii, in one of the most daring and dangerous midnight adventures recorded in the annals of war- fare.

But, alas! with the boy-like innocence due to

his age, in his own unbounded adoration for the beautiful goddess, Kalanikupule erred in supposing that a proud woman's love once won, is won forever. And as familiarity with even a goddess begets indifference of her dignity and her power — in a vaulting human soul — it came at length to pass, in after years, that when beset by numerous and insurmountable difficulties, the Boy King murmured aloud with profane tongue at the seeming neglect of Pele, and, in losing her favor, lost his life and his throne together.

This sad event took place on the eve of a great battle with his traitorous uncle, the warlike king of Kauai. The forces of Oahu had become discouraged and decimated by the long continued wars with Kamehameha on the one hand, while now the well-chosen army of Keao, of Kauai, was about to attack them on the other. The hour was indeed dark and boding for Oahu. Where was Pele with her friendly word of cheer, her usual assurance that all should yet be well? For the first time in his life she had failed to show a single torch-light from her craters, or a single quake of the earth-crust, or other vestige of remembrance of her young hero, in this his direst need.

Alas! alas! in a jealous mood the young king believed Pele had deserted him for his rival; when, goaded by his anguish, he suffered himself to cry aloud in fierce disdain of her all-powerful love, and even in bitter derision of the help she had bestowed upon him in the past wars.

Worst of all, this scene took place at one of the
most sacred of the *wahi kapus* on the Isle, where
the king and his young queen had retreated to
invoke the divine blessing of Pele. They had
been worshipping by moonlight, at the Goddess
Fountain, in the sacred orange grove of Nuuanu
Valley; when Kalanikupule's imprecations angered
the Goddess, and in a form of living fire she leaped
up from the fountain, and stood 'neath the crest
of the spray, as she retorted upon the dismayed
king as only an outraged woman can do when
scorned. The summer moon hid its face in darkness, and the stars grew tremulous with fear at her
anger. The orange leaves withered upon the
trees because of her fiery breath, and their yellow
globes jangled like alarm-bells because of the terrible passion of a goddess when defied by incon-
siderate man. The very waters of the sacred
fountain whereon she sat hissed and boiled, and
jet forth in fiery tongues like envenomed snakes,
so awful is the wrath of deity when justly enraged.

From that hour the fame of Kalanikupule was
dimmed forever. The mistake of that one moment
was irrevocable to the end of his being. Yet Pele
so far relented, even in the hour of her wrath, as
to leave her loved young hero a god-given spear,
which served to win him the victory over Keao in
the unequal contest of the coming morning.

But, as the proud and terrified young king made
no reply — no show of relenting — to either the
wrathful justification or persuasive admonitions of

2

the Goddess, the bright sword of unending victory, which Pele had forged with her own hand for her young hero, was suffered to dangle a moment before his eyes, glistening with its rare jewels and tawny gold, during her tirade, then dropped disdainfully back into the fountain, until the igneous earth far down beneath should reclaim its rare metals and precious stones again.

Thenceforth the rising destiny of Kalanikupule's rival was unending and unquestioned. Kamehameha's fame rose from that hour with unwavering splendor, until the name of the " Lonely One " of Hawaii filled the world with glory. Though the older and more sagacious king was uncomely in aspect and rough in demeanor, yet was he gifted with a subtle cunning and patient obeisance toward the sex, which stood him well instead of his young rival's physical beauty and knightly prowess. Thus the name of Kamehameha Nui (the Great) has been transmitted to posterity, not wholly for his warlike deeds, but rather because of his greater duplicity to a fickle deity, else were some descendant of the noble Kalanikupule now ruling his fair kingdom of Oahu to-day.

Yet prior to this ultimate event we have described, both of these warlike kings were greatly beloved by Pele ; while such was her innate love of tumult, and the clash and din of war, that she not only instigated, but presided over their warlike contentions. Thus the battle-deeds of those barbaric monarchs necessarily became heroic types of daring and endurance; fit emblems of their day, to be commemorated, held in ever visible perpetuity by the grandest mountain peaks which monument their volcanic Isles.

Here the dread Pele still dwells, and still rocks the hollow earth with her terrific earthquakes as of old. Here she continues her volcanic warfare against heaven and .earth and sea, smiting the midnight sky until her lurid flames dart above the mountain snow-crests, like serpent tongues snapping at the stars.

Here, upon her palace home of Loa, are still witnessed the most gigantic eruptions of the globe, where red fountains of molten lava turn the blackest storm-night into day by their brilliance; rolling in roaring rivers of lava down the mountain side, to do battle with its greatest antipathy — the sea.

It is no fictitious legend, however wild and improbable it may seem to us now, that the fierce War-goddess of Mauna Loa did sometimes preside over the great battles of her favorite heroes in those long-gone days of which we write. We might rest the authenticity of this statement upon a single momentous event, where Pele, with her destructive might, utterly annihilated *every man* of one wing of an army, with her equally miraculous salvation of the opposing army, while fighting under the command of her favorite warrior, though they were in equally exposed situations with their foes.

Alas, that we are compelled to record it of one so mighty and so wise, it did seem at times as if the divine ignipotent of Hawaii suffered her dual affections for human heroes to fluctuate from one rival warrior to another — a womanly prerogative, however, still tenaciously claimed by her sex.

Just previous to the time of which we write — a few brief years before — Kalaniopuu, the aged king of Hawaii, died, leaving the half of his island kingdom to Kamehameha, the foremost warrior chief of the whole Polynesian world. The other half of his kingdom Kalaniopuu left to Kiwalao, his rightful son and heir. This act was consummated with the distinct understanding between the dying king and his powerful war-chief, that the latter should promise to maintain Kiwalao on his throne against the probable contentions likely to arise after the old monarch's death.

Keoua, the warlike brother óf the dying king, was known to be unscrupulous and ambitious, and it was feared by king and people that the young Kiwalao would have but small chance to maintain himself against his intriguing uncle.

Thus Kamehameha, from being only the leading war-chief of the reigning king of his time, stepped at one bound into possession of a kingdom. Kona, Kohala, and Hamakua was transmitted to him; while Kau, Puna, and Hilo fell to the lot of Kiwalao. But war soon sprung up in the fruitless endeavor to dispossess Kamehameha of his rightful crown. The first contention was brought on

by Keoua and Kiwalao over the still unburied
manes of Kalaniopuu. It ended in Kiwalao being
killed in battle, and Kamehameha getting possession of the whole island of Hawaii.

Keoua and his great chiefs retreated to the
mountain fastness, and kept up a desultory warfare
for years. Tiring at length of the desperate struggle against the invincible Kamehameha, Keoua
voluntarily surrendered with several of his great
chiefs, under promise of protection, when eight of
the noble warriors were assassinated while in the
act of landing from their canoe at Kawaihae, in the
very presence of Kamehameha. This act of despotism remains an indelible stain upon the character of the usually humane conqueror; and it acquires additional interest from Keoua being *one* of
the many reputed fathers of Kamehameha, though
Kahekili, king of the Leeward Isles, and father of
Kalanikupule, sustained the best claim in this
knotty question of promiscuous paternity.

Thus the sudden rise of Kamehameha not only
created great jealousy among the ambitious war-
chiefs of his own island, but also drew down upon
him the bitter enmity of the old line of kings of
the Leeward Islands, ending with begetting the
long and bloody wars by which he finally came
into possession of all the " Eight Isles," whose
present appellation is: *Hawaii Nei pae aina* —
" these Hawaiian Islands."

'Tis midnight on the stormy sea!
   The night is dark as hour of doom;
The scud flies swiftly down the lee,
   Like demons of the murky gloom.

The gale is fierce with shriek and wail!
   The billows run to mountains high;
Before the wind *one* scudding sail
   Tears through the storm it dares defy.

Hark! to the crash, as thunders roll
   With every peal of lightning's glare,
Till awed becomes the human soul
   With all the terrors gathered there.

   .   .   .   .   .

Now rends in twain the inky sky!
   With lava-floods from Kilanea;
Its glare would blind an eagle's eye,
   Such fierce and furious lava-fire.

Like some tremendous Pharos-light,
   God-sent, to guide the bark aright;
For on that ship the boatswain came
   Who prompts Hawaii to warlike fame.

CHAPTER II.

T was a weird, wild storm upon the opening night of our story. As furious a tempest as ever howled over the Pacific was beating upon the Hawaiian shore. A dark and starless midnight, black as ever confronted a mariner, with pelting rain and shrieking wind — such a night of terror as causes even the bravest to cower, and turn with trembling supplication to the Father above. Heaven and earth and the mad sea were rocking with earthquakes, and made deafening with loud thunder-peals following fast upon the red lightning's glare.

The low-lying scuds were flying swiftly over ship and sea, as is their wont in such equinoctial storms in the tropic. The great seas rose to enormous heights, as if intent to out-bellow the thunder, and out-rumble the earthquakes. These stupendous waves are easily accounted for by the ready facility with which storm-billows build upon trade-wind seas when driven into such frenzy by a hurricane.

Though at times the deluge from the clouds ceased for a moment, it was followed by a saline one as drenching from the torn-up ocean below.

23

So terrific was the force of the wind that the ghastly, seething foam-crests were torn from the mountain billow-tops, and hurled along the writhing face of the black waters with the force and fury of hailstones.

None but the smallest and the strongest of the storm-sails could be set upon the one solitary vessel now scudding before the gale. She was the only foreign ship at that time in all the Hawaiian seas. God help her! and preserve her crew, for she bears Keone Ana, the noble sailor, yet destined to become the noblest chief in all the land.*

That it was a night of the sublimest horror was evidenced by a glance on board the Elenora, for every soul of her terror-stricken crew had lashed themselves about the fife-rail of the mizzen-mast, or beneath the precarious shelter of the wheel-house, clinging with tired arms, endeavoring to resist the pitch and roll of the vessel; displaying pallid faces and anxious eyes during the yellow gleam of the lightning, as they clung awaiting the uncertain doom impending over them all.

Two strong seamen were struggling with the helm, active and alert to forecast for the ever-veering ship as she hung poised on the tops of the careering seas. With bare and brawny arms, and

---

* John Young, an English boatswain, came to Hawaii in the Elenora, and was restrained from going back to his ship by Kamehameha upon the occasion of Kameeimoku's capturing the "Fair American." Young was made a high chief, and, more than any other white man, was conducive to the final conquest of the islands.

swollen biceps, tough as springy steel, they spun the wheel starboard and port with a terrible energy, born of the tempest and engendered by the perils. Presiding over the helm stood brave John Young the boatswain, the future chief and counsellor of the great conqueror of Hawaii. Prudent and brave, he too was lashed by the topsail-halyards to the weather rail, while he conned the helm under the directions of the captain, who was perched on the hurricane-house above, where he had lashed himself to the mizzen-mast — the only man on board fully exposed to the storm.

The Elenora was running to make the Upolu Passage, the strait separating Hawaii from Maui, and to deviate a single point from the true course would be to run upon the one rock-bound shore or the other. It was truly a perilous position, even without the added horror of the gale. But it was a situation where the boldest strokes of the best mariners oftenest prove the safest in the end.

The mere matter of a clear gale in a landless sea is but pleasant pastime for competent seamen. But a foul gale, trending upon a lee shore, with impenetrable darkness and blinding lightning to contend with, made a situation sufficient to terrify the boldest. It places the mariner face to face with eternity, until the voice of God possesses his soul as in the final hour of dissolution.

Such scenes of terror have often blanched the heads of young seamen prematurely gray. Rarely was ever such a pandemonium of ocean horrors gathered about one devoted ship, as here. Hark! to the fierce crescendo of the storm, shrieking among the wet ropes and twanging shrouds like the utmost voices of a thousand winged demons, enhungered for their prey.

In the brief interval between the maddening fury of the strongest squalls, there wails a hoarse bassoon among the great shrouds and tarry stays, verily like the multitudinous voices uprising from ocean graves. These intervals are soon followed by the oncoming blast, tearing the very sea to tatters; when every strand of rigging becomes strained to its utmost tension, creating a dissonance too frightful to be told. It is then that each rope and shroud and stay — each, after the measure of its size — shrieks with demoniac yells sufficient to terrify the boldest on board.

At such moments, those least overcome by their fears, with one accord fling their gaze aloft with fierce intent to discover the infernal demons who have beset them. But useless all, for no mortal eye can pierce the gloom above the catharpins, or forward of the bowsprit. Beyond these limits of vision, all is inky blackness, riven only by the red lightning which leaves the black night blacker still from the blinding effect of its flash.

How roar the great curling crests of the toppling seas, rolling their spiteful waters over the laboring vessel, as if with intent to sink her where many a one has gone down before! — now flooding over the one rail, and now the other, until the tossing, tumbling ship is often buried waist-deep under the seas.

Though fleeing at her utmost speed before the mad wind and mountain-seas, yet occasionally some great oncoming wave overtakes her, and poops the flying ship as it boards by the stern, deluging all on board as it rolls forward and retreats by the bows.

Though this action of the mammoth waves upon the stern accelerates the speed of the ship to the utmost for the moment, it also veers her to the one side or the other, when down crashes the next following wave over bulwarks and rail, rolling like a mountain avalanche across the careening deck, to the imminent peril of whomsoever is in its path.

Frequently, when the belabored ship goes plunging down the steep incline of the larger seas, because of the black darkness a wild illusion seizes upon the minds of all that the vessel is rushing headlong to certain destruction, never again to rise up to the level of day.

But luckily in such peril, safety lies in the insufficient speed of the ship, being rescued from her downward plunge by the onrolling billow which passes her, until she is next seen climbing the steep hillside on the rear aspect of the passing wave, with bowsprit pointing to the sky, like an appealing hand outstretched to heaven.

The captain of the luckless ship had lashed himself to the mast where it protrudes above the hur-

ricane-house, conning the ship from his elevated
position with his utmost vigilance. While all others were permitted to seek shelter beneath the hurricane-house, the brave master took his stand in
wild solitude above the deck, where he was pelted
by the driving spray torn from the sea-tops, and
exposed to the rake of the cutting wind and the
frequent drenching rains.

But it was an hour when the master-mind can
depend upon no other lookout but his own. For
when the land *is* discovered — if discovered it can
be in such a night — his action must be immediate, or of no avail to save his ship and crew from
instant destruction.

With a courage above all praise, the dauntless
Captain had thus chosen his station well ; for it is
a knowledge intuitively imparted to most men,
that moments of great peril are best endured
when sustained in companionship with others of
our kind. Yet there he sways to the wind and
the sea, girt by the wet lashings that secure him
to the creaking mast. There he strains his anxious eyes, peering into the black gloom ahead,
endeavoring to discover the dread land, which,
though it were but a ship's length before them,
could only be distinguished during the brief interval of the lightning's glare.

Could the Elenora once pass the Upolu Strait,
she might ride out the gale in safety under the
mountain land of Hawaii, near the Kohala shore.
But it is a question with all minds on board whether

the ship is running toward the Straits or on to the
land, it is so easy for a vessel to deviate from a
true course, owing to the unknown currents encountered in strange seas.

If the swift-rushing ship was not heading for the
opening between the islands, there was but one
other dreadful alternative awaiting her, for they
were dashing with mad speed upon the one rock-
bound coast or the other. This is a peril such
as only the hardiest mariners can contemplate
with equanimity, för wreck and a terrible death
lie open-armed to receive them. Who can depict
the long-sustained anguish of such a moment, with
such a harrowing fear added to the heaped-up horrors of the storm ?

Presently, as if the previous terrors of the storm-
lashed seamen were not already complete in abundance and kind, there came the awful shock and
crash of another earthquake, more terrible than
any before, coming as if the earth had rent asunder
directly beneath their feet. Lo ! how the ship rocks
and rolls, and rears as with sentient madness, quivering from truck to keel in abject fear, as if shaken
in the monstrous grasp of a hadean giant.

How quail the terrified seamen, deeming the last
moment of earth-life has come ! The rain ceases
its down-pouring upon the instant, and there comes
a moment's lull in the mad howling of the gale, as
if the concussion of the earthquake — rolling seaward from the land — had met and breasted back
the wild storm with unrelenting hand.

Again and again come the renewed shocks of a
rending earth and an oscillating sea, — vibrating in
mammoth waves through atmosphere and ocean,
quelling the rush of wind and the mad roll of waters
until the black night seems convulsed as if in labor
with some Plutonian god.

At length the wild tumult ceased. The hush of
impending death broods over the stilled winds and
the crushed waves. The anguished throes of par-
turient Nature, seem to have brought forth, partus
with some voiceless demon, which fails to utter the
expectant cry of the new-born. "What is in store
for us now?" is the tremulous heart-cry of every
soul on board.

One moment only, — one long, lingering moment
of windless air and waveless sea they were held in
suspense, — then the mad winds piped on again,
increasing to the wildest frenzy the ship had yet
experienced.

Suddenly there was a dim and ghastly illumina-
tion discovered through the inky blackness directly ahead, of the ship, — faint and portentous as
some midnight paraselene when presaging a storm.
Growing at length to a ponderous glare, it was
soon seen flickering and beating against the Egyp-
tian darkness, growing brighter and brighter, until
it increased to a gigantic pillar of fire, leaping six
hundred yards up through the unearthly gloom of
the midnight sky.

It was as though the whole western heavens were
rent in twain to recall a benighted world, opening

a wild chaos of seething fire whose furious heat
eats up the darkness, as a tropic sun dispels the
dawn. Simultaneous with this appalling sight
there comes the frequent shiver of a perpendicular * earthquake, vibrating upward through sea
and ship with a motion that stuns the human
mind, serving to further appall the frenzied seamen with an added conviction that their hour of
dissolution had come.

Steadily the red rift in the western sky seems to
broaden and brighten and lengthen; advancing
upon the ship until neither its distance nor the
force of the strong wind prevents a glow of its
incandescence reaching the faces of the seamen as
they stand aghast awaiting the consummation of
their doom.

Awful beyond conception is the lurid glare which
cleaves the heavens from sea to sky, sundering the
black night with a fiery radiance red as human
gore; rimming the jagged blackness above and
around it with serpent-tongues of flame that flash
into the inky gloom like the gleam of ponderous
scimiters in the hands of Pele's avenging gods.

Though Hades might have been deemed but a
priestly fiction prior to this hour, by which to af-
fright the sinful world and sequester the elect,
doubt reigned no more among the scoffing seamen

---

* As is well known, the vibrate of most earthquakes is a
horizontal motion following the convexity of the earth-crust.
But the writer has encountered some of these perpendicular
motions which will lift a ship half out of water.

of the Elenora. Their superstitions had become
their masters, until they stood awed and horrified,
involuntarily muttering unseemly oaths, or murmuring long-forgotten prayers — each according to
the texture of his soul. Hope fled alike from the
sinful and the sinless, though it is true that the
"pure in heart see God" through the utmost danger and the profoundest gloom. Yet in this hour
strong men stood aghast and trembling, and the
bravest and the best were so appalled by this new-
found fear, that they would gladly have fled back
like frightened birds into the Plutonian darkness
and the frightful storm they had just encountered.

To the sin-loving and the scoffing — now so over-
mastered by their fears — the fiery chaos before
them seemed the long-expected pandemonium of
their dreams. For it is a law of our natures that
evil-doers live in continuous expectation of a coming retribution, and end with becoming their own
severest judges when impressed with the conviction that their final hour has come.

Hideous indeed must have been the sight and
sound and sense of horror pervading air and ocean,
that the black demons of the storm should again
slink back crushed and cowed; hushing their unearthly noises as if they, too, would hide in fear
among the caverns of the deep.

Even the gigantic waves now beheld their master,
and stilled their loud-mouthed bellowing, slinking
down like creeping curs beneath the impending lash,
unpluming their proud crests, and disrobing their

wild fury, for there had come forth upon the sea a greater tyrant than the storm which had aroused them.

To those of less mental disquietude than their fellows, those having courage sufficient to search boldly into the hadean sea of fire before them, there was occasionally visible a grand and graceful creature in woman's form, dancing exultingly on the crest of the fiery ebullition, or flitting daintily across from one black border of the lurid scene to the other. This was Pele, the sublime goddess of volcanoes, ever presiding over the eruptions of Loa, and the earthquakes of the nether world; and who was now exulting at her victory over the rude storm-king who had assailed her kingdom at the instigation of Moa-alii, the dread god of the sea.

Nearer down to the water was visible another sight, terrible enough to appall even the dauntless. A huge and hideous figure, now seen boldly outlined in black shadow on the blood-red sea, as it stalked in silhouette across the lurid glare, and now beheld lurking like an ambushed foe behind the red-rimmed blackness of the borders of the fiery caldron. This colossal figure was Kaonohiokala, the " Eye of the Sun," or the Angel of Death, whose mission is to conduct the " spirits of men to Po," there to be eaten by the gods, — a huge black-winged monster, with large glowering eyes hideous enough to curdle the life-blood of a nation.

Kaonohiokala was indeed an awful personation

3

of Death. His long black wings were ever indelibly stained with human gore, while the cruel glowering of his insensate eyes was such as only human victims can appease. Doggedly and sullenly the Death Angel flapped his slow, deliberate wings, as he guarded the doomed track of the approaching ship to the wreck that awaited her, ambushed to intercept all who would pass without the countersign from Pele. Though already gorged with human prey, as seen by the laggard motion of his wings, he was alert for more, like the black buzzards on the Death Towers of Bombay, which ever stand watchful to devour the Parsee dead.

CHAPTER III.

How weird and wild the crater gleams!
'Tis angry Pele's blood-red streams;
Her molten rivers spurn the sea
With shocks of earthquake revelry.

They have passed through the fire and the tempest;
Were they demons of horror and hate? —
Rather warriors who've scented the battle,
Casting all on the promptings of Fate.

HEN first the stupendous eruption was discovered bursting from Mauna Loa, it seemed but a lingering flash of far-off light from the sky, dim and indistinct as a transient gleam of sunlight through a storm-cloud. But light travels quickly, and soon the fierce glow of the great eruption grew upon the beholders, illuminating the ship and the furious sea about her, as with the glare of noonday. Seen amid such a night of storm, the colossal eruption was an added horror to the people of the Elenora, even more demoniacal than all the terrors they had endured before.

In the brief interval, while the far-away light was approaching the vessel, several eyes on board discovered the godlike figure of Pele dancing on the very top of the volcanic light. Some thought it

35

was but the wild delusion of their own minds, knowing nothing of Pele and her ignipotent rule of the land. Some conceived what they saw was but a fanciful storm-cloud, assuming the shape of a woman, flitting vision-like upon the red-lava fountain seen in the sky.

Before their doubts could be solved to the satisfaction of all, — if doubts there were, — the attention of all was called to other living, moving figures seen upon the upheaving water, between the scudding ship and the volcanic light beyond.

Looking closely down the lee, numerous objects could be distinguished in blackest silhouette, dancing like madmen on the curling crests of the seas. One moment they were seen with vivid distinctness, and then were ingulfed in the cavernous troughs of the great billows.

When first seen against the lurid background of the rifted sky, belief obtained among all that they were veritable demons of the storm, battling with invisible weapons against the furies of the night. But when the full glare of the vast eruption had penetrated down to the Elenora, and out into the sea beyond, then all were made aware of the true nature of the objects before them. A large double war-canoe, impelled by sixty naked savages, was brought fully into view, paddling with might and main directly across the track of the approaching vessel.

It was the forward-striking motion of paddling that created the delusive appearance of the savages battling with some foe before them. It seemed at first impossible that boat or men could live for a moment in such a sea-way, and such a gale.

But a double-canoe — well separated by strong outriggers — cannot be capsized when fairly managed. The two canoes before them seemed to be decked over with some water-proof material, leaving only the necessary apertures occupied by the sixty nude warriors in possession. Perhaps the amphibious propensities of the Hawaiians deserve to be considered, lest we transcend the credulity in depicting such daring; yet the courage required to tempt death in such a night of elemental war seems almost superhuman. The adventure calling forth these swarthy warriors must be of momentous importance, to induce even such heroes to seek battle with a human enemy amid such accessory dangers.

None on board the Elenora had deemed it possible for aught but a scudding ship to live in such an infernity of wind and waves. As the fountain of molten lava rose higher and higher, and grew larger and larger, invading the murky gloom with its noonday glare, the red warriors discovered the ship near aboard in the offing. With a shout of " *Moku! Moku! — Haole moku!* " (the white man's ship,) sixty suspended paddle-blades pointed to the Elenora, and the great canoe was left to toss and roll on the crested seas as the astonished savages gazed upon the approaching vessel.

Instantly a youthful warrior — evidently the
guiding spirit among them — sprang up from the
stern of the windward canoe, and waved his paddle with a furious gesture of friendly warning.
His signal was imperative for the vessel to luff
away from some yet undiscovered danger. And
none too soon had come the providential light and
the friendly warning. For while yet in the very
act of bracing up the yards, preparatory to luffing
to the wind, there appeared the black, beetling
crags of Hilo, lying directly across their course.

The ship was running to certain destruction,
instead of into the Upolu passage as they had
thought. Ten minutes more running in the darkness would have discovered a wrecked ship, shattered into fragments by the momentum of her own
speed, and her crew of twenty hardy mariners
strewn in mangled corpses along the rock-bound
shore.

Loving Father! how tender is thy care, how
paternal thy providence when witnessed in such
hours of peril upon the sea! Who can portray the
tender light of God-given thanks instilled into the
hearts of those awe-stricken seamen at such a time?
The sudden rapture of that storm-pelted Captain—
lashed to his mast — as with choked voice he hoarse-
ly bellowed his orders through his trumpet to the
mate :

"Brace up! Down helm! Come by the wind
with port tacks! Work with a will, or we are
lost — lost!"

To the eyes of hovering angels in that moment
of peril — to whom darkness is as light — that
noble captain was visible, clasping his horny hands
in fervent, outspoken prayer; when words become
as living things in the mouths of men, and lives
are as tinder just snatched from devouring flames.

What to him were the cutting talons of the
shrieking wind, as the ship luffed to meet its furious onslaught! What to him the cold dash of in-
gulfing waters, as finding something obstructing
their path the great waves rolled madly over the
wallowing vessel, as if still impelled to hurl her
upon the adjacent shore!

Though they were lost in the next moment it
could not detract from the convictions of that
brave man that he had been a subject of remembrance by his God; that he was still an object of
the special care of the Father.

After thankfulness to God for their own miraculous escape from wreck, came that other momentous question, of interest to all: Who was that
kingly youth, and his rude warriors, that they
dared the peril of such a night? Heedless of his
own danger, how intent had seemed the beardless
warrior to warn the vessel away from the adjacent
rocks!

The enlightened world said they were cannibals,
and had just devoured Captain Cook, who, from
being worshipped as god Lono, and fed gratui-
tously with shiploads of provision, suffered himself
to dismantle the sacred temple of Lono for fire-

wood. And because of the theft of a paltry boat,
with the act of a passionate despot he seized upon
the aged Kalaniopuu and Kiwalao, his son, and
endeavored to transport them to his ship, to be
held as hostages. While enforcing this brutal act
he lost his life, and for a century the blame has
been put where it does not belong. And yet these
savages in the canoe were endowed with sufficient
nobility to forget their own danger and warn another *haole moku* — another Lono and his ship —
away from a greater peril than their own.

As the red light of the volcano gleamed upon
the waving paddle of the manly chief, himself and
his grim giants were so rimmed about by the lurid
glare that they might well have been taken for
ocean demons struggling up from the subterranean
world. Yet they were human heroes instead, intent upon surprising a gigantic foe, though camped
among his hundred chosen warriors, and otherwise
guarded by the best of all security, a furious equinoctial storm.

The captain and boatswain of the Elenora had
been in these seas before, and were not long in
recognizing the young warrior as Kalanikupule,
the Boy King of Oahu. From a child the young
Prince had been nurtured in arms, and was permitted to accompany the great Thunderer, his sire,
to every battle on their Isles. Now Kahekili was
dead, enshrouded in "black tapa," and the daring
young king was seeking to beard the Lonely One,
the gigantic Kamehameha, in his remotest lair,

attacking in an hour when an assailant could be least expected.

The swift canoes were dashing along under the black crags of Wailuku, near the entrance of Hilo Bay, the fairest stronghold of Kamehameha. Though the grim chiefs of Oahu were all giants in stature and skilful in warfare, what could a double-canoe and sixty nude warriors expect to accomplish against the fiercest fighters of the Hawaiian king? for Kamehameha was conceded to be the most powerful and savage and sagacious warrior among all the Pacific Isles. What indeed! but to show to the hated bastard of Kahekili — his own father — that Kalanikupule was as fearless in war and as enterprising in seeking battle as himself!

It was the immature conception of a young Hannibal, thus bearding his powerful enemy upon his own soil. True, he came not with strength sufficient to fight a decisive battle, but with daring sufficient to strike terror into the soul of his foe; confronting him with a hardihood of courage and a spirit of adventure rarely equalled and never surpassed in the annals of warfare.

He sleeps! the fierce Kamcha' sleeps,
  In palace hut on Coco Isle;
While watch and ward the tempest keeps,
  And not a chief stands guard the while.
There are who never come too near
This Giant King, but come with fear;
Who think him born of Pele's kin,
And tremble when his presence in.

But one now comes from Molokai
Who swears to conquer him — or die.
A monarch's look sits on his brow;
A warrior's deeds his name endow.
A heart, that never knew to quail
  Within the ken of mortal view;
A soul, that never knew to fail
  In any task it bent to do.

CHAPTER IV.

HOUGH the effect of these monstrous eruptions of Mauna Loa, and the frequent earthquake shocks that ever accompany them, is sufficient to crush the strongest gale in an instant, it can rarely continue its subjugation only for a brief time. And while the wind-moter that has served to build up the great waves is hushed into silence and driven seaward for a time, still the huge billows are left turbulent and tossing, though deprived of their crests, rolling with more chaotic confusion than ever.

Thus the favoring influence that kept the ill-fated Elenora from being dashed upon the wave-beaten coast alee, was the occasional earthquake oscillations still sweeping out from the land, acting like a strong undertow upon the vessel's keel. Though the teeth of the gale were drawn, the wind yet blew too hard in the intervals of terraqueous vibrations transmitted from the crater, for the ship to show much canvas in beating. So the task of clawing off from the foam-lashed shore which threatened them, as yet imparted but little hope to cheer them.

The tall cliffs yet visible under the lee of the ship were the rocky crags of Hilo, between the Wailuku River and the "Swimming Gulch;" the latter, a long, deep ravine, down which the crimson lava-flood was pouring furiously, leaping like a mad river of blood into the sea, till the white, foaming breakers hissed and boiled with increased fury by the contact.

The Waipunalei, or the Swimming Gulch, is now the pilot's landmark for inward-bound vessels; steering for it, they are enabled to avoid the dangerous reef-point making out from Leleiwi, which comprises the sole projecting arm of Hilo Bay. With this knowledge the Elenora might have kept away to the south and soon found anchorage under Coco Isle, though wholly exposed to the rake of the wind.

The war-canoes had disappeared the moment they passed the lurid track of volcanic light. When last seen entering the black night beyond, they were plying their sixty paddles with a savage energy promising soon to land them under the sheltering lee of Coco Isle. There, Kamehameha slept in his armed camp, which was felt to be more secure than the peopled shore of the adjacent bay; for the thrifty Hilo district had but recently been conquered from a rebel foe.

In the midst of a semicircle of neat grass houses built along the windward shore of the palm-clad isle, where dwelt the great king and his chosen body-guard of three hundred savage warriors,

there nestled a charming cluster of more preten-
tious habitations, where towered the tallest palms
of the cocoa-nut grove along the inland shore of
the little isle. This was the palace-home of the
wise and comely Kaahumanu, the "love-queen"
of Kamehameha.

With the queen dwelt Pelelulu, a natural daughter of the Hawaiian king, whose half-divine mother
justly claimed family connection with the goddess
Pele, and still abode in her mountain-home among
the volcanic fires at Kilauea, the palace-home of the
family of gods. The intelligence and beauty of
Pelelulu were the pride and wonder of the Hawaiian world. The heart of the Boy King had
long been enamored with her fame. The task he
had now set himself to do, was to slaughter her
savage sire and his chosen warriors, and make the
lovely princess his slave. To his great war-chiefs,
Kalanikupule had placed the desire for battle
before the romance of his love; but deep in his inmost heart the gallant young king had given precedence to a wish to possess Pelelulu, above all the
other motives of his life. In this innate preference
for beauty before glory, we recognize the ever-
present tenderness of a valiant heart; a heart that
does its best battling to win the high guerdon of a
noble woman's love.

The swift war-canoes, keeping to the shelter of
the windward reef, dashed through the tumultuous
waters of the Wailuku, where the fierce mountain
river forced its way through the long line of break-

ers into the bay. Stealing onward with hushed
voices and impetuous paddles, the ghostly war-
party darted like a black shadow along the very
edge of the reef, where the last of the huge rollers
fell in great sheets of milky foam, whose dazzling
phosphorescence served to light their murderous
way. Softly as a cat's-paw on a summer sea they
glide along the romantic shore of Coco Isle, still
unheard and unseen by their slumbering foe.

Beneath the sheltering palm grove, where the
long fronds droop tenderly over the palace-home
of the Hawaiian queen, the warriors of Oahu
moored their canoes and adjusted their arms for
the deadly combat to follow. The darkness of
the night grew yet more impenetrable, because of
the gathering of hadean spirits who ever lurk adjacent to murderous deeds. The wail of the wind
through the swaying trees became plaintive as a
dirge above new-made graves. The great breakers
that floundered with voices of thunder on the far
windward shore, stilled themselves into an aqueous
lullaby, so harmonized were the elements in this
last dread soliloquy of death.

Sixty such grim warriors as these of Oahu, led
on by their impetuous young king, who had grown
up by their side in the din of battle, — lithe as a
panther and fearless as an eagle, — was sufficient
force to crash like an avalanche through any body
of assailants who might bar their path.

Men who had come a hundred miles through a
terrible tempest to seek foemen worthy of their

steel were full of a purpose as irresistible as a thunderbolt; and terrible indeed must be the shock of battle if they meet their equals in the coming assault.

Of the three hundred chosen warriors slumbering in the camp of the Lonely One — their king — there were some of the bravest fighters and strongest men the world has known. Yet among them all, gigantic as they were, the hugest and the strongest was their ferocious leader, Kamehameha the Great.

But sixty men, awake and eager for battle, may prove more than a match for many times their number, when the foe is being roused suddenly from sleep. Sixty ferocious men, glowing with warlike thoughts that burn like living fire, their strong arms made supple by the labors of the night, were not to be resisted by any number; for they came to win, or to die! And when does Victory not abide with noble souls, savage or civilized, whose only alternative, self-allotted, is victory or death in a battle planned with no provision for retreating.

Moored beneath the shelter of the little isle lay twenty huge war-canoes of Hawaii, which must first be demolished, scuttled, and sunk in the five-fathom harbor to prevent immediate use being made of them in pursuit after the battle. Though Kalanikupule and his chiefs well knew that a sunken canoe, were it drowned in a hundred feet of water, was no difficult task for their country divers, men, women, or children, to unlade of their lava blocks or coral stone, and bring to the surface again. So this precautionary task was not deemed permanent, only sufficient for the time, to prevent pursuit during their home retreat.

The enemy's canoes once disposed of, and their own swift ones headed to the north, with paddles in place ready for the homeward flight of all who survived the battle, one of the least mighty of their number was left in charge. Then the Boy King called his savage chieftains about him, giving his last orders before they took their positions for assault.

One trembles when contemplating the tempestuous passions of sixty such stark, mad men as were gathered about their magnetic young leader in the darkness of that Plutonian grove. Fire is not hotter than the roused heart-blood that coursed through their veins. The ferocity glowering in their dark eyes borrowed something from the electric flashes preceding the thunder-peals above their heads as well as from an unsatiated thirst for battle. Though their great muscles could be worked with the elasticity of steel in the hour of action, they were now tightened into a tension rigid as iron until the vise-like hand-grip upon their spears and dagger-hilts were but a cruel waste of muscularity. As they listened to Kalanikupule's whispered orders and inspiriting words, every lip was muttering imprecations, and every finger becoming a talon intelligent with murderous thoughts to grapple the throat of the sleeping foe.

There is a sublime grandeur in the inhuman passions of a giant savage, standing thus statuesque, with foot advanced to leap upon his foe. But alas!

it is the one link of nature forcibly reminding us
of our kinship with the beast of the forest.   What
a dark gulf yawns between such condition of savage madness, whether in Christian gentleman or
cannibal native, and the Christ-like spirit of prayer
we commend to whom we love !

As the scene of coming combat was made so
dark by the deep gloom of the cocoanut palms,
being unrelieved by either the volcanic eruption or
other light, it was thought best to assail the camp
only from the lee-side entrances, lest coming from
opposite directions they might mistake some of
their own party for the foe.

True, this plan of proceeding left open the
chance of some of the enemy escaping through
the inrolling surf on the weather shore.   But
against this argument it was agreed that the body-
guard of Kamehameha were of a kind not to seek
method of escape when fighting for the safety of
their king.

The queen's palace, the temple containing the
family idols, and the cook-house, were near the
beach where the war-party had landed.   As the
mission of the Oahuans was more for the purpose
of striking terror into the hearts of the Hawaiians
than for any great havoc they hoped to accomplish,
Kalanikupule was intent upon carrying off their
queen, as well as the semi-goddess, Pelelulu, as
visible trophies of his valor.

Thus, when every warrior was in position before
the houses of the Hawaiian chiefs, Kalanikupule
4

and Boki, his *puua hele* (bosom companion), stole into the palace and seized and bound Kaahumanu and Pelelulu, and bore them to the canoe. This was but the work of a moment, sleep being but a pleasant condition of anæsthesia to a healthy woman. And before the queenly lump of adiposis and the lithe and graceful Pelelulu were fairly awake, they were carried hastily to the canoe, and left in charge of the warrior boatman.

The abduction accomplished, the King and Boki sprang to their allotted task of grappling with the giant Kamehameha. Every door of the circle of huts facing the bay was already guarded by twos and threes, ready to assail the incumbents. The more imposing hut of the savage king was in the centre of the cluster; there stood Kalanikupule and Boki with drawn swords and native *paloa* (dagger) in hand, ready to give the signal of attack. Not a soul was visible in the intense darkness, yet in the black hair of every chief shone a starlike piece of phosphoric agaric — the *Agaricus muscarius* — gleaming above two savage eyes that flashed with electric warfire. This trick of the agaric, together with a band of white tapa about the right arm, were the distinguishing marks by which to know their party in the darkness of the night.

With the first gleam of lightning sufficient to bronze into tawny gold the group of dark warriors before the huts, the young King waved his glittering sword in the electric sheen as the signal to attack, and himself and companion sprang in upon the slumbering Giant with the demoniac yell of wounded tigers battling for their young.

Only the ghostly light of a few slumbering embers in the centre of the room showed where lay the sleeping monarch, nude-limbed, upon his low couch of soft mats and pulu pillows. Suspended from the neat basket-work walls of the royal hut hung spears and javelins, and *pahi* (sword) and *paloa* (dagger), made with unusual ponderance for a giant hand. But nearer within his reach lay upon the floor the great warrior's favorite *Laau palau* (war-club), the dread of every chief who had battled with the Hawaiian king.

It was not in the nature of Kalanikupule to stab a slumbering chief. Hence the yell of announcement, given with some sense of fairness; and an intuitive wish that his herculean foe should realize who were his daring antagonists ere death should sunder them forever.

With eyes of living fire, the aroused Giant glowered with the utmost rage upon his youthful foe as he fairly awoke to the sound of the hateful war-shouts of his assailants. His large white teeth ground together with savage vehemence, amidst the muttering of muffled imprecations at this sudden surprisal. The hideous scowl upon his fluted forehead was terrible to behold; while his hairy scalp contracted until the coarse black hair erected with ire, waving and curling in the flickering fire-light like tortured serpents.

Not a muscle of his great savage face gave evidence of aught akin to fear. Not even were the ferocious eyes permitted to protrude, or the ugly mouth to gape asunder as a token of dismay. Kalanikupule would have given his right hand to have seen but a single trace of cowardice pictured upon the coarse visage of his hated rival. But it was only by an instant's glance that either could measure the mental calibre of the other in that moment, as Kalanikupule sprang into the middle of the *hale* (house), seeking to find better scope for the swing of his descending steel.

Planting his left foot fairly upon the ponderous war-club of the Hawaiian king, Kalanikupule smote down a double-handed blow with his long *pahi*, cleaving deeply into the head of the giant as he rose quickly from his couch.

Kamehameha was a man of intensest action — active in thought and plan, and instant in execution. Though taken at the utmost disadvantage as he was, he displayed a sublime courage amounting to the most savage ferocity. Although receiving a terrible sword-cut while in the act of springing to his feet, the gashed and bleeding king groped blindly about in the doubtful light of the flickering embers for a spear, and did such gallant work as a wounded warrior may. But the odds and the weapons were against him, and he fell wounded and bleeding at the feet of the young King whom he had so often sought to dispossess of his throne.

Instantly a glorious white radiance, more intense

than sunlight, flashed through the gloom of the
dark hut as the great monarch fell with the crash
and momentum of a Koa-tree of the forest.

Though abashed and blinded by the sudden
effulgence, it was permitted to Kalanikupule and
his companion to behold the divine face of a beautiful goddess bending tenderly over the kingly
form, as if with intent to recall the dying monarch
back into life again.   This accomplished, she lifted
her gracious countenance with persuasive condescension to the face of the Boy King, with something very akin to a smile of satisfaction rippling
over her beauteous face.   Though she snatched the
fallen warrior from the death he was dying, she
suffered her blue eyes to soften into more than
human tenderness as she looked her approbation
of the heroic daring of Kalanikupule.

One instant the Goddess suffered the abashed
eyes of the young King to dwell upon her, un-
dimmed by the divine glory that usually veils godhead from human eyes; then with a small, imperious hand, whiter than the snow-sheen upon her
own mountain-tops, she motioned the young warrior to begone!

It was Pele! the beautiful ignipotent of Mauna
Loa, whose mandate is the law of the earth, and
whose divine bequest constitutes the utmost happiness when bequeathed to the sons of men.

To have tarried longer when thus dismissed, or
to endeavor to get possession of his fallen enemy,
would have called down upon his head a volcanic

flame that could burn him to a cinder. With fear, and trembling at the supernatural sight they had beheld, the King and Boki withdrew out into the black night again, where, as soon as they could recover from the effect of the divine radiance within, they sprang among their fellows to grapple with other foemen.

And it was well they came to the rescue as they did; for the first gleam of lightning showed need of help at more points than they could fill. The warriors of Oahu were being hard pressed by over-numbers, and were falling fast in the fray.

But the King and Boki each chose a weak point to retrieve, and let fall their fresh blows with telling effect, shouting, as an inspiriting cry to their followers, " *Ue Make Kamehameha! Ue Make Kapu Alii!* " — (Dead is Kamehameha! Dead the Sacred Chief!) This struck dismay to the Hawaiians, who instantly changed their battle-cry to wailing.

Then Oahu's braves struck home with renewed energy, until the remaining Hawaiians lost hope and fled into the adjacent breakers, and the royal camp of Coco Isle was won. Only wailing women and shrieking children were left to mourn over the heaps of dead and wounded braves.

It was now time for the decimated warriors of Oahu to gather up their dead and wounded, and fly. For in spite of the roar of the surf and the lingering tumult of the gale, the loud shouts of the embattled hosts, and the shrieking wail of the

women, had roused the people across the bay on
the Hilo shore. Lights were now seen along the
whole crescent of the bay, from the roaring waters
of the Wailuku to the peaceful Waimea; and during the brighter flashes of lightning, or the dying
gleams from Kilauea, numerous canoes could be
seen embarking fresh warriors for the defence of
their king.

Applying the torch to the palace and its out-
houses, and to every warrior's hut forming the
camp, Kalanikupule manned his canoes with the remaining moiety of his chiefs, and departed by the
light of the burning houses, the volcanic eruption
having nearly subsided.

Hugging the inner line of breakers, where the
tremendous surf fell and floundered on the inner
border of the reef, the thirty unwounded braves of
Oahu plied their paddles lustily for the mouth of
the harbor. The great surf, curling its ghastly
crest thirty feet above their heads, showed with
terrible magnificence in the gleam of light from
the house-fires of their foe, serving also to shelter
the retreating Oahuans from observation, while in
no way endangering their safety because of proximity; for while the breakers rose in awful grandeur high above them, they broke and fell so abruptly on the inner verge of the great coral reef
that the fleet canoes could make use of the smooth
and snowy sheen of foam directly under their lee.

Ere the weary warriors had fled an hour upon

the homeward track, the wild gale of the night
died fairly away, and the grateful land-wind began
to assume its aromatic sway. Creeping slowly
down from Mauna Kea, through wide fields of
fern-trees and mountain flowers, the delicious land-
wind brested back the lingering gale until it fairly
withdrew seaward to its ocean caves.

As the canoes passed the "Swimming Gulch,"
the wild waves along the shore were seen steaming
from their hot tussle with the fiery lava. Though
the eruption had ceased far back in the mountain,
there was yet left miles on miles of flowing lava to
find its way down the mountain to the sea. The
color of the fiery river in the gulch was already
cooling to a cherry-red, and would soon grow slug-
gish and interrupted in its flow, and cool to a
shining black.

It was by this intrusion of the flowing lava
upon the sea that the long East Point was made,
now extending fifteen miles out into the deep
ocean. Thus the volume of some of these lava-
rivers from Mauna Loa exceed the utmost conception of one who has not looked upon them for
himself. Though the eruption we have described
flowed but a day, it is more often the case that
they flow for weeks and months, shining by night
with a radiance that can be distinguished a hundred miles away.

As soon as the land-wind had gained sufficient
strength, so that the constant tossing on the fitful

seas would not spill the wind from their sail and make it useless, the great mast was stepped in its place, and the tri-cornered sail was set, causing the swift canoes to take wing with the speed of homeward birds.

On Kea's crest the sun arose,
And crowned with gold his wintry snows;
As were a yellow mamo cast,
To hide the throne of Midnight past.

How long the Princess watched for day;
To learn her fate — be what it may.
Unclothed her virgin budding breast
    In unaffected nakedness;
Yet round her nude young form she prest
    Her raven locks — her only dress;
Disclosed her bosom's rise and fall,
While his dark eyes held her in thrall.

Not long she mourned her Hilo home,
For ere they'd reached Upolu's foam,
She learned she was Kalani's prize,
    The noblest king 'mong all the Isles;
Who turned on her his kingly eyes,
    And taught his heart to love her smiles.
But touch the master-chord of love,
How glad most maids from home will rove.

CHAPTER V.

WHEN day dawned upon the weary warriors they were already forty miles away from the scene of their fight in Hilo Bay. Then Kea put on his crimson crown to greet them, gilding his wintry snows with bewitching ruby in kingly commendation of their deeds. Fairer morning never dawned upon the volcanic snow-peaks of Hawaii.

In this kindly greeting of nature Kalanikupule recognized the fostering care of Pele, who had promised him success before the outset of his undertaking. She had indeed shown him greater recognition than was ever proffered to earthly king before. It was thus left to the Boy King of Oahu — above all men born of woman — to rightly interpret the smiling symbol of three gigantic mountains crowning their heads with gold and ruby to greet him on the morning of his victory.

Kea and Loa and Hualalai, rose-tinted all by the refracted rays of the yet unrisen sun, were greeting the youthful victor and his scarred and bleeding braves as never was victorious king greeted before.

Grand and beautiful rose the tripple mountains in solitary grandeur into the morning sky, lifting

so clear cut against the blue ether that they seemed
within the easy reach of whomsoever would climb,
yet they were successively one and two and three
score miles away.

Below, where all was yet lying in shadow along
the mountain's base, misty valleys and far-off forest lands lay robed in purple haze, now fast growing soft and softer in the morning sheen; and now
becoming gold-tinted and tremulous with the first
lance-thrusts of the reflected light in the Orient,
where met blue ocean and bluer sky.

More than ever after the wild storm of the previous night do these monarch mountains impress
the reverent beholder with their exquisite sense
of repose. Power and grandeur lie hushed in
brooding revery — not slumbering — but half re-
cumbent as one roused from repose, reverent and
rapt, in peaceful contemplation of a waking world.

Whether savage or civilized, the heart of man
ever acquires a God-ward lift while contemplating the primordial majesty of lofty mountains.
To Kalanikupule and his war-worn braves the
titanic peaks above them were but emblems of the
majesty and the might of Pele. They saw the all-
pervading influence of their goddess in the very
aspect that the kingly heights put on.

In the rainbow hues, slow dawning upon the
snow-crowned peaks, they beheld the tripple smile
of their special deity exulting over the human carnage her earthly warriors had wrought in battling
with their foe.

Goodness is never a component part of a barba-
rian's creed of divine greatness, or of almighty
power. Evil overtops all their conceptions of
Deity. A god who does not terrorize his worshippers fails to arouse or retain the obsequious homage of the savage mind.

Though the awe of a savage is easily aroused by
the sublime and majestic in nature, being born with
the same innate reverence inherent in all men, yet
it is always overtopped, outflanked, and followed
after by a long train of demoralizing, grovelling
fears.

In the blue column of gyrating smoke curling
lazily up from Loa's volcanic peak, the ardent worshippers of Pele behold her in a suspicious state of
inaction, — with nought of peace or repose, — but
cruelly brooding over some new evil by which to
terrify or destroy the sons of men. They ever
judge their dread Creator by what she creates in
her hour of wrath ; as a warrior is judged by his
fierce deeds in battle -- not by his amenities to his
fellows in times of peace.

As the day dawned fairly upon that little band
of fleeing warriors, with their ghastly rows of stark
dead and numerous wounded laid out upon the
platform-deck between the canoes, the eager, kingly eyes of Kalanikupule and his captive princess
met for the first time in their lives. It was the
supreme moment in all their young experience of
life. Though Pelelulu had been snatched from her
sleep during a midnight storm, and borne to the

canoe of an invading enemy in the midst of the war
of elements, and a darkness made lurid by lightning's glare and volcanic eruptions, yet the keen-
witted maiden had not been long in discovering
who had captured her.   And where in all the
" Eight Isles " of Hawaii was there a maiden who
would not rejoice to be captured by the heroic son
of Kahekili — the Thunderer ?

Born of a semi-goddess, Pelelulu's kinship with
Pele made her almost superior to human fear of
human things ; so that even the fearful scene she
had listened to of clashing spears and frightful
shouts of frenzied men in battle, and even the sor-
rowful report that Kamehameha was dead, had not
so dismayed her as might seem, for she now sat
fearless and self-possessed in spite of her captive
situation.

Watching with all a youthful maiden's curiosity
for the dawn of day, Pelelulu had awaited with
the utmost eagerness to behold the young hero
whose fame had already filled the Hawaiian world.
The dawn of a tropic day is long in coming, its only
prelude being the deeper darkness of the antelucan
hour.   But it came with its usual abruptness at
last, and four alert and sparkling eyes met as human eyes have rarely met before.

One pair of these large, soft orbs looked to see
the fierce eyes of an exultant warrior glowering
down upon her with something of the lingering ferocity that dominated while her captor was slaughtering her sire.   But the look of rudeness or fierce-

ness Pelelulu looked for was not there. Instead, there beamed a swift look of compassion upon her; a kindly glance that fast took on a degree of soft- ness and tenderness, that over the whole wide world of human experience has yet found but one name holy enough to consecrate its sentiment.

As the gray dawn fairly unveiled her captor, all that is grand in physique, and noble in intellect, seemed to Pelelulu to be grouped together in har- mony of form and face in the Boy King before her. The athletic exercise of steering the flying canoes by the deft use of his paddle, imparted a glow to his olive face, and displayed his nude and hand- some figure to the best advantage in a maiden's eyes. Tutored or untutored, the gentle heart of woman is the same everywhere; and we may not wonder that the large gazelle eyes of the maiden princess were found revelling in the manliness of the heroic King.

As these noble scions of royalty were both de- scended from the Spanish maiden Opala, who was wrecked on Pele Point two hundred years before, they both partook of similar characteristics, exalt- ing them eminently above their subject peoples.

Though the young King was but eighteen at this time, yet he was more than six feet in stature, pos- sessing the finest degree of adiposic symmetry con- sistent with such great strength and wonderful activity as he ever showed upon all occasions de- manding prowess.

The face of the young warrior at this age was

frank and open, his whole appearance being impressive and attractive, full of youthful grace and majestic mien, such as would distinguish its possessor in any rank or in any land. His well-poised head was crowned with black and curly hair. His eyes were dark and piercing, easily penetrating the designs of whomsoever he looked upon. Before his ireful glance in the hour of battle the fiercest chieftain among his warriors quailed as before a demigod.

It will be readily conceded that here was an ideal type of barbaric man, endowed to win the confidence and secure the homage of his warlike people, and one to captivate a maiden's heart upon the instant of contact. What wonder that the young princess, endowed with kindred beauty and equal intelligence,—though the daughter of his bitterest enemy,—should look upon her kingly captor as a god!

Had he not dared the wild tempest of a stormy sea when the fiercest known gale was abroad upon the midnight deep? Had not the divine Pele given him a supreme token of her love and fostering care, illuminating the midnight darkness and the storm-lashed ocean as with the sun of noonday?

For his sake, had not the dread Pele hurled her earthquakes against the contending elements, till the loud-mouthed winds hushed their brawlings, and the monstrous waves slunk back into the caverned deep to let him pass! — the inky darkness retreating before her glance like cowering wolves before the fierce eye of the hunter.

Before the recent advent of Kalanikupule there
had been no rival to the gigantic prowess and warlike genius of Kamehamaha. But now, had he not
slain the Lonely One with his own hand! Kamehameha, titanic in stature above all men; monstrous
in his might as the leviathan of the deep, and fiercer.
than a whirlwind in his hour of wrath; a warrior
before whose blows the great chiefs of Oahu had
fallen like trees before a tempest!

Ah! how the young heart of the captive maiden
glowed, while swift, delicious thrills mounted up
into cheeks and eyes as the morning light suddenly unveiled the warrior-king to her longing
eyes!

Now that the combat was over, who could be
more gentle and tender in his every aspect than
this same ferocious warrior of a few hours since?
The compassionate softness she discerned in his
dark eyes seemed borrowed from the cooing wood-
doves Pelelulu had left behind. There was tenderness, almost tremulousness, in the resonant
tones of his voice when addressed to his captive —
his slave. The kindly smile upon his kingly lips
when speaking to her seemed but the veriest ripple
from an ocean of warmth within, delving down into
the maiden's heart like a sudden sun-burst after a
storm.

When the King spoke to Pelelulu on that dread
morning, his words seemed something more than
words — however warm and winsome words may
sometimes be; — he spoke to her with emotions,

5

winged like springtime birds when seeking among bees and blossoms for a mate.

As young flowers when bursting from bud into bloom open eagerly to receive the warmth of the morning sun, and nurture in fond dalliance upon the wind and dew, so the heart of the captive princess opened its inmost petals to the warrior's smiles as she fed with girlish delight upon every word uttered by the youthful King.

While such were some of the essentials in the character and appearance of the King, Pelelulu was in no respect his inferior; possessing every endowment of imperious beauty attributed to her clime, winsome in manners, with the quick intelligence one might look for in the daughter of a great monarch, and a semi-goddess on the maternal side.

Those who knew the young princess best dwelt most upon a magnetic charm which ever captivated the stranger before she spoke. In this quality, more than her matchless beauty and dulcet voice, the people recognized Pelelulu's kinship with Pele.

However much Kalanikupule may have been influenced by this ever-prevading magnetism of his captive, he seemed to dwell most on her soft, dark eyes, and the delicate tinting of her pearl-white cheeks, as they glowed into swiftly-recurring damask under his ardent gaze.

The first act of the abashed young princess, when day dawned upon them, and she found herself so prepossessed with Kalanikupule, was to free, with her rosy fingers, the wet tangle of her long, black, wavy hair. Though Pelelulu was as nude as Godiva — but for this trailing vestment of mid-night tresses — yet because of her untouched purity she was not in the least abashed by the rude presence of Oahu's barbaric warriors. In her case there was no need to constrain the eyes of either the curious or the connoisseur, — as in the instance of the Norman noblesse, — for all know that primitive innocence is a far more impenetrable vesture for a pretty damsel than self-conscious virtue. For this latter vestal is often a cunning adept in the knowledge of man's love of contour, and of her own abundant insufficiencies ; thus her own numerous abnormalities — real or supposed — serve to excite her blushes, which might otherwise have been controlled before an unobtrusive admi-ration of her self-satisfying charms.

Smoothing her jetty locks from off her girlish brow, with many a furtive glance at her royal captor, Pelelulu draped her luxuriant masses with a dawning sense of modesty about her unrobed form : a figure that might well have served as a maiden-model for the Cnidus Venus of Praxiteles.

Her simple toilet thus completed, by trailing her one only garment like a banner of night about her, Pelelulu suffered her proud eyes to dwell im-periously upon her kingly captor unquailing and undismayed. She gazed as one meeting the ques-tioning glance of her equal ; like one attired as best comported with her youth and beauty and rank ;

even sufficiently becoming for the august presence
of a King and his victorious warriors.

This unterrified demeanor in his pretty captive,
together with the charm of her remarkable beauty,
so won upon the receptive heart of Kalanikupule,
that, she whom he had snatched for his slave, and
as a token of his scorn for her sire, grew to be
contemplated as his future queen. Wishing to
know more of her mental calibre, he addressed her
with this purpose in view :

" Wahine! I am Kalanikupule of Oahu. I
snatched you from the side of Kaahumanu, to make
you my slave. What say you, Wahine ? " — girl.

With dark eyes flashing with scintillant lights,
and a tempest of supremest scorn curling her
voluptuous lips, Pelelulu made instant answer
with look and gesture, while prudently tarrying to
restrain herself with queenly dignity before re-
plying.

" Sire, it is the part of a captive princess to
obey. Pelelulu, of Hawaii, will demean herself as
becomes the daughter of Kamehameha the Great,
whom you have slain."

" It is the duty of a victor to sacrifice his
prisoners in the wahi kapu — sacred places — of
Pele. As Kaahumanu has escaped, you are Oahu's
only prisoner, by which to propitiate the gods.
What say you, proud maiden ? "

" Pelelulu is the prisoner and the slave of
Kalanikupule. It is truly the duty of so noble a
king to remember his just immolations to the

goddess — the great Pele who loves him, and
makes his arm strong in battle. The great king,
my father — whom you have slain — would have
sacrificed a noble warrior to his country's gods.
But a less noble than he may content himself
with sacrificing a wahine — a girl ! ''

The glorious scorn of those impious young eyes,
while answering, acquired an untold charm for the
King to look upon ; prompting his ardent heart to
clasp this resplendent creature to his bosom without more ado. But he forbore yet a little while,
to further prolong the new pleasure he had
aroused so successfully.

" You speak truly, Wahine. And Kalanikupule
must strive not to be less noble than his father's
bastard son. Pelelulu, you are fair as the dawn
that comes blushing over the sea-tops yonder, to
greet you as its peer. Your cheeks are tinted like
the rose-crest on Kea's snowy crown. The lightnings that lit my way to battle were less vivid
than the glittering scorn in the dark eyes of my
captive. Wahine, my heart warms to you! I
would proffer you the half of my name — than
which there is no greater in the Eight Isles — and
make you my queen. Would it like you, maiden,
to be called Kupule, and be made the queen of
Kalani, of Oahu, the fairest Isle under the sun ? "

The choice phrases of a king are as drops of
gold to his people. A maiden's ears ever lie open
to her heart in such an hour ; and a monarch's
words flow like a rivulet into her soul. , The heart

of Pelelulu was not shut to this praise of her beauty,
and the scorn, yet lingering in her eyes, gave
place to soft tints caught from the mellow clouds
in the Orient.

"Oahu's King is a great warrior. Pelelulu has
often seen yonder mountain peaks brighten with
glory, as now, on the morning of the victories of
Kalanikupule. He is the best beloved of Pele,
else he could not have slain the Lonely One. It
becomes a great King to wed with his peer. An
Alii Kapu" — sacred chief — "should not suffer
himself to wed either a *prisoner*, or a *slave!*"

This noble reply of the young girl served but to
add fuel to the flame of the King's admiration.
His voice softened to the cooing of the fragrant
winds that now wafted them over the seas. His
dark eyes grew tender as he listened to her proud,
sweet tones. Here was a maiden who could not
be had for the asking. She must be won, and he
would win her.

"True, Wahine. I hear the voice of Alohalea
in your tones. You speak with the wisdom of one
so near akin to Pele, who has often spoken to me
of you in my dreams, and bid me go seek you for
my queen. And now that my ears are open to the
music of your words, I know you are indeed born
of a goddess, and very near akin to Pele. I have
seen that you are beautiful, and I have learned
that you are fearless and noble. None but a
great King should possess you. If there is a
greater in all the Isles than Kalanikupule, and you

love him, breathe his name, and I will forsake the
homeward track and take you to your lover."

"You are indeed great and good, and the gods
have not sung your praises wrongfully. None but
Pele has heard Pelelulu breathe the name of him
whom she loves. But while I remain your slave,
your captive, it does not become me to disclose the
name of the favored one ; for, while in bondage,
Pelelulu is unworthy of a noble lover."

"But you are a slave no longer ; you never
were a slave ; for a spirit like yours cannot be
held in thraldom. Liberty is a bird that will sing
on though imprisoned in a cage. It was only the
darkness of night that imprisoned you, for since
the dawn crept up over the hilltops of the sea, you
have been free, and the best beloved of Kalanikupule. Is the name of Kupule unpleasant to your
ears ? "

"Kupule is a pleasant name. It greets my ear
like the songs of singing birds and rippling waters.
She who possesses it should be noble and brave,
as she will be happy in the love of Kalani, the
bravest warrior in all the Eight Isles."

"You have called me Kalani ; you have robbed
me of the sweetest half of my name. You have
transgressed a sacred law of our country. Do you
know that there can henceforth be no more Pelelulu among all the wahines of Hawaii ? "

"I know that the name of my girlhood is no
more ; it was buried beneath the foam-crests far
behind, in the track of your swift canoe. It is

the will of Pele, and the law of the land, that
Pelelulu shall be spoken no more in Hawaii."

"Then Kupule is your name, and you shall become the queen of Oahu. When one name binds
two hearts, they are indeed made one."

"There can be none sweeter, for it is the half
of your own. I can already see it written in let-
ters of gold upon the crests of the seas, and the
night shall disclose it rimmed with stars in the
sky. Behold it on the mountain tops, waving in
red banners of glory. Alas! if my ears were not
dull, I could hear the birds make music of Kupule!
Kupule! the whole day long. It will sing in my
heart for ever; and it shall know no dishonor from
the daughter of Kamehameha — the dead king of
Hawaii."

"It is well. The canoes speed more swiftly
because they bear the young queen of Kalani.
Our love shall date from my great victory of Coco
Isle. I will henceforth be to you father and
mother; in Kalani you shall find a husband and
lover in one. From this hour you are Tabu for
Kalani. It shall hereafter be death to whomsoever permits his shadow to fall across your path.
Proud chiefs shall bow down when you pass, or
their heads shall fall as over-ripe fruit from the
tree, and be sacrificed to the gods, because of their
breaking the sacred Tabu of their King."

"Yes, it is well. And Kupule will love her
King as no other wahine in Hawaii could love
him."

"Aye! it is indeed well. And you shall be my queen; and because of your wisdom, your voice shall be heard in my council. Pele has long since told me of you; she has so charmed my heart that I could no longer delay, but gathered my great chiefs and went forth upon the war-path to take you for my queen."

"Kalani is a great warrior; his battle-deeds will never be forgotten. And because Pele is your friend, there can be none found to resist you in battle. She filled all the dreams of my girlhood with thoughts of Kalani. When I swam in the Wailuku, my heart was full of music because of you. When I coasted the great breakers on the reef, I learned to be brave that I might be fitted to become your queen. Did not Pele whisper to you of my love?"

"When Kalani stood upon the shore of Maui, and looked over the wild Upolu sea to the mountain land of Hawaii, the divine goddess has whispered your name into his ear. In my fair isle of Oahu it came to me in bird-songs. There the trade-winds sing of your beauty the whole day long."

"You make me happy; so full of joy I fear my heart will burst with delight before we reach my new Oahu home. Our bards sing often of your sweet Nuuanu vale."

"The valley of Nuuanu is the heaven-land of our Island world. In the Goddess's Fountain, on the sacred hill, the great Pele has permitted Ka-

lani to look often upon thy fair face in the holy
waters of her fountain.   And because of thy
beauty, seen therein, I strove from my boyhood to
become a great warrior, that I might win you for
my queen."

"If Kupule is fair to look upon, she is glad,
because of the love of her King. Pele has made
me what I am only to match the kingly fancy of
Kalani. We will love her for this goodness to her
children. We will worship her ; for there is none
greater than Pele, the goddess of volcanoes, the
creator of the world."

"Great is Pele, the goddess of Kilauea!
Greater than Lono, who is the crazy god, and
comes to us in great mokus (ships) — like Cookee
— and devours all the food of the land, and kills
the Kanakas while they are worshipping him in
the temple, and filling his ships with pigs and
taro."

"Great indeed is Pele! Greater than even
Moa-alii, the terrible god of the sea ; the devouring god who overturns the canoes and feasts upon
multitudes of Kanakas. But for Pele, my young
warrior would never have reached my Hilo home,
and won his greatest battle, and snatched his willing bride from out the darkness. For was not
Moa-alii angered because of your coming ? and
did he not tear the wild winds into tatters, and
lift his mad seas into mountain billows, that they
should hurl Kalani upon Kohala's shore ? "

"But Moa-alii is a coward! For when the di-

vine Pele arose in her might, did not the fierce
sea-god, and his angry winds and his mad seas
cower like whipped curs, and slink away into the
caves of the wind and the depths of the ocean?"

"Great indeed is Pele! She has made the
heavens and the earth, and brought the sun from
Tahiti to shine upon us all." *

"In our kingdom of Oahu we will worship Pele
above all the gods of the world. In my great
temple at Waikiki we will sacrifice heaps of *kane*,
puaa, and *hua* (men, hogs, and fruit). And Paao,
the great high priest, shall make a Tabu until all
the land of Oahu shall become dark at midday,
and Silence shall steal over the land like a white
ghost; and no voice shall be heard to speak in the
sunny vale of Nuuanu, or the misty valley of
Manoa, or along the white beach of Waikiki. No
voice shall be heard but that of the Alii Kapu
(sacred chief), praying to Pele in the great heiau
at Waikiki."

"Auwe! auwe! how brave is Kalani, to come
over the wild Upolu sea, to find a little wahine for
his queen. Did not the heart of Oahu's King
beat loudly at the anger of Moa-alii, and the black
storm with which the fierce god covered the
waters?"

"The heart of Kalani is not a maiden's heart.

---

* Kana, disliking the darkness of his day, walked through
the sea to Tahiti, where lived Kahoaalii, the sun maker. Having obtained it, he returned, and Pele placed it where it has
since remained, for the benefit of the world. — *Hawaiian
History.*

Because Pele bid her young warrior go and capture a beautiful Queen for Oahu, he knew no fear.
When Moa-alii's storm seemed about to swallow
Kalani and his great warriors, then Pele remembered her promise, and showed her face to her
Alii Kapu, lighting the pathway of our waa
(canoe) as with a thousand suns."

"And did Pele, the beautiful goddess of Mauna
Loa, become visible to my King? And did she
dance upon the fiery billows of lava, and ride
upon its fountain top where it leaped into the sky,
as I have seen her do when the Lonely One was
out upon the war-path; and when my mother took
me in her arms to Kilauea, and left me to pick
berries with my infant hands on the brink of the
crater, while she leaped down into the *Hale-mau-
mau* to swim on the boiling lake with Pele."

"She danced with delight on the red crest of
the lava, to gladden the eyes of my warriors.
And as my young Queen in her girl-days plunged
down the great falls of the Wailuku, so Pele, tiring
of dancing on the fountain jets of her lava,
plunged down the rushing river of fire into the
Swimming Gulch, there to greet her young warrior as he passed — he and the great Chiefs of
Oahu. Even then in the hour of tempest, when
Kalani's ears were deafened with the mad winds
and the roaring seas; when the earthquakes
rocked the Isles like ships on the sea, — even then
the good Pele whispered in my ears of a *wahine*

maikai ! — a beautiful girl — on Coco Isle, sleeping by Kaahumanu, and dreaming of her warrior."

"Ah! great King; and now I may tell you that such was indeed my dear, sweet dream, when you snatched me from slumbering beside the queen. I knew not then it was you, but now I know it was Kalani, the noblest and the bravest of kings. My dream was of a great war-canoe coming over the sea from Maui; the *waa* was full of warriors, and one, nobler and grander than all the others, smiled upon me as I sat on the Hilo shore; sat watching the swift canoe being drawn by flying gods having eyes of red-lava and wings of fire. What wonder that I love you, you who are like a god !"

From Maui's shore to Kawaihai
The war-canoes are passing by,
With full intent to battle meet
If Hawaii dare to meet their fleet.

Or on the sea or on the land
  A vastly busy scene we view,
Among the fleet or on the strand
  Confusion marks the most they do.

The sacrificing Priest we see
Red immolate to fierce Moa-alii;
High on the cliff the blood doth flow,
The carcass hurled to gods below.
They pray Moa-alii smooth the sea,
And bid Eurus guide from dangers free.

As those of eld Eolus cry,
  Who bags them up his leading gales;
They rend the bags and let them fly,
  When tempests tatter all their sails.
Thus in Cathay the boatmen burn
  To Joss, their god, the perfumed prayer,
Where'er the yellow rivers turn
  Some castled hill, or Pagod fair.

CHAPTER VI.

URING the morning hours the great war canoe had been sailing at tremendous speed along the Kohala shore, freighted with her dead warriors and wounded chiefs. Among the grim and exultant chiefs sat Kalani and Kupule, discoursing with bright eyes and tender tones upon subject-matters mostly appertaining to themselves.

They had now arrived off Upolu Point, the extreme northwest cape of Hawaii. The black cliffs, so full of terror on the night before, were objects of fear no longer. The huge undulations heaving in from the eastern board — the recent storm-billows shorn of their crests — now serve to lash the whole northeastern shore into such stupendous breakers, that the enemy could not embark in pursuit if he would.

The swift canoe now overtook and passed the Elenora, the ship Kalani had saved from wreck the night before. The vessel was now bowling along under all her light kites, speeding on her way through the Upolu Strait, thence on to Kealakeakua Bay, where Captain Cook had been killed some few years before.

79

In the casual events of life, how often we seem
to approximate some condition of things or individual influence, by which or by whom our whole
future life *might* have been changed for subsequent
good. The meeting of the ship and the canoe;
of John Young and Kalani; was a remarkable
instance in question. The influence of no man so
impressed the future destiny of the King of Oahu
for evil, as Keone Ani, after he was restrained from
returning to the Elenora, and made a great chief
by Kamehameha.

It was this sagacious boatswain who counselled
the enemies of Kalani to build up a strong fleet,
and drill a thorough army, officered and led on by
white men; and to bide their time for conquest
until they could arm both fleet and troops with
European weapons of warfare. And it was by the
skilful use of Keone Ani's cannon that Oahu's
rampart walls were eventually broken down during
the final conflict. And it was also by this same
Keone Ani's hand that the Boy King met his gallant death at last, while fighting the desperate
battle of the Pali.

Had Kalani possessed the foresight and sagacity
of Kamehameha, at this time, he would have induced the Elenora to go to his capital port of
Honolulu. It needed but the asking, when they
met thus in the Straits; for at that time there
were no greater admirers of Kalani and his warriors than the captain and the noble-hearted boatswain of the Elenora. The king's war-party had

saved the white man's ship from certain destruction, and they would gladly have become his friendly advisers at this juncture.

But the young King's experience with other white people and their ships had not been pleasant, thus he failed to see the immense advantage that might be derived from his association with the better class of maritime foreigners. By so doing he too could have obtained munitions of war, and induced skilful white men to enlist in his service; thus enabling him to compete with his great rival of Hawaii. But failing to see the importance of this in time, the unrelenting fates pronounced his sad and cruel doom.

The canoe now left the land, and stretched out into the rough waters of the Upolu Sea, where strong winds and swift currents contend between Hawaii and Maui. The land wind had served them well thus far, but was now becoming baffling and unsteady. Now blowing in wild gusts from out the mountain ravines, and now giving way to the strong onset of the freshening trades, which struggled bravely to secure their right of domain over the Upolu Sea.

In the intervals of calm, between the battling of the land squalls and the sea wind, Kalani ordered his unwounded warriors to bring their paddles into play, himself taking a paddle, as Kupule volunteered to steer; for the lithe young princess was handy with surf board or canoe, fish-spear or paddle. And it was with a lover's delight that

6

Kalani watched the deft young creature guide the great war-canoes, with an exquisite show of muscle and skill. It warmed the hearts of even the wounded warriors, to see the ravishing young blood leap into the pearly cheeks of the maiden, as every muscle and sinew of her girlish figure was brought into extremest play. Her eyes sparkled with roguery, and her bosom heaved like a young billow with exultation ; while the trailing masses of jetty hair forgot their office of vestment, and streamed like a black banner in the wind alee.

She was overjoyed to be of service to her dear young King, and delighted to receive the grim approbation of brave and bleeding warriors, who forgot their pains, and ceased their maledictions and their groans, in watching this charming creature act the steersman, where naught but the nicest application of subtle skill could serve in the place of the usual muscle and brawn expended by a steersman.

When at length the trades struck down the passage strong and steady, Kalani took the guidance, steering across the rough Straits, and soon reached Kana-loa, the southernmost part of his kingdom of Maui. They soon found themselves coasting along under the shelter of grand old Halakala — the "House of the Sun." In a few hours they passed between Isle Molokine and the Kula district; the wind following favorably after them through between the islands, until they approached the low level of Wailuku, between the

towering Halakala and the lesser mountain of Eka.
Here the fierce "wollywaus" tore through the
gut, and whitened the smooth sea along the beach,
until the great canoes tore on with utmost rapidity,
and soon passed Opilu Bay and the Island of Ranai.

The moment the flying canoes passed the last
point, and approached near enough to be distinguished by the people of Lahaina, it was seen that
many a missing one was laid low. Then a wild
wail of mourning broke from the gathering group
upon the beach, sweeping in dismal cries over the
sea, and up the steep slopes of Eka's sunburnt
side, whose peaks were just then robing themselves in the sombre hues imparted by the setting
sun.

It was well known to all, that every warrior
who went forth to battle with their King, was
chosen from among the noblest and the bravest
chiefs in all the Isles. Hence the wild grief of
the people ere they knew who were dead. For
whosoever the dead ones might be, they were
worthy of the profoundest grief, and would receive
a great national mourning.

But, as the great double canoe approached
nearer, and was at length run upon the black
sand beach abreast of the Maui palace, one of the
chiefs, hailing from the bow of the canoe, proclaimed that Kalani — their loved young King —
was safe and unwounded; and Kamehameha —
the terror of the Isles — was dead! Then the
mournful wail was at once turned into a tumult

of joy — alike for the death of the giant king and
the safety of the living one.

And when their young monarch sprang joyfully
ashore, leading proudly by the hand the royal
princess of Hawaii, proclaiming her as Kupule —
the "Queen of Oahu!" — the shouts of the glad
populace were deafening, in the wild exuberance
of such various emotions ; for the laugh of a tran-
sient mourner is the more hearty because of the
grief that has gone before.

The fame of the princess of Hawaii for beauty
and wisdom, and kindliness to the down-trodden
people, made her beloved throughout the group.
And her presence among them told at a glance
that Kalani had won his battle, else he could not
have borne off from the camp of their arch enemy
the charming Pelelulu, the "Haaheo ō Hawaii!"
—Pride of Hawaii.

Wild was the jubilation, and joyous the feasting
on that eventful night. While here and there
grouped the ostentatious mourners making the
tropic night hideous with their cries. Those of
the dead warriors belonging to Maui were given
into the hands of the tabu priests of that Island,
a tabu being proclaimed, and a cruel human sacrifice instituted over their manes. Those of the
dead chiefs belonging to Oahu were sent on to
that Island, with orders for Paao, the high priest,
to bestow honors and sacrifices upon their obsequies.

The news that Kamehameha was slain filled the

whole land with rejoicing. His resistless feats of arms had made him a constant source of dread throughout the leeward Islands. Freed from the dread of encountering the savage Hawaiian in future battles, the war-like chiefs of Maui at once began to instigate a plan for the invasion of Hawaii, with a view to taking possession of the Island before the panic-stricken people could organize under a new king.

This ambitious design was finally acquiesced in by Kalani. A small, but well-equipped army, with canoes sufficient for their transportation, were hastily got ready in Maalea bay. In less than a week the army was ready for embarking, starting out from that part of the Hana district lying opposite to Kohala.

Even with many prayers and numerous sacrifices to the gods, Kalani had not been able to establish communication with Pele; thus he was compelled by the force of events to embark upon this bold expedition, without having obtained divine sanction, or sufficient secular encouragement for hope of success. But the ambition of young hearts bends everything to their wishes, and Kalani was at length determined to undertake the conquest in spite of the ominous silence and probable disapprobation of the dread Goddess of Mauna Loa.

Failing to awaken the sanction or sympathy of Pele, the last hours before embarking were given to the timely worship of Moa-alii, the fierce sea-

god. From every headland about the Kana-loa
rose the sacrificial flames; and rended limbs and
gory portions of human subjects were tossed from
the cliffs and capes to Moa-alii, and his ravenous
tribe, awaiting the savory repast in the blue sea
below. This example of dual worship is by no
means confined to the Hawaiian Isles. The first
solicitations in all lands are usually offered to a
people's best conception of the divine, and overruling One. But, failing in immediate response
to the wishes of the supplicator, how frequently
is the lesser conception, the underruling One
appealed to; lest our human schemes for human
aggrandizement should fail for want of extraneous
aid.

Moa-alii was thus often indebted to Pele's tardy
recognition of the warlike schemes of her people
for many of his gory repasts upon human manes.
Yet so wedded were the king and his people to
the belief that Pele's sanction was all-important
to the success of any warlike enterprise, that it
was with many misgivings that Kalani now made
his final preparations for embarkation; and this
secondary worship bestowed upon the sea-god was
not entered upon with relish, nor found quite sufficient to awaken the desired hopes of success.

The obsequious attention of Kalani's Alii Kapu
to Moa-alii, at even the eleventh hour, served to
ensure a prosperous voyage across the ever-rugged
waters of Upolu; and with this hope to sustain
them, fifty double canoe loads of warriors em-

barked before dawn, while the trades were yet blowing lightly.

The straits were crossed ere the sun had tipped the snows on Mauna Kea with their diurnal glory. Keeping along the adjacent shore of Kohala, a landing was made at Kawaihae without any resistance from the scattered forces of the enemy. The native soldiers stationed here being wholly unprepared for invasion, fled in hot haste to the mountain fastness.

But messengers were dispatched in every direction ; and in a few days an army of Hawaiians more than twice the strength of the invaders was concentrated in the mountain ravines, which was duly reported to Kalani by his numerous spies and local friends from the Kohala and Kona districts.

The fame of Kalani was already such that even the out-numbering army of Hawaiians hesitated about attacking his irresistible warriors, led on by such an impetuous hero. Thus demoralized by their fears, they resorted to uses of cunning and stratagem. Sending out small war-parties, they gathered here and there upon the foot-hills above the Oahuans, endeavoring to tempt them to battle, with a purpose of drawing the invaders into an ambush among the mountain gorges by this display of weakness.

But the scouts of Oahu were frequently coming in, reporting the continuous reinforcement of the Hawaiians, until a great army now lay ambushed among the hills. By the advice of a war council, Kalani had sent to Maui for more men, as it was

considered imprudent to attack at a disadvantage
in an enemy's country.

Though Kalani was too proud to retreat without
giving battle, yet he now hesitated with more than
usual misgivings, because there had come no pro-
pitious signs from the volcanic world, or other au-
spicious concurrence of events to intimate the needed
sanction of Pele. Thus situated, the priests now
proclaimed a terrible *Kapu Kane* — man tabu — and
taking possession of the great heiau at Kawaihae,
they sent out their ferocious *pepehi Kanakas* (man-
killers) in every direction, entrapping a score of
natives too old to run, or too young to fight, but
sufficiently acceptable to sacrifice to the obdurate
Goddess of Kilauea. Throughout the whole night
long the hours were made hideous by the sad wailing of the mourners and the howling outcries of the
priests invoking divine aid from Pele.

While the numerous priests were thus wrestling
with the gods, and the wise diviners were disem-
bowelling the dead, during the process of the sacrificial rites, Kalani had immured himself in the
holy of holies, the sacred house within the enclosure of the Temple, and given himself to fasting and prayer, and that degree of dramatic entertainment most acceptable to the sex of his dread
divinity.

With the King was the royal *Akua pua* — his
divine bird-god — richly decorated with rare feathers and costly pearls; together with the brilliant
jewels long since descended to the kings of Maui —

heirlooms from the old Spanish priests wrecked in their rich argosy upon Pua Pele centuries before.

As an ardent maiden decks herself in finery to please the lover's eye, so the Boy King now adorned himself in best attire, ready to receive his beloved Gôddess in state. Upon his head was the proud helmet worn by his great father, — the fierce "Thunderer," — richly adorned with yellow feathers, the kingly color, and gayly plumed with the crimson tail-feathers of the tropic bird.

Depending gracefully from his shoulders hung the far-famed Mamo of a long line of kings, yellow and glistening as polished gold. This exquisite mantle was made from the hair-like feathers taken from the weird little iiwi birds, whose wildwood notes are as strange and guttural as their name would imply. Not the richest fabric ever woven for European monarch could match this costly war-cloak of the kings of Oahu.

Tired of his long, prayerful obeisance, Kalani was now seen posed like a gladiator on guard to receive his foe. In the one hand glittered the tremulous point of his long *paloa*, and his two-handed broadsword was in the other. Both sword and dagger were presents given to Kahekili by the courtly Vancouver, whose judicious influence over the savage kings was much more humanizing than that of the ill-fated, injudicious Cook.

Cutting and thrusting at an imaginary foe, Kalani had possessed himself of an appearance of savage fury, as he menaced and manœuvred before his

unseen antagonist, in futile endeavor to attract the
attention of Pele, either by the adornment of his
manly person or the imposing postures of a warrior
in act of battle. Alas, alas! was this heroic godson of Pele right in supposing that the divine ones
of either heaven or earth could be imposed upon
by such an exhibition of vanities? Judge him not
harshly, for he was wiser than we know.

Exhausted with his manual exercise in pantomimic battle with a mimic foe; his fierce lunges
and swift slashes with his jewel-hilted sword; the
wary feints and cunning stabs with his keen paloa
into some grim battle-ghost of his brain, — Kalani
at length sunk down upon his divan of soft lahala
mats and pulu pillows, and was soon overcome
with profoundest slumber.

How long Kalani slept, he knew not. But suddenly the whole outer world was convulsed with
throes that shook the rocking sphere to its centre.
Was it a divine behest, or a dread retribution at
hand? To those without there came at first a
long, low muttering as of distant thunder. Then
the light of the stars was put out, quenched upon
the instant as by the black outriders of a coming
tempest.

Then followed the quick succeeding earthquakes,
rolling with terrific noises down from the high
mountains to the wave-lashed shore. Down top-
pled the lesser mountains, rent to their base. Torn
were the great cliffs along Kohala's shore, until
they tumbled headlong into the sea.

It was Pele! She had awoke at length to the impending necessities of the hour. She had divined with the swift retribution of godhead, that evil was predominant, and justice must be meted upon whom it would fall. The fate of the Island nations trembled in the balance, awaiting the divine adjustments of her hand.

Kalani had dreamed that he was being ingulfed by a red river of fire, rolling down from Kilauea. But as the swift-flowing lava approached, and seemed about to overwhelm him, a voice from out the starless gloom spoke to him, saying: "Aloha! Kalani. Fear not. Is not Pele the godmother of Oahu's king?"

And the fiery river divided about him, and went roaring down upon the one hand and the other; destroying the two ambushed armies of the enemy; harming neither himself nor his embattled warriors: no, not so much as singeing a hair of their heads.

A WHIRR of wings aroused the King's surprise!
  In voice divine he heard the Goddess call,
And there — *unseen* — stood Pele 'fore his eyes,
  Her godlike silhouette discloses all.

Wind-blown her tresses — pinions in repose —
  Her hands upon his shoulders, *cold and chill!*
A woman's form her sun-made shadow shows,
  Whose lips upon his own awake a thrill!

Dead lay the army, stricken by her might,
  No living soul e'er woke to tell the tale!
What awful power disclosed to human sight;
  Well might the warrior King recede, and quail!

Some died with hope-illumined faces seen,
  Their feather mamos wrapt about the head;
Some died with horror, prostrate on the green;
  One sulph'rous breath from Pele laid them dead!

CHAPTER VII.

AND in Kalani's dream, one in the semblance of a fair woman came and sat by him; and with her dainty lips, crimson as the red ohea, she snatched away his breath as he slept, saluting his sensuous mouth with her hallowed kisses. Such was the ardor of the fair one of his dreams, that she awoke the sleeper from his vision of love and glory.

And he awoke. And the eyes of Kalani opened upon a blaze of intensest light, dazzling him near to blindness with its brilliance. In a rolling cloud of white sulphurous smoke and yellow flame stood the beautiful Goddess, even Pele! the creator of the heavens and the earth.

Bending like a loving woman over the half-awakened King, the lustrous blue eyes of Pele looked tenderly down into the dark orbs of the boy warrior, as she impetuously bid him arise, and hearken to her counsel and commands:

"I am Pele! I have come to counsel with my young warrior of Oahu. I have come to admonish him that his ambition is too lofty — vaulting into the domains of godhead — for if an eagle soars too near to the sun, his pinions will be seared, and he

93

will fall maimed back to the earth again. Be wise
in time, for the days of all men are numbered.
Enough ever lies at hand to enrich the noblest;
beware, lest you reach too far off for plunder; or
stretch your hand over the domain of Godhead.

"Kalani has brought his fleet of brave warriors
across Upolu Sea, without sanction or assent from
Pele. He has feasted Moa-alii—the hated sea-god
—and come abroad to capture the great kingdom
of Hawaii, whereon stands the fiery throne of Pele.

"But there lives a greater than Kalani in this
land of mountains and rivers of fire, and Hawaii is
his kingdom. Kamehameha, who was slain by the
valor of my Boy King, though he was dead, yet
is he alive again! This land is his. I have said it!
It is Kamehameha's, and he shall rule it; though
there fall the heavens, and the earth is rent in
twain; he, and his noble descendants, even to the
tenth generation of men.

"My hero of Oahu: there are others for you to
flash your *haole kane's paloa* upon (white man's
dagger). Even while I counsel with you, a powerful king and great warrior is preparing to wrest
your own beautiful kingdom of Oahu from your
rule. Go home to the new *wahine* I have bestowed
upon you, arouse you, and behold the battle afar
off, lest you be found wanting in the time of need.

"Hear me, Kalani! The young moon is now at
hoaka (two days old), roaming among the stars
like a thready crescent of gold; yet an hour before
the time of *kulu* (full moon), ere she has filled her

maiden zone with glory from devouring many stars,
see that your battle-line is formed on the steep
hillside of Nuuanu, or the offspring of the Thunderer will be known in the land of Oahu no more.

"Open your ears, that you may hear; for it is
Pele who lifts the veil of *poeleele* (darkness) before
you. I will hang the yellow kulu in the western
sky, till her white sheen lies like a roadway of silver
between the gap of the great breakers leading into
your harbor of Honolulu. Watch you in that hour,
— you, and the fair young Queen I have given
you, — for afar off upon the sea you shall behold
the *waas* of Kauai, bringing Keao and his warriors,
who are more numerous than the whistling plovers
on Waikiki's sandy shore.

"Fight the battle which I now *permit* you with
the ambushed foe among the mountains, — lest
your gay plumes droop like a fowl's in a storm, —
then hasten to your own fair isle. Bid every warrior whet his weapons into its utmost keenness;
mend his spears and paloas, for the blood of Oahu's
braves shall flow in your beautiful valley of Nuuanu, until its streams shall be redder than the hue
of my rivers of lava.

"But out of much evil may come some good,
even to those who suffer and toil; such is the
method of the gods. In that day the battle shall
not go to the strong; else my loved young hero
must go down. In the hour of your final victory
you will love whom you love with a devotion you

cannot bestow to-day, for she is wiser and braver
than you know ; for is she not akin to Pele ?

" Be cunning, and watchful, and full of the circuitous wisdom of the serpent, in your warfare
with the sons of men. As the battle is not to the
strong, so the race is not to the swift. The sharp
eyes of a great warrior spies the end of battle afar
off, and layeth deep his cunning pitfalls before the
footsteps of the foe. He appears to his enemy in
unexpected places, until fear possesses the heart
of whom you would ensnare, lest the one pitfall
he has discovered should be only one of many.
Lest, because his one weak flank has been assailed
and crushed, so the other likewise may be in
danger from a hidden snare he cannot discover.
Thus your foe flies because of your greater cunning in the hour of battle.

" You, and your *Alii kapus*, should have praise
because of your frequent worship at my *wahi
kapus* (sacred places), and your numerous sacrifices of kanakers at the great *heianu* at Waikiki.
Above all the sons of men my Boy King of Oahu
is the pride of my heart ; fierce in battle as the
mountain eagle, and swifter than the wind when
he pursueth the retreating foe. Yet other battles
shall he win, greater than all that have gone before ; and Pele will guide her young warrior's
hand in the hour of combat, and shield him from
peril in the thickest of the fight. Though Kalani
shall yet fight and win ; because of my love he
shall die young, and become a god.

"But Kamehameha is also my lover, and his worship is pleasing to my sight. He only has had courage to climb my lonely mountains without fear, and sit on the fiery brink of Kilauea without trembling. Even the black night and the mountain storms do not appall his great heart, for he has witnessed the wild revels of my gods of Kilauea, when I have spoken to him with tongues of liquid fire, and whispered to him with my voice of many earthquakes. Thus, because of his love for me, harm shall come to him no more from the hand of man — not even from Kalani — and his kingdom shall increase because of his bravery in battle, until there are no more kingdoms in the Eight Seas to conquer.

"Because of Kamehameha's love of the solitude of my lonely mountains, he is called the 'Lonely One.' But he came with a wish to see my face, and a great heart may bend the heavens to its will; and I came and sat by his side, for the gods love whomsoever can venerate without fear.

"Thus it came to pass that in the reign of Kalaniopuu I conversed in person with the Lonely One, — as I now make myself visible to Kalani,— and promised him the kingdom of Hawaii. On the death-bed of the old King, I bid him send for Kamehameha and bestow the half of his kingdom upon him. And he did it, and died. Kamehameha's battles with the rightful heir, Kiwalao, accomplished the rest; and he is sovereign king of

7

Hawaii, he and his descendants to the tenth generation.

"But Kalani is my hero, in whom I take delight. His beauty is a joy to Pele, and she has given him a princess such as the world of men has not seen before. The valor of my Boy King had won the heart of the wahine, and she loved him long; and you shall make her your Queen, and Oahu shall rejoice in her wisdom and her beauty.

"Be not vainglorious, for behold already your fame is enthroned among the stars. Because of your heroism, and our mutual love of warfare, Pele will now permit her young warrior to go forth and win a battle over the Hawaiians. They are already gathered in legions among the mountain glens above you; ambushed after the best manner in the knowledge of men.

"But because they have become too vainglorious, and have performed no Kane kapu (man tabu) in my sacred places, Pele will now show her almightiness to her people; such a witness of divine retribution as shall live forever in the memory of men.

"Go forth, Kalani! climb the steep sides of Kea with your small army of Oahu braves. Seek the fierce hordes of Hawaiians in the central of the three valleys; you will find them eager to meet you by the one, and ready to ambush you by the two. Of the two armies lying ambushed in the valleys on the right hand and the left, take ye no heed; though they think to pounce upon your rear, and

destroy you, Pele will set the seal of her might
upon them, for they are ungodly men. That
which we accomplish in your aid this day, shall
make your battle of Mauna Kea the most famous
in the warfare of men.

"On the one army to the left, Pele will lay her
hand lightly, as when a sea-hawk swoops among
the winged fishes and seizes but a few; not all of
these shall die, because of their leader, who has
worshipped me often in secret. But upon the
army ambushed to the right, exulting in vainglory
and scorning the gods, the weight of our just indignation shall fall. Though the sunlight shall
lie brightly upon Kalani and his battling warriors,
those of his foes to the right shall die. For I will
breathe with my fiery breath upon them, and they
shall drop down one by one like men in sleep;
singed and burned like a moth in the camp-fire,
and not one of all that host of fierce warriors
shall awake unto life again.

"So go forth to battle, and fear not for the
result; for though your foes are quadruple your
army in numbers, not one of that proud army
which most could harm you shall live to fight you.
It shall be a token to all the world that Pele is
mighty in her wrath, the one dread power above
all others, most terrible to behold in the day of
retribution.

"To Kalani of Oahu, the love of Pele thus bestowed, shall become the mightiest power of his
kingly crown. Kalani is my best-beloved hero

among the Isles, because of his youth and manly
beauty, his invincible courage in the front of battle,
and the religious abundance of human sacrifices in
the great Heiaus of his kingdom.

" I depart now to my palace home in Kilauea.
But in the hour of battle I will sit upon the mountain top and watch your great feats of arms. When
the battle is done, you and your blood-stained
warriors shall go and look upon a whole army of
dead Kanakas, retributed for a cause. Take warning by what you see !

" The token that Pele is pleased with her young
hero in that hour, and that she stands invisible by
his side in womanly admiration of his deeds, shall
be the dark spot I will lay upon the sun while I
abide with you. This, and the more visible token
of one lone puaa (hog) being seen rooting, swine-
like, among the dead warriors whom I have slain,
because of their sins and my great love for Kalani.
Aloha! kuu hoa Kalani." (Love to my friend
Kalani.)

With a smile of unearthly sweetness, and a lingering, tender glance from fond eyes of iris hue,
the flame-cloud in which Pele had sat, rose heavenward in majestic splendor, fading slowly and
almost imperceptibly away.

The stillness of death reigned in that little
sanctuary after the departure of the divine guest
from the great *heiau* of Hawaii. The thoughts of
Kalani were as thoughts of molten lava; his
young soul was fired with the brilliant deeds of

valor he would accomplish in the presence of the
divine goddess of Mauna Loa. He questioned, in
his heart, if the figurative language of Pele was to
be accepted as having a literal meaning. Would
she indeed enter in person into this unequal warfare with the Hawaiians? Time alone could tell.

In the outer world all was again calm. The
shock of earthquakes had ceased, and the heavens
had become cloudless, and the morning stars were
twinkling the last good night to their dancing reflections in the tranquil sea. The stern voice of
Paao — the great high-priest — was heard wailing
in sadness and sorrow, because of his insufficient
prayers, or ungenerous sacrifice of human victims,
having failed to bring acceptable acknowledgment
from the gods. And yet his human holocaust had
numbered his victims by the score.

Paao had received no sign as yet of the divine
presence of Pele, and knew not that she had
veiled her proximity from the lesser *Alii Kapu* by
the earthquake, and dealt alone with their young
King within the holy of holies, and gone forth to
her mountain throne again. But suddenly the
tones of Paao's mournful outcries were changed
into exultant cries of joy; for without the rumble
of an earthquake, or other indication of Pele's
being aware of his anxious oblations, there, upon
the dawn-touched snow-crest of Mauna Loa, jets
the red lava with its finger of fire into the sky,
rolling down the mountain side in a river of blood
toward the sea.

For an hour the fiery eruption flowed forth in red vomit that outcrimsoned the dawn, and then went down as suddenly as it came. The priest now proclaimed his glad tidings to the army without the walls of the heiau; announcing by the loud-voiced heralds that because of his long wrestling in prayer, and his holocausts of dead *Kane*, Pele had at length come to their aid and promised them victory.

Paao was still kept in ignorance of Kalani's interview with the Goddess, which was held secret because of the prophetic counsel imparted, that might perhaps serve to discourage the less brave chiefs of the army. For had not Pele imparted to Kalani the dread news of her having restored Kamehameha to life again? Had she not also asserted the renewal of her love for the grim and hideous giant of Hawaii — than whom none were held in such unseemly fear, because of his murderous havoc in battle, and his cunning policy in peace? And had Pele not further announced that the kingdom of Hawaii should remain Kamehameha's, and subsequently be permitted to grow on until it swallowed up all the other kingdoms of the Eight Isles?

Alas, had she not told Kalani that a great king and brave warrior was already secretly preparing an army to invade his beautiful kingdom of Oahu? Who could it be but Keao, his traitorous uncle, the fierce old king of Kauai. Here was a danger, indeed!

The brother of Kalani's dead father, knowing
the weakness of Oahu's army, from the long continued wars with Kamehameha, was designing to
steal, like a tempest at midnight, upon the coveted
kingdom, while Kalani was abroad contending
with the Hawaiians. This news would greatly
dishearten every warrior in the five kingdoms, for
Keao was known to be terrible as a thunderbolt in
the first shock of his battles; and but for the past
aid of his allied forces, the army of Oahu could
not have sustained themselves against the terrible
onslaughts of the Hawaiians.

Above all, had Pele not warned Kalani that he
should die young; that he could not be permitted
to outlive the latest deed of his coming glory?
Alas, alas! with all the world so bright and
beautiful before him, to die young and leave his
charming Kupule, whom he had already learned
to love better than his life.

Alas! to die and leave his fair isle of Oahu, with
its fruitful valleys, and its sea-gardens of rare pearls
and countless ocean treasures. Oahu, with its
odorous forests of sandalwood; its countless groves
of yellow orange, and red ohea-trees, where sing
the o-o and the royal iiwi. An Isle so precious in
the sight of deity that Moa-alii — the terrible sea-
god — is set to guard it, caverned in his subterranean den, deep down under the great coral reef
near the sacred heiau of Waikiki!

Well might the young King exclaim, in bitter
anguish, as he contemplated the brief span of life

allotted him by the Goddess: "Auwe! auwe! Aloha, kuu Kupule; aloha, kuu aupuni o Oahu!"

At the earliest dawn of light, Kalani called the leading chiefs of his army about him, simply informing them that he had received a revelation from Pele during the night, and bid them prepare to march with all haste upon the Hawaiians. They were soon upon their way, pressing forward up the deep central valley of Waimea, leading to the mountain fastness, where the enemy were seen flaunting their banana leaves, and brandishing their spears in defiance.

With a strong rear-guard in charge of Boki, ready to face about and defend the rear from a hidden foe, who were expected to close in upon them from the valleys on either hand after they had passed, Kalani led on his foremost rank of chiefs in person, because of some misgivings expressed among his more prudent warriors.

Marching straight up the central valley of the three, which debouched from a common centre on the steep mountain-side, hoping to fairly encounter the middle corps of the Hawaiians before their two ambushed wings could be brought into action upon his rear, Kalani found the cunning enemy steadily falling back, decoying him up the valley, with a view to their flanking armies being brought into action before battle was offered in front.

Still Kalani pressed boldly on, while the curcubita drums and bamboo fifes did their utmost to enliven his dispirited army, who liked not the certain peril of their position. They had marched nearly up to the head of the valley before the retreating enemy showed signs of coming to a stand and offering battle.

There were ominous clouds shrouding all the great mountain peaks above them, as they pressed on in breathless haste for conflict. Kea was hidden in more than midnight blackness. And from the more remote brow of Loa came an angry muttering, in prophetic keeping with the threatening clash of arms, as the serried ranks closed in upon each other for a death grapple at last.

The terrible blackness which so lowered upon them was not that of a thunder-storm, for no rain fell, and no lightning was visible. Momentarily the gathering gloom increased, creeping down more and more upon the valleys, until no man could fairly distinguish the face of his fellow. As the dismal blackness closed in fairly upon them, the sulphurous fumes blew into their faces, until every soldier stood aghast with weapon in hand, cowed by a peril more deadly than that of war.

Suddenly this horrible cloud rent asunder, and the storm of gray ashes fluttered down like snow-flakes upon the grass and trees. Above them showed a narrow, cloudless rift, through to the heavens beyond, down which burst the morning sun; until the birds sang, and the swaying fronds of the countless fern-trees glistened in his ray.

Then the two awe-stricken armies rushed into combat, fighting hand to hand with the utmost

desperation of frenzied men. Each of the contending nations accounted the sudden rift in the sulphurous cloud as a good omen, intended especially
for themselves. Both were worshippers of the
divine Pele, and it is not an unusual occurrence in
this world of ours for both the saint and the sinner
to each think themselves the most worthy of sancti-
fication, to the utter exclusion of all others.

As the contending armies fought on, swaying
to the one side of the valley and the other, they
heard the hoarse rumbling of earthquakes in the
adjacent valleys, invading their ears like muffled
thunder. It was apparent to all that Pele was
angered with some one, and was abroad upon the
war-path, bent upon destruction. And because of
the conceits of men, each thought the dread Goddess was about to chastise the other. Only the
favored King of Oahu knew the true meaning of
the clouded heavens and the rocking earth. And
knowing the tender, cerulean eyes of the beautiful
Goddess were looking down upon his swift deeds
of war, from her mountain eyrie above the clouds,
Kalani fought upon this eventful morning as never
young hero fought before. One after another of
the savage chiefs of Hawaii, deeming it their special mission to slay this over-valorous foe, leaped
from the ranks to confront him, and went down
before his flashing pahi, as falls a gnarled tree
before the blast of a tempest.

Soon the ranks of the Hawaiians were broken,
and they fled, hiding themselves in the thickets of

fern-trees and among the lateral ravines of the valley. As yet nothing had been seen of the dual army that was expected to close in upon their rear from the adjacent valleys. "Where are our ambushed forces, from which so much was expected?" was the question asked by the numerous skulking Hawaiians, as they listened with anguished hearts for some sound of combat down the valley, when they hoped to again take courage, and fall upon the doubly-beset Oahuans.

But only the song of summer birds among the fern-trees, and the hum of prolific bees among the hollyhock and hibiscus flowers, met the anxious ear. The sun still looked brightly down upon the Oahuans as they gathered up their wounded and returned cautiously down the valley. Yet still the black clouds rocked and rolled to and fro upon their either hand, and occasionally a breath of sulphur fume invaded their pathway as they returned below.

A few dismayed prisoners were taken as the Oahuans retreated, the bewildered scouts from the two divisions of ambushed Hawaiians. Some of these prisoners told a frightful story of some of their division to the right having been swallowed up by an earthquake, and the rest were hurrying down the mountain to escape further destruction; their leader sending on these scouts to warn the other division not to attack the Oahuans with hope of being supported. But what had happened to the left-hand division none as yet knew.

Leaving a guard with the prisoners and the wounded, Kalani now wheeled his army through a ravine leading to the other valley, with a hope to encounter the laggard division of the Hawaiian army. He had not marched far before he did encounter them indeed; they had fought their last fight with Pele, and were now an army of dead men! Not a soul in all that warlike host remained alive to fight or flee from the victorious soldiers of Oahu; dead, dead everywhere!

Rooting inquiringly about the gallant corpse of Kapiolani, their gigantic leader, was the one lone hog spoken of as the token that Pele had remembered and accomplished her promise to Kalani. The astonished swine next turned his attention to the brave and beautiful chieftess Moimoi, as she lay clasping the hand of her dead chief, and pressing her ashen lips to her dead lord's. So they had died; expressing to the last an affection that death could not sever.

Some of the noble chiefs appeared calm and without trace of lingering fear, as though they had dropped quietly to sleep by the wayside. Some were found in the attitude of supplication, but with naught of fear on their heroic faces — supplicants who demand justice, not mercy, when they plead with a cruel and relentless god.

But the faces of most of those of the common order were contorted with the most abject expression of fear; such men as die prematurely from apprehension, before the final death comes pleas-

antly to their rescue, — men who die twice with
every deathbed. The brave had died with a lingering hope upon their faces, lying crouched down
upon the mountain grass in best position to retain
their breath, awaiting hopefully for the sulphurous
cloud to pass away that they might attack their
foe; but a greater than Kalani had assailed them,
and they died.

One fair young couple — a youthful chief and
his winsome warrior wife — lay reclining against a
great rock on the hillside, locked fast in loving embrace, pressing nose to nose in fond national salutation ; each clasping the dear loved one confidingly, until the lamp-of-life went out, ushering such
as they to a brighter than earth can bestow.

Seeing the live hog rooting among the dead warriors, reminded Kalani that it was one of the tokens
which should denote the divine presence of Pele.
Turning to the sun, which just then burst through
the inky pall of cloud that still hovered over this
valley of Death, there, also, he could readily distinguish the dark spot upon his face of fire, which
was to comprise the token of double assurance that
the divine Goddess of Hawaii would be round
about her hero King.

In spite of the heat of battle he had undergone,
and the torrid sunshine pouring down upon him,
instantly a cold thrill of awe crept over the stalwart
frame of Kalani, as the awful conviction dawned
upon him that the dread Pele — the arbiter of battle, the creator of the world — was standing before

him in the broad light of day ; but in such complete
invisibility as not to be distinguished even by one
who knew her to be there.

Strong and piercing were the glances of his dark
eyes, as he flung his questioning look above and
about him everywhere. How his great heart leaped
with desire to look upon the beautiful Deity, with
her hair of woven sunshine and flame, and her eyes
of a kindred hue with the summer skies. But nothing in the form of godhead was visible to his human eyes.

True, the sunshine failed to reach down upon
the grass and flowers within an irregular circle at
his feet, though there were neither tree nor cloud
to intercept his burning ray. And yet the shadow
was not dense and strongly outlined, like the shade
cast by material things, only that it took on the
figure of a graceful woman, uncumbered by other
vesture than her abundant hair. Though only this
impalpable shadow could be defined, nevertheless,
every intuition of Kalani's roused young soul ad-
monished him of the presence of the one only god,
above all other gods in the land.

As the young King stood thus, in the tremor
and pose of expectation, suddenly two light hand-
touches were laid daintily upon his shoulders —
soft, ghostly, invisible hands — followed by the
loving pressure of two cold lips upon his own red
lips of fire. Tenderly and lovingly they clung, as
when two earthly lips are about to whisper their
farewell " Aloha ! "

Although Kalani knew it could be none other than Pele thus saluting him, yet he shrank back appalled, chilled to the heart's core with supernatural apprehension. Was it reality or some trick of fancy that so impressed the warrior King? Was it but a cold snow-breath creeping down from Kea's wintry crown that perpetrated this osculation upon him, so like to the kiss of a loving woman? Or might it not have been but a damp wind-gust stealing into the sunshine from the densly wooded ravine before him? Who can tell?

Still the flimsy shadow of a graceful, womanly form lay upon the alert grass and the exultant flowers. And while yet he questioned the Divine Shade with yet more watchful eye, he beheld it swell and sway; now to the one side, and now to the other; like the respiratory oscillations of a living being, or perhaps in answer to the keen interlocution of his soul, as eye may answer eye when other lovers stand questioning face to face.

Presently a change took place in the outline of the shade upon the grass, and the added shadow of two uplifted, fluttering wings were plainly distinguished; followed by the gentle fanning motion of the hot air impelled against his upturned face, — as when a dove seeks sudden flight, — and the shadow was seen upon the grass no more.

But as Pele winged gently upward, on her way to Kilauea, there came a loving message fluttering back into Kalani's tensive ear, saying, in the melodious voice of a singing bird, "Aloha, ka'u

Moi!" (Love to you, my King!) Adding what
could only be interpreted by loving ears, as, "Be
brave! Be strong! For is not Kalani of Oahu
beloved of the gods?"

And the dread presence of the divine Goddess
was felt no more. Turning his eyes with a questioning look to the sun, Kalani saw that the delusive spot upon its face was gone. And his
respiration deepened, and his tensile muscles relaxed, so that his rigid limbs became supple again.
And as the blood-stained young warrior regained
self-consciousness, he ordered the retreat of his
victorous army, for his far-famed battle of Mauna
Kea was won, and recorded among the stars.

Leaving the many hundred dead warriors thus
slain by Pele, to their transcient sleep of death,
Kalani returned to Kawaihae, and filled his canoes
with plunder. At night, when the strong trades
of the day went down, the great fleet, with their
war-worn and weary, set sail with the favoring
land wind for Maui. There they related their
tales of daring, and the miracle performed in
their favor by Pele, which thus enabled them to
win their great battle of the Mountain.

From that hour their Keiki Moi (Boy King) was
almost deified by his people. The influence he
had acquired over the dread Goddess of Kilauea
was unprecedented in the knowledge of men.
They little knew of the terrible weight of prophetic wisdom borne in the heart of their young
monarch, because of the introspective glance Pele

had permitted him to catch of the irrevocable
future.

Oh, the kind wisdom of the Creator, in dropping
an impenetrable veil over the future in the lives
of men. Though his curtains are flung wide,
down the remotest Past, untrammeling our retro-
spect in whatsoever direction we would gaze.

8

See the home of Kalani!—long the palace of kings—
How 'twill gladden to-night o'er the Beauty he brings!
There the sweet-singing O-o will sing to my bride,
And our dark-eyed Wahines come sit by thy side.

Look there on Nuuanu! enchanting it lies,
Like a dream-land of beauty dropt down from the skies;
There the orange and plantains luxuriant grow,
And the streams from the mountain exultingly flow.

See the palms of Waikiki lean over the sea,
Their fronds in glad welcome are waving to thee!
On its bay of blue waters thy *waa* shall ride,
And the Mermaids of Pearl Garden sing to my bride.

CHAPTER VIII.

EAVING a small force in charge of Maui, Kalani hastened the departure of his army for Oahu. He took Kupule along with him, together with several young chieftesses who had become attached to the beautiful princess during her sojourn at Lahaina.

Word had just been brought from Kauai of Keao's disaffection, and that he was rapidly collecting a great army for the purpose of capturing Oahu. Rumor stated, that because of Kalani's ambition to possess Hawaii, Keao feared that his warlike nephew would next undertake the invasion of Kauai. So the fierce old warrior had aroused, and now hoped by a bold stroke to possess himself of Oahu, while Kalani was away upon his foreign invasion.

Taking the flower of his Maui army along with him, and leaving a few of the least serviceable chiefs behind, Kalani spread his sails to the fresh, fair trade wind, and the great fleet winged their way along the southern shore of Molokai.

Early in the afternoon the foremost vessels of the fleet passed Koko point, and skirted Kona's fertile shore, where the wind became light, and it was approaching night when they passed Diamond

Head, and coasted just without the long line of
gigantic breakers abreast of Waikiki. Every canoe
feeding out their hoarded morsel to Moa-alii as
they passed his caverned home under the reef-bed
in front of the great *Heiau* built in the mouth of
the Manoa valley beyond.

Here first Kupule saw her new Oahu home,
peering out from among its great king-palms and
large bread-fruit trees, far up the beautiful vale
of Nuuanu, than which nothing is more charming
in all the Hawaiian world. While the evening
was approaching, and they were coasting along
the unbroken surf, stretching from Leahi (Diamond
Head) to the harbor's mouth, Kalani pointed out
his seaside palace, seen in the midst of the great
cocoanut grove at Waikiki.

To the right of the palm trees rose the massive
walls of the great *heiau*, with its temples and
towers, and sacrificial places within; where in the
terrible Kapu Kane, thousands of human offerings
were sacrificed in the service of Pele and Moa-alii.

To the left of Waikiki glowed Puawai — the
Punch Bowl mountain — in the setting sun, looming like a monstrous storm-billow dropped in unbroken grandeur upon the plain. Where its
frowning battlement of jutting rocks, and turret
peaks of gray lava, overlooked the town, was now
flung to the breeze a yellow tapa flag, to signal
the approach of the King.

On sped the fleet with the soft-blowing trades,
clinging to the white line of coral reef, and keep-

ing just without its roaring, floundering breakers,
whose crests were now gilded like oriental domes
by the dying day. Kalani's heart was made glad
as he passed countless scenes of happy boyhood
days, while he pointed out to his blushing bride
elect his fair kingdom of Oahu ; his royal palace
of Nuuanu — the barbaric home of a long line of
warrior kings.

Here luxuriant nature seemed to have completed
a grateful task of love. Grouping together in the
fair Nuuanu vale her utmost beauties for a kingly
home. Here flourished every fruitful tree and
prolific vine, and grew the greenest grasses and the
rarest flowers, with heaped-up rugged mountains
to overlook and overawe the completed whole.

A wide-mouthed valley, blue-marged by the
sea, and blue-rimmed by the distant sky ; narrow-
ing downward from the far skyward hills, where
the mountain gateway of the dizzy Pali opens above
the sea into the sky beyond. Green with the
ceaseless perennity of a thousand varying hues,
the Nuuanu expands as it descends in easy slopes
down to the reef-barred harbor of Honolulu.

The green lawns of the valley are only separated
by a coral sand-beach from ocean's rarest madreporic sea, wherein the thousands of sun-swarthed
children swim, from the hour of birth to the octo-
genarian days of decrepitude. Here the youth of
adolescent age, whether *wahine* or *kane*, may dive
in playful pastime for the gaudy shells, the rare-
hued corals, and the opulent pearls. Here they

fish from the inner reef-edge, whether for pleasure
or profit, with never a doubt of abundant pastime
for the children, or of readily accorded sufficiency
to the lazy housewife's demand.

Crowning a palm-clad knoll upon the east side
of the valley, Kalani had already pointed out the
vine-covered palace of his sires. About its numerous outbuildings were fine old bread-fruit trees,
with their dark green foliage, looming stately and
grand among the more graceful palms, the gnarled
pandana and the symmetrical Kukui trees.

To the east of the palace rose the frowning
Punch Bowl, a grass-grown crater, brooding over
its ancient days of fiery splendor now long gone
by. Back of this towers Tantulus, overlooking
the Punch Bowl, and densely tree-clad to his top.
Beyond all rises grand old Waolani, the nearest
approach to Kea and Loa that Oahu can show.

Just back of the busy palace knoll uprose a
higher hill, sacred to the gods, and tabooed with
the utmost rigor for the use of priest and king;
its whole rounded crest and sloping sides were
clothed with a dense grove of orange trees, ever,
as now, presenting a countless abundance of blossoms and fruit the whole year round.

On the very apex of this sacred hill there leaps
up a charming natural fountain, emerging from
out a mound of vine-covered rocks, jetting forth
from a clear, never-failing spring, and running the
zigzag course of a mountain brook down the valley
to the sea. From out the cool, crystal waters of

this grass-grown, flower-verged fountain, it is said that many mystic and unearthly sights have been disclosed, in divine answer to priestly oblation and royal prayers. It is the *Kiowai o' Pele* (fountain of Pele) sacred to the gods.

This sacred grove has been the holy of holies of a long line of noble kings. A tabooed resort where the reigning monarch has sought for solitude during the various phases of the midnight moon, when interceding with the gods for divine aid during contemplated wars.

Here also came the cruel Alii Kapu — the tabu chief — when his king was depressed in body or mind, with the fear of death upon him, and in the belief that some sorcerous enemy was praying him to death — a current belief of the time. Here came the great High Priest, and after fasting and prayer, would necessarily discover in the fountain the treacherous visage of the wicked *Kilo*, who was secretly praying his king to death. And when thus discovered, it was a natural sequence that the body of the impious sorcerer should be needed as a victim in the next *Kapu Kane*, proclaimed for the good of the state at the sick king's command.

Above and beyond all these lesser hill-tops arises another, where leaps a wild cascade down the rocky declivity, emerging from a densely wooded glen above, ravined and craggy with jutting rocks tumbled from the mountain by the earthquake shocks in years gone by. Below the wild cascade and the noisy stream, the waters broaden out into a mountain mere, and end in a wide, smooth waterfall, where the western orbs of night and day glass their seven prismatic hues in rainbow sheen or Luna glory. While in the windless waters of the tiny mere, the jagged peak of Waolani may mirror his rugged beauties with every eastern sun.

From another little lakelet, skirting the foot of the palace knoll, flowed the murmuring mountain stream valleyward, in eager haste to the sea. And because of the dislike for fresh water, of the fastidious polypi, who reared the great coral reefs, the Oahuans are indebted to this stream of Nuuanu for their novel and beautiful harbor of Honolulu, or Fairhaven.

True, it was the work of centuries for this little stream; but small means, with constant application, may tear a mountain from its base. And no better illustration can be shown of what may be accomplished by small things than this work of the Nuuanu brook, in excavating a roomy harbor, and an outlet, through the great reef-bed, though the sea-girt shore was defended by the inrolling avalanche of its ponderous breakers.

Not only is the harbor novel and compact, but the anchorage is made a safe one by the deep, tenacious alluvium deposit made by the stream while working patiently at its subterraneous excavation, and making its subsequent assaults to pierce through the barrier reef-bed, making a commercial gateway to the sea.

Through this one narrow opening, cleft through the gigantic breakers, which uprear in dangerous proximity on either hand, Kalani's long line of war canoes now found entrance into the harbor; steering in as the swift shades of night shut down, by the flickering lights of an hundred camp-fires up the Nuuanu, where the new levies of Oahu's army lay roasting their bread-fruit as an accession to the usual evening meal of poi and lawaia — fish.

Wild and uproarious was the welcome flung over the water from a thousand voices, as their doubly victorious King debouched with his fleet through the watery gateway into the harbor. Though numerous dead warriors were distributed throughout the canoes, yet they were deemed but tokens of the desperation of his battles, and the wailing, as yet, was muffled and low, lest the glad welcome they would tender their Boy King should be marred.

Among the crowd of chiefs and priests gathered about the landing-place to greet Kalani, were seen crippled warriors of both sexes, hoary grandsires, and tottling children, all coming to shout their praises of the warlike deeds of their heroic monarch, and sing their hymeneal song of rejoicing in glad welcome to Kupule; the story of her goodness and beauty being well known among them all.

The same demonstrative scene of joy and and grief was here undergone as that which had transpired at Maui. It was well into the evening hours be-

fore Kalani and Kupule could break away from
the endearments of the people, and take the homeward valley path along the flowery banks of the
babbling stream leading up to the palace of
Nuuanu.

Here a rich repast awaited the King and the
numerous Alii Kapu, whom he had invited to partake with him. For grave matters of state must
be discussed ; and the threatened invasion of Keao
was a topic of moment, sufficient to detain chief,
and priest, and warrior, far into the night.

Kupule and her numerous retinue of charming
young wahine alii (girl chiefs) were entertained
by themselves in the women's eating-house. For
among the Polynesia it is not only a breach of
etiquette, but a most heinous sin for male and
female — of whatever rank or state — to partake
of food together, or even in the same house. It
was a *kapu nui*, and death was the penalty in very
many cases.

As the night seemed warm to the Hawaiian
princess, after supper Kupule led the way out
among the grand old trees for better air. At her
dear old Hilo home they were always refreshed by
the cool mountain breezes from Kea's snows during the evening ; while here in the Nuuanu, the
night winds are ever soft and fragrant. But Hilo
is located upon the windward shore, while Honolulu lies under the lee of the mountains.

Kupule and her favorite companion, Manona,
seated themselves beneath the tutui trees, sur-

rounded by many another maiden attached to her household. The days of *muku*, (no moon,) had passed, and before the laughing wahines hung *hoaka*, the thin crescent of the moon, reflecting herself in the little lake beneath, and dancing a merry *hula-hula* in every ripple of the mountain stream, down to the sea, where every crest of the great breakers adorned its crown with a crescent of luna gold.

The palace stood just where numerous deeply-cleft forest glens found their way into the broad valley of Nuuanu. From out these cool ravines — now the trade winds were stilled down for the night — there stole the grateful perfumes, distilled throughout the day from the wild-grown fruits and spontaneous flowers. Coming now, hand in hand, with the tottling night airs like baby lovers, hurrying to greet the infant moon, they blunder into the faces of every laughing maiden and wooing lover, as they wander in pairs, ever-welcomed guests, over the whole valley in the light of the moon-sheen.

In spite of these cats-paws of fragrance and zephyrs, the cloudless night was calm and peaceful. The lizards sang dreamily in the great algaroba tree near by, prompting the maidens into song; those low sweet *meles* made up of the countless harmonies around. The rumbling surf, floundering on the reef-bed, and the resonant waterfall tumbling tunefully from the crags, were the only two obtrusive soliloquists that would not

become hushed sufficient to comport with the
placid night scene.

But for the flashing of camp-fires across the
valley, and the occasional passionate invective of
some grim old warrior against Keao, for his
threatened invasion, none might have deemed there
were such elements of discord as war and ambitious strife among men.

In due time the maidens retired to the royal
sleeping house of the wahines. While the King
and his wise old war-chiefs lingered far into the
night hours, perfecting their plans so as to increase the thinned ranks of the army, to enable
them to successfully resist the powerful force
likely to be brought against them by King Keao.

At the suggestion of Paao, the great high priest,
it was thought best to proclaim a mild tabu on the
morrow; a kapu puaa (hog taboo) being thought
sufficient for the occasion, which was also the
final completion of the obsequies of the dead
chiefs brought from Hawaii. The dread *kapus* of
the Polynesia were as important an element to the
obsequies of a great chief, as were a profusion of
oboli at a Greek burial. The dead soldiers not
being of sufficient importance to encumber the
fleet, had been fed to Moa-alii from off the cliffs at
Kawaihae, as a small propitiation to the sea god.

The present tabu was made a light one, so that
the chiefs, not immediately connected with the
dead, might attend to hunting up every spearsman
within their districts. It was also necessary to in-

voke the labor of every woman in the land, to dig taro and make poi sufficient to sustain an army, should they become besieged by the invaders from Kauai.

Up to this time Kupule had not been proclaimed as Queen, nor had any public marital ceremony been performed. When the King gave the princess Pelelulu the half of his name, while making passage from Hilo, by so doing he publicly engaged himself to her. When he at the same time pronounced her tabued to the King, it would have been considered just cause of death for any one to essay to woo her; as well as death to the maiden herself should she attempt to win any other chief, as it is considered right and etiquette for any free maiden to do in Hawaii.

When, just before landing at Maui, Kalani tore off a strip of his yellow tapa and tied it about the neck of the captive girl, it became the royal badge, the King's tabu — the Star and Garter of Oahu. And upon the day of his departure, when going to invade Hawaii, when in the presence of the great chiefs and the high priest, Kalani plucked out one of the red plumes from his war helmet, and publicly placed it in the dark hair of Kupule, the King invested her with present authority during his absence, and the permanent rank of Queen in case of his death while away.

Yet so far the royal princess was looked upon as only the Queen elect. A preliminary state of things quaintly expressed by the one word *hoaho*, a

unique etymon in a language having no term implying chastity. Hoao, literally meaning a state of
trial, with a view to marriage ; a custom in common use by the chiefs, and in some measure by
the people.

On the third day after the arrival of the army
at Oahu, as no further news was heard from Kauai,
and the trades were now blowing too strong for
canoes to make headway against it, a *kapu hua*, or
fruit tabu, was announced, and Kupule was proclaimed, by heralds, throughout the island, as
Queen of Oahu.

A great feast had been prepared for the occasion, and three hundred of the noble chiefs, and
their families, were in attendance, with several
thousands of the common order. Hundreds of
whole hogs, dogs, fowls, and fishes, were baked
in the monstrous earth-ovens, made by hot stones
and green leaves, together with all the usual ac-
companiment of vegetables, bread-fruit, bananas,
etc., which were cooked with and served at the
same time with the meats.

Palm wine and *awa* were in extensive use, adding greatly to the hilarity of the lordly chiefs,
and imparting an unbecoming jollity and state of
limpidity to their lymphatic wives. Dances and
games, and feats of arms, were entered into with
the greatest zest, and the royal wedding was made
the occasion for one of the merriest times known
for many a year.

The marriage ceremonies of the Hawaiian Islands conformed to no law, other than the pleasure of the parties most interested. A most revolting custom sometimes compelled the high-chiefs to marry the next in rank, though the person were a cousin, an aunt, or a sister. This arbitrary custom was not approved, as incest was considered disgraceful, and usually these unnatural marriages were in mere nominal compliance with the distasteful law — not sufficiently binding upon either party to prevent one taking a new wife and the other a new husband.

Dancing at festivities was as universal as swimming, enjoyed by people of all ages and both sexes. These dances (hula) assumed various characteristics; the *hula alaapupa* was accompanied by chants and a chorus, the chosen subject being the warlike achievements of the king; and in the present instance the happy love of Kalani for his youthful queen. Usually professional dancers took the lead, the males being decorated with necklaces of human hair, adorned with sharks' teeth and the fangs of dogs. The women were prettily wreathed with flowers, and wore necklaces of shells, corals, and pearls, encircling their limbs with anklets and armlets, beautifully fabricated from colored feathers of rare birds. At wedding festivals the girls garlanded their long flowing hair after a most tasteful fashion; the youthful *wahines* rightfully priding themselves upon this feature of beauty, emulous of the long black tresses of their Queen, for the silken hair of the princess had not been cultivated in vain.

But upon this, her bridal day, Kupule's regal garments were of greater value than the robes of an empress of the Orient. And yet the number of her vestments were but two. The páu, or kirtle, worn upon this happy occasion, was constructed of the rare golden-yellow feathers of the iiwi, of which the gorgeous mamos of kings are made. Kupule's glistening páu reached only from the waist to her knees. About her legs were clasped beautiful anklets of tiny shells and rare bits of red and yellow coral. Her small, arched feet were left rosy and bare, and surely no civilized *kane* could have the heart to wish them concealed in the modern deformity of shoes.

Over her shoulders was thrown with careless grace the small mamo, glistening like a vestment of woven stars. This war-cloak, or cape, of a royal chieftess, implies a wish to take rank not only as a queen, but as a warrior wahine. The mamo was also fabricated from the priceless iiwi feathers, previously described; only two of the tiny feathers being found under each wing. More than ten thousand people were employed in trapping the birds and weaving this mamo and páu of Kupule's. About the bottom of this free-flowing war-cape there were festooned more than a thousand royal seed-pearls.

About the neck of the blushing bride there depended a triple string of the most opulent queen-

pearls found in the ocean. From the front of this
necklace hung the noted cluster of diamonds which
had been handed down by the kings of Oahu, an
heirloom from the old Spanish wreck, from whose
grandees they claim their descent, and from whose
cloaks their mamoes were patterned.

The long silken tresses of the maiden Queen
were put simply back over her ears, and left flowing in wild magnificence to her knees, their only
bondage being a wreath of wild hibiscus-flowers.
Secured to the wreath upon her forehead, clung
the crimson plume of the tropic bird, given her at
Maui by the King, who bestowed it as a badge of
her queenly rank.

About her plump and rosy arms Kupule wore
several of those exquisite bracelets made of " Pele's
hair," being almost as golden as the feathers of her
mamo. These wind-blown locks of the goddess are
flung wide over the land and the sea, during every
volcanic eruption ; tokens to remind the people that
Pele is the one god, supreme over all, unto whom
daily reverence is due, and frequent *kapu kane* is
required to insure her favorable remembrance of
men. None but one claiming kindred with the
Goddess would have the temerity to deck her person with these sacred locks, which are secured to
the *heiaus* as holy emblems of worship.

Sometimes these tresses are blown far out to sea,
and fall upon the decks of vessels. Woe to that
ship if aught of irreverence is done to this " Pele's
hair," for as sure as the sun shines, death comes to

9

one or more on board; or Moa-alii is importuned
to wreck the ship itself for any great delinquency.

The dress of Kalani upon this august occasion,
was only that of a warrior in full battle array.
Marriage, on the part of a great chief, was considered as a lordly condescension, rather than a
necessary rite; hence the festal display upon this
happy occasion argued well for Kalani's love. He
only wore his kingly mamo, depending to his knees,
with his graceful war helmet upon his head, and
the usual *malo* worn by all men, being a narrow
girdle about the waist, extending down before and
behind.

About the neck of the King was suspended a
huge carved tooth of the sperm whale. Though
this ornament was a little ostentatious in weight
and size, it was considered the rarest and most
costly adornment among the isles.

The last young King of Hawaii, Kiwalao, lost
his life in the hour of battle, because he left his
fallen enemy half dispatched, in his eagerness to
rob him of his cachalot's tooth. Seeing the situation of his favorite warrior, Kamehameha sprang
to the rescue of Keeaumoku, giving opportunity
for the prostrate chief to rally and spring up and
kill Kiwalao, the king, — thus saving tooth and
life both, items of about equal value with many.

When the great feast was ready to be served,
and all the royal chiefs were seated in a great circle under the trees, the kane Alii being gathered
among the palms, and the wahine Alii clustered

under the tutuis, with the great algaroba in their
centre. the King arose and went from among the
chiefs into the Queen's house.

Soon the wild shouts of the people filled the
valley with joy. Kalani was seen leading the
radiant Kupule forth, followed by her maidens, on
his way to place her in her circle of women,
awaiting to begin the repast. As the young couple
came forth, Paao, the high-priest, led the way
before them ; dressed in his official garb of black
tapa, and bearing the king's god, Pua, before him,
before which all men bow their heads in reverence
and fear, and all women cover their faces and
humble themselves to the earth. As they passed
on, numerous war-heralds ran about everywhere,
repeating the words of Paao:

"This is Kupule! the beautiful Queen of our
warrior King. Pelelulu of Hawaii is no more.
By the will of Pele she is our Queen. Whosoever
lets his shadow fall across her path, shall die!
Proclaim it, ye *Lunapai!* that he that hath ears
may hear ; and the eyes of all men may see."

Thus were they wedded, in presence of all the
nobles of the land. Leaving the blushing bride
to feast among her maidens, within the great circle
of the fat wives of the chiefs, Kalani and Paao
returned to the grove of king-palms, and gave the
signal for the hungry warriors to begin. The food
being served upon great green leaves and sea-
shells, the liquids and semi-fluid foods being con-

tained in bottles and every variety of dishes made from gourds.

After the feasting was over, Kalani went for the Queen, and together they took their seats on the veranda in front of the palace. Then a general reception commenced. Most of the many thousand people present came up after the chiefs and the priests, and greeted the royal couple, bowing low, and striking their breasts vigorously in token of their allegiance, as they passed.

Thus ended the ceremony, binding in wedlock this much-loved couple of Oahu. The remaining part of the day was spent in games, and feats of arms; the soldiers joining in mock battle with long spears, and short, barbed javelins; the chiefs wielding their great *laau palaus*, or the unsightly *pahi*, two-edged, with jagged sharks' teeth.

As the evening shut down over the Nuuanu, the youngest of the people joined in the fantastic *hula hula*, many a dancing group being formed throughout the valley. While the warriors and the more thoughtful ones of the seniors gathered about the white-haired Puaaihi, the blind old bard, who upon momentous occasions came down from his hermitage far up the misty valley of Manoa, where the daily rainbows hang their bows of promise over the sightless poet's home, as if in poetic commiseration of his blindness.

It was in the province of Puaaihi to relate in song the remote pedigrees of both the royal families, now united by wedlock; singing, as none

other could, the wonderful prowess of some of
their more celebrated ancestors. It was also the
gift of the bard to peer with lynx eyes into coming
events, and lay bare the awful forecasting of the
future. But being on the eve of a great battle,
where the nation needed their utmost courage to
sustain them, in fear that Puaaihi might disclose
too much for the public conscience to bear, Kalani
had whispered in the ear of the gnarled old
prophet to confine himself to the immediate coming events, lest by some chance he should discourage the chiefs and strike a panic upon the
common people, by disclosing that which Pele had
imparted to himself in the heiau at Hawaii.

Strange and mysterious as it may seem, nothing
of national importance had ever yet transpired in
the memory of man that had not previously been
foretold by Puaaihi. Therefore the young King
was not surprised to find his meaning was at once
comprehended by the wise old bard, who had evidently long since been the repertory of Pele's
irrevocable horoscopy of events.

As lightning bursts from out the midnight gloom,
 So Pele flashed, on those within the grove;
Her face was sad, like one who bears a doom
 Convoked by sins the Godhead *must* reprove!

On fiery clouds the haughty Goddess leans —
 As might an earth-maid lie on flowers fair —
A rolling, sulph'rous cloud of flame, that screens
 The Goddess save where falls her golden hair.

Abashed and awed the trembling lovers bow;
 For none can look on Pele's face divine!
She who so loved the King, records her vow:
 " Revile the gods! and sudden death is thine."

" How fair thy Queen! thy Kingdom, fair to see;
 Thy Fame invades the star-robed skies above!
But *pride* has tempt to sin — lost victory !
 And robbed my *Keiki Moi* of Pele's love."

CHAPTER IX.

NEARLY a fortnight had now passed since the army came from Maui. The King and his great war chiefs had applied themselves with assiduity·in reorganizing and drilling their newly recruited forces, until the army was now considered in such state of discipline as to justify the leading warriors in believing they were more than a match for Keao.

Thus far the trade-winds had blown boisterous, favoring Oahu. For with such strong wind and rough seas, the army of Kauai could not embark upon their threatened enterprise. The people of the Pacific Islands name many of their days by the moon phases, and prognose with great accuracy upon all important accessions of wind and weather by the devious changes of the weird lunar orb.

The glorious night of Kulu had come, the broad, full moon ; and the trades had dropped away into cooing breezes, with barely strength enough to sway the long pendent palm-leaves ; while brook-side grasses and flowers were left to mirror themselves in the tranquil pools, placid as even the star-flowers in the sky.

135

The sea lying between Oahu and Kauai had now become smooth enough for the fierce old Keao to undertake his treacherous invasion if he desired. It was but a stretch of eighty miles, and the Kauaians were possessed of the largest and best canoes in the world, and none doubted but the old king would attempt a landing during the night.

It was becoming late in the evening, and the great saffron face of Kula had long since looked down into the Nuuanu from above the highest mountain peaks, and she was now fast chasing the black shadows from every western aspect of Waolani. The young Queen and two of her favorite maidens, Manona and Leleha, seemed the only ones awake about the palace grounds. The trio still lingered under the tutui trees awaiting the return of the King.

Kalani and Boki had long since gone across the Nuuanu to inspect the condition of the army, and satisfy themselves that the chiefs were alert and the outposts were placed against any possible surprisal.

It was the general belief of all that Keao would land before morning. But whether he would disembark at Ewa Bay or at Honolulu, remained uncertain. So the look-outs were stationed along this interval of coast, and also upon the highlands above where the army lay. This precaution, together with the thoughtful one of anchoring a canoe upon the Middle Ground, a shoal spot just without the harbor entrance, would seem to insure them against surprise.

The hours flew fast, and it was already almost midnight before Kalani came in sight, from where two loving eyes were watching before his palace door. As he leaped the brook at the foot of the knoll, Kupule sprang down the hill and ran to meet him; bounding like a young fawn, with her fresh, fond heart beaming tenderly in her eyes. She had already acquired a strong influence over her liege lord and King by her quick intelligence and native charms.

Kalani flung wide his golden mamo to receive her, tossing it from his shoulders, and extending his arms to his darling as she ran to meet him. Taking her flushed young face into his hands, after he had embraced her, he pressed his kingly greeting warmly, but soberly, upon lips that glowed carmine even in the moonlight.

Gazing with mingled pleasure and pride into the soft, dark eyes that delved so keenly into his own, searching anxiously for the troubles of state that had disturbed him throughout the day, Kalani entered at once into the gratification of those orbal questionings, now expressed with such delicate intrusiveness by his darling.

"Has my little Queen turned owl, that she watches so late into the night for her lover King?"

"Does the moon-flower of Oahu sleep, while the beautiful Kulu sits upon her throne among the stars? Then why should Oahu's Queen slumber,

with a cloud lingering upon the kingly brow of
Kalani! Have the good gods not answered your
prayers, my King? Has the divine Pele failed to
respond to your every wish? 'BE BRAVE! BE
STRONG!' *Auwe, Moi* Kalani, *na ke aloha o* Pele!*
For all things come to pass as the gods require,
not as men desire."

" '*Be brave, be strong!*' who put those admonitions of Pele's into the mouth of my Kupule?
They have rung in Kalani's ears since the battle
on the mountain, so uttered by the invisible lips
of Pele in the land of Hawaii."

" Then treasure them in thy soul, *auwe, ko'u
Moi!* (oh, my King!) for Kupule knows not
whence they came. Have you done with your
warriors to-night, my love?"

" Ae oia, Oluolu!" (yes, Sweet!) " I have done
with them, unless their war-bugles call me to
battle. What would my Kupule with her King?"

" I would my Kalani should come with his little
Queen to the tabued grove, and sit in the light of
the moon by the Goddess' Fountain. It is the
hour when the gods are abroad in the sacred places
of the Isles. Kupule is troubled in her heart lest
her *maikai Moi* (good king) be not with her after
to-night. Let us be to each other all we may in
these last dread hours before the battle."

Kalani twined his arm tenderly about the slight
form of his darling, and in sadness and silence
together they found their way up the steep foot-

---

* Oh, King Kalani, for the love of Pele!

path by the tumbling rivulet, and entering the orange grove on the sacred hill, they seated themselves by the dread Fountain of Pele, in the still midnight hour.

Where the grass rose green and the flowers grew bright, and the clambering vines garland the rocks and the trees, there the sacred pool of the gods was found, rimmed round about on its farther side by the overhanging ledge. While up from the spring on its rock-bound side leaped the plumy jet of a natural fountain, flashing back into the pool and over the trees, spraying the grass and flowers and vines that were trained there by unseen hands.

Along the path by which the lovers had come, leaped the stream from the spring, singing with a babbling voice as it ran bounding like a roe down the hillside on its way to the sea. It was indeed a fairy spot, this rock-bound fountain, so nestled among the fruit-bearing trees. Above all other spots, it seemed fit seclusion for the weird, wild worship of tabu priests and warrior King.

And it was indeed the chosen place of meeting of the Visibles and the Invisibles of this and other worlds. Here met the unseen spirits from the depths of nether earth, and those more subtle ones from the ambient air. Here congregated those evanescent qualities and impalpable things which rule over the destinies of men ; often materializing themselves into visible shapes, human or divine,

and imparting their joyous bequest to the one, and
their fearful maledictions to another.

That our couple were found seated in the silence
and the solitude of such a place, beneath the
mystic charm of a midnight moon, implies they
are gifted with hearts where courage and resolution reign supreme. Kalani had come willingly to
counsel with his wise little monitress, and answer
her intuitive entreaties as best he could.

As it approached very near to the midnight
hour, the time of the appearance of whatsoever
and whosoever were to come, the lovers were seen
to cling a trifle closer, and hush their breathings
into almost indefinite respirations, as they involuntarily became disturbed by the frequent and
various vibrations of the air above, and the earth
whereon they sat. If a shadow came over the
face of the moon, it was not for human eyes to discover the cause, for not a cloud or other visible
thing could be seen. If the fruit came tumbling
rapidly down from the trees, because of the hurried
descent of those who came late from above, it was
not fit subject for human wisdom to investigate,
lest harm should come out of it. Even when the
previously tranquil pool suddenly overran its
flowery marge, whereon they sat, showing every
appearance of unusual ebullition on its moon-
touched surface, it would be considered perhaps as
insufficient evidence of the numerous baneful
spirits hurrying up from the nether world, like all
evil qualities, impatient to dispose of whatsoever

of malevolence they brought, upon whomsoever it must fall.

But arousing, at length, from the overshadowing awe so often cast by supernatural things, and in moral assertion of their equal right of occupation, Kalani addressed himself to the business of consultation which had brought the human part of the congregation to this sacred place.

" Darling, it is a busy night about the fountain. But never fear, we will attend to that which brought us here. Has my young Queen harbored thoughts that her *koa Moi* (warrior King) will fall in the coming fight with Keao ? "

" The wings of Kupule's thoughts are not drooping with the doubts that burden them. The pinions of her soul are alert and fluttering, like the tremulous wings of a wounded bird, because of the terrible dread which wraps itself about her heart, colder than the wintry snows on Kea's yonder crest. Tell me, Kalani — tell your little Queen — has the good Pele sanctioned your fighting with Keao, and promised you victory, since the terrible *kapu kane* of yesterday ? Certainly Paao sacrificed a goodly number of poor victims to propitiate the Goddess."

" Neither to Paao nor Kalani has the dread Goddess made herself visible since our return from Hawaii. The great heart of Kalani is troubled lest Pele has bestowed her whole affection upon the ' Lonely One.' "

" Auwe, my Moi ! this cannot be."

"Did not the mighty warrior of Hawaii lay dead, cut down by the swift blows of my sabre! And is he not now alive again, and building a great fleet to invade Maui? Because of this my brow is shadowed, and my heart is full of sorrow, knowing I am forgotten by Pele; and yet the hour of battle is near."

"No King in all the Eight Isles has ever received such aid in battle as Kalani of Oahu. Why should Kalani distrust the good Pele, when the wounded are not yet healed, who fought where the dread Goddess slay the half of an army to pleasure her godson."

"Has not Paao sacrificed scores of my people, now so much needed in battle, to gratify Pele's greed for the blood of man? And yet she has not smiled upon our immolations, nor condescended even a rumble from Kalauea, nor a torchlight of lava from great Loa's brow. We are forgotten! A great King is forgotten by his god in the hour of direst need."

"Auwe, moi Kalani! Would the gods be divine were they at the beck and call of men? Does the love of a great Goddess go out like a flickering taper? Does it set, like the yellow sun in the sea, not to rise at its will on the morrow? Believe me, believe your little darling, who you know is akin to the gods; whom the gods love, may be tempted with trouble, and tried with care, but forgotten, never! Never!"

"But the hour of battle approaches, and not a

star-fall from the sky to denote that my cries have been heard at Kilauea. The hideous Kamehameha has taken Kalani's place in the affections of Pele. But is she not a Woman? And is it not the nature of all womankind to be *fickle* and *false?*"

With a look of the wildest terror, Kupule sprang up, and with a cry of anguish pressed her hand over the mouth of the King. Instantly there was a swift disturbance in the air, and a bustle among the trees, like the whirr of many wings, as the countless lesser spirits made haste to depart, in abject fear of the coming greater ones. And Kupule clung to the King, and cried aloud bitterly :

"Auwe! auwe! na'u Moi! na'u Moi! Pele! forgive my Kalani, he knows not what he sayeth. He seeth not that which is clear as the moon above our heads. Cry 'Pardon!' my Moi; lest the heavens fall and crush us where we stand! lest Oahu's fair Isle should sink into the sea, because of your blasphemy."

Even while she spoke, the great Island shook to its foundation. Waolani's mountain peak rocked and swayed against the stars, as if it were toppling to its fall, and would soon plunge headlong down the Pali into Koolau's garden land.

Afar off the red lava streamed up from Loa's top, and lit the reeling world with fire; like some monstrous beacon-light put forth by the hand of God. The pool, that had already grown tranquil since the departure of the nocturne-spirits, had again become ruffled as by some unseen wind ;

bubbling up from beneath as from the breathing
of some subterranean monster in his rage.

At length the loud rippling of the spring voiced
itself upon the ear in melody, seeming to purl
itself into low, indistinct notes of music, like the
melodious singing of shells beneath the sea.

Again the hill whereon they stood shook with
agony ; followed by a long, low rumble of earthquake. The orange trees swayed and rocked in
the windless air, tumbling their golden fruit about
them ; plashing their yellow globes into the fountain, and among the swaying grass and the drooping flowers.

The fountain now flung its jet higher than ever,
throwing its spray even above the tree-tops. The
water of the pool took on renewed agitation, flowing with sudden haste over its border, trampling
the long grass and bending the night-blooming
flowers as it rushed frantically down the hillside.

A dark something now came suddenly over the
moon, leaving the royal pair clinging to each other
in the midst of blackest darkness. Not a star-
beam reached to the earth, nor ray of light from
anywhere. There now came a clear, sweet voice,
speaking to the King from the direction of the
fountain. And the grove, and the fountain, and
the vine-covered rocks beyond were illuminated
as by the light of day ; for it was Pele !

> And the cliffs were rent, as with fires of hell!
> And the orange-groves rung a funeral knell ;
> For the blue-eyed Goddess, with hair of flame,
> To rebuke Kalani at midnight came.

The trembling lovers were impelled to turn and look, when with shaded eyes they beheld the majestic figure of a woman, a creature of supernal loveliness, standing in an illuminated cloud beneath the falling fountain. Beyond this rolling fire-cloud was seen a glow of incandescence that could not be looked upon. They could only see sufficient to distinguish that the great ledge of rocks were rent asunder, showing a fiery gateway leading down into the volcanic earth beneath. Here, indeed, was a new horror in their midst; and but for the thought that some master-mind was present, fears were awakened that a crater was opened ready to consume them with fire.

Leaning against the fiery cloud, as upon a bed of flowers, stands the beautiful Ignipotent, with a look of divine sadness and sorrow predominant upon her face. Her feet are whiter than alabaster as she stands upon the ebullient waters as upon the solid earth. Though the music of the rippling waters has not died away, it seems not obtrusive, so blended with the divine cadence of Pele's voice, like the chorus of a heavenly choir.

By the tender blue of her large, soft eyes, and the golden magnificence of her shining hair, both the King and Queen knew the blinding vision before them to be Pele, the Creator of the world! It needed not the halo about her head, nor the almost blinding radiance of her countenance, to convince any one that it was the Goddess of Kilauea.

10

In her right hand glistened a spear, having a long tremulous stave contrived of twisted sunbeams, with a quivering head of blue volcanic flame. In her left, hung dangling a gleaming sword, made massive and two-handed, and dazzling with the brilliance of its sheen. The lambent glances of her sweet, sad eyes, floated about over the grove like falling stars. Though her ungarmented form did not obstruct the upward flow of the fountain in which she stood, yet for effect, or otherwise, the crest of the water was permitted to toss her yellow locks until they flashed like vivid lightnings in a storm.

When Pele spoke to her trembling subjects, the almightiness of her voice was subdued in the awful terror of its tones, falling upon the human ears before her like the softest music of singing birds. Addressing Kalani, she said: *"Auwe! koa Moi o Oahu! Poino, poino na ouku!"* Was it for the Boy King I love to revile the ·goddess who so kindly presided over his birth? Who but Pele could have strengthened the young arm of Kalani for battle? shielding him with more than a mother's fondness in the thickest of the fight. Is it for Kalani to forget that while yet a boy he was suffered to enact the heroic deeds of men; leading armies, and overcoming the great warriors of Hawaii?

" Who but Pele could have protected you on the night of the great tempest at Hawaii, when

* Oh! warrior King of Oahu! Alas, alas for you!

the terrible Moa-alii did his utmost to uproot my Eight Isles, and hurl my young warrior and his great chiefs into the sea?

"Tell me, thou sinful boy, who but the great Goddess of Kilauea could have imparted strength of heart and arm for you to contend with the giant king of Hawaii?—he whom Pele loved before you were born. Though Pele suffered Kalani the glory of slaying the great Hercules, she could not but snatch back her first love into life again. For a greater than Kamehameha is not known among the sons of men.

"Does the memory of her young hero fail him, that he assumes the credit of the victory of Mauna Kea, where two cunning armies were ambushed upon his rear? Is it so easy to forget that, but for Pele's aid, Kalani and his whole army would have been destroyed that day? His manly beauty so maimed by the spearsmen foe that the mournful stars would have wept blood, staining the snow crests of my mountains with their just sorrow.

"I am Pele, the Creator of the earth! The queenly mother of all the gods in the land. Being a *wahine Akua*—a woman god—I became the godmother of a baby king, who touched my divine love with his beauty. But, being a woman, I am 'FICKLE AND FALSE!' so says Kalani.

"So be it, *auwe Moi!* It is the message of Pele of Kilauea, to Kalani of Oahu, that *ke wahine Akua* will be *fickle* no more. Open your ears, that you may hear. Henceforth kings shall contend for my

kingdoms and the weakest shall fall — though it
rend my heart to see the loved one slaughtered —
and the wisest shall rule over my Eight Isles, he
and his sons and his daughters, unto the tenth
generation of men.

"I see in your heart great wonder that Pele
heard your reviling so far away. But your Goddess sat upon the spray of the fountain as you
spoke; myself, and a thousand servitor spirits who
came to do your bidding. It was Pele who moved
your queen to bring you here, that she might
whisper much divine counsel in your ear by the
soft voice of Kupule.

"See what I have brought. Behold this gleaming *pahi* (sword) with its scabbard of gold, and
its hilt formed of the rarest gems of the earth,
whose blade was forged deep down in the nether-
most centre of my kingdom of fire. It is the
sword of Peace! Whomsoever shall possess this
blade of fire and this scabbard of gold, shall rule
without wars to his dying day.

"Because you have profaned the name of the
Goddess who loved you, it shall not be yours.
Open your eyes that you may see. Behold, I drop
it back into the incandescence of my earth-fires
again. Where blade and scabbard and dazzling
hilt of gems — such as the eye of man hath not
seen — shall resolve back into the elements from
whence they came; as the bodies of dead kings
shall resolve back into dust once more.

"Keao is now upon the war-path. His canoes

outnumber the stars in Orion, and his warriors are
more numerous than the whistling plovers on
Waikiki's shore. Keao is a great warrior, and his
chiefs are valiant in battle. But for Pele's aid,
the warriors of Oahu could not resist the strong
army of Kauai.

"For this once, Pele will aid Kalani in the coming battle. But there shall be other battles where
the weak shall fall, for my Isles shall be given up
to wars, and the strong shall win. There shall
come a greater than Keao, and Pele will sit in
judgment on her mountain-tops, and witness the
final battles; where the victor and the vanquished
are the best loved of her heart. And because
there is a beginning to all things, so there is an
end; and the end is death.

"Whoso wins in the last and greatest fight to
come, unto the survivor, Pele, in the might of her
omnipotence will bestow the *pahi* of Peace, and
great wars shall be known in the land no more.
Then the Conqueror shall rule my Eight Isles as
one kingdom.

"Then the *nui mokus o ke haole* — the great foreign ships — shall flock to my shores, countless as
the white swans from the north. From the far
land of *Lono* shall the *mokus* come, for the pearls
and the shells on the reef-bed will become as gold
and silver in the hands of the king.

"Then the sweet-smelling sandal-wood shall be
sought by the *haole*, and shall be transported to
Cathay for much gold; and the *nui Alii* — the

great chiefs — shall be robed as kings because of their riches. And the *wahines* shall deck them-selves in *kapas* (clothes) hued like the clouds when the yellow *la* (sun) lies down in the sea, and sings *aloha* to Pele upon her far mountains at Hawaii.

"And the *haole wahine* shall come, from the land of Lono shall they come, and the white-skinned creatures shall bring their Akua (God) hidden in their hearts. And the red blood of Kanakas and the white blood of *Haoles* shall mingle like the stream and the sea. And the *nui Akua* of the *haole*, who lives beyond Pele's stars, beyond the *la* (sun) and the *mahina* (moon), in his *lani hale* (heaven-house), shall smile upon Hawaii, and look down to woo the soft heart of Pele. And Pele will love the white *Kane's* God, and my people shall learn to worship his unseen face in the sky.

" But when that day shall come, Kalani will not be here to see ; and Pele will have wept in secret as she sits on her fiery throne, because of the in-gratitude of her *koa Moi;* him whom she loves with the affection of a thousand mothers.

"Auwe! auwe! who in all the world suffers such sorrow as the mother who has lost her son ; the Goddess who is bereft of her hero king, because of his becoming too arrogant for the world to contain ; thus, falling in battle, he dies and hastens to the dark shades of Po.

" Poino, poino ! — alas, alas ! — would that Pele

had taught her young warrior the great dual lesson of life: 'That a woman's heart maketh room for the love of many in her time. That ingratitude to the gods is a monstrous iniquity, sufficient to darken the light of the sun, and fill the land with war and famine.'

"Would there were power in the supremest godhead to undo the daily sins of men. But it may not be. The world must roll on, and the gods abide by their decrees, lest a wild chaos seize upon the spheres, and the sun be flung down from the heavens.

"But once more in life shall your young eyes look upon the divine face of your Goddess on earth. When you have fought the great fight— the battle of the Pali—and your heroic heart lies ebbing its red current away, then Pele will sit by your side once more. The last sound that greets your dying ear,—heard above the shriek of the wounded, and the wail over the dead,—heard even above the love-plaint of your darling, shall be the last love-message and divine forgiveness of the Goddess who watched over your birth, and instilled the war-spirit into your boyhood.

"One word more and I go. Cherish the royal maiden Pele has perfected for your throne. Seek her counsel in troubles of state and dangers from foreign foe, for her wisdom is inspired by the gods, and the heart of the *wahine Moi* is stronger than your own. There is a divine quality in her blood never before imparted to woman, and her human affection surpasseth the knowledge of man. Through your queen you may still be linked with the gods.

" Kalani of Oahu, thou son of the Thunderer, lift up your face into the light of godhead! Behold I leave you this spear, forged in the terrible *Hale-mau-mau* of Kilauea, and tempered by the hand of Pele to find the heart of Keao. But against Kamehameha it shall not avail. Aloha! Moi Kalani. Aloha, Moi-wahine! Receive the spear, ere it sinks in the 'Kiowai o Pele' (Fountain of Pele), for it is the last visible god-gift of one who has loved you all too well." ·

As a broad gleam of summer lightning flashes down the evening sky an instant, and is gone, leaving greater darkness from its brief presence, so Pele's cloud-throne blazed into greater effulgence for an instant — too dazzling for human eyes to look upon — then vanished through the rock-rent gateway into the fiery gulf beyond, and was seen no more.

When human vision was available once more, the rocky crag and the clambering vines beyond the pool were seen apparently untouched and unharmed. There in the turbulent spring stood the glistening spear, standing upright in the water as Pele had left it, its pointed head flaming with blue light, lurid and fitful as the ghastly gleam on Mauna Loa. But for that, and the numerous ripened fruit tumbled from the orange trees about where the lovers sat, and over the surface of the

spring, there was naught to indicate the supernatural visitants — seen and unseen — that had
recently invaded the Sacred Grove.

Ah! who can depict such a sorrow as now
crushed this royal pair? Who portray the cruel
wreck of their kingly aspirations and their regal
love? A bereavement so sudden, so severe, that
the black darkness about them becomes peopled
with sympathy for their woe. Even the gentle
song-birds — the tabooed pets of the grove —
nestle uneasily in their leafy covert, so awakened
to grief, oft changing their roosting-places ner-
vously from twig to twig, rumpling their tropic
plumage with birdish-look-folorn, as they repeat-
edly twitter their sorrowing nocturnes over the
lovers; thus joining in the chorus of sibilant
whispers which now people the grove; voices
coming from dusky figures too impalpable and unearthly to court human inspection, though engendered for human ears and awakened by human
bereavement.

She sprang to meet the King's embrace!
　Upon Kalani's neck she clung,
So awed by Pele's angered face,
　Who'd burst like flames themselves among.
She sought to snatch the King from grief ;
　Who said : " Ere morning's sun shall rise,
Keao will pass the harbor reef,
　And when we meet in war — he dies ! "

" 'Tis Pele's wish you use her spear
To win the fight approaching near ;
For Kauai's king must then be slain,
Or my dear King in death be lain."

So she compelled herself to speak,
Till carmine grew her olive cheek,
And lip and eye with beauty glow,
Her royal love entranced her so.
Kalani caught the Queen in arms,
　And peering in her comely face,
With kisses ravished all her charms,
　And held her in his strong embrace.

CHAPTER X.

ALANI stood as one transfixed in tawny marble in the sacred grove after Pele had departed. Bowed was his kingly head, and clenched in strong agony his warrior hands. His forehead was fluted as though he had aged during this one brief hour, like one crushed with convicted sin, or become disconsolate with an inconsolable grief. He had indeed committed the one unpardonable transgression against godhead; and Pele, the supreme one, had forsaken her young *koa Moi* forever.

The sobs which reached the ear of the Boy King were not alone from Kupule; for above his head in the starless gloom, and round about him everywhere in the black darkness of the grove, the whole place was palpitating with great sobs of woe; such introit wails as come to us from the ambient spirits in all the great sorrows of life, if we have but the soul to comprehend and the introspective eye to discern them.

The vibrant leaves bent tenderly over the pride-crushed king in this first great sorrow of his life, whispering audible consolation into his ears, while some mysterious something riding upon the spray

155

of the fountain sobbed louder than ever the grief-stricken Queen from out the darkness. The dew-laden grasses leaned lovingly about the naked feet standing there in their midst, while the flowers hung their pensive heads, bedewed with floral tears of sorrow for the King.

Thus the maternity of Nature is ever aroused by a great transgression. And whether the subtle sympathies of her visible elements or unseen things are apprehended, is according to the intuitions of the transgressor, or the condignity or condolence of his sin.

But in the midst of this general expression of sympathy, it was left for Kupule to rescue Kalani from the effects of his sorrow and shame. While she groped about for him in the sudden darkness caused by Pele's departure, the moon, which had been blotted out by the divine effulgence of deity, ventured timidly forth again. Not with the broad white radiance of an hour before, but with a sub-dued and tender light — so considerate in the busy lunar orb — as with a gentle, loving purpose of shielding the young King even from the intrusive light of the merry stars, and the condolent spirits of the place.

Springing to his side, Kupule twined her loving arms about the neck of Kalani, and pressed her hot young cheeks to his own, as she bent herself to the task of recalling her new lord and master back to his regal duties.

" My King, my darling ! Because one has com-

mitted a great wrong against deity, must one also
commit another, that two black wrongs may
witness against us, following you about everywhere in life, like those ominous sea-birds whose
presence ever portends a storm?

"Pele has left my *koa Moi* a spear—the cunning work of her own hand—with which to resist Keao until he cries aloud, '*Leuka-lua!*'—
(beaten.) Would my Kalani wrong the divine
Goddess again, that her coming vengeance shall be
hastened in its fall upon our heads?

"Seize it! seize the god-given spear; for while
I speak it is sinking slowly and irretrievably back
from whence it came. Poino, poino!—alas, alas!
—if the priceless god-gift is suffered to sink in
the 'Kiowai o Pele,' then woe to Oahu! Woe to
my King! For he will be slain on the morrow
like a timid boy by the treacherous hand of Keao."

The sting of the last thought proved the touch-
stone to awaken the crushed young hero again.
Rousing as from a lethargy, Kalani sprang into
the fountain and snatched the sinking spear, which
blazed yet a moment like a sulphur-flamed torch
in his hand, then went slowly out like an expiring
taper, filling the grove with a sulphurous mist, and
casting a veil of green and gold over the face of
the moon.

A moment more, and the ghastly mist caused
by the spear-flame was gone, and again the resplendent moonlight flooded the tropic Isle; dropping its robe of gold, veil-like, about the lovers,

whose two young hearts sought to beat in unison in glad remembrance of this act of half recognition by the gods.

Like an earthly paradise lay Nuuanu at this moment, so lapped in a delicious swoon of gladness beneath the yellow moonbeam. How quivered the long plumy fronds of the palm-trees in the upper air, bending their pensive heads in reverence to the hallowed night, and whispering their leafy benediction to the stars!

From out the cool depths of the mountain forest stole the wandering airs, floating on laden wings of perfume down the enchanting valley to the sea. From the ripened fruit, and the odorous blossoms in the orange grove, commingled a rich aroma, toying in playful dalliance with the rifts of yellow moonbeam from out the sky.

From afar off, beyond the breezeless bay, came the plaintive murmur of the sounding surf, as if endeavoring to hush its own noisy footsteps upon the reef-bed and the shore, yet beating against the white silence of the slumbering valley like the droning hum of multitudinous voices from afar. Answering back to the subdued roar of the great breakers there came the ceaseless rumble of the waterfall above, whose white curved arch hung like a bow of liquid silver in the abundant sheen.

Calm and bright lay the glittering harbor across the mouth of the valley. Here and there were seen the ghostly outline of canoes on guard, hovering like forbidden spirits about the harbor's entrance, or fluttering like unhallowed ghosts across the shimmering waters of the bay, paddling as they were with unseen blades, that dropped phosphoric gems of gold whenever they crossed the moon-glade.

Along miles on miles of white coral reef rolled the great breakers, their crested tops quivering with an ever-changing sheen of burnished gold as they rolled in the midnight ray. On Diamond Head slept the tawny night-beam, robed as with an Osman's turban of cloth-of-gold about its craggy head, shining as if her rays were attracted there by the glitter of those fabulous gems, said to have existed in the crater of this wonderful headland. Such was the tropic night about our lovers, so transformed from the darkness of transgression of an hour before.

With a tender love, such as only a noble woman can proffer in times of need, Kupule clung to her lover with a voiceless silence, in keeping with the night, which often affords the best consolation in grief. Though her sympathy and affection were inaudible to the ear, yet how much more impressive was the voiceless language of her intumescive heart, as she clung with love's expressive endearments about the neck of Kalani; now so crushed in spirit by his prophetic doom, and the awful rebuke of Pele.

With the sanguine temperament of all youthful heroes, Kalani had performed such deeds of valor — seemingly with his own kingly might — that

he fell into the too human error of depreciating
the divine source of love and power which so
overrules the destinies of men ; ending, at length,
as we have seen, with measuring himself by the
divine capacity of might and mentality only
meted to deity.

Terrible indeed was the humiliation of being
made to feel himself too human, too parvenu, in
the queenly presence of the woman he adored.
Kalani's aspirations had vaulted so high — winged
so proudly above his fellow kings — that he came
at length to poise too high for human strength of
wing, and now fell to a depth commensurate with
his eagle-flight among the stars.

How often are such human vicissitudes the result of an overweening ambition in the lives of
men ! Ere the royal lovers parted that night in
the sacred orange grove, the Boy King was a boy
no more. It is a quality inseparable from the
youth of all men, to aspire to the premature coming
of manhood — the acme of young dreams in adoles-
cence — mapping out the far future with plans re-
quiring an interminable length of years to mature ;
plans sadly bereft of their qualities of splendor and
utility by the first great grief of our lives.

Snatch the image of godhead from a hero's
shield — though his young fame may have grown
to divine stature — and the youth of a warrior
withers in an hour, like summer grasses when
assailed by fire. Thoughtless deeds and empty
words must henceforth become things of the past

with Kalani, for the acts of a doomed king must
necessarily become weighty and wise.

Now for the first time was he learning the
priceless value of a wise woman's love. He had
snatched his new Queen as a gem to adorn his
throne, a new toy in a cluster of many; but he
had now learned that all love should not be rated
as a toy in the palace of a king, — that the intuitive counsel of a true woman, when prompted by
a regal affection, is all-worthy of a great warrior
and a noble king.

Roused at length by the recollection that the
nation was upon the eve of a great battle with
a powerful foe, Kupule sought to infuse something
of her own heroic spirit and wise methods of view-
ing his misfortune.

"Come, my King! — my warrior above all
praise — let gentle love win you tenderly back to
deeds of state again. It was indeed a ruthless
wrong for my noble Kalani to chide the good Pele,
because the *Alii Kapu* received no answers to
their human immolations and long-drawn prayers.
Paao and Moi Kalani well knew that Omnipotence
is not subject to the beck and call of men.

"Darling, it was thy huge ambition overleaping
itself, overmastering even the wisdom of a *Kapu
Moi*. But the years lie tender and few on the
head of my Kalani, else he were not so tempted
to match his human mandate with the awful
power of godhead."

"But I will be a boy no more. Let the past

11

begone! I crush it from memory, as I crush this
fruit in my hand. The future of Kalani lies but
a few brief moons before. The far mountains of
glory that I had built up to the stars greet my
young eyes no more.

" The end of existence has so advanced to meet
me — so hedged me in with brief years — that
well may Kalani of Oahu question if life is worth
the warlike toil to win it. Pele has henceforth
cast great Titeree's son into the tumult of alter-
nate wars between Keao and Kamehameha. She
has bannered his young life with her frown, and
made yonder Waolani his cenotaph even before he
dies. Doomed to lose his battles before he fights
them, why should your Kalani strive to win?"

" Nay, nay, my Moi, my Aloha! Your dear
eyes were blinded, and your proud head was
bowed with the weight of your first transgression,
that you would not look up into the loving face
of deity. The Goddess chid you for a great
wrong; but, dear one, it was as a noble mother
chides a darling child. Pele was not *huhu nui* —
greatly mad — there was no tinge of wrath in look
or tone. She bade Kalani weigh the value of her
friendship by the past, and thus learn to judge his
loss. She who could have slain my King with a
glance of her azure eyes, has but laid his sins in
judgment at his feet; bidding him monument
these great wrongs against his god by valiant
deeds in the future; that, dying, Kalani of Oahu
shall receive Pele's forgiveness in the hour of his

greatest glory. For dying is not to be forgotten; but to so martyr a warrior's achievements by death, that his fame shall rise higher than Wao-lani!"

"But Pele has disgraced Kalani in the eyes of all the world, and made him feel unworthy of the very breath he breathes. Though withdrawing her divine aid, she has bid me cope with the two mightiest warriors among the Isles. The final defeat at the Pali means many a battle lost before that day; for he that fights seeking death will not tarry in his warfare, nor husband his deeds of valor. Tell me, loved Queen, is it worth a doomed warrior's while to fight for the pleasure of pos-terity?"

"Auwe, wiwo ole Kalani! (Oh, brave Kalani!) Take you no pleasure in the glorious deeds of Titeree, your sire?"

"Yes, my Moi-wahine. Kalani is proud of the warlike fame of his sire; and he also despises the paltry cowardice of the sick king, when he per-mitted himself to beg his life of Kamehameha, and to barter away his kingdom in this craven message to the Lonely One: 'Wait till the black tapa covers Titeree, then his kingdom shall be yours.'"

"Are there no loved ones whom Kalani would elect to do battle for, that his name should shine down the far generations with glory?"

"Ah, my Kupule, you have indeed struck the key-note to a warrior's heart at last. To brighten

thy dark eyes with pleasure and pride, Kalani will
do such deeds of battle as shall make the Isles
ring with his name."

" Thanks, my King.   Your little *moi-wahine*
will treasure your valiant deeds above all others —
except Pele.   Remember, dearest, *ke maikai* Pele
has forged a spear for her young warrior from out
her own mountain lava, with which to win the
battle against Keao.   Forget not the beautiful
goddess in this hour of trial."

" Poino! poino! — Alas, alas! — has she not disgraced me?   Henceforth, Kupule, my beautiful
Queén, shall become my battle-god ; by the light
of her dark eyes Kalani will win or fall."

" Remember, *auwe Moi!* (O King!) that only the
god-given spear of Pele can find the heart of Keao.
Does my proud Moi wish to hear the craven cry of
'*Luka lua! Luka lua!*' — beaten, beaten—shouted
from his own warriors, instead of from the Kauaian
foe ? "

" *Aole! aole!*   It shall not be, if Kalani lives to
fight out his battle."

" Then pleasure the little Queen who adores you,
and the good deity who loves you still.   Arm your-
self with the beautiful weapon of Pele, that your
father's treacherous brother shall die — for Pele
has said it!"

" It shall be as you wish.   The eyes of Kalani
are at length open to your beauty, and his ears are
awakened to your wisdom.   If I fall, I will die
worthy of your love.   If I win, the glory shall be

Kupule's — *ke moi-wahine o* Oahu " (the maiden queen of Oahu).

A faint smile — the first of the night — flitted over the sad face of the young monarch as he caught his little Kupule in his strong arms, and crimsoned her glad lips with his kisses.

They had risen to go, and were standing together by the western margin of the spring, ere Kalani had been won from his stubborn resolution to fight the coming battle without the aid of Pele's spear. This error of judgment overcome, he found relief, and looked about him with freedom and pleasure once more.

The graceful shadow of his pleading Queen had caught his eye, where it lay upon the surface-sheen of the fountain, limned by the great luna orb in the western sky. Nude almost as Aphrodite stood the fair young *Aloha moi-wahine* — (Love Queen),* — pleading before her King, like Venus newly risen from the wave; with only the vesture of her abundant hair, and a short, flimsy *pau* of tapa garmenting her voluptuous figure from waist to knee.

Awed by the supernal beauty of the Goddess while her august presence had dimmed the moon, in wonder and worship Kupule had dropped her tapa robe; standing there transfixed and statu-

---

* Kamehameha and most of the other kings had their queens of state, — by whom they begot their heifs because of their high rank, — and also their " love queens," one or more, who were their resident queens. Such was Kaahumanu, the wisest and worthiest of Kamehameha's queens.

esque, while the resplendent light of Pele's countenance had beamed down upon her comely face
and graceful figure.

As human beauty once embellished by the hallowed light of Deity, cannot wholly divest itself
of the added charm acquired from the approximate
presence of godhead, Kalani now recognized for the
first time the voluptuous beauty of his maiden
Queen.   And when Kupule also arose supreme in
courage in the midst of this terrible maranatha of
Pele's, he could not fail to plainly distinguish the
quality of semi-godhood with which he had linked
his fate and his fortune.   And when she also showed
herself so wise in counsel and so intuitive in prescience, it were not to be wondered at that the
bright young creature succeeded in lifting her hero
King back into the region of his once high hopes
and lofty aims again.

Rallied by the inspiration of his love, — so new
and unlearned in the sense he knew it now, — Kalani had been compelled to confess the wisdom of
Pele in permitting him to enrich his country with
heroic deeds, and his name with glory, in partial propitiation of his sin.   And Kupule could
not but exclaim with delight at the wholesome
change :

"*Ka! Aloha;* now Kupule beholds her *koa Moi*
(warrior King) again.   His royal kisses cling like
the touch of the laden bee to the fiery-tongued
ohea-flower.   To your little Queen it is a sure

token that the great heart of Kalani is warmed
back to heroic life once more."

" Thanks to *ko'u moi-wahine*."

" Thanks to your own noble soul ! As I look
into your face, those fond eyes give back my love
with double lustre ; as the reflected smile of the
mahina (moon) in the spring, outshines the heavenly orb in the sky. Now Kupule feels thy answering heart-beat against her bosom, responding
throb by throb to her own, as yonder echo among
the mountains answers back to the wild pulses of
the sea."

" My darling Queen, life with Kalani would be
dark indeed but for the lesson of love you have
taught him in this hour. You have snatched him
from a gloom blacker than the shades of *Po !* Who
but Kupule could have taught her King that a
wahine's love is sweeter even than ambition ? For
this will Kalani take courage, and battle for his
Love-Queen on the morrow, as never great warrior
fought for his *Aloha* before."

" Auwe Moi Kalani ! my hero lover. You have
grown to be a god in the eyes of your little Queen.
Your great battle-deeds already shine prophetic
before my vision. When the bugle calls, the love
of Kupule will take wing like a bird, and follow
her warrior through the thickest of the battle.
When my Moi strikes home his swift blows, the
dark eyes of his Kupule will be upon him, count-
ing on her fingers the many wounds inflicted by
her hero."

" You stir the blood of Kalani till he becomes impatient to behold the foe."

" And woe to that foe when he stand before thy path. But when Oahu is free, and Keao lies dead before thee, and his warriors cry ' *Luka-lua!* ' then remember to whom victory is due, and bow thy great heart to Pele. In that hour her voice of terror shall be heard among the mountains, and great Loa will light his torch of joy."

" The words of Kupule are as words of fire to Kalani. You make my coming deeds to shine in my soul, as the stars shine in the glad waters of the fountain. Your voice is as the music of running waters to Kalani."

" And will not Kalani confess how great is the love of Pele? Did she not make him brave in counsel and strong in battle? And has not the beautiful Goddess given her own terrible spear into thy keeping, by which alone the king of Kauai can be laid low?"

" Kalani is made glad because of the love of Kupule. But the heart of Pele has become as stone to her young warrior; and Mauna Loa will forget to light her torch-fire in the hour of my victory."

" As the mother's love returns to her wayward child because of visible repentance, so Pele will watch thy battle-deeds with delight, and remember her *Keiki Moi* (Boy King) in time of need.

She who moulded your soul to greatness, and
taught you the cunning use of armies, may justly
chide you for *a* great wrong. But forget you —
never ! Unlove you — NEVER ! "

It was a glad sight to see the inspired young
Queen thus plead for deity, and uphold the trailing banners of her warrior King.

Oahu's city sleeps to-night!
For scarce a cur-dog's bark is heard,
Much less the din of noisy word
To jar upon the moonlight bright.
She sleeps — as if she knew no harm
To keep her Warrior's eyes awake;
Sure — danger casts before a charm
Like that around the venomed snake!
'Tis but the calm before the storm:
To-morrow, with the dawn of light,
Keao, with all his fearful swarm,
Will dare Oahu forth to fight!
And ere yon moon shall look again
Upon Waikiki's peaceful plain,
For many, she will shine in vain!

At times the watch-fires light the bay,
When rude some hand their embers spurn,
Then flicker faint, and die away,
With but a glow to show they burn.
The " Punch Bowl " hill rears o'er the town
And casts his fearful shadow down;
Abruptly springs from out the plain,
As billows rise from out the main.
Protective o'er the mountain springs
And casts his shade to ocean's marge,
As when some guardian warrior flings
O'er form he loves his battle targe.

170

CHAPTER XI.

THE night hours had passed slowly and sadly away to the lovers, as they clung to each other, sitting there by the fountain on the sacred hill. Yet at length the terrible night of maranatha was almost ended, and the dawn of an eventful day was fast approaching.

Across the Nuuanu the camp-fires burnt low, and the spirit of peace seemed hovering over the slumbering warriors, as they slept beside their long spears and murderous paloas. Though as yet not a gleam of the approximate dawn was visible in the orient, yet the land-wind had suddenly aroused — the earliest harbinger of a tropic day — descending from the mountains upon stronger wings than it ever acquires during the night, when its ostensible object seems to be dalliance with perfumes and fondling with flowers.

Awakened to a spirit of rebellion by this sudden resistance of the land-wind, the great breakers along the shore rose up in their might, bellowing like angry demons disturbed in their lair. Aping the hoarse thundering of the floundering surf — as small intelligences ever pattern by the greater

171

—the tuneful waterfall now roughened its voice into a wild bassoon, rumbling down its jutting crag as if seeking to obtrude itself among the roused up dissonances of the approaching dawn.

Kulu, the yellow moon, had sunk low down in the tranquil west, fringing the crests of the breakers more than ever with shimmering rims of the palest gold. The long line of glittering moonglade spanned the western sea from Isle to horizon, like some heavenward pathway leading to the land of the blessed.

Except the furious uprising of the surf and the answering waterfall, ever roused by the first breath of the land-wind, all was yet calm and peaceful over land and sea. Naught but the fitful flickering of the dying camp-fires reminded one that such human madness as war existed on the earth.

But at length there came a low, ominous sound from afar; the mingled vibrates of many voices seemed creeping faintly up from the shore and sea. Simultaneous with the foreboding sound, and imparting to it a menacing meaning, there flashed the gleam of a hundred kindling signal-fires, as hilltop and crag and mountain footspur lit their beacon-lights, stretching away from Nuuanu to far-off Ewa Bay.

Though these first indistinct notes of proximate war were the merest vibrant murmurs on the air, they were sufficient to cause the royal lovers to spring up from their seat, where they had long twined in silence only broken by sighs and responsive heart-beats whilst awaiting the morning.

From the earliest childhood these two had been inured to the signals and watch-cries of inter-Island warfare; thus their keen ears had instantly caught the alarm before it had taken apparent shape or meaning. Though the lookouts from the coast-hills, and the watch in the guard-canoes, had discovered the approach of Keao, as yet nothing could be discerned by Kalani or his sharp-eyed queen.

Soon the war-cry from the shore became mingled with the murmur of multitudinous voices across the valley, where a giant had been disturbed in his slumber, for the army had been awakened. Rousing with a muffled cry of portentous evil, augmenting and increasing into an angry roar that swept across the valley, akin to the resonant thunder from the surf-beaten shore.

Rude hands now stirred the dying embers, till the camp-fires made a thousand silhouettes of the swarthy warriors, as they eagerly sought the in-dispensable pipe-smoke before the battle. How flashed the bright spear-heads of shell, and glit-tered the sabre-blades of the chiefs — innovations from the armature of the Christian brother from over the sea!

Dark objects suddenly peopled the opposite valley side, as though the very earth had opened its caverned sources, and the hillside had rent open and spawned its evil spirits, reeking with human gore, and murderous with terrible inten-tions — ever the hideous offspring of war and rapine.

Suspense out-demons a thousand lesser ills ; and
the last hour before day is ever the most ghostly
of the night.   A rude, weird dissonance had crept
like a thief over the peaceful valley, until the
shudder and chill of awe smote the inmost soul
of man.   Even the heart of Kalani beat tumult-
uously, and would not still ; and brave little
Kupule was filled with dismal intuitions of impending danger, ambushed horrors, lurking among
the shadows everywhere.

But at length the head division of Keao's canoes
came one by one into sight, dispelling the incubus.
A long line of dark objects dotted the golden
sheen of the moon-laved waters.   They were paddling toward the land furiously.   Impelling their
great war canoes with incredible swiftness, hoping
to secure the harbor-entrance by surprise before
their approach should be discovered by the warriors of Oahu.

But it was no part of Kalani's plan to defend
the harbor, or prevent the landing of the army of
Keao.   He was open to a trial of strength, and
wished the battle to be decisive for the one army
or the other.   His war canoes had been withdrawn
to Waikiki Bay, and his army to the valley, with
a purpose of giving Keao perfect freedom to land,
that he should not be tempted to burn Honolulu.

Kalani and his great war-chiefs well knew that
this plan would imply a fear of the enemy, and
lead Keao to deem the army of Oahu to be weaker
than it was.   But this would also serve their pur-

pose of decoying the Kauaians up the Nuuanu and away from their own canoes, that in case of defeat they should not all escape by sea. For Kalani fully meant it to be a battle of extermination for the one army or the other, that the question of supremacy might be settled forever.

Keao, being a great warrior, gigantic in stature, and ferocious in temperament, had ever thought lightly of the army of Oahu and the Boy King, his nephew; though doubtless this erroneous judgment took rise in the decimated ranks of the one and the extreme youth of the other. Thus it was thought that the usually wise old King of Kauai would be easily tempted away from his base of action — his canoes and the harbor front — to where the army of Oahu were encamped, near their stronghold, and could fight with their flanks in unassailable positions.

When the Kauaians found themselves in possession of the mouth of the harbor, the foremost canoes rested on their paddles, awaiting the arrival of the whole fleet and army. At length one hundred great war-canoes were seen collected in the harbor, and hastily marshalling themselves in battle array, preparing to force a landing upon the beach against whatever resistance might be offered. For while the Oahuans could plainly distinguish everything transpiring in the broad moonglade, the conformation of the Nuuanu left the valley in deep shadow where the army lay.

It was a spirit-stirring sight to Kalani, as one by

one he counted the great war-canoes as they debouched into the harbor; for if he won the battle he might count upon possessing himself of many of these finest specimens of naval architecture, for the Kauaians excelled in canoe making.

When the first shouts of the far-away lookout jarred upon the peaceful silence of the valley, Kalani leaped to his feet with the spring of a tiger. His nostrils dilated, and his manly chest rose and fell quickly, while eager thoughts possessed his soul, linked with the coming battle. As he stood shading his eyes, scanning the west along the moon-gold sea, endeavoring to catch the first glimpse of the coming foe, Boki came in search of him, to learn what disposition should be made with the army.

This matter settled, according to the plans already agreed upon, Boki sped across the valley to assume command during the absence of the King. Kalani waited upon the sacred hill until Keao's whole force had passed through the reef, marshalled in battle array, and were seen paddling steadily and swiftly for the beach in front of the town. When each canoe was seen leaving its track of quivering fire on the tranquil surface of the bay, and each of the five thousand paddles were seen scattering their phosphorescent gems — emeralds, and opals, and rubies — with every lift of the glittering blades from the hyaline sea, then the warlike young monarch prepared to depart.

Turning to Kupule, with a flash of living fire in

his eyes, and something of the old warlike spirit in his tones, Kalani flung wide his stalwart arms to receive his loved young Queen ere he left. It was possibly the last meeting of two noble souls on earth, and their varying emotions in that moment of separation were a mingling of the heroic and grand, the loving and the tender. There was an exquisite harmonizing of kingly affection and warlike exultation in the heart of one, and a womanly pride and girlish adoration in the other.

Smitten with an innate love of combat, and the delirious joy of conquest, Kalani, with all his wealth of love for his new-found darling, was impatient to be gone, and for the moment, possibly, his love for the Queen was unfairly divided in favor of the god-given spear, which now blazed anew with his magnetic grasp upon it, in the enthused exultation of his soul.

But before the swift flitting visions of Kupule, in the fresh, pure affluence of her love for the doomed young King, there arose the ever-impending perils of battle, when fought between two such ferocious spirits. Thus with the probable death of Kalani ever obtruding upon her, her girlish arms were found strong enough to retain her lover to the last moment, while her soft, black eyes, devoured every rising expression of his frank open face, and her rose-red lips clung to his, as we press the farewell kiss, and look the farewell look upon the dying.

But the call to arms grew deafening, and Kalani's

12

impatience grew strong, and with a tender parting
he tore himself away. Seizing the long glittering
spear, bestowed by Pele — who grew in his love
as his war-spirit rose — Kalani tested the supple
texture of its slender staff; and with something of
his old gallantry, proffered his radiant young
Queen the flashing spear-point for her parting kiss.

Bidding the Queen watch the coming battle
from the Punch Bowl mountain — so suitable in
position and conformation, being almost inaccessible from the harbor — Kalani sprang down the
hillside swifter than the headlong stream by which
he ran.

Passing within hail of the palace hill, on his
way to join the army, the King gave swift orders
for the Queen's wahines to await her coming; but
to the hundreds of gathering women and children,
families of the great chiefs who were with the
army, he gave orders to join the Queen's party
when she went upon Puawai, where they could
not be harmed, and if need be could easily flee
into the higher mountain forest for safety. For
should victory fall to the lot of the foe, great rudeness would transpire, and terrible excess in the
first frenzied hours of conquest.

Kupule remained a while in earnest prayer to
Pele, pleading for the safety and the success of
her darling King. And when she arose to go to
the adjoining mountain, she found the whole bowl-
shaped top of Puawai covered with women and
children; among whom were a few crippled or

superannuated Kanakas — a human commodity not over numerous, thanks to the overruling intelligence of the frequent *kapu kane* days.

Kalani and his great chiefs leisurely organized the army into two crescent lines in front of the walled stronghold; their convex aspect fronting to the foe. The front line being wholly armed with spears and paloas; the second with short halberts and slings. The great Alii Kapus carrying the *pahi, paloa* and huge *laau palau* — halberts made to strike or thrust with — a formidable and favorite weapon with Kamehameha and Keao, the two most gigantic chiefs among the Islands.

When all had thus assumed their position in the order of battle, the chiefs gathered about their young King, together partaking of their morning repast; while Boki, and his subordinate chiefs of staff, permitted a certain number of inferior men from the ranks to provide breakfast for the others, who ate their meal and smoked their pipes on the grass, without falling out of the line of battle.

After Keao had landed, and hastily taken possession of the deserted town, his army was permitted to prepare their morning meal and stretch themselves a while upon the grass, to recruit their strength before marching to battle.

When it was found that no resistance was offered to their landing, it was considered as a positive indication of weakness if not of fear, by the Kauaians, engendering great contempt for the prowess of their foes, and made the savage old

Keao too unwary and impatient to receive the surrender of Kalani and his army. So far the young King had made a good point against his usually sagacious enemy.

Keao did not attempt to burn the town nor the scattered houses about the valley, as was the custom when an invader had no intention of holding the conquered country. Neither did Keao leave a single kanaka to guard his noble fleet of canoes, for a thought of being defeated had found no room in the mind of the proud old warrior.

As day broke over the eastern mountains, and the rose tints of dawn lit up the jagged peaks of Waolani, the valley-ward position of the army of Oahu was fully discovered to Keao, who soon sounded the call and led on his forces up the valley. It was the custom in those barbaric days for the great chiefs to lead their armies in person when entering into battle.

Kamehameha, with greater military sagacity than any before his time, had adopted the better plan of directing his armies from the rear, while they were led into action by his best chiefs, reserving his own gigantic strength to rally and re-form any weak part along his lines. Kalani had seen the merit of this method in his numerous encounters with the Lonely One; or perhaps had also acquired it from Pele's counsel, as his rival had done, and usually adopted it in his battles.

But Keao was too stubborn and conservative to adopt new notions from younger chiefs, and now

stalked with gigantic strides at the head of his
dusky warriors, with young prince Kaumualii, and
several old chiefs following close about him;
though the prince was currently said to be more
of a gallant than a warrior.

The example of his traitorous old uncle in heading his army, well suited Kalani's purpose on this
occasion, as above all things else the young hero
most wished for a hand to hand encounter with
this villanous brother of Titeree's. Kalani's little
army was now finely positioned upon a low rise of
ground, directly in front of his trenches and the
entrance to his walled stronghold, which imparted
confidence to his new recruits. His wings were
thrown back; on the one side against the steep
crags of the hillside, and on the other against his
rampart wall, within which were stationed some
superannuated old warriors with slings and spears,
making this left wing also unassailable. Thus
cunningly posted, here he awaited to receive the
oncoming foe.

While the proud Kauaians marched steadily and
grandly up the valley, showing the finest discipline
and unbroken array, tramping to the stirring
music of bamboo fifes and numerous carcubita
drums, the undismayed Oahuans stood sternly to
their posts, in the ominous silence that best portends the coming storm.

How beat one little heart on the frowning crag
of Puawai, as the great army of Kauai marched
up the Nuuanu where Kalani's small body of in-

ferior men awaited them! But for her trust in
the divine power of Pele, Kupule could have no
hope in the coming encounter, with such great
disparity of forces. But whom the gods love shall
win; and in this precept lay the hopes of the
young Queen, and many a chieftess and child
about her.

The hour of daybreak in the tropics is one of
exquisite charm, so filled with the swiftly changing
aspects of light and shadow, in the ever impulsive
leap from darkness into dawn. The land-winds
ever freshen at this hour, the first forerunner of
the coming day-god, hastening from the cool
forests and the deep dells down the valleys to the
sea, ladened with newly awakened perfumes of
ripened fruits and bursting flowers.

Never had a more delicious aroma pervaded the
Nuuanu than upon this peaceful morning of the
murderous battle with Keao. The palm-trees
swayed gracefully in the breeze. The tall algaroba waved its feathery foliage, so like the long
drooping plumage of emerald birds. The great
hau-trees tossed their star-colored flowers in the
wind and sun, swinging bell-like in merry unison
with the jubilous songs of the newly awakened
birds. But the fierce invaders scented no perfume
but the blood of their foes, and saw no beauty but
the prophetic one of dead men slain by their
spears, as they marched sternly on eager for battle.

As the armies approached very near to each
other, Kalani flung off his golden mamo, which

flashed back the rays of the morning sun, and the two Kings advanced a few paces in front of their respective forces, with the usual intent of greeting each other, like murderous duellists in other lands.

Both monarchs were armed alike with sword and spear and dagger. Both were nude, with the trifling exception of the *malo*, a narrow waist-cloth worn by all men. This unrobed condition served well to display the supple, sinewy muscles of the one, and the brawnÿ, brutal strength of the other.

Keao was a herculean, savage-looking warrior, with deeply furrowed cheeks, and corrugated, frowning brow; of treble the weight, and double the strength of Kalani. But though the younger King lacked the gigantic prowess of his foe, yet a single glance disclosed the grace of the crouching leopard in his fine physique, while the lithe, springy motion of the panther was suggested by his every movement while in action.

As the Kings came to a halt, face to face with each other, Keao glowered down upon his boy antagonist with the murderous look of a demon from the nether world. He was infuriated by the fearless audacity he witnessed in his nephew, whom he thought to crush with his presence and devour with a look. But instead, in the calm, dark eyes of Kalani he beheld the piercing gaze of a young eagle who has learned to swoop with unerring talons upon his prey.

It was thought by some of the watchful old

chiefs about Kalani that the hard lines in Keao's
rugged face softened and unbent, somewhat, as he
traced the kingly likeness of a once-loved brother
in the fearless young warrior before him. Be that
as it may, such thoughts were not given voice,
nor suffered to harbor long in his stony heart.

It was usual in Polynesian warfare, in those far-
gone days, for the leaders to thus advance to the
forefront and hurl a spear at each other, by way
of salutation in opening the combat. But when
Keao had approached within half a spear's cast of
Kalani, hearing a rude rattle of weapons among
his warriors behind, he stopped, and raised his
own terrible spear with a thundering imprecation
for his men to halt and be quiet, while he addressed himself to Kalani :

" Keiki Moi o Oahu ! " (Boy King of Oahu !)
" We have come over the sea, following the yellow
moon-path made for us by Pele. Keao and his
great warriors have come to take Oahu, and Maui,
and Molakai. Open your ears — you and your
army — that you may hear. Surrender your
Island, and submit to us, or I will suffer my strong
chiefs to thrust their great spears through you all,
as we would spear the fat fish in your harbor."

Kalani's thin lips had hued to a livid, ashy pale-
ness ; curling into a proud, derisive smile, withering as a torchfire. He had heard Keao to the end.
But now his eagle eyes were flashing forth living
fire as he replied with scorn and contempt to the
brutal salutation :

" The Kanakers of Kauai have grown fat and
dumpish from lack of wars, and eating too much
poi ; and I doubt not have come to Oahu to learn
how to fight. If Keao were to look at himself he
would die with fright, so old and ugly has he
grown. If he were not in his dotage, his hideous
ears would long since have heard the world ring
with the fame of Kalani."

" Beware, Keiki ! lest Keao slay you for want
of respect to your father's kingly brother. Surrender your Island, or I will take it ! "

" You came like a thief to steal my kingdom in
my absence. You find Kalani most glad to receive
you. Take Oahu, and begone ! Have your dull
eyes become blind that you cannot see it lying at
your feet ? Seven feet of the sacred Isle shall be
yours before we part."

" Cease, vile Keiki ! Should Keao become *huhu
nui* — very mad — he would crush you in his
strong hand, as he has crushed many a foe in his
day."

" We of Oahu have played with spears from our
babyhood. We teach our warriors that two can
play at taking kingdoms. Keao carries a huge
spear, large enough to blot out the sun, but I
have heard that it is harmless as a reed in the
hands of a wahine."

" Dog ! You talk bravely for a Keiki Moi ; but
talk will not save your kingdom. Do you not see
that my mighty warriors are growing impatient to
slaughter your army ? They long to throw your

fat carcasses to good Moa-alii — the fierce god of
the sea — who brought us in safety to your shore."

" But Kalani has promised Moa-alii that he shall
feast upon the clumsy carcass of Keao, and Kalani
will keep his promise to the great sea-god."

" Hearken, if you have ears. Because you are
the son of the great Thunderer, Keao would spare
your life and save your army, that you may join
the brave Kauaians in fighting Kamehameha, who
claims to be the born King of all the Eight Isles.
Will you surrender? or shall Keao fling his keen
spear through your soft body, as a signal for his
impatient warriors to slaughter your army ? "

" There is no word like surrender known in the
sweet tongue of Oahu. Kalani would witness if
so old a King as Keao can handle a spear. Behold
how you tremble at the mere mention of weapons
of war. Are you indeed so much afraid of Kalani
as to shake at his presence ? "

" Surrender! or die. At them, my chiefs!
Sweep them from the earth ! "

And Keao shook his great war-spear with terrific meaning, while a look of terrible vengeance
darkened over his wrinkled face, so maddened was
he by the saucy taunts purposely inflicted by his
youthful foe ; shook the poised weapon in his
giant hand, and hurled it with the utmost ferocity
at the naked breast of the manly boy, who had so
aroused his ire.

Swerving gracefully to one side — yet without
moving an atom from his footsteps — Kalani

caught the great spear as it rung hurtling through the air, whistling like a bullet. Turning the cumbrous weapon in his hand, Kalani hurled it back at Keao, who also swerved and caught his weapon as it spun by his head. Kalani calmly folded his arms and scornfully awaited another attack.

This is indeed a courageous act and cunning art of the great chiefs of Polynesia. The Alii Kapus of Kauai were connoisseurs in such achievements, and their keen eyes saw at once that their too impetuous King had found more than his match at this game. And lest harm should come to him in [3]such perilous trial of skill, six brawny chiefs — the skilful body-guard of their old monarch — assumed cross positions in front of Kalani, and together hurled their keen-edged weapons in murderous concert at the audacious King; the six being followed closely by the more ponderous spear of the now frenzied Keao.

With folded arms and flashing eyes the Boy King stood alert to receive them ; ducking, dodging, and swerving gracefully away from the six previous weapons — thrown in such cunning crossfire — reserving himself to again catch the ponderous weapon of Keao, which he tossed contemptuously behind him, as being unworthy of his further attention ; the art of catching so weighty a spear being the severest test known among feats of arms.

Both Kings being now of one mind, maddened with an insane wish for the death-grapple, drew their swords at the initiative given by Kalani, and rushed furiously towards each other for a hand-to-hand encounter. But suddenly, before they could cross swords, the whole earth shook with the awful reeling and rumbling of an earthquake, till men tottered as when drunk with *awa*, and the earth rent asunder at their feet, separating the two combatants by an abyss that neither could leap. This awful occurrence stayed every hand in both armies, leaving them stunned with horror at what had happened.

Simultaneous with this convulsion beneath their feet, occured another above the head of Kalani. Above the noise of the earthquake, and the tumbling of earth and rocks down into the chasm, was heard a mysterious cooing in the air, together with the fluttering and fanning of great unseen wings, as when doves suddenly alight, followed by the never-to-be-forgotten voice of Pele, whispering in Kalani's ear:

"He Ihe! He Ihe!" (The spear, the spear!) "*He makana* o Pele." — The gift of Pele.

Swifter than the winged lightning did Kalani poise the blue-headed gift of the Goddess, and hurl it with the ring of a scimitar across the fast-closing abyss, piercing the savage heart of the mad-mad king of Kauai, as he stood on the farther brink of the chasm, frothing at the mouth, with the awful rage of battle upon him.

With a hideous groan of mingled rage and pain, the huge body of the old king was seen to reel and stagger and tumble headlong into the deep earth-rent below. Slowly and steadily closed the rough chasm over the dead body, with the spear of Pele still clinging to his heart ; both King and weapon lying buried fifty feet beneath the field of battle.

While yet the air rung with the wild shouts of exultation from the army of Oahu, even before the yawning earth was wholly closed up between them and their foes, Kalani waved his sword in the sunlight, and led on his fierce chiefs and eager spearsmen against the Kauaians, half stunned at beholding this direct interposition of the gods in favor of Oahu. Desperate and bloody was the fight that ensued, for the wrath of maddened men, like the foam on the crest of a storm-billow, does not quickly subside.

About Kalani fought the great war-chiefs of his father's reign. Fighting to shield their *Keiki Moi* from the wild rage of battle ever centring about his kingly presence. These grim old warriors loved their hero because of his likeness to the noble old Thunderer, and his unusual favor with the gods.

The leading chiefs of Oahu were the most cunning warriors among the Isles ; long trained in the advanced arts of barbaric war, wielding their weapons with coolness and consummate skill, sufficed to make them more than a match for the passionate fury of their more numerous foes.

With admirable tact Kalani had succeeded in fully enraging the fierce Kauaian chiefs, until they

now flung themselves too heedlessly into the thick
of the fray. Being less skilful than their wary
antagonists in the use of weapons, they spent
their strength in many a futile blow; until, at the
end of an hour's fighting, hundreds of the burly
forms of the invaders lay dead or wounded upon
the green slopes of the Nuuanu.

This condition of things, together with the terrible accessory of Pele's having shown visible
preference for the army of Oahu, discouraged and
dispirited the brave Kauaians, and they now began
slowly and steadily to retreat toward their canoes,
still fighting with a bold face to the foe.

The combatant who dares take the first step
backward, proclaims his loss of heart and hope to
his antagonist, and imparts renewed vigor and
strength of arm to the enemy from whom he retreats. With the yell of a thousand demons the
Oahuans now pressed the stubborn foemen back
with gory spear-point, and war-club and sabre,
down the valley, strewing the whole line of retreat
with the dead and dying.

With the eye of an eaglet, watching from her
eyrie, the Queen had watched every incident of
the battle from the overhanging battlement of
Puawai, and with more than human wisdom had
decided the battle as won for Oahu, when Keao
received his death from the god-given spear. And
now the quality of her semi-divine blood asserted
itself to some purpose.

Calling about her hundreds of the warlike wives

of the great chiefs, and bidding them each select some brave spirits from among their retinues of women, to the number of a thousand or more. Kupule pointed down to the harbor beneath their feet where lay the great fleet of war canoes unguarded, and with flashing eyes bid her army of wahines to follow her to the rescue.

There winds a steep and perilous pathway down the very front of Puawai, where few but the bravest men like to trust themselves in times of peace. But now it was a time of war, and what Kupule was to do must be done quickly, for the Kauaians were already retreating; and she chose the perilous footpath and led the way, followed by at least twelve hundred brave women.

With the speed of a bounding deer the god-born daughter of Kamehameha led the way down the steep front of the mountain. Keeping the groves and the taro-patches between themselves and the retreating enemy, they quickly reached the shore, unseen by the Kauaians.

Few but her own chieftess maidens were equal to the example of swift-footedness set them by their daring Queen, and they soon reached the canoes, followed steadily by hundreds of other fearless women, matrons and maidens, all eager to save a canoe, though the horrid din of battle was fast drawing toward the shore.

With the leap of a winged creature the young Queen sprang into the royal canoe, where lay the robes of state of the dead Keao, followed by a

dozen of her fleetest maidens. Thrusting off from
the beach, each seized a paddle and plied it with
strength and skill, as all wahine kanakas are
trained to do. Rounding Papu Point, and following the trend of the shore inside of the great
breakers, they sped away for Waikiki, five miles
distant, where the canoes of Oahu were moored
and guarded.

Swift example is ever the best incentive to induce energetic action in others. And it now
became a stirring sight to see eighty great war
canoes leaving the harbor, and impelled along the
shore by lithe maidens and fat women, their long
black hair streaming in the now freshening trades.

All but twenty of the canoes were afloat and
away, before the rearmost of the approaching
Kauaians discovered the cunning proceeding.
Breaking from the ranks they flew to the rescue,
smitten with panic at the thought of their retreat
being cut off. Those who first reached the remaining canoes hastily manned them and fled
from the harbor, without waiting to see the final
result of the battle.

Hemmed in between the boatless shore and the
victorious army of Kalani, the weary and wounded
Kauaians saw themselves at the mercy of their foes,
and cried out: "*Luka-lua! luka-lua!*" — Beaten,
beaten; the least courageous fearful lest they
should be slaughtered to a man.

The bravest are ever the most generous in the
glorious hour of triumph after a great battle is

won. Kalani's noble heart was touched with pity
at the desperate condition of his brave antagonists,
and he now rushed like a fiery meteor along his
own lines of blood-stained warriors, and struck
down sword and spear and paloa, bidding his grim
chiefs and infuriated men to forbear.

When the wild tumult was stilled, and the
angry spear-points on the one hand, and the weary
weapons on the other had dropped to the earth,
then Kalani stepped forward and addressed the
crest-fallen, though yet stern and sullen invaders,
who stood firm with an evident intent of selling
their lives dearly if called upon to do so :

" Kaumualii ! and you, the great war chiefs of
Kauai, it lies with you to say if the battle of Nuuanu is ended. My warriors are famishing for the
blood of the invaders who came to deprive us of
our homes. Kalani would save you, if you prove
yourselves worthy of his clemency. I see many a
loved kinsman among your ranks ; and I offer
Kaumualii and his army, peace, upon full sub-
mission.

" You are witness that Kalani has not sought
this warfare. You can also witness the great
wrong my father's brother sought to perpetrate
upon my people ; and Kalani ought, perhaps, to
permit his outraged warriors to slaughter you to a
man. You are witness to the great love of the
gods for Kalani ; and you saw that the mighty
spear of Keao could not pierce whom the gods
would cherish.

13

" Would you peace, or war, Kauaians? Kalani
of Oahu awaits your reply." Whereupon Kaumualii and several of the older chiefs stepped forth to
make answer.

" Noble King, and great warrior! I am Kaumualii, the son of Keao, and I speak in the name of
my people. I was not one of those who wished to
come to Oahu to fight my noble cousin. But the
warriors of Kauai remembered their duty to their
king, and joined Keao on the war-path, — following over the yellow moon-path which leads to Oahu.

" Those who made the plans to capture Oahu
were wrong, and they are all dead; by this we now
know that they wrought against the wishes of the
gods. Kaumualii asks what is expected of us if
we surrender? for we are a band of heroes, and
would rather die fighting than live to be unjustly
dealt with. I bend my ear to listen to the wisdom
of Kalani. For whom the gods love must be wise."

" You speak wisely, as becomes the new King of
the great Island of Kauai. Keao is dead, and Kaumualii is King. I have said it, and it shall be so.
Kalani makes no claim to your kingdom. Oahu is
in want of great warriors to fight against Kamehameha : who, though he was slain, is alive again.
The Lonely One seeks to take all our islands to
make a kingdom for himself. He is a mighty warrior, and he is loved of the gods. He will rule over
us all unless we join hands to resist him.

" I offer Kaumualii a palace-home in Nuuanu;
and land and homes shall be given to his warriors

from among my possessions in Oahu. Your young
warriors may find wives among my dark-eyed wahines, and your great chiefs shall send to Kauai for
their wives. And we will join our armies and endeavor to save our kingdoms from the monster
warrior of Hawaii. The heart of Kalani warms to
the young king of Kauai. Speak: is Kaumualii
my friend, or my foe?"

"Kaumualii is the friend of Kalani. He will
lead his warriors to battle against the ugly giant
of Hawaii. The great chiefs of Kauai have not
shut their ears against the fame of Oahu's King.
The themes of our sweet bards are the wonderful
deeds of Kalani. Your victories have stirred our
hearts with a love for war. My ears have ever
been open to hear the bards sing of your battles,
and my voice has ever been the loudest in your
praise.

"When Kalani dashed through the storm like
the sea-eagle, fearless of the black night and the
sea-tempest, and slew the great monster Kamehameha Nui, the heart of Kaumualii stood still with
wonder; and he looked, and behold your name was
placed among the stars. And but for Keao, Kaumualii would have come with our young warriors
and fought beneath your banners, as our old chiefs
once fought under the tapa flags of the great Thunderer."

"Kalani has heard what you have said, and it
has lingered pleasantly in his ears. But my sharp
ears hear a murmuring of voices among your war-

riors. Is it the muttering of thunder which portends a storm? or is it the roar of pleasant waters that would slake our thirst for war? It is the wish of Kalani to hear a voice from among the great chiefs of Kauai. Would they again join battle with my impatient warriors? or is there wisdom in the counsel they have taken with each other?"

Pepehi, a noble old warrior whose voice was ever for peace (though his name implied *killer of men*), stepped forth from the ranks to speak for his companion chiefs. His breast and arms, and even his grim and wrinkled face, were bleeding with many wounds; proof that Pepehi had been in the forefront of battle, and was skilled to save his life from the points of many weapons.

"I am Pepehi, of Kauai. When a young warrior, I fought under Titeree, the kingly father of Kalani. Though I now come with my command to invade Oahu, I have watched with joy the rising fame of Kalani, who is the best-loved of the gods. If Kalani cannot save us from Kamehameha, who in all the islands can we look to? I have counselled with the chiefs, and we are of one mind. We would join the brave warriors of Oahu against Kamehameha. It is the wish of our hearts to be at peace with Kalani, for we are wounded and sore, and suffering from the shock of battle. This is the voice of Pepehi."

"You have spoken well. Pepehi is a great warrior, and many of our brave Kanakas have gone down before his strong arm. Pepehi was the joy

of the king, my father, and he shall come to find
delight in the eyes of Kalani. Koleamoko, our
great medicine-man, shall bind the ti leaf on
your wounds. Let us greet, and rub noses, and
be brothers."

And setting the example for his chiefs, Kalani
advanced with extended arms to embrace Kaumualii. And those who had fought with the utmost
fury against each other, now mingled in friendly greetings, and joined in dressing each other's
wounds.

Returning up the valley with Kaumualii and
Boki, the King ordered Paao and his priests to
hasten on a great sacrifice at the heiau in Waikiki;
with directions to gather up all the dead spearsmen of Kauai, and make a *kane kapu*, confined to
the Manoa valley and Waikiki shore. And Moa-
alii was to be remembered; feasted upon numerous of the abundant dead at his caverned lair under
the reef-bed. The tabu should not extend to the
Nuuanu, which should be given up to feasting and
joy.

True, the wounded were being gathered under
the shade of the great bread-fruit trees, and beneath the singing palms, whose long fronds tossed
merrily in the brisk trades. Hundreds were lain
upon the grassy banks of the mountain stream,
where they could slake their feverish thirst, and
find such companionship with the brook-side flowers as never before.

Though Nuuanu was a valley of groans, because

of its numerous prostrate braves, yet, above the
cries of pain from the wounded and the wail over
the dead, rose the shouts of jubilation everywhere,
because of their deliverance from the powerful
invader.

Thus it was in keeping with time-honored custom for Kalani to order a great feast prepared for
the night. There the two young Kings and their
great chiefs met together under the tutui trees,
before the palace, eating to repletion of the baked
hog and dog, and drinking largely of the strong
awa that loosens the tongues of silent men, and in-
culcates the senseless tattle of parrots.

Kaumualii and his great chiefs were assigned
houses for themselves, while the soldiers of both
armies were camped together over across the
Nuuanu.

Kalani had witnessed the brave doings of Kupule
and the wahines. He had missed the graceful
figure of his little Queen from the grass-grown
rim of the crater, and while yet he wondered at
the absence of the dark-eyed maiden, and why she
were not watching her Keiki Moi drive the fierce
Kauaians to the shore. Lo! the wahines appeared
from behind the houses of the town, and were seen
capturing and escaping with the rich trophies, the
far-famed canoes of Kauai. To what extent this
fine piece of strategy influenced the close of the
battle none can tell. But as possession is legal
property for the victor in time of war, to his darling Kupule the proud young King was indebted

for the permanent possession of the fleet, if not for the easy solution of the final postulatum — out of which the treaty arose — that the one army were victors, and the other beaten beyond hopes of retrieval.

The heart of the victor-King warmed at the thought of Kupule's wisdom and daring. And when peace was agreed upon, Kalani sent to Waikiki for the return of the Queen and her chieftess maidens, to join in the coming feast, and for all the other wahines to come to the Nuuanu, for many of them were expert in dressing the wounds of the warriors.

When the King's messenger reached Waikiki, Kupule's toilsome task was almost completed. One by one the great war-canoes had been dragged from the water into the cocoanut grove. Here they were safe from intrusion by the sea, so walled in by the great surf, there being no other outlet through the reef than that at Honolulu.

For this deed of gallantry, in the immediate presence of the enemy, — with the horrid din of fighting in their ears, — the brave and beautiful Queen was long held in such esteem as augments with time, and acquires romance during centuries of repetition.

It is even told that none but a god-born wahine could have conceived a deed so daring, and none but a kinswoman of Pele could have inspired a thousand wahines with instant courage to follow the lead of a stranger, or to arouse the latent

energies of fat and lazy women, sufficient to act
promptly and skilfully — so distracted by their
fears in the proximity of battle.

And now Manona and Lelela followed the
Queen to the palace, up the mountain way, leaving
other scores of maiden chiefs, attached to the
royal household, to head the noisy procession of
two thousand wahines, marching back to Honolulu
and up the Nuuanu. And to this great company
were added more by the way; for after the
bravest of the chieftesses had captured the canoes,
others from the Punch Bowl and elsewhere suddenly acquired that curious accession of courage
which ever induces many to seek share in the
spoils after the conquest.

When this great concourse arrived in the valley,
they scattered about in groups among the camps
and forsaken hamlets throughout Nuuanu, seeking their dead and wounded friends, rejoicing
aloud over the living, and wailing with a wild cry
of uncontrollable grief over their loved dead and
dying.

Ten thousand wailing voices made the night air
dismal throughout the Nuuanu at the end of that
terrible day. While, with their piteous faces upturned to the moon, a thousand baying dogs joined
the cry of grief, for scenting the dead from afar
off ever awakens the sympathetic howl of *caninus*
in all ages and in every land.

But not all of these loud-mouthed mourners
wept the true tears of grief, for among the Poly-

nesia there is an honored avocation of mourning; a trade held in excellent repute among those too lazy or indifferent for grief. The more dismal the tone, and the more prolonged the howl of these hired mourners, the more acceptable they become among the fat widows who dislike such vocation, and cannot arouse themselves sufficient to search out the small atoms of merit in the deceased.

And even Kaumualii was one of those who, in this instance, forgot to weep for the savage old father who had left him a kingdom. This young King had at heart but little love for fighting, and was never over-ambitious even in the thickest of the fight; often permitting his father's warlike chiefs to lead the van in his stead. Hence his wholly unwounded condition at the end of this day's fray. And hence the unusual wailing by the hired mourners over the sacred spot where fell Keao under the heaped-up mound made by the earthquake.

But about the palace grounds, and in camp across the valley, there was feasting and rejoicing, and smoking the frequent pipe of peace, without thought or heed of who were dead or who were living. Grim old war-dogs were seen fraternizing with those who were their mortal foes a few hours since.

CHAPTER XII.

See the Queen in her skiff!
  Bending low o'er the tide;
Peering down into Ocean
  Where the Mermaids abide.

Tell me which is most beautiful,
  The most graceful and free;
The fair maid in the boat?
  Or the maid in the sea?

 FEW weeks of feasting, in honor of the important victory won by Oahu, and with the cunning intent of learning some of the characteristics of his new allies, and, if possible, to endear himself to their battle-scarred leaders, and Kalani was prepared to sail away to the seat of war at the Windward Islands.

The fine army Kalani had now organized from the two combatants, gave him reason to hope he might resist any force Kamehameha could bring against them. He took with him Kaumualii, now become king of Kauai by the death of Keao ; and all the captive Kauaians, who the more readily joined their conquerors from having previously fought in the army of Oahu in the reign of Ti-teree.

It was an anxious hour for Kupule when separating from her loved young King. The fame of Kamehameha was daily increasing, and he was now winning almost every battle fought under his own command. And it was now known that he had been equipping a powerful navy, as well as an army, and among his fleet were many white men with fire-arms and cannon, led by the sagacious boatswain of the Elenora. Though John Young had been detained against his wishes in the first place, he and Davis and others now found it greatly to their profit to abide with Kamehameha, who had made them chiefs and given them large landed possessions.

Kalani was thus hastening his fleet and army to Maui, before the Giant of Hawaii should swoop down upon the Island and capture it during his absence. Kupule and the great *kapu Alii*, Paao, were left in command of Oahu during the King's absence in Maui; the High Priest being subordinate to the Queen, young as she was, for her recent display of heroism in capturing the war-fleet of Keao, had not only endeared her to the popular mind, but had elevated her greatly in the esteem of the chiefs and the love of the King.

Anxious days followed the departure of the army, for Kupule, above all others, believed that the genius of her father would eventually prevail over any opposition thrown in his way; for had not Pele foretold it in her presence, that Kamehameha should yet possess all the Eight Isles; and when did the dread Goddess fail to fulfil her bequests to the kings of men? The whole nation had awakened to the fact of Kamehameha's growing favor with their divine ruler. For had not Pele snatched the giant King from death, after Kalani had slain him in single combat? But the real reason of Pele's suspending her affectionate watchfulness over the Keiki Moi of Oahu, only those who sat by the Kiowai o Pele on that terrible night could tell.

To none but the politic young King and Queen was it yet known how the arrogant Goddess had then rebuked her favorite warrior; and even they could not yet believe that the avenging Ignipotent would be as relentless as she proved. But they lived long enough to learn that a wahine Akua — female god — never forgives loss of faith in her affection, or contempt of her power.

An hour before Kalani's rebellious utterances in the sacred grove, he stood pre-eminently above all others in the divine esteem of Pele. But his defection in that one hour of thoughtless apostasy proved his downfall; and thenceforth his father's illegitimate son wholly usurped his place in the fickle affections of Pele.

This half-defined belief was becoming all too current; acting to depress the people, and somewhat the warriors of Oahu. But never for a moment had it deterred Kalani, or his noblest war-chiefs, from making their final preparations for battling with the utmost desperation, though beaten in many a battle before the final one.

Thus, when the army was gone, and the young Queen came to feel the full responsibility thrown upon herself, — together with the terrible secret harbored like an incubus in her bosom, — she sought to inspire Paao and the other tabu priests with constant attention to their religious duties at the great Heiau of Waikiki.

Their first sacrifices were due to Moa-alii — the Neptune of the sea — inducing him to carry the King's great fleet safely over the sea to Maui. And when the army was fairly embarked, Paao went away to the great Temple, and promulgated a brief *kapu puaa hea* (a hog tabu) to propitiate the fierce god of the sea.

Kupule took it upon herself — aided by many of her maiden chieftesses — to make many and frequent oblations to Lono, whose sylvan heiau was built among the adjacent sandal-wood forests, Lono being the only god suitable for the worship of women. To this gentle god, fruits and vegetables, and flowers, were the only sacrifice required to propitiate his kindly remembrance, and lead him to continue abundant fruit and plenty of taro, the root out of which the national food, poi, is made.

Though he ever answers to the prayers of his adherents, yet in what far country good Lono resides none can tell. Being a great chief in his day, and having a beautiful wife, — so beautiful that a neighboring gallant coveted her, — he came home one day to his house in Kealakeakua bay, and heard from the tall cliff near by the gallant calling to his lovely Kaikilani, "Oh, beautiful wahine! your lover salutes you: Keep *this*, remove *that*, and one will still remain." Meaning, kill Lono, and I will wed you. In a moment of frenzy Lono smote his wife, and she died. After years of mania and grief he left the country in a canoe, promising to return some time in a great *waa*. For this he was deified ; and thus Cook was taken for Lono returning to his people.

From Diamond Head, and many other headlands and sea-side crags, the sacrificial offerings went on, with prayers for the prosperity of the fleet. But when word came from the windward that the army had reached Maui, having crossed the rough Pailolo sea in safety, then the terrible Moa-alii was held in less veneration than before. And now, the stray hogs and yelping curs, required less watchfulness in their sagacious endeavors to escape the murderous lariat of the Pepehi Kanaka — man-killer — of the tabu priests.

After a few days respite, a *kapu kane* was pronounced for the future welfare of the army, when the great Heiau was a scene of terrible human sacrifice, priestly wailing, and loud-mouthed prayer to Pele. To none other did these people worship with such earnest zeal and inhuman oblations, as to the dread Goddess of Mauna Loa. To the fiery Ignipotent all bowed with fear and trembling. There were so many visible events and imaginary accessories ever transpiring to arouse the superstitious, and remind the people of the awful and relentless power of Pele, that her worship was never likely to be forgotten or imperfectly accomplished.

If but a tiny star wings its way earthward, spending its transfusive life upon the bland tropic air, it comes like a warning voice to thousands of quaking souls, lest it marks their doom in the black record of the *Kapu Kahuua* — tabu priest. But whether to priest or peasant, it is a reminder to all that the Goddess of Kilauea is abroad in Spirit; and whether this visible expression is to be construed into a dread phantom, or a peaceful gratulation, is a subject for the dread Augurs to decide. So the life of many a poor wretch is thus dependent upon the good or bad digestion of the ever-cruel Hoopiopio of the temple nearest at hand.

If by chance a bluish-green meteor explodes in the sky, and illuminates the heaven with its lurid gleam, crashing down with its unearthly splinters of grayish-green rock into sea or soil, then indeed the consternation is dreadful, and the whole world of Polynesia leap to their feet, agape with wonder and agog with fear. Thousands fall upon their faces in abject abasement or maniacal terror, pleading piteously for the dread Goddess to mitigate their sin of omission or commission; the aroused conscience of each delinquent applying the meteoric warning to themselves.

Let but an earthquake jar upon the tranquil tropic night, undulating the thin earth-crust of the Islands, until the surface rocks and rolls beneath

the feet, like the great billows of the sea; then
all agree that something is happening to the army,
and the whole land is filled with wailing — as
upon the death of a king.

But weeks passed and nothing happened to jar
upon public tranquillity until one calm morning,
when Loa was seen belching forth a sulphurous
cloud, until it hung like a funeral pall over the
sunlit day. Then indeed all were alike convinced
that a great battle was transpiring, pending weal
or woe for their army. The zeal of the priests
was awakened to a frenzy, and Paao at once proclaimed the necessity of a *kapu kane* to appease
the angry Goddess in this hour of terrific war.

As none knew who the unlucky ones would be,
thus suddenly required by cruel mandate, all fled
to the sea, or climbed to the mountain fastness
with the utmost desperation. An hour after and
the whole land became depopulated of its movable male population, leaving only the aged and
the crippled from which to choose. But the immolation was made. If the choice had to be made
from a few, the selection required the merit of
expedition, and this was ever a consideration where
thousands of quaking souls were watching for the
welcome appearance of that ghastly *peculiar smoke*
from the Heiau, indicated by human sacrifice. As
hunted foxes sneak from their holes, and once en-
snared birds peer forth from their coverts, so the
stealthy canoes paddled in from the sea, and the
forest-hiders crept down to their homes and scared
loved ones once more.

Often the cunning old Tabu Chiefs predoomed the people long before the coming sacrifice; in such cases the doomed ones were always entrapped just before they were wanted for the holocaust. This comprises another and more devilish form of living dread for the banned ones; living a life more hideous than are a thousand deaths to the brave.

This hereditary doom becomes a part of the daily existence of every male of low degree. Therefore, if a priest or one of his low-browed Pepehi Kane, but look askance upon a peasant-man, who by any possibility deems himself of little value to the crown, either for purposes of war or progeniture, it is sufficient cause for him to believe himself doomed for the next immolation; and in such case he often sickens, and declines by a slow, lingering death, wholly the effect of fear.

But there were days when all went well; when news of partial successes came down from the Windward Isles, making all hearts glad; happy in the hope that each battle might be the last; for with days of peace there were less occasion for human sacrifice to their cruel gods. At such times the less anxious among the banned proletarian class forgot their abnormal fears of daily personal jeopardy, and entered into the pleasures and pastimes of others about them, but with ever a furtive glance at the volcano and the heiau.

In these happy interlucent days, old and young, kane and wahine, spent many a joyous hour frolicking in the wild surf, or floating lazily about

14

upon the passive waters lying between the great
breakers and the tranquil shore ; the reef being
well out from the beach, and reaching from Diamond Head far down the western shore, left within a smooth coral sea, usually unruffled by a billow.

In these oblivious days wandered merry troops
of tender girls and obesitous women, through
fruitful groves and the flowery fields. But most
they loved to search the deep cool valleys for the
purple figs and the yellow papaya, and hear the
sweet-voiced o-o sing. Or climbing yet higher
among the mountain fastness, where grew the
wild tutui, and the red ohea pomiferous with crimson beauty. Here they wove themselves baskets
from the pandana leaves, to fill with juicy ohea
apples, ever so palatable to a thirsty wanderer ;
gathering armsful of gay hibiscus-flowers or yellow
blossoms from the hau trees, from which to wreathe
their heads of shining hair. Hying homeward,
only with the western sun, each with their gay
leis (wreaths) of red and purple, yellow or green,
as best suits their poetic fancy.

Among those who best loved bathing and boating, were countless youthful maidens, mostly led
by the wahine Aliis — the chieftess girls. Of
these, some would fish for hours upon the reef ;
varying their vocation by leaving their anchored
canoes and bathing in the surf, or diving for
shells and pink pearls, and tiny clusters of blood-
red coral, bits of which were used to deck their
ears, or string as beads to adorn their brown necks,
or clasp about their fat arms.

Still others there were among the proud high-chief maidens — girls full of poetic revery, whose young lovers were away in the army — who loved best to drift in their canoes whither the wind took them, or the tidal currents might bear; finding pleasure in noting the varied and exquisite beauties of color and growth among the wonderful formations of the coral bottom.

Among these latter maidens — who ever found solitude thick peopled with delightful fancies — was the youthful Queen. She loved best to paddle out alone in her own tiny canoe, seeking communion with self upon the unruffled waters of this rare madreporic sea. Sometimes Kupule was accompanied by either the gay Manona or the sweet-voiced Leleha, two bits of maiden-beauty almost as charming as their loved young Queen. But oftenest she dismissed even these loved young attendants, and, with a sobriety above her years, sought out the mystic *Mona Kihapai* of Waikiki, a forbidden spot — tabued to all but the high-priests and the royal pair.

None but the King and Paao ever knew the whole mystery of Kupule's so loving to frequent this one particular spot, far down Waikiki reef toward Leahi's frowning headland. It had been reputed as a haunted spot in the sea for centuries. This *Mona Kihapai* (Pearl Garden) was made sacred by the strongest spells of sorcery known to the mystic rites of priestcraft; so Tabued, as to invoke instant death upon whomsoever were found

within its limits, except they were accompanied
by one of the Kapu Alii or the royal family.

The Pearl Garden was in the vicinity of the
place where so many poor peasants had been
dragged by the lasso to feed Moa-alii, in times of
sacrifice. Sufficient reason in itself why others of
their class became not too curious to encroach upon
the dread domain, or spy upon its awful mysteries
before *their* time of slaughter.

It was called the Pearl Garden from being the
rarest spot of coralline sea known in the Pacific ;
where were found the largest royal seed pearls
trafficked in commerce ; but its other mysteries
were known only to the few. Yet it came to be
observed by the knowing ones, that when even
one of the royal divers tattled too much of the
marvels of the place, he soon disappeared from
among his friends, and his face was seen no more
upon the earth. When the priests or the sooth-
sayers were questioned about the lost divers, they
attributed the disappearance to their being devoured by some of the numerous guardian monsters of the tabued spot.

Be that as it may. Those who dared breathe
their thoughts about this matter ever whispered
them in trembling and fear, having seen the
peculiar smoke of human sacrifice ascending from
the heiau after the previous loss of their companions, hinting that the less said about the matter
the better for all concerned, lest still another tat-
tling tongue should be missed from among them.

People grow wise as dangers thicken ; and un-
ruly gossips learn best to guard their tongues in
these countries where death is the penalty. Where
even the gentle moon and the merry stars seem so
many fiery-eyed spies, watching in the service of
the vengeful Goddess of Kilauea. How else are
so many snatched rudely from existence within the
very hour of disclosing some tabued subject ?

Many a day Kupule and her maidens would join
the sporting wahines, swimming in the great breakers, or on the still waters of the harbor near the
town. But when tiring of this sport, and often
after only watching the other wahines, without
entering into their aquatic pastime, the Queen
would dismiss her court maidens, and stepping
lightly into her own frail canoe would dart out
to the very verge of the floundering surf, till its
flying foam-bubbles flecked her jetty hair as she
spun swiftly along. Thus paddling or drifting,
Kupule gradually approached the tabued spot
which bore such a dread for every other wahine
in the land but herself.

As we have seen, Kupule, though but a winsome creature of sixteen years, was a wahine of
heroic mould. A natural daughter of Kamehameha
by a mountain mother, said to be near of kin to
Pele, she was gifted with a heart where fear was
but a fugitive emotion, which came not often nor
tarried long. Semi-goddess as she was, the love
of daring deeds became the very spirit of her
existence.

It may well be conceded that in the frequent
conditions of such a mind the tumultuous rumble
and roar of the great breakers found an answering
resonance in her soul. Its stupendous barytone
served well to lift a pondering mind above pigmy
things, and was often in exquisite harmony with
the grandeur of Kupule's warlike imaginings, while
conceiving deeds of valor for her loved young
King. For be it remembered that the Queen was
born in an age and of a race where many a dark-
eyed chieftess fought, from preference, side by side
in the ranks with their noble lords.

The first day of Kupule's courage being severely
tested by any remarkable discovery in the Pearl
Garden, though she had previously scanned miles
on miles of rare coralline growths, was when coming suddenly upon the caverned lair of Moa-alii.
She knew that his awful den was somewhere under
the great reef-bed, but thought it was nearer Diamond Head, upon which his largest temple was
erected. She was not at that time searching for
the hidden mysteries of the nether world; but
rather seeking to gratify her craving for poetic
beauty in the coral habitat of the sea.

But upon the day in question she discovered
something which paled the rich carmine in her
olive cheeks, and roused her native superstition
to the utmost. On the following day it was noticed by her maiden companions that after a long
interview with the high-priest, Paao at once proclaimed a yet more strict tabu of the *Mona Kiha-*

pai; extending its bounds and increasing its penalties. And it was rightly guessed by the people that the Queen was the sole cause of it. It became a secret subject of gossip for months after, and curiosity was not wholly allayed until some of the males among the gossips were found kidnapped and fed to Moa-alii.

Had not Kupule so recently endeared herself to her new subjects, this event would have created great prejudice against her. But as the pearl-fisheries belonged exclusively to the King, and he never had farmed out the Pearl Garden to any of his chiefs — as he did other fisheries — it came to be believed that the new tabu was solely to protect the unusually large pearls of that part of Waikiki Bay. Upon that conclusion it was accepted as a pardonable piece of female vanity in the Queen to restrict others from going there.

On the day in question Kupule had paddled farther down the reef than usual, occasionally drifting quietly over some of the rarest spots in the Pearl Garden below, where the exquisite coloring of the coral, and its endless variety, captivated her poetic mind. But whatever the charm we may encounter in the sunniest days of life, it is an inherent characteristic in such ideal minds as Kupule's to still search on with an ever increasing incentive for something yet more beautiful than this life contains. So the Queen continued her searching, ever onward, brooding in the delicious revery of an ardent maiden endowed with a kingly love.

At length she drifted with suspended paddle over some new charm; and by the added flush upon her pearly cheek, and the unusual look of animation portrayed by every feature, it must be something strange or novel to so attract her from her dream-like revery. The meridian sun was just approaching a point in the zenith where it casts its minutest shadows, until even now Kupule's toy canoe was casting but a tiny shadow-speck upon the sheeny whiteness of the coral temples beneath.

The startled creature was at that moment hovering over the forks of the five-road channel below, a spot known to be frequented by beautiful mermaids, as well as hideous eeries and other sea-monsters, positioned due south from the high tower in the great heiau, and probably the most curious and beautiful sea-bottom thoroughfare found in any madreporic sea. The young Queen bent more and more earnestly over the low gunwale, composing herself intently for yet another scrutinizing search into the dim mysteries of the supernatural world below.

After the closest attention Kupule could clearly trace the singular conformation of the beautiful sea-bottom beneath, and distinguish many a half-defined creature in human form, 'mid the deepest chasms over which she was drifting; though the general level of the Pearl Garden was but a few fathoms beneath the surface, so shallow that a maiden could easily dive down and pluck shell or coral anywhere at her pleasure. But from where the canoe now lay there could be seen a broad, deep channel, making out in the direction of the outer reef, where the increasing tumult of the great breakers crashed and roared with unusual significance, imparting a terrible meaning to the human ear when heard in such a place.

So deeply creviced into the ocean-floor was this strange aquatic highway, that but for the vertical rays of the midday sun the human eye could not detect the snowy whiteness of the coral sand, which served to relieve the terrible gloom of the great abyss below.

By the description she had received from the old bard of Manoa Valley, Kupule knew that she was now in the immediate vicinity of the dread " Moa-alii's Den ; " the place of terror above all others for the fishermen who went beyond the reef to fish ; for it was not an infrequent occurrence for the poor fellows to be tossed from their canoes and swallowed at a gulp by the savage sea-god.

From her present position Kupule could only distinguish a light-blue archway at the far end of the deep sandy roadway, out toward the breakers, reaching in under the great reef-bed to the sea beyond. But it is said that by the aid of a low-lying western sun, one can discern light through the deep, dark cavern — an unquiet, disturbed light — agitated and broken by the movable black shadows of great monsters within.

This caverned den of Moa-alii was held in the utmost horror by all the natives of the Islands ;

the rapacious Moa-alii being the cause of much
human sacrifice in times of war. Occasionally the
hideous sea-god appeared in the quiet waters of
Waikiki Bay, snapping up some native bather, and
retreating with him to his caverned lair ; leaving
a terrible trail of crimson in the disturbed waters,
through which he had rushed like a meteor in the
sky.

Upon such occasions the cruel priests would add
to the public grief, for deeming the occurrence one
hinting to the Kapu Alii that they had been re-
miss in their religious duties to the *Moana Akua*
(ocean god), they would at once order the sacrifice of numerous other victims to appease the voracious maw of the ravenous monster.

Thus it will be seen these many elements of
terror might well serve to arouse the latent superstition of even the god-born Queen, when she discovered into what dread domain she had drifted.

Overhanging the steep sides of the ocean chan-
nel-way, beneath her canoe, hung delicate shrubs
and stately coral trees, leaning with precarious
foothold out over the deep abyss below ; as
gnarled old trees are sometimes seen to overhang
a rocky cliff or deep ravine, until we almost watch
to see them fall.

These overhanging coral growths served to
deepen the gloom of impenetrable shadow far
down on the white sea-bottom, casting so many
black veils over the dismal lurking places of the
unsightly denizens of the deep. Hideous mon-

sters! whose vast proportions are only guessed at by the jagged outline of their shifting shadows, occasionally thrust stealthily out into the torrid sunshine, denticulated in black silhouette upon the snow-white sand below.

Unshapely creatures! so *almost* visible in their deep ocean lairs as to create a loathing, and a cold, creeping horror, by the mere reflection of what they possibly *might be*. Even the boldest cannot but shudder when thus spying down upon the nether world; gazing awe-stricken and eager, until one's flesh creeps and crawls at the very thought of possible contact with such unshapely, slimy monsters.

Rarely in this world have human eyes been permitted to look searchingly into one of these frightful haunts of the monstrosities of the sea. Sometimes a fisherman, bolder than his fellows, has acquired a taste for looking into these unhallowed mysteries; but, alas, his life was short, and his ending dreadful.

But the god-born Queen supposed herself exempt from the frailties of common humanity, and though her superstitions were easily awakened, her courage was undaunted. And to one imbued with a courage that quails at nothing, and a patience content to bide its time, there is much to be discovered with all things favorable.

While Kupule was thus hovering over the deepest and widest part of this thickly peopled chasm, watching with the utmost stealth and stillness, there appeared just beneath her canoe, in frightful proximity, a great snarl of long, slimy tentacles — hooked and clawed with a thousand writhing talons — reaching out sixty feet into the sunlit channel. Floating thus stealthily out upon the inflowing current coming through Moa-alii's Den, these tentacles seemed as instinct with murderous intent as a squirming snarl of monstrous serpents.

Kupule soon learned the meaning of this array of sandy-gray arms; which, but for the dense waving shadows they cast upon the sunlit bottom, might have been taken for mammoth growths of floating sea-weed, they were vibrating so snake-like in the swaying motion of the current. A large fish came sauntering in from the sea, feeding from the coral branches, where a medusa or other radiate had caught, when incautiously striking against one of the tentacles, instantly two other tentacula closed upon him, and he was drawn struggling into the hidden maw of the gigantic Octopus thus ambushed like a highwayman under the overhanging bank.

The young Queen shuddered at what she had seen, and with a few strokes of her paddle thrust herself away from the spot; gently approaching the Five-Forks again, from which a trifling occasional air from the shore had wafted her canoe away. Though Kupule had thrust the ugly Octopus away from her sight, and brought her eyes to dwell once more upon the charms beneath her, yet the frightful creature she had seen clung like an incubus to her mind. She could not but remember its stealthiness, for never for a moment did the gigantic Devil Fish venture its monstrous body out into the light of day. Neither did other of the mammoth creatures show anything but their dim shadow-shapes ; and these uncertain reflections were only made visible as they crawled stealthily around some submarine projection, in passing from cavern to cavern, leaving the awed observer but little to judge of what manner of creature they might be looking upon.

Puaaiki, the old bard, had told Kupule of many a fearless diver in the employ of the old king, who had innocently gone down in the vicinity of these haunts, in search of rare pearls, never again returning to his loved ones on earth. But directly about the Five Forks where Kupule now was, the water was less deep, and the hiding-places less capacious ; sufficient reason, she thought, to wholly exclude the larger denizens of the deep, and induce hope of having an interview with Oluolu, the queen mermaid of the Five Forks.

Between the jutting forks of two of these shoalest sandy reaches, leading deviously away toward the shore, there grew a stately Pinna-coral tree ; large as a pandana, and crimson as the gaudiest sunset of their clime. So red and diffusive in color was this great sea-shrub, that it cast a soft vermilion glow over the white coral about it ; even imparting a faint crimson tint to the far-down bottom of white sand in the reaches — verily like a pink carpeting of apple-blossoms wind-strewn from their tree.

Partly sheltered behind this stately crimson tree, waved the delicate mauve-colored foliage of a graceful Fan-coral; its broad and beautiful leaves fancifully perforated like the magic fretwork of some fairy temple. Some of the long frónds were so thin and elastic that they swayed gracefully in the current, like the bending swale in a meadow stream. Upon these broad, mauve-colored leaves could be traced many a quaint design, delicate as lace-work, as if woven by the consummate art of a cunning hand.

Growing about everywhere upon the coral shrubs and porous rocks, clung the great pearl oysters, wherein nestle those princely gems which captivate the world. In the more open spots, where the eye could pierce down through the coral foliage to the bottom, could be seen numerous rare shells creeping merrily about, as if at play with the broken sunbeams.

Here breed those delicate Pinna Pearls, or crimson "wing-shells,"— divine conceptions of the wondrous æons of the deep, — which produce the exquisite pink pearls and the lustrous red nacre so rarely seen out of the Orient, being too priceless for the general mart. And as if to add to its wonder, the byssus, or beard, by which the Pinna is anchored to the bottom, is a costly cable of rich-brown silk. From this silken byssus the wahine chiefs plat themselves necklaces and bracelets — like that about Kupule's neck, to which her pearls were attached. In India, gloves and many other fabrics are woven from this byssus, though rarely seen outside of the harems.

Round about the gorgeous Pinna-tree grew countless sea-flowers of every conceivable combination of colors; and when Kupule remembered that every minute corolla was the charming *products of a life* (not a vegetable growth), being not only sensible to pain, but also instinct with visible life and passionate emotion, — lives capable of receiving exquisite pleasure from the sunlight, and which are prompted to loving companionship by the subtle Luna orb, whose mystic influence affects all viable creation. Well might the gentle Queen find intelligent companionship among these pretty polypidoms — "daughters of ocean" — and love to watch the conscious beauties preen and perk in the sun, swaying playfully in the clear blue tides, joyously as land-flowers swing in the wind and sun.

The god-born girl had early taught herself wise lessons by observation, as she daily played from early childhood in the coral sea among the swimming polyps and matured corolla, with their royal mauves and purples, and delicate carnations and deeper crimson petals; all *living products*, not senseless marine growths as are generally supposed.

And here in her queenly home she again made playmates with the charming sea-flowers, watching them bud and blossom and produce seed out of which sprung animate animal life in floral form; being gifted with keen intelligence and quick perceptions in choosing their friends. True, they were not herbaceous, having woody stems like her palace-flowers, but, more wonderful still, they were horny or calcareous. Every rosette or sea-flower will be found instinct with hunger, and may be daily seen feeding, gathering their own food by the aid of tiny arms, or long tentacles, searching warily about in their brief limit, and devouring whatever small animalcule they can seize upon.

Thus being a lover of these wonderful marine anthology, Kupule had long since come to the knowledge of judging by the form and color of the young *swimming larvæ* what manner of submarine shrub or sea-flower they would become at maturity, selecting those kinds she liked best to transplant in her sea-garden near the Waikiki palace. Choosing one of the slim, translucent pearl-colored larva to transplant for " Music-Coral " — the most beautiful of the anthozoa when seen in full blossom.

The larva of the " Neptune's Cup " is a deep vermilion, while others of the polyzoa are a dark brown, or robin's-egg blue. Ever choosing the thick-rumped, clumsy little milk-white larva, which swims backward with great activity, and are more numerous than all others, to plant for the shrub-border of her madreporic garden. Having to seek days sometimes to find one of the rare dark-rumped, gray-bodied larvæ with tiny pink eyes, from which grow the gorgeous Pinna shrubs —

tipped with their enchanting pink corolla — which serve to transform the clear turquoise sea into scenes of Oriental splendor.

Some of these baby polypi can be caught while swimming nimbly about — always stern foremost — while others, a trifle more matured, are plucked from their eternal anchorage, after having fastened upon a rock purposely or by accident. For after a brief existence the young larvæ adhere to whatever they touch from a plastic lymph which exudes from the rump for the purpose. Once caught, they build a coral temple about themselves — thenceforth flowering and fruiting, each after the manner of their kind.

Like gorgeous birds among the tree-tops of a tropical forest hovered the innumerable colored fishes everywhere. Flitting in and out among the coral branches and the drooping leaves, they flashed their various hues like butterflies among flowers. Occasionally these rainbow-colored fishes would be seen shooting suddenly upward in a cloud from among their coral covert, darting above the foliage with many a furtive look behind, as if they had been driven away by some common impulse of fear — like a flock of startled lories in the palm-grove — so intimidated by the sinister movement of some vindictive sea-god.

But when all became quiet again, hundreds of these red parrot-bills would be seen feeding from off the snowy foliage of the stately corals, seeming verily like the crimson blossoms of fresh-blown

15

flowers; while deeper down among the winding
avenues of the coral groves roved countless shoals
of gold-fishes, dazzling♦ with yellow brightness in
the torrid ray, as if they themselves were but rov-
ing sunbeams.

Here was a scene of wondrous life and beauty
well fitted to captivate a less poetic soul than
Kupule's. Though born in a crater, and reared
accessible to the great reef-beds of Hilo Bay, the
Queen here found such fascination as joyed her
young soul. But she who, while yet in maternal
arms, had seen the flame-clad Pele dancing like a
gypsy in the volcanic fires of Kilauea; and had
since looked face to face upon the divine Goddess
in her hour of wrath; was endowed with courage
to delve among the monstrosities of the sea; and
perceptions sufficiently delicate to open her inmost
soul to the exquisite charms of the scenes here
opening upon her.

And who could guess better than this god-born
girl that as yet the presiding spirit of this enchanting spot had failed to disclose itself to her human
eyes? For well she knew that out of all perfect
elements, whatever their nature, there must ever
arise a presiding spirit, a divine æon or incarna-
tion, born of its own ethereal essence in quality
and in kind. And in search of this essential spirit
Kupule still prolonged her stay. Though her girl-
soul had filled to repletion with what she had already seen, still was she thirsting, like a wanderer
in the desert, for the one complete fulfilment of

that which had already baptized her young soul in beauty.

With a touch light as a seabird's wing in the sea, Kupule dipped her light paddle in the still water, changing her canoe about from one enchanting spot to another, yet finding no view so beautiful as at the Five Forks, where the crimson coral rose queenly and grand above its white companions.

Kupule had now become so fascinated with the place that she cared not to tear herself away from the spot, especially as she continually caught glimpses of something strange and unusual, dim, human-like creatures moving stealthily about in the black shadows of the subterranean by-ways. How they stirred her on to continued search! Some of these shadowy disclosures would silhouette verily like human forms upon the sheeny whiteness of the ocean floor. Sometimes she caught veritable glimpses of small, girlish upturned faces and tiny outstretched hands, as if the half-defined sea-nymphs were themselves spying upward to herself and her canoe, endeavoring to lure her below.

In such moments the enthused young Queen would catch her breath, and press her fair hands wildly upon her ungarmented bosom, wherein her tumultuous heart beat loud and strong with certain expectation of soon beholding the unholy mysteries she sought. But the timid sea-people are ever shy, and abound in cunning ways to pre-

vent a full exhibit of themselves. Though, like
the earth-maiden above them, these habitans of
the deep are ever curious to peer forth into the
upper world; but lest they should be seen are always receding from one place of lookout, and appearing stealthily at another. Might it not be
that the roused human gaze so concentrates upon
a half-discovered mystery as to project a pungent,
electric shock, terrifying the object of our investi-
gation? For certain it is that once the human
eye rests strongly upon one of these shadowy figures, they melt away before the gaze like dew before the sun.

Who of us ocean wanderers has not thus found
himself gazing down among the coral groves of a
tropic sea, with a sometime half-assurance of soon
beholding an embodiment of our fantastic visions
of the unknown folk-people in the luculent depths
of ocean?

Yet when searching these stalactic caverns and
madreporic gardens of the sea, who can tell whether
the shadowy shapes we discover are viable realities
or born of the hour within our own teeming brains?
For the human mind is capable of being aroused
into most profound conditions of awe by the very
weirdness of its own conceptions.

It was thus Kupule peered down into the sandy
reaches and sunlit grottoes, her wide eyes flashing
about with momentary expectation. Watching
until her young heart stood still, so awed with
wonder at the near approach to the *unseen* rather

than at the visible ; gazing until her quick respiration hushed itself into the smallest available breathings.

While Kupule was thus attributing every waving motion imparted to the delicate sea-grasses, the red dulse or the mauve-colored flowers, to the stealthy movement of some dark-faced Eerie, — such as often haunts the conception of us all, — suddenly a single note of exquisite music vibrated against the bottom of the canoe, as Kupule leaned low down over the gunwale, with her flushed young face mirrored in the sea. The startled girl was thrilled by the sweet strains as by an electric spark, so tense and tuneful were the delicate neuroses of her soul in such a moment of awe.

The melody that had aroused her was a simulate of the clear, sweet tremolo, made by a wet finger rubbed upon the vibratious rim of a glass bell. And again it came, rising higher and higher, swelling at length into the softest pianissimo of a far-away human voice.

So intent had Kupule been upon the beauties of the Pearl Garden, that she had not noticed the sun's creeping up to the full meridian day. Nor until this moment had she remembered what the fishermen and the old bard had told her of the *Meles o ke Kai* — songs of the sea — heard only at midnight and midday, somewhere out in the vicinity of Moa-alii's Den.

That it was music she heard, and music of the strangest, sweetest melody, there lingered no doubt in the mind of the startled Queen. But whence it came, and who gave it utterance, as yet she could form no conception. Thus far the exquisite cadence was detected and determined as much by Kupule's roused sense of *feeling* as by her hearing; by its vibrations against the thin bottom of the canoe, rather than against the tympanum of the maiden's ear.

The whole soul of the young creature became thrilled by the witching strains. Her long black hair crackled as from an electric spark, waving with life-like excitation in the windless air. Her dark eyes sparkled with a look of sweet content, flashing like the mirrored sun in the sea. She sat entranced with wonder at the psychic spirits she had aroused.

Kupule's first thought was of ambient spirits in the adjacent air. But not a cloud was visible in all the summer sky, on which to perch a kindly spirit or an evil spook. Look where she would, there was naught to bequeath her wandering conceptions upon.

Was it Pele — she asked — calling to her from Loa's distant peak? For something, such strains had been heard in the Kiowai ere the Goddess came forth. It was not probable that it was the dread Goddess, for Loa and Kilauea were slumbering in the utmost tranquillity; and one of these craters were always aroused and active when the divine Pele was abroad.

Wearied with her long watching, Kupule at

length became terrified by her own superstitions; so annoyed at the thought of hearing repeated strains of music out there upon the open bay, that she seized her paddle and spun her light canoe swiftly to the Waikiki shore.

While hastening to the beach, cleaving the blue water and tossing the foam, though all unconscious of the occurrence at the time, Kupule acquired a distinct landmark by which to find the Five Forks again. Two pandana trees were in exact range with the tower in the great Heiau; and she afterwards remembered the trees and the tower when she eventually wished to retrograde her track.

Kupule grew calmer ere she reached the shore, and with a thoughtfulness above her years, determined to keep her own counsel, and not disclose what she had seen and heard; settling into the conviction that the ocean melody she had heard was a part of the supernatural agency ever around her, Kupule adhered strictly to her first conception of secrecy, imparting nothing of what had transpired to even Manona or Leleha, the two best-loved among her *wahine Aliis*. As we have said, only relating her discovery to the Tabu Chief, requesting Paao to not only confirm the present *Kapu o Make* (tabu of death) about the Pearl Garden, but also to make it more extensive in its aqueous bounds.

On the *unseen* brink of a world unknown,
Met the earth-born Queen and an Elf from her zone;
Each were queens in their clime, and met with delight,
Yet were awed with wonder, and chilled with fright!

From the Fountain sprang, conjured up by pray'r,
With her azure eyes and her amber hair:
She sat 'neath the spray, with the moon on her face,
A vision of beauty and fairy-like grace.

Ah! this meeting of Spirits from worlds remote,
Is a terror to dread, more than words denote;
E'en the stars blushed gold! and the moon grew cold!
Yet they wove for the Elf-queen a raiment of gold.

And the orange-bells, and the fronded palms,
Chimed a song of delight o'er the Elf-queen's charms;
And the surf and the sea, and the fountain's spray,
Played an anthem of joy on the lunar ray.

232

CHAPTER XIII.

N the following morning the trade-winds struck down strong, and continued so throughout several days following Kupule's visit to the Pearl Garden, thus debarring further investigation of the mysteries of the dread *Mona Kihapai* until smoother times.

But roused by the past mysterious occurrence to more zealous attention to her religious duties, the Queen now frequented the Kiowai o Pele in the sacred grove, for both orison and vespers; the place having become doubly sacred to her since Pele's appearing there face to face with herself and the King.

Yet woven conspicuously into the subtile weft and warp of her recent religious duties, was an ever ulterior motive. Is not such an under-current of frequent occurrence in very young devotees of her sex? Believing that the divine strains she had heard emanated from Pele, and if addressed solely to herself, exalted her to a high place among the elect, Kupule now sought to learn by earnest watchfulness and frequent prayer, if the imperious Goddess would not submit to further communication. And as the sea was too rough for boating, — debarring her from the Pearl Garden, — she ingen-

iously asked : Might not the divine strains be
vouchsafed to her prayerful supplications at the
sacred Kiowai?

But although Kupule's superstitions were exalted to the utmost, and in numerous visits she had
watched with patient assiduity in the only small
space left smooth by the falling waters of the fountain, yet only the charming image of her own fair
face had responded to her gaze. And except the
tinkling notes of the falling spray, never a sound
of melody had reached her ears from the fountain :
only the quickening heart-beat of a hushed and
reverent maiden, kneeling there breathless among
the marginal flowers, was ever heard upon the palpitant air.

Though the Kiowai had failed the Queen in her
appeal for divine interposition, it could never be
other than a sacred place of reverence and mystery, after what she had witnessed in company
with Kalani. While sitting upon its border, Kupule was ever repaid by a flood of wild, strange
thoughts, glowing with poetic fervor. There she
ever seemed in the viable presence of supernatural spirits, those all-pervading Invisibles which
so mould our destinies, and advance or terminate
the lives of nations at their will. Among such in-
fluences, the thoughts of this god-born girl would
climb to the stars, or delve down into the utmost
recesses of the seething earth — following the beautiful Ignipotent into her fiery element, down to the
roaring sea of incandescence beneath.

Not wholly satisfied with her numerous day-visits to the sacred Kiowai, Kupule thought to test the charmed hour of midnight by the mystic light of the moon. The night orb was now at *Hoku* (nearly full), when her mysterious influence was approaching its most subtile consummation; that baleful hour when the bodiless spirits of the nether world quicken from their brief embryotomy, and take sudden wing to infest the world with evil, or endow it with good works, each according to their kind.

Rising softly from her simple couch of *luhala* mats and *pulu* pillows, Kupule groped her way from among her slumbering maidens, — grouped about their Queen like a constellation of lesser stars, — and flinging a robe of flimsy tapa about her nude young form, the heroic creature climbed alone to the sacred hill in the orange grove.

Following retrograde by the babbling brook, — which was an acceptable companion in the stillness of starlight, — Kupule groped her way among the dark trees, and at length seated herself by the fountain to await the coming moon. The shaggy peak of Waolani yet hid the approaching Hoku, and left the brave young Queen sitting in the deepest shadow.

Ere the mystic noon-of-night reached its throne in the zenith, the inquiring face of Hoku was seen peering down from the mountain top; flinging her yellow locks about the hatless head of Waolani, who sat frowning upon the world below. Soon the welcomed moon began weaving her gorgeous

mosaic of broken beams among the whispering
trees, and over the pensive flowers by the fountain's rim ; reserving the yellowest of her moon-
kisses for the upturned face of the maiden who
greeted her coming so gladly.

Whether purposely or by chance, we know not,
but then, as now, there was a small open space
among the encroaching tree-tops above the fountain. Though the rising night-queen had not quite
reached the altitude where she could bathe her amber locks in the waters of the spring, yet ever lav-
ish with her effulgence, she was playfully weaving
her abundant gold-beams among the topmost jets
and falling sprays of the sacred Kiowai ; as when
some loving hand in playful dalliance may weave
her rosy fingers among the flowing locks of the
loved one, at greeting.

Was it the rose-flush of fever that crimsoned the
maiden's face, or a gentle and not unpleasant awe-
terror, parching the throat of the Queen, in that
hushed moment of expectation ? Whatever it may
have been, she craved a frequent lip-touch of the
cool waters of the spring, and leaned over to quench
her sudden thirst, sipping from the dainty dipper
formed by the hollow of her hand. And again she
reached **for a** second drink. But why does she so
hesitate? tarrying with hand suspended and eyes
more lustrous than the stars !

Fixedly she sat, with heaving bosom and rapid
breathing, looking intently down into the still
shadowed waters as yet illumined by only a few

twinkling stars, and the one small glimmer of
broken moonbeam that has found its way to the
spot of still water wherein she gazes. Is it only
her own reflection the startled Queen has discovered, limned in softest silhouette by the stars?
Who can tell?

Being there for the sole purpose of conjuring up
the divine Pele to an interview, or, failing in that,
some sylvan spirit or harmless wood-nymph from
the viewless world about her, what wonder that
her young heart should so flutter with trepidation
at thought of the supernatural beings she might
convoke about her, and not even her darling *paua
hele* — bosom companion — Manona, or her loved
Leleha there to witness her being spirited away —
perhaps to return to her beautiful Oahu home no
more!

Kupule was born of a warlike race, and like all
of her human kindred was a fervent worshipper
of Pele. Her kinship had also imbued her with
yet greater reverence for the goddess, which was
still more increased by the remembrance of Pele's
condescension to herself and Kalani, when the
fiery ignipotent made herself visible to their human
eyes. After such an experience, and in the consideration of her birthright, it did not seem too
much for the maiden to expect that Pele would in
some way respond to her inordinate wish for
another interview. And upon this she was intent,
gazing with the utmost vehemence of her soul.

Throwing her unbound tresses from off her face,

and casting her tapa robe from off her fair round
shoulders, Kupule nestled down upon the dewless
grass and among the sister flowers — herself the
fairest blossom among them all — and bent with
the utmost eagerness to the task of defining what
had so aroused her attention deep down in the
spring. Leaning with the wild reverence of a
devotee over the dark waters, she searched again
and again for yet one more glimpse in duplicate of
her own weird imaginings.

What romantic maiden, in love with herself, or,
better still, with another, has not undergone in
some measure Kupule's experience? Striving thus
with outstretched hand to lift the mystic veil that
hides the mirrored future from her view, peering
with supplicating eyes into the starlit sky for want
of some better media. But upon more momentous occasions, when love becomes laggard, and
the heart yearns for companionship, seeking some
remote woodland spring, with better assurance of
accomplishing her fond divination, and thus still-
ing down the wild unrest of her bosom.

While thus gazing in a delicious flutter of ardent
hope and beleaguering fears, Kupule had been
startled by what seemed at first but her own simple reflection, seen deep down in the tremulous
waters of the shadowed pool. Yet after gazing
with greater intensity, seeking further assurance,
what was her amazement to see the supposed reflection retreating furtively away from her too eager
quest — sinking slowly and stealthily away from

its first position of apparent nearness, down, down into the rayless gloom where human vision cannot follow.

And this was Kupule's terrifying experience. Well might she become startled and dismayed when awakened to the full conviction that what she had seen was really some sweet-faced elf-girl of the spring coming timidly up to greet her, until frightened rudely back by the sudden eagerness of the earth-girl's gaze. But so wholly had the elf disappeared — if an elf it was — that Kupule became in doubt whether she had really seen anything or not.

It becomes a matter for physicists to determine whether these mystical visions so often encountered in moments of mental delusion are really glimpses of supernatural beings such as people the aqueous and pneumatic elements, wherein all frenzied minds are wont to seek them, or whether they are the divine conceptions of our own creative minds when exalted and enthused, conceived in answer to ardent search and intense desire.

Perplexed and bewildered for the moment, Kupule covered her face to shut out all further deception from her deluded eyes, while she waited, silent and trembling, the rising of the moon sufficient to fully luminate the fountain. The next half hour was spent in wondering revery at what had transpired. And as all delusions grow out of what they feed upon, she soon came to possess the strongest possible conviction that if a veritable vision had not been seen, certainly one was yet in store for her.

And while she thus waited, fortifying herself for the coming event, whatever it might be, the broad, bright face of Hoku crept up over the tree-tops, glinting the shining leaves with yellow radiance, and deepening the golden hue of the orange globes. And when Kupule unveiled her eyes, Hoku had mirrored her own wahine moon-face in the still water beside the face of the girlish Queen.

With a look of wild expectation Kupule withdrew the hands from her face, intent to peer down once more into the spring beneath her. But a muffled cry of joy rose to her lips as she beheld a slight, fair creature sitting in the moonlight, arched over by the falling spray of the moon-gold fountain.

The Elf maiden sat upon the ebullient water light as a bubble floats on the air, a tiny counterpart of what Kupule had dwelt upon during her waiting for the moon. Not like one sitting at ease sat the evanescent Elf-girl, but like a startled bird with wings alert, half flexed to fly, in grave doubt whether to abide or depart.

What wonder that the tiny creature showed such timidity when thus confronted by a human maiden with staring midnight-eyes voiced with terror, and orbed like fire! What a contrast were these two from adjacent spheres. The tiny girlish face of the Elf beamed like a star, her lustrous beauty serving to form a shining halo about her

head.   Her long yellow hair grew more than
golden, so tenderly imbued by the moonlight.

It was indeed she, the fairy Queen of the Elves,
who ruled over all the elfin tribes of Oahu.   She
had come not wholly in answer to Kupule's prayer,
but rather on a mission of love and pride, for it
had long been in dispute at the court of the elves
as to who was the most beautiful, Kupule or Nani,
their golden-haired Queen.   So true it is that the
gossips of air, and the unseen elves in the fountains and rivers, are moved to dispute over the
graces and virtues of earth-born maids.

Henceforth who will smirk, with so many to
see?   Who will prink and preen in brook or spring
when a thousand bright eyes are sure to be near.
Think of these Elves patterning by our smiles
when we mirror our coquetries in brook or pier;
aping our graces of manner or mien, when we
adorn for some loved one of high degree.

How they peered at each other, like strange
birds met by a stream; this Queen of the Isles and
this Elf of the spring!   How like to each other in
feature and form are these pretty types of nature's
best handiwork!   But how unlike in all else!   One
so tiny beside her sister Queen; blue-eyed and am-
ber-haired, with red lips like the baby-buds of
unblown roses.   To Nani, how full of questioning
wonder seemed the large dark eyes of Kupule;
and what terror in the massive hair, dark-hued as
a tempest, dancing and writhing with electric excitation in the quivering moon-silence of the night!

16

There sat the Elf-queen so timid and sweet and tiny, arrayed in no vesture but the yellow flocks of her sunbeam hair, till the kindly night-queen, with maternal thoughtfulness and an affluent hand, flung down over the Elf-girl a robe of amber beauty that was dazzling to behold — a garment of moonbeam rich spun with gold, rayed over with starlight and gemmed with opals from the fountain's spray.

The longer Kupule gazed upon Nani, the more the dim and half defined Elf-maiden attained to perfect shape and graceful contour. The fair, sweet face — so unearthly in its beauty — which at first appeared so ghostly and uncertain to human eyes, now came to beam with intelligence, answering swiftly back to Kupule's orbal questionings — like the faces of coy human lovers confronted in some rustic lane.

How the soft blue eyes of little Nani question and stare at the expression of amazement still lingering on the face of Kupule! How her small red lips rimple into timid smiles at detecting something so akin to terror in the awe-touched face of her companion! She, the dark, majestic Queen, who dared to conjure up whomsoever would appear; fascinating the little Elf-queen up from among her elfin mates; why should *she* fear a creature so frail and so fair?

Thus they sit and stare and study, showing a mimosa-like shrinking of mutual fear lest they should startle each other away. Something verily

like a human maiden's blushes come and go over
the tiny moon-touched cheeks of Nani, flitting and
glowing like the autumnal aurora discerned in the
far northern skies.

How Kupule longed to question the young immortal with audible voice and vocal words, but
dare not lest she fly at the tones of her voice. She
so wished to reach forth two loving hands and
gather the enchanting vision to her side. But she
rightly felt that with the first spoken word, the
first aggressive movement, the spell would be
broken, and the fountain would call back the
transcendent creature forever from her gaze.

So, with her breath hushed back to the softest
respiration, and her human emotions chained down
with all her imperial will, she watched and waited,
and questioned with her wondering eyes; while
Nani answered back some of the infinite thoughts
of her soul. Time, to these two, had been as
naught; sitting there upon the flimsy border of
the great unknown, while the invisible curtain
was lifted, by what power we know not, for a few
brief hours' gaze.

Suddenly, with an outcry almost of pain, Kupule sprang up and leaped with outstretched arms
into the fountain; but, alas! only to clutch the
empty waters in her frantic hands. All unob-
served by the maidens, the moon had dropped
down the west, until the tops of the overhanging
trees suddenly shut out her beam from the spring
to the terror of the Fairy; and as a bubble floats

swiftly away on the air, so had receded the beautiful Elf-queen from the enraptured gaze of Kupule.

When Kupule thus found herself alone under the falling spray of the fountain, she dived swiftly down in search of Nani, groping about the rocky bottom of the spring; but the Elf-maiden was gone. The heart of the young Queen sank within her as she came empty-handed to the surface, sorrowing that the visible and the invisible had thus met in sweet accord; and yet no word had been uttered — no key-note imparted — by which to again lift the invisible veil, and conjure up some answering spirit to her call.

A hush as of universal death came over the night in that hour. Silence lay like a white pall over the land and sea. The ever unceasing fountain now stilled down its falling spray until its tinkling waters fell with velvet footsteps upon grass and flowers. The leaves upon the orange trees hung limp and tremulous, as with the fear of impending dissolution. Throughout the grove the orange globes swung like funeral bells, tolling a requiem unheard by human ears. The moonlight flooded the Nuuanu cold and chill and ghostly as if Death were dead! The wail of the far-off surf on the shore sounded wild and unearthly, like the mournful echo of some funeral dirge over the much-loved dead.

Even the garrulous rivulet became less sportive in that hour, hushing its dulcet symphonies, so awed by the momentous occurrence of the night,

tinkling a solemn nocturne to its playmate flowers
as it ran stealthily through the ghostly moonlight
on its way to the sea. Ah! it is indeed an intuitive ear that can interpret all the inarticulate voices
of such a night; whisperings too unearthly to
court inspection by unhallowed ears; utterances
of flitting, fluttering Spirits never fully outlined
to timorous souls, nor ever wholly invisible to
ideal minds like Kupule's!

Swimming out from the fountain, and wringing
the water from her masses of hair, Kupule took
the hillside path which led back to the palace.
Silently she stole in, with a hush over footstep and
breathing, for stillness had acquired a new meaning in that hour. She had not been missed by her
maidens, for the slumber of girlhood days is inno-
cent and sweet and unbroken. Without waking
even Leleha to her aid, the reverent young Queen
dried her hair, murmured an invocation to Pele,
and crept softly into her couch for slumber and
dreams.

'Tis mid-day on the ocean blue!
　The winds and waves are hushed to sleep;
Kupule guides her light canoe
　Where noontide slumbers on the deep:
Watching the dusky forms below
Flitting like spirits to and fro.

The dauntless Queen explores the sea
　Far down among the corals rare,
Where green-eyed monsters flit and flee,
　With monstrous Eeries everywhere:
Paling the maiden's cheeks with fear
Lest dread Moa-alii should appear!

Remote from all the haunts of men
　Oahu's Queen thus drifts and dreams,
Intent to search with fearless ken
　Where mid-day sun intrudes his beams:
Watching the beauteous Sea-queen swim,
Far down among the caverns dim!

With bated breath she peers below,
　Half terrified while she explores;
Where gleam the corals white as snow,
　And blue and crimson madrepores!
Mermaids appear at length in view,
Luring the Queen 'neath ocean's blue.

246

CHAPTER XIV.

HEN morning came, the strong trades of the past week had died away. The gigantic surf was rolling in with unusual turbulence, the lingering effect of the strong winds during the past days. Though the great undulations were still heavy without, yet within, the bay lay calm and unruffled, and off Waikiki beach the Pearl Garden was smooth and glassy as a mirror.

Kupule's plans were at once made for the day, when seeing how tranquil it had become. Next to the importance of ruling the kingdom during Kalani's absence, was the growing necessity of solving some of the mysteries of the tabued sea lying off the great *heiau* at Waikiki. Throughout her young life, in her far off Hilo home, Kupule had ever tasked herself with such labors; but now she required the vertical sun to facilitate her search, and impatient hours must pass before she attempted her voyage to the mysterious *Mona Kihapai.*

From the old Bard we learn that it was the daring child-girl, Pelelulu of Hawaii, who knew most of the surf wonders on the reef at Hilo, and

247

of the cliffs and caves and waterfalls along Wailuku's romantic river.   It was Pelelulu who succeeded in winning the timid Luna-Sprite of
Anuenue (Rainbow falls) into many an interview
beneath the full-orbed Kulu ; a sweet mist spirit
who would never remain visible to any one but the
god-born princess, when they entered her cave,
deep in, under the bended bow of the Falls.

It was also Pelelulu who so loved the wild
haunts about the *Pei-Pei* Falls, that its broad
sheet of tremulous waters would sing like a chorus
of spirits at her approach.   But above all, it was
the same daring Pelelulu who set the first example
of swimming through the dark water-galleries of
the *Puka-o-maui :* those terrible subterraneous
caverns through which the Wailuku compels its
mountain torrent in reverence and aqueous worship to Pele, who has channelled this temple of
gloom through the black rocks of their waters.
And now that the princess of Hawaii has become
Kalani's Queen, she is exploring yet another and
more wondrous field of supernatural agencies ;
seeking companionship with those evanescent
spirits — numerous in all elements — so beautiful
in conformation, and so charming in the influence
they possess over our lives.   For it was as true
in those far-gone days as now — "The pure in
heart see the gods."

From the palace hill up the Nuuanu, hundreds
of merry wahines and happy children could be
seen swimming in the harbor or sporting on the

great rollers of the monstrous surf. After the
morning meal, Kupule and her maidens went down
to join in the pleasant pastime, and frolic like
dolphins in the blue waters of the bay.

Thus passed the morning hours in luxurious delight. When at length the swimming was ended,
and Leleha had dressed the black masses of her
mistress' hair, while Kupule sat on the mats under
the *moi pama* — king palm — on the point, the
maidens were sent away to the forest. Most of
the Queen's wahines were already gone to the
Kaliki valley to gather the red Ohea in which they
delighted. But now, Manona, the sweet-voiced
puua hele of the Queen, was also sent away with
the rest to gather the fragrant hibiscus flowers to
make *leis* — wreaths — for them all, while the
Queen stepped lightly into her tiny *waa* to wander
by herself about the charming bay.

Kupule was impatient to again enter upon her
search among the mysteries of the *Mona Kihapai*.
She was exulting with renewed hope of once more
listening to the strains of exquisite music that had
so enchanted her the week before. As the Queen
spun her little canoe away from the shore, and
sped like a bird across the bay, her heart beat
wildly at thought of the weird pleasure awaiting
her. But what was her surprise to find herself
accompanied by a large *Anuenue ia* (Rainbow
fish), by far the most beautiful of the piscatory
habitans of the coral sea.

Whatever direction Kupule took, and whether

paddling fast or slow, the following Anuenue was ever by her side, flashing its brilliant crimson in the sun. Though the great fish was half the length of her paddle, there was nothing about it to excite apprehension, for its whole appearance was friendly, only that there was a knowing, impish look of human intelligence about the creature that was rather startling to contemplate, and ended with inspiring a degree of awe in Kupule that she could not quite throw off.

If Kalani was dead she might not doubt that her new companion was the disembodied spirit of the King. But word had come that very morning of his safety, which led the intuitive girl to believe that the friendly Anuenue was without doubt her little Nani, the pretty Elf-queen of the fairies, else why did it look so knowing when called by her name; and why wag its silvery tail, and turn its great golden eye up to Kupule with a look of something more than friendliness.

Paddling her light canoe close along the inner reef-bed, where the blue waters lay as tranquil as crystal beneath her eye, and the tropic sun delved down into the mysterious depths, unveiling the gorgeous cities of the sea; well might the joyous Queen forget all else in her delight and wonder.

Here she discovered fresh clusters of glistening shells that had been hurled over the reef by the wash of the furious breakers. There, flashed away frightened swarms of colored fishes — startled by the approach of the *waa* — flushing the turkois sea with the hues of sunset clouds.

Now she came where the corals were crimson and blue and green; which, with the waving mauve-colored madrepores, and the blood-red dulse, comprised a scene of Oriental enchantment for the eye; while the unconscious ear was ever captivated and held in thrall by the hoarse bass: on of the rumbling breakers; which, while it lulled one into revery, ponderings of things seen and things unseen, it also awakened a sense of awe that overshadowed even the noonday sun. Fit accessaries were these to arouse the requisite intuition for exploring such a spectral sea. Yet how strange is the fact, that not only the sublime and terrible in nature, but also the charm of its exquisite beauties connected with the sea, ever arouse the most sombre reflections in the mind of the idealist.

Though Kupule did not realize just where she had been upon the previous days, when she retreated in such haste to escape her superstitious fears, yet she at once recognized the arched entrance of Moa-alii's Den when she neared it; when, following inshore on the range of the pandanas *on* with the temple tower, soon brought her to the desired spot over the Five Forks. With a soft backward stroke of her paddle-blade, the awed young Queen stilled her little *waa* until it lay motionless on the hyaline sea, just where she required it; while the still following Anuenue swam quietly under the canoe, and rested motionless against its bottom, satisfied to be in loving proximity to her companion.

How the ardent soul of Kupule stood reverent and alert in this moment, like a startled bird with lifted wings ready for flight! With a lambent gleam pervading her dark eyes, and ears alert to catch the first strain of the unearthly music she came to hear, Kupule looked long and eagerly about among the novel nooks and shadowed niches in the coral rocks, and among the madreporic trees. But not a note of the exquisite cadence came to greet her ear.

Only the roar of the bellowing surf claimed the attention of the impatient girl, as the undulations floundered in unrelenting fury on the obtruding reef. Only this, and the muffled songs of birds in the adjacent palm grove of Waikiki, and the more distant songs of children, and the bleat of the far-away mountain goats; as the one played upon the palm-fringed shore, and the others called down with plaintive cry from the jagged battlements of frowning Puawai.

Only these divergent sounds greeted her ear. But the sun yet lacked something of meridian, so Kupule fell to searching the surrounding madreporic region beneath with closer attention than she had found patience to bestow before.

But what has so suddenly aroused the attention of the watchful Queen? For presently, as she leaned in graceful pose over the frail canoe, the faintest, flimsiest, outline of a strange nondescript in half human form grew slowly upon her vision as she gazed. She had suffered her canoe to drift

a little away from over the Forks, wafted shore-
ward by the strong concussion coming from the
resounding surf, and was now lying over one of
the narrow sandy gulches so closely overhung by
the various coral growths.

The half-defined creature Kupule had discovered
seemed maliciously inclined at first as it stealthily
approached the canoe, coming cautiously up from
its deeply-caverned haunt. With many a furtive
glance from its great green eyes, it slowly emerged
from among the calcareous rocks and etiolate foliage, when, changing its purpose, it swam slowly
away in the direction of the Forks with many a
backward, angry glance, like that of a cowardly
dog who slinks sheepishly away for kindred aid,
to assail whom it would attack.

Seeing the great sea-beast had not courage to
attack her, Kupule followed slowly back whence
she came. The uncouth creature that had gone
before seemed half fish and half human, with a
coarse, gross, and hairy face of the most hideous
aspect. Though the eye could trace an apparently
positive outline to the shape of the mammoth
creature, yet the ghostly thing was possessed of
less substance than a morning mist. For neither
its great saucer-like eyes, nor its long sharp fangs,
seemed attached to anything tangible; only assuming the normal position of teeth and eyes; as did
the heart and stomach, which could be seen without impediment from the transparent body.

Kupule's dislike of this monster was increased

by the apprehension displayed by the little Anuenue, which at once took position close alongside the
canoe, with a look of fear at the ugly sea-god, and
many an appealing glance at Kupule. Nestling
close under the paddle-blade, even with its wildly
erect dorsal above the surface, it suffered the hand
of the Queen to stroke its head, while it rubbed
its nose affectionately against her palm. And from
this moment, Kupule became confirmed in her belief that it was her little Nani, who had thus assumed the shape of the beautiful *Anuenue ia.*

Who among us could thus gaze unterrified upon
such an unhallowed denizen of the deep? A shape
without substance. Yet the very quality of its
partial visibility chained one to the perilous task
of exploring its invisibleness. Well might the
courageous Queen quail and quiver, with something very akin to disgust and fear, to thus find
her unhallowed wishes so strangely answered by
the unearthly powers she had invoked, when this
dim, dark Eerie became thus outlined before her
human gaze.

This almost human-shaped creature, evanescent
as vapor, what could it be? A seeming body,
though bodiless. Having an apparent quality of
visibility, though impalpable as the sunlit air. So
truly bodiless was this uncouth monster, that it
was seen to swim through and through the dens-
est foliage among the great coral trees; passing hither and yon without causing the slightest
disturbance to itself, or deranging the flimsiest
growth through which it passed.

Other of these terrible Eeries began now to congregate beneath the canoe, taking courage by the example of their cowardly companion, all alike curious about this charming visitant in the upper world. But in whatever number they gathered, it was seen that neither one nor many of their substanceless bodies served to shut out from view anything lying beneath them. This shadowy quality of the loathsome Eeries came at length to impress Kupule with the belief that they might be but some shadow-reflections of aërial Spirits above her, hovering between the sea and the sun.

And yet this could not be. For she saw that the reflections — if such they were — were wingless, and flew not. While the monsters were seen to swim with very human-like motions, and with the outlines of what seemed to be very human-like arms and hands; except that the latter were seen to be strongly taloned with long cat-like claws.

Their ghostly faces looked fierce and coarsely masculine; and seen in the strongest light appeared bearded, with large and cruel eyes, and mouths fanged like serpents. As the half-human appearance of these terrible Eeries became better distinguished by the more vertical sunlight, Kupule could not help recoiling with a thrill of horror, occasionally receding back into her canoe while she questioned what their purpose might be, in making themselves thus visible to her.

Sitting thus, furtively watching the bodiless creatures, lest she should attract their attention

too much, and induce them to attack her, Kupule
gradually became aware of feeling an occasional
thud of something against the bottom of her canoe.   Her first thought was that it might be Nani ;
but she was lying still as a mouse close alongside,
but without touching the canoe even by the occasional motion of her large pectoral fin.   Was it the
Eeries?   Great Pele ! the thought sent a cold chill
over the maiden, and a feeling of sickening repul-
sion crept over her to think of being in their grasp.

But when she poised her paddle and was about
to fly from the spot, she suddenly became aware
that it was a rhythmical vibration beating musi-
cally against the bottom of the canoe.   Venturing
to glance over the side, Kupule saw large bubbles
ascending from beneath the great mauve-colored
fan-coral directly beneath her, and striking the bottom of the canoe.

With a quiet stroke of the paddle, the canoe
was thrust softly away.   Instantly the notes of
music she had previously heard burst upon her ear.
Bursting into concentric rings and spreading far
and wide as they ascended, the bubbles diverged
into melodious ripples sweeter than bird-songs.
Low and indistinct at first, like the droning hum
of far-off bees, but steadily increasing as the musical bubbles grew larger and ascended with greater
momentum.

Here then was an explanation of the mysterious
music Kupule had listened to before.   As it increased in volume, rising into surprising volée,

the melody seemed less to come from the sea than from the sky, as upon the previous day, when the Queen * chanced not to be so nearly vertical to its source as to discover its cause.

The mystical cadence Kupule now listened to seemed pitched in a different key from that heard on the previous day. It seemed less clear but more vibrant, having less of the sweet, swelling resonance of bell-like music. It was more like the low murmuring notes of an Æolean just touched by the summer breeze, when made slightly tremulous by the fluttering media of multitudinous leaves.

The charm of the music had entirely attracted Kupule's attention away from the frightful Eeries, from whom she was about to flee. When at length she came to look for them, they were gone. But not so the dread they had impressed upon her, for every thought of the loathsome creatures imparted a chill to the maiden. And Nani had also discovered their absence, for the crimson beauty had quietly taken her position directly under the canoe.

While the eager eyes of the Queen were fastened intently upon the spot whence came the musical bubbles, strange and hideous shapes were indistinctly seen flitting about the coral glades. Was it the pibroch of the terrible sea-clans she

---

* The melody we seek to describe is similar to that of the "Singing Shells" heard in the sea at Batticaloa, of which there are several species, the principal of which are the *Littorina lævis* and the *Cesithium palustre.*

17

heard — marshalling their sea-folk to war, perhaps upon herself? The roused and awe-stricken maiden was watching to see.

At length the slow, cautious movement of a graceful swimmer attracted Kupule's attention. She saw but the slightest undulatory motion of the long sea-grasses at first, then the wave-motion of a swimmer against the calcareous leaves; but being an amphibious maiden herself she knew their import.

With shaded eyes and quickening breath the excited girl bent low down over the water, and there, indeed, between the great fan-coral and the crimson tree could be distinctly seen the small shapely head and bust and pliant arms of a veritable Mermaid. One of the fairest of God's handiwork among all the wonders of the sea.

The gentle, human-looking Sea-girl was now seen floating slowly and timidly upward, from a deep sandy reach to the north of the Pinna-coral tree. The pretty grotto under the great mauve-colored coral was her home, surrounded by the rarest beauties in this most charming quarter of the Pearl Garden.

It was the beautiful Sea-Queen of Oahu, that Kupule had discovered by her patient search. This was made evident on the instant of her appearing; for Nani darted away from the canoe at once, and with one swift plunge placed herself beside Oluolu, the Mermaid Queen.

It was Oluolu's busy hands that had gathered

so many rare sea-growth about the Five Forks.
It was the dainty Sea-queen who had taught the
countless thousands of gorgeous fishes to feed unharmed about her charming grotto, freeing the red
dulse from the gnawing sea-bugs which usually destroy it; and foraging upon the ravenous grubs
that so love to corrode the delicate meshes of the
beautiful fan-coral, that here grew with such thrift
above her door. Here the piscatorial tribes found
themselves unmolested, partly by Oluolu's protection, but more from the dread tabu, which freed the
beautiful fishes from their ever pervading fear of
anything wearing human semblance.

Well might Kupule long to descend beneath the
clear blue tide, and greet the charming Sea-queen
of whom the old bard had sung; there to spy out
her grotto, the sea-palace where she made her
aqueous home; gemmed about with every beauty
found in all the madreporic sea.

Upward and upward floated the little Mermaid, and louder and clearer grew her sea-song as
she rose. Though evidently wishing to approach
nearer to the sweet human face bending so tenderly over her abode, her native timidity forbade
her coming beyond the thin, perforated leaves of
the fan-coral, under whose drooping fronds she
tarried.

There beneath its topmost mauve-colored leaves
Oluolu lay, with Nani beside her, spying upward
through the blue sea to Kupule, and at intervals
voicing her little heart in song. Music being the

medium by which she expressed a Sea-girl's longings for the sunbright world above: as we on
earth may melodize our prayers for sympathy from
the dear unseen spirits above our heads.

It was with a wild thrill of joy that Kupule had
discovered this intelligent creature, when she had
almost come to believe that the sea was given
wholly up to hideous and unhallowed forms. And
when she became certain that she had discovered the Sea-queen, and that her little Nani was
friendly with her, her delight was doubled, for she
felt that her kinship with the god-world would accomplish the rest.

Kupule now remembered the stories the old bard
had told her, of music being sometime heard at
noonday, far out on the *Mona Kihapai*, near the
den of Moa-alii — the awful god of the sea. And
she also remembered his other tales of greater marvels still; relating that often by the midnight
moon, when Kulu (full moon) was sitting on
the topmost bough of heaven, the song of the
Sea-queen grew the loudest. Adding, what had
seemed the most unlikely of all, that sometimes it
was permitted to the eyes of the great Alii Kapu
to behold the singing girl of the sea sitting on the
Waikiki shore.

But Puaaihi usually terminated his tales or his
songs on this subject by something too startling
to be believed, exclaiming: " Auwe! auwe! Poino,
poino!" — Oh! oh! Alas, alas! " Such an event
always signifies the death of a king. May it be

long before the *blind* eyes of Puaaihi may *see* **a** singing sea-girl upon the shore of Waikiki!"

Though Kupule well knew that the priests and the bard were given to relating strange stories, in their endeavor to arouse the superstitions of the Kanakas of low degree, and that the higher chiefs were not expected to give full credence to all their wonders, related for special purposes ; yet here was a complete verification of one of the most doubtful legends sung by the white-haired old minstrel.

Soft and sweet continued the occasional magnetic strain of Oluolu's song, so like the alluring melody of human heart-beats, when tenderly elicited by the gentle impulse of love, that Kupule could not but respond in kind, singing some of her own wild Hawaiian airs.

The effect of the Sea-queen's music upon Kupule was what all ocean travellers have found it ; for it grew to act with a degree of fascination upon her, that was fast luring her into the blue bewitching depths below. She became so charmed at length, that it required constant restraint to keep herself from dropping swiftly down to Oluolu, to embrace her little sister of the sea.

How strange it is that underlying every note of a Mermaid's song is a sad and solemn undercurrent of sorrow. Though Oluolu's melodies sometimes rose into exquisite interpretations of a Mermaid's joys, yet they, too, oftenest dropped into a sad adagio of unutterable longings ; almost wail-

ing for a companion from the bright upper world,
to love and abide with her forever.

Here was an instance of the same exquisite sense
of fascination which one interprets when listening
to a wild bird's singing; when being together
with them in the deep gloom of a primeval forest.
Watch a little songster hop nearer and nearer to
you, between the frequent interludes of his song,
until at length he sits confidingly at your hand,
peering trustingly into your eyes — eyes made
sympathetic by his singing — appealing with a
subdued twitter of long-drawn, entreating notes,
charming us, in spite of ourselves, from the too
human predilection to kill.

Just as plainly was the tender solicitude of the
little Mermaid addressed to the sympathies of
Kupule. Oluolu pleaded for her companionship,
until at length the fascination of her alluring
songs, together with the magnetic charms of the
pretty Sea-queen, ended with Kupule's laying
aside her paddle, and casting off her *pau*, (skirt of
pendulous leaves,) dropping like a plummet from
the leadsman's hand over the side of her canoe,
Kupule swam with outstretched arms to greet her
little sister of the sea.

It is well known that the Hawaiian maidens are
as much at home as the fishes, in the sea; being
about the most expert divers in the world; so that
Kupule's act of going to the Mermaid beneath the
water was done under as free an impulse as she
would have gone to her upon the shore.

Swift as a fish-hawk from the summer sky,
Kupule dived down through the intervening fathoms of clear blue brine. She descended until she
could cling like a swaying bird on the topmost
boughs of the red coral tree. There in the current
she planted her small red feet upon the redder
branches of the kingliest growth in all the ocean
forest, at once seeking to entice the Mermaid-
queen out from under her leafy covert, beneath
the bending fronds of the fan-coral, where she
peered out upon the new-comer as shyly as a timid
child from among the homestead vines.

The Queen's abrupt descent scattered the countless gold fish from about her meteoric path; startling the red parrot bills and the green macaws, till
they flashed away like glowing aërolites in the
evening sky; the fishes, as well as their pretty
queen, amazed at this new acquisition from the
divine regions of the sunlit air.

Judging, also, from the swift hurrying away of
dim, dark objects, from beneath her, as she dived,
hugely formed creatures who swayed the calcareous
grasses, and tossed the plumous sea-flowers rudely
away as they ran, Kupule's unannounced descent
was making a profound impression everywhere in
this elysian habitat of the Eeries, and among the
ghostly sea-Gnomes perched among the etiolate
branches below.

Even the eager and expectant Mermaid, though
evidently prompted to an ardent friendliness by
the little Nani, shrank timidly away at Kupule's

first approach, amazed at the swift descent of the nimble swimmer, and perhaps appalled at the sudden and unexpected consummation of her wishes for companionship, as a human soul would be who had called an angel down.

But the enticing face and alluring arms of Kupule instantly reassured the Sea-queen, who soon ventured timidly up, face to face with her winsome sister of the upper air. But not until little Nani had transposed herself from the crimson Anuenue into the charming Elf-queen of the Sacred Fountain, and swam boldly out from under the long fronds of the fan-coral, and taken her stand beside Kupule, did Oluolu gain courage to assume her former position again.

What a meeting was this! A consorting of the three typical affinities of Earth, Air, and Ocean. The tiny Sea-girl was but a darker miniature of her larger companion. The hair and eyes of the representative maidens of earth and ocean were black as midnight, though Kupule's hair was softer and more abundant, floating out over her bare shoulders like two raven wings half spread for flight.

This meeting of the three Queens was not unlike that of other stranger maidens, meeting by chance upon the terrestrial sphere. Their faces expressed mutual attraction and honest admiration of each other; and the fact of their being queens of three elements made them abounding in curiosity, as other wahines might be from different countries.

In the shapely busts and bodies of the three, they were not unlike, except in size ; tiny little Nani not being even a quarter the size of Oluolu. But here the similarity ended between the two larger queens, for in place of Kupule's plump and taper limbs, and dainty feet, — only a little less rosy than the red coral whereon she stood, — the Mermaid's tapering extremity was similar to that of a porpoise, ending in pliant and graceful flukes, with which she could swim at great speed.

But the graceful flukes of Oluolu were amazingly handy in their briny element, for many other purposes than swimming. For while the fairy-like Nani, in girlish mimicry of Kupule's majestic poise, stood with her tiny bare feet, tottling upon the rough foliage of the crimson coral, the Sea Queen, with her broad and bending flukes, stood with greater freedom upon even the delicate fronds of the swaying fan-coral, without harming its exquisite arabesque in the least. And while both the others required their hands to support them in the flowing current, the affectionate Mermaid used hers to stroke the glistening backs of the several gold fishes and purple mullet, who fondly sought companionship with their loved Queen during this audience of consorting sovereigns.

Kupule's observations soon began to be withdrawn from her companions. She had not been the least disturbed by the quick gathering of countless fishes, representing more colors than all the coral or sea-flowers about her, even though

the finny creatures came spying about in such
close proximity, venturing even to nibble, not only
at her long elf-locks floating on the swaying tide,
but also tasting daintily of the soft warm flesh of
various unprotected parts, made prominent by her
standing, clinging upon the arboreous foliage.

But the matter grew more serious when the
very sunshine began to be darkened by the ominous gathering of many brutal-faced Eeries above,
between Kupule and her canoe; rallying as if in
fear for the safety of their loved Sea-queen.
While from every caverned lair other monsters
had stolen suddenly out, together with numerous
strange and ghostly sea-Gnomes, who now thrust
their uncouth visages between the coral branches
and among the waving dulse leaves everywhere
about their Mermaid-queen. But, worst of all,
the very waters began now to quiver and quake,
vibrating with angry mutterings; the rising wrath
of unseen monsters who bellowed like maddened
bulls at the current report of danger threatening
their much-loved Queen.

At this juncture the two minutes of time usually allotted a diver for submergence had about
passed. But Kupule had remained long enough
to win the love and confidence of the Mermaid-
queen, by exchange of pantomimic courtesies, and
had been contemplating the necessity of going air-
ward for breath; when suddenly she discovered
the ominous gathering of the monster habitans of
the sea. And when to this sight of terror was

added the hoarse rumbling caused by the swift approach of some other gigantic creature of the nether world, then, indeed, Kupule realized her peril.

Terror now took the place of smiles on the face of the Sea-queen, and with a forward movement of her flukes, and a swift back-stroke with her pretty hands, she shrank back beneath the fan-coral, with an expression of distress for the safety of her queenly guest. Waving her little hands impetuously, Oluolu pointed upward for Kupule to begone!

Nani, beside herself with fear, had already changed her fairy figure into the Anuenue again, and was now nestling close to Kupule, sheltering under the floating tresses of her dark hair. Thus aroused, the heroic Queen took in the perilous situation at once.

Catching the meaning of the Mermaid's warning, and little Nani's terror, with the strong impulse of an agile swimmer Kupule spurned the crimson coral from beneath her feet, and sprang swiftly upward toward the surface; while Oluolu, seeing her guest had gone, turned and shot like an arrow down into the ,sunlit gloom, between the coral shrubbery, to her grotto of rainbow sheen.

Glad was Kupule to see the great man-faced Eeries make way for her coming, as she rose; though it was only as a cowardly dog retreats to the rear, intent on renewing his warfare; for as she passed them like a meteor, they sprang furi-

ously back upon her, snapping with their fanged
jaws at the long black shadow of the up-shooting
maiden, with an unpleasant clang of their enhungered maws.

Her face being turned seaward as she rose, looking out toward Moa-alii's Den as she neared the
surface, the brave Queen was horrified at sight of
a queen-eyed monster of hideous mien. Approaching furiously, with gnashing teeth and gloating
eyes, the gigantic creature seemed maddened with
intent to devour this bold intruder into his watery
domain.

But, luckily, there was not a fleeter swimmer in
all the " Eight Seas " than Kupule of Oahu. And
with the utmost rapidity she now approached the
small black shadow she took to be her canoe.

Remembering the old bard's story of Una and
the lion, — for all the most wonderful legends of
antiquity are familiar to the indigenes of Polynesia, — Kupule kept her brave eyes fixed intently
upon the approaching demon, for the brief time it
took her to leap to the surface, and spring like an
agile leopard into her canoe ; the same bound taking the Anuenue in by her side.

Seizing her paddle with frenzied hands, Kupule
plied her blade, heading swiftly for the shore;
eagerly as an escaping sea-bird swerves from the
downward swoop of a hungry eagle, the brave
Queen plied her paddle for the land.

With a wild leap of demoniacal fury, the swift
pursuing monster breached out from the foamy

water, at the very spot where the nimble maiden
had disappeared within her canoe. But neither
canoe nor maiden were there. And Moa-alii had
tossed the blue ocean into an avalanche of foam all
too late, in the mad fury of his pursuit.

Biting savagely at the shadows of the low-soar-
ing sea-birds as they silhouette upon the water
about him, Moa-alii tore on in mad pursuit of the
retreating canoe ; rolling his angry green eyes like
flaming fireballs as he ran. Before Kupule could
reach the Waikiki shore, he was upon her. Rang-
ing up alongside of the canoe, the fierce sea-god
showed intent of upsetting the frail boat and devouring its contents.

But the royal creature within that canoe was a
Wahine Moi! a *Tabu Alii!* as the great green-eyed
monster soon discovered, when he rolled savagely
up to the surface to inspect his prey. Or was it
little Nani, who now sat by the side of Kupule in
her new role of the Elf-queen, who thus informed
the enraged Moa-alii, and shamed him from his
pursuit?

Instantly the whole demeanor of the awful sea-
god changed. He put off his ferocity with the
nimble alacrity of a trained courtier, becoming the
mildest-mannered monster that ever fed upon human manes!

With the true gallantry of a veritable Sea-god —
a most courteous Neptune of the sea — Moa-alii
escorted the tabued Queen and her canoe as near
to the shore as he could swim, without grounding

his huge carcass upon the côral rock; and then, with a look of almost human admiration, turned, and shot with unbecoming swiftness — implying shame of his transaction — back to his caverned lair under the reef-bed.

Though the danger from which Kupule had just escaped roused her heroic heart with an intense emotion, something akin to the human fear of any other maiden, yet now the sense of danger was passed, there arose in its stead a sudden leap of human exultation, only known to the successful warrior in his hour of triumph. An element of new beauty possessed the queen in that moment, as proud lip and flashing eyes kindled into a semblance of godhead when she remembered that even this ferocious sea-monster had been cowed by his intuitive perception of her pre-natal affinity with the immortals.

When the peril of the moment was passed, either from Moa-alii or other monsters of the deep, Kupule slowed down her paddling, and headed farther on up the shore in search of a little brook-bed into which to draw her canoe. Still nestling by her side sat the little Elf-queen, whom Kupule stooped to kiss as they sped along the shore; contemplating a charming time together after landing. And the golden-haired Nani seemed delighted with every attention bestowed upon her by her loved companion.

Shooting her little craft into the creek, where it would be secure from wind and wave, Kupule laid aside her paddle, and turned to bestow her attention upon the little Queen of the Fairies; but lo, she was gone! With a look of sorrow Kupule's eyes sought her everywhere. She remembered to have just felt an affectionate purring upon her cheek, as she stooped to fasten her canoe, like that of a very young kitten; when, turning to answer Nani's fondlings in kind, she was gone.

Only a swift-flitting shadow could be seen hurrying away over the grass tops, and just bending the flowers as it passed; speeding away in the direction of Nuuanu; such a small, fleeing shadow as is made by a passing bird in the air. But there was no bird in the sky to cause it; and it could be none other than the invisible Elf-queen flitting away from flower to flower — like butterfly or bee — on her way to the Kiowai o Pele.

With a look of real sadness portrayed upon her flushed young face, Kupule donned her tapa robe, and adjusted her *pau* — skirt of leaves — and quietly took her way to the palace. Her disappointment at thus losing Nani could not be got rid of; and if a bird swayed a shrub as she passed, or a bee bended a honeysuckle from its poise, Kupule was stirred with a momentary hope that it might be her little Elf-queen returning. But she arrived at the palace without learning anything more of the fairy.

After hearing something of the day's adventure from her maidens, the Queen dispersed them all, and sent for the High Priest for the purpose of consultation. When Paao arrived, and heard the

Queen's experience, he at once showed great dismay. He agreed with Kupule, that Moa-alii's appearing to her in such a manner boded no good to the nation. It was Paao's belief that some great King of the Islands was about to die. And both Priest and Queen feared it might be their own noble Kalani, who was being hard pressed in his wars to windward.

It was agreed to withhold the knowledge of this warning not only from the people, but the King; who was now daily expected, returning with a shattered army and in broken spirits, because of his many defeats. He must soon return to his last stronghold, and prepare to fight his last battle. It would require superhuman efforts to rally another army, and prepare for a final defence of his kingdom against the victorious Kamehameha.

Paao also advised the Queen to remove her household to the Waikiki palace, there to await the coming of the King, and where she could be near the Heiau during the coming days of sacrifice to Moa-alii, interceding with the god to protect the homebound fleet when they came from Maui.

CHAPTER XV.

Oh, Queen of the deep!
  Come forth from thy grotto;
Almost do I weep
As I sit by the deep,
  Because thou comest not — oh,
  Comest not from thy grotto.

The moon on the sea
  Lures thee forth from the water;
And I'm waiting for thee
By the murmuring sea,
  Oh, sea-god's pretty daughter!
  Waiting here by the water.

Awake from thy cave,
  Pretty Queen of the Ocean!
Hasten forth from the wave —
From thy madrepore cave —
  Ere awakens the motion
  Of thy turbulent Ocean.

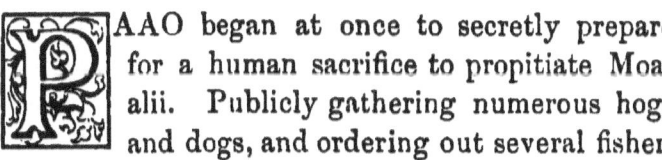AAO began at once to secretly prepare for a human sacrifice to propitiate Moa-alii. Publicly gathering numerous hogs and dogs, and ordering out several fisher-men for an early morning catch; while himself and other Alii kapus consorted in the Heiau, to doom a few Kanakas so as to impart a true value to the oblation to follow. Yet, it must be con-

fessed, these priestly shepherds of the flock evinced a nice consideration in dooming only those too old for future fighting purposes.

Even the most exemplary Alii kapu ever exerts scrupulous care in this frequent matter of thinning out his lambs for slaughter. Ever guarding the thrifty and the noble-born with the most judicious consideration, upon the usual secular principle of giving to those who have in abundance, and unto those who have not, demanding a gift — even the gift of life; a priestly weakness frequently known in other lands, when discriminating in parochial affairs.

The mind of the Queen was full of her captivating interview with the beautiful Sea-queen and little Nani; and of those terrifying experiences with the unhallowed eeries and the man-eating Moa-alii. Something of the pleasant part of her adventures Kupule related to her wahines, greatly exciting their wonder, and unduly rousing their national superstition.

But only the great Tabu Chief and the loved old bard of Manoa ever knew the whole story of their young Queen's encounter with those hideous monsters of the deep. For it was held to be of sacred significance that a kapu Alii was able to discover that which is wholly invisible to the common people. It linked the great chiefs with the gods, in their own esteem as well as in that of the people, and even sanctified them in the eyes of priesthood.

With the early dawn Kupule went up to the Kiowai for prayer, ever renewing her supplication that Pele would relent in the prophetic doom she had pronounced upon Kalani. Returning, she breakfasted with her young wahine Aliis, and together they made their plans for removing to the Waikiki palace immediately after the expiration of the present religious observances at the Heiau.

For in the dark hour preceding dawn the dread kapu kane had been proclaimed by the *kapu elele* — tabu heralds—for a period of two days' observance; and the hush of death now lay like a pall over all the land. Not a soul was visible about their usual occupations on the bay or about the valley. None but the priests and the *kapu Aliis* were permitted to be abroad.

The very hogs were housed lest they should squeal and bring death upon the owner of the *puaa*. The cocks were hooded that they could not crow, while the fowls were hidden away in calabashes. The mouths of the dogs were tied up, lest the fractious yelp of a cur should cost a human head. So terrible is the gloom caused by a kapu kane, that the very sun is dimmed by a macula; and the mournful face of nature seems bathed in tears of sorrow because of the sacrifice of her people.

In these dread Tabus it is a crime worthy of death to light a fire, bathe in the sea, or to launch a canoe either for fishing or transportation; and no noise is permitted to either man or beast, lest they come to grief.

Except the priests and their murderous man-killers who officiate about the temples, and the royal family and other tabu chiefs, all must keep within the shelter of their houses through all the tabu days, whether they be few or many. Should they leave their enclosures for food or drink, it is at the risk of their lives.

To infringe any of these rules during the strictest tabus would displease the gods, break the holy sanctity of the tabu, and be sufficient cause for the death of any person implicated; the method of death being procured either by priestcraft or sorcery — praying to death or otherwise.

As Kupule and her two favorite wahines sat together under the tutui trees on the palace hill, there came a sudden wail of anguish from the Honolulu shore. The Queen and Manona sprang up to learn the cause, fearing lest some bad news had been received about the King or from the army. And swift-footed Leleha was sent away to see what it might be.

But the outcry, when discovered, was found to be caused by the murderous *Pepehi Kanaka* of Paao, lassoing a white-haired old native, and dragging the pitiable old man to the shore, where he was strangled and cut in pieces suitable to feed out to Moa-alii and his tribe at the mouth of their den. Other natives had been privately kidnapped during the night and taken to the Heiau, among numerous *puaas* and *ilios*, though the hogs and dogs had been taken openly. But this venerable old grandsire was needed to supply an after conclusion, and was the best that could be had at the time. What had been done with the others might be guessed by the *peculiar* gray-blue *smoke* seen ascending from the Heiau ; a never-to-be mistaken indication of human sacrifice, that sufficed to blanch the˙ cheek of whomsoever beheld it.

The wailing at the foot of Nuuanu came from the aged wife and numerous daughters of the kidnapped peasant. The old man had been a serviceable warrior in his day, and had the reputation of being a kind father and good provider for his family. But, per contra, he was old ; his days of public usefulness were over ; thus the discriminating judgment of the High Priest had assigned him the high honor of being sacrificed for his country's good.

Under these circumstances the grief of the numerous mourners was expected to be a considerate and subdued grief, not *too* loud, lest it excite animosity against priestcraft, and be deemed sufficient cause to confiscate another tender lamb from the family.

In the dread lands of *Kapu Kane*, the public sympathy is capable of exquisitely delicate adjustment; being considerately limited to the nearest connections of the afflicted family. And it is a remarkable phenomenon to those who have observed with what nice discrimination the proper line of exact consanguinity may be defined ; for when personal peril is involved, the degree of propinquity becomes remote in the exact ratio of the danger apprehended by the wailing relative.

Among the people most subject to the edict of priestcraft, whose heads had just escaped confiscation, the choice of the tabu priest was defended with animation. He was proclaimed as being the best judge in making choice of subjects for sacrifice, even though the recent choice did happen to be a *very dear* friend of their own — for had not they been spared for the time?

In the present case, Paao's *Pepehi Kanaka* had been less secretive than usual; having openly lassoed the aged peasant in the presence of his family; though having previously cunningly decoyed the old man to his door by the imitative squeal of one of his own pigs.

A more frequent method of doing these murderous deeds by the holy church would have been for the ill-visaged *Pepehi Kanaka* to secrete himself; remaining ambushed behind some rock, or bush, or family cluster of banana leaves — from whence food must be secretly sought — and pouncing upon his victim, kill without outcry; while other noble assistants of the priests hid themselves by the frequented path between villages, and from their ambush lured the approaching victim by some piteous outcry of pain. And woe to the decoyed one — woe to whomsoever has sufficient humanity to answer an appeal of anguish at such times, for he is caught by the cunning lariat of the

Pepehi, strangled, and taken to the Heiau, or fed out to the sea-gods from the cliffs.

After the recent incident had been discussed, and all became tranquil once more, the royal wahines returned to their previous occupation of packing, preparatory to removing. The sea-shore palace of the kings óf Oahu is charmingly located in the midst of the cocoanut grove at Waikiki ; and thither the Queen and her numerous retinue of wahine chiefs, and household servants, removed at the expiration of the tabu days. There they would remain until the King's return, which was now daily expected.

Kupule loved best her Nuuanu home, with its wild cascades and mountain streams; its wooded valleys leading into the cathedral gloom of the primeval forest, where she loved to stray ; above all, the charming orange grove on the sacred hill, where grew the freshest flowers and the greenest grasses about the tabued Kiowai o Pele, where she loved so well to worship the divine Goddess of her land.

And yet, because of an ulterior motive in her little heart, she had acquiesced in the wishes of Paao, and now removed to Waikiki, inwardly delighted at the thought of being constantly near to her new acquaintance, the pretty Mermaid Queen. Both Puaaihi and Paao had reassured Kupule that moonlight nights were the favorite times for the timid water-girls, and other nameless sea-gods, to sport in the Waikiki surf, and frequent the tabued shore abreast of the great Heiau of Pele.

Their first day, after the removal to Waikiki, had been a busy one with the Queen and her chief-girls, bathing and fishing, and riding on their *papa* upon the surf. The afternoon was spent in the misty vale of Manoa, gathering wreaths for the head, and paying a visit to the blind Bard. Later in the day they climbed to the top of Puawai, to scan the eastern sea, looking for the expected fleet and the King. And not until the sun lay low in the west, glinting his fierce rays from the glassy surface of the harbor up into their faces, as they lay on the jagged battlement above, did they leave the Punch Bowl for the Waikiki palace, where a supper of bread-fruit and fish, and poi, awaited them.

Kupule had moored her own little *waa* close to the beach in front of the palace, with the intention of keeping up frequent communication with the Queen of the Pearl Garden. From the tiny canoe fluttered a small white *puawlu* of tapa, which served to tabu the little craft from the approach of any one.

After the swift tropic night had shut down over Oahu's mountain Isle, and a hush had gathered about the sylvan homes at Waikiki, the Queen and her girl-chiefs clustered about under the great palms standing nearest the moonlit shore, there to receive the numerous evening callers. Aged chiefs came to inquire about the last news from the army, and proffer advice arising out of their long experience in affairs of war and state. The

wives of great warriors came to glean some hope
about their absent braves, and some of them were
imprudent enough to express belief that Oahu's
prestige in war was dimmed.

During the evening, Paao, the grand and courtly
Priest, dropped in upon them, to communicate a
few ominous·prophecies to the Queen, which he
had derived from the gods, concerning the absent
army ; after which the Priest returned to his habitation in the walled precinct of the sacred Heiau,
to enter into other yet more profound divinations
for the public weal, and perhaps to indulge in a
rich repast upon the poi-fatted dog — fed from the
mouths of women, and baked in the ground ovens
— the baked bread-fruit and the luscious poi, made
from the nutritious taro root — the *arum esculen-
tum.* The tables of the tabu priests being usually
furnished sumptuously by the obsequious people —
that class whose precarious lives depended upon
the will of the priests in the all too frequent days
of *Kapu Kane.*

And dare we whisper it of an exalted member
of such holy order, — even at this remote period
of time and geographical distance, — probably Paao
would end the night in slaughtering some trembling victim, who had just replenished his Highness'
larder with roasted pig, or a munificent calabash of
poi, both prepared with a trembling hand and heart
of prayer, because of some sinister glance bestowed
by the haughty priest upon the lowly peasant.

At length the old minstrel was sent for, to re-

gale the Queen with sweet music from his black
bamboo flute.   And after a while Puaaihi ended
his evening entertainment by relating some of his
own strange experience with the terrible sea-monsters of the adjacent bay; ending with a fascinating recital of his numerous personal interviews
with the singing mermaids of the Waikiki shore.
Beautiful sea-girls! allured from their coral grottoes and enchanting caves by the charms of his
music on flute or harp, when discoursed from the
beach, or his lone canoe out upon the moonlit bay.

To all but Kupule these tales of the singing sea-
girls were too marvellous for belief. But there was
a charm in listening to the old poet's recital of
their beauty and their exquisite songs of the sea.
Such romantic stories told of weird, mysterious
creatures, when related in the wild, dramatic manner of the old bard of Manoa valley, might well
cause the young chieftess maidens to cluster into
close proximity about the rime-haired Puaaihi.
His sightless eyes turned upon the moon, as if in
admiration of its beauty; his pale face, corrugated
with age, contorted by the varied emotions appealed to in his theme; his deep voice, resonant in
many keys as his tones rose and fell, chimed well
with the quick recurring boom of the breakers,
and the muffled echo answering back from among
the palm-trees about them.

How alert was every maiden to catch the slightest accents of the story as it ran; leaning intently
forward as they clung to each other, with supersti-

tious fears aroused to the utmost! They formed a novel group, this score of young chieftesses, so quickened with emotion; hedged about the white-haired minstrel with awe-stricken faces; their weird, black eyes flashing with lambent gleams, now scintillant with delight and now lurid with terror; ever emotioned at the will of the cunning old bard.

Sitting thus in the deep shadow of the whisper-ing palms, the wahines were only distinguished by the mystic light of broken moonbeams, filtered down through the long plumy fronds; their long black hair draped about them helped to mystify the appearance of their dusky figures. Seen thus, they are made to resemble the *eleele uhane* — sable spirits — of the grove, centred about some pro-phetic ghost of the past.

As the night advanced, the black shadow of Puawai crept like a thief away from the whisper-ing margin of the sea, where it ever comes during an eastern moon, coming to spy in grim silence upon the white-footed tidal spirits, as they romp and ripple in playful frolic upon the coral sands along the shore. The mist-veil gathered down across the valley of Manoa, as if to exclude all further ingress after the old bard had tottered away to his hermitage, deep within its covert of sandal-wood and flowers.

The people of the neighboring hamlets dropped away one by one, straggling into their thatched *hales* for slumber. While those living in the cocoa

grove either followed their example, or covered
themselves with a thin tapa, or lauhala mat, and
lay down for the night under the canopy of palms,
hushed into dreams by the soothing lullaby among
the swaying fronds.

When the royal group by the shore had somewhat thinned out, leaving only the Queen and her
best-loved maidens, Kupule sent her companions
to their rest, and herself strayed away along the
shore to indulge in that which she most loved —
a midnight revery by the spirit-peopled solitude of
the sea.

It was a night when heaven stoops down with a
loving nearness over its foster-children, the green
earth and the blue sea where they meet in kindly
brotherhood upon the lonely shore. A night when
the countless invisibles of earth and air — which
ever seem so far off in the garish light of day —
approach on viewless wings, hovering so near unto
us as to invade our thoughts by their plaintive
whisperings, as they stand with vibrant heart-beats
and folded pinions by our side.

Kulu, the great yellow moon, had filled her
horns with glory, imparting a witching sense of
enchantment over the wave-rocked ocean, and
throughout the flowery fields and fruitful forests
of Oahu's mountain Isle. Diamond Head lay
basking like a slumbering monarch in the tawny
beam, his brawny chest breasting the great breakers
like a proud swimmer in a mimic sea.

Afar off, in the utmost distance through the

skies, shone the gigantic snow-crest on Kea's lordly brow, gleaming like a throne of polished silver
high up among the golden stars. There sits to-
night a crowned Theophany upon Kea's moon-
touched throne; transmuting the orbal harmonies
to man's requirements, and dispensing all things
in the spiritual need of life with an affluent hand.
How yon Spirit King is crowned we know not, for
his head is high above the stars, only there glints
a diffusive stream of rosy rays from off his glittering crown — unseen though it be — transmitted to
wave and waterfall; to tiny brook and roaring
river; laving the whole illumined hemisphere in
Luna-loveliness.

The heart of Kupule was afar off with her absent King, as she strolled the lonely beach on this
night of beauty. Wandering over the shining
sands, she lived over again some of the fond endearments of her wedded love; now made doubly
dear by the terrible maranatha of Pele, the ultimate of whose prophecy was fast drawing nigh.

In sadness almost akin to sorrow the young
Queen trod the impervious sand lying between
the grove and the sea, until at length she approached the guiding pandanus, whose range-line
denoted the direction of the Mermaid's haunt in
the Pearl Garden, and the ever to be dreaded
vicinage of Moa-alii's Den.

But with a brave attempt Kupule withdrew her
meditations from the fateful future awaiting her
loved one, and flung aside with a touch of imperi-

ous will all thought of the anomalous creatures of
the deep, and proffered her undivided attention
to the witching beauties of the night.

In soft tranquillity lay the waveless waters of
Waikiki Bay, mirrored at her feet, as she strolled
along the shore. Beyond the bay rose the vast
breastwork of coral reefs, encircling the harbor like
the ponderous arm of some monster of the deep.
Against these reefs roll the long lines of gigantic
breakers — heaped up billows of furious waters —
crested with playful foam, now gleaming like
molten gold in the meridian-moon.

How roars this great surf on such a night of
silent sheen and slumbering beauty! How echoes
the whispering palm grove and the wooded valleys
with its monstrous tumult, answering back to the
sea in the hoarse murmur of ghostly voices from
out the sylvan shades. Even the far mountains,
sombre and silent in the windless air, fling down
their surly answer to the bellowing sea; while
such is the concussion of the breakers against the
trees, that the long, drooping palm-leaves are made
tremulous and murmurous, quaking as with fear
of the muffled thunder of the sea.

Coming to the end of the cocoanut trees, Kupule now entered upon the dread *Wahi Kapu* —
the sacred place in front of the great Heiau, where
no mortal but the *Alii Kapus* dare intrude upon
her solitude. Here she seated herself reverently
by the tremulous rim of the tidal sea. Sitting
upon the silvery sand so close to the shimmering

waters that she dipped her dainty feet into the
slumbering tide, while she pleaded to Pele to
watch over her warrior King.

In her hours of sadness how closely the young
Queen nestled down upon the sand, lying very
near unto the throbbing bosom of the great Ocean.
Kneeling thus by the murmuring sea, with clasped
hands and outstretched arms, Kupule invoked yet
one more of its hidden mysteries to quench the
human craving in her saddened soul.

How attentive was her listening ear to the
ghostly whisperings of the palm-fronds above her
head ; and to the rhythmic pulse-beats of the sea,
where the countless footsteps of the playmate-tide
come pattering up the shore to greet her! Watching long and wonderingly into the blue, translucent waters at her feet, Kupule at times extended
her gaze out over the moon-touched surface, with
an eager quest not limited by distance or the mere
scope of human vision. Who has not thus questioned some of the passive imports of the slumbering Ocean, when so rocked to its centre by the
subtile moonbeam ? Watching for its meaning,
and hearkening for its mysteries, which are as
countless as the stars ; but, alas ! how few outspoken messages are ever given back in response
to our quests !

Receiving no answer to her appeals, either ocu-
lar or auricular, all unconsciously Kupule came to
thinking almost wholly of her recent experience
with the Mermaid Queen. At first it obtruded

itself with unwelcomed frequency into her anxious
thoughts about Kalani; weaving itself into the
sombre visions of her wifely revery, with the intrusive insistence of moonbeams, raying the blue
waters with their harpstrings of gold.

But, hark! what has so suddenly possessed our
brooding Queen? As if her own eager thoughts
had given birth to the inmost wish of her soul,
there come fluttering across the glassy bay a few
prelusive notes of the little Sea-girl's song. Kupule sprang up, with thought to see the Mermaid
on the water close at hand; so clear was the tim-
bre of her alluring voice, and so seemingly near
was the soft pianissimo that fluttered on tremulous
vibrates of melody to the shore. But not an object could be discovered over all the moon-gold
sheen of the slumbering bay.

Crouching down again close upon the coral sand,
where it touched the polished mirror of the sea,
Kupule hushed her own heart-beat, and listened
with awakened soul to the pulsating throbs of the
great heart of Ocean; laying her flushed young
cheek against his tidal bosom, listening, as saintly
ears in all ages have leaned heavenward, hoping to
entice the angel voices down.

Soon the weird song-notes rose softly over the
resonant waters again, dwelling in Kupule's ear
with a fascination that chained her to the spot.
Coming low and soft at first, the rhythmic cadence
soon rose distinct and clear as the purest utterance
of a minstrel's flute. Sometimes the music ap-

peared to come from the water, and sometimes to be wafted earthward from the upper air. Though the little singer still remained unseen, yet the volume of her melody increased with an ever-growing sense of nearness that was startling indeed to an awe-thrilled listener, because of the continued invisibility of the singer.

Such exquisite strains of music, when heard at midnight on the lonely shore, accompanied by the surly tumult of the surf, and the answering echoes from the grove, were like the enchanting melodies one may abstract from the bewildering mazes of a great master's score.

With an ear less attuned to the most delicate perceptions of melody, such a hidden cadence coming from an unknown source, when heard amidst the wild crescendo of the breakers, might have seemed but the distant hum of a droning bee. But Kupule was so linked from birth with the unseen powers of earth and air, that it was ever the underlying sights and sounds of hidden nature that most captivated her soul.

And when lying as now nestled by the hushed waters of the slumbering sea, a mystic chord was touched in her untutored mind until she finds companionship in the prattling tides and the murmuring Ocean, and receives its imprint as a loving child receives the assuring kiss of the mother.

Nearly a half hour had passed since the last song-notes of the Mermaid were heard. Kupule had tired of peering so eagerly into the sea, and

19

had dropped into a trance-like revery; looking
with appealing eyes up into the face of Kulu, addressing herself to the reflected face of Pele, ever
visible in the full-orbed moon. As the moon had
passed the meridian, and was now reining her amber chariot down the west, the Queen was contemplating returning to the palace, as post-meridian is
deemed too late to call up the unseen, or to allure
the sea-gods to land.

As she was about to rise from the beach, her
attention was directed to a dim, dark object seen
swimming along the bottom, and approaching
stealthily where she sat. Owing to the strong
Luna-light upon the sea, dark objects, when seen
on the white bottom of coral sand, were unduly
magnified by refraction, and drawn out to an interminable length. This delusive light imparted to
the approaching creature a meandrous motion, giving rise to a serpent-like appearance that was startling to behold.

Kupule sprang up with a bound, ready for flight
if attack was intended. But once upon her feet,
the swimming creature took on another appearance. Seeming now verily like a young girl sporting on the sandy bottom — perhaps one of her own
wahines — swimming timidly up from the deep sea
toward the beach where stood the Queen; presenting a sweet face, upturned appealingly to Kupule's.

What was her delight to find it was Oluolu, the
Mermaid. Her long black hair acquired its waving motion by the act of swimming; shining like

glistening scales in the gold-beam of moonlight. Not having quite the courage to swim directly in to the shore, the little Sea-queen swam back and forth along the bottom, with her sweet, entreating face turned to Kupule's; as a bird may approach timidly and circuitously to attract our attention ere it alights for companionship.

The Mermaid had evidently been cognizant of the Queen's presence during the singing, and was now purposely approaching Kupule to gaze once more upon her human beauty. As Kupule sat down again at the very verge of the sea, and extended her arms down to the timid creature, the pretty Sea-girl rose at once to the surface; staring with her large and wondering eyes, she swam hesitatingly a little nearer to the shore, where she stopped in doubt about approaching nearer.

With outstretched hands, and low, sweet-voiced entreaty, Kupule succeeded in coaxing the timid water-girl slowly to the shore. Little by little the graceful creature crept up the steep beach, until only her flukes and a portion of her small lay in the azure sea; looking, with every pause she made, with such heart-touching entreaty into the face of her sister Queen, as if with a latent fear of being harmed.

Uttering a plaintive cry of childish delight, Oluolu twined her pretty arms about Kupule's neck, and nestled confidingly upon her bosom. The round, girlish face of the Sea-girl beaming with a mingled expression of affection and admiration for her earth-born sister Queen.

This meeting between such remote types of life was as though a human maiden had climbed to a mountain top and allured a loving angel down. So startled and alarmed, amidst her wondering admiration, was the timid Mermaid; while Kupule stroked her glossy hair and patted her chubby cheeks; endeavoring to win the sweet amphibious creature from her apprehensions, arising out of her novel situation and companionship.

With the keen intuition of all womanly natures, Kupule sang to the trembling Mermaid a low, sweet lullaby; endeavoring to induce Oluolu to sing in return, by the example she set for her; as well as to reassure her of safety, and the real love she bore to her. How the tender eyes of the little Sea-queen softened with quickened affection, as she listened with her heart in her eyes. While an almost human smile crept into her small red lips and nut-brown cheeks, her mouth opening sufficiently to show the pearly whiteness of her small, sharp teeth.

Sitting thus upon the shore, with the midnight moon shining upon their faces, their fond arms twining about each other with the ardent zest that ever enhances a new affection acquired in the tender days of girlhood, Kupule warbled her plaintive song with her utmost sweetness, while Oluolu clung to her, questioning with her large dreamy eyes, alert and intuitive to catch the every import of the tone of the song and the look of the singer.

SONG.

> I heard a Mermaid singing!
>   Her voice was sad and sweet;
> Like silver bells a-ringing,
>   When wedded lovers meet.
>
> The moon was on the water,
>   The winds were hushed to sleep;
> I heard old Ocean's daughter,
>   Whose home is in the deep.
>
> Now hark! I hear her coming;
>   Oh, would that we might meet!
> Alas! 'twas th' ripples drumming,
>   Young Tides, with snow-white feet.

As Kupule's cradle-song died gently away, and the white silence and tawny moonlight together laid their ghostly hands upon the two hushed maidens, nestled there by the shimmering sea, Oluolu showed she had caught the intention of her companion; beginning at once to sing one of her own elfish songs in reply. Then it became Kupule's turn to look and wonder, at the tenderness and sweetness of the Mermaid's strains, as she sat and contemplated her unearthly companionship with this charming little Elf-girl of the Ocean.

The clear, soft notes of Oluolu's song were as thrilling and melodious as those of the white singing-mice of India; which, when well trained, vie with a Hartz-mountain canary in volume and volée. Though her singing rose at times into a resonance

as vibrant as bell-music, rivalling the ecstasy of a
lark in his matin song; yet oftenest sinking into
low pianissimo, similar in key to the notes of the
singing-shells of Batticaloa. As near as human
ear can translate, this is her song.

THE MERMAID'S SONG.

Come under the sea,
Pretty Queen, to me,
Where the pearls and sea-shells grow;
I've seen thee afloat
In thy pretty boat,
And so longed to lure thee below.

Come down to my grot —
'Tis a pretty spot —
Where the wealth of Ocean lies!
Where gems, and bright gold,
Lie in heaps untold,
And rare corals greet thine eyes.

We'll gather the beams
Of the sun in gleams,
And we'll wreathe his gold in our hair;
Deep under the waves
We'll search in my caves,
For the wonders treasured there.

While the Sea-queen was singing, so intent was
she upon her song, that assurance soon took the
place of previous timidity, and she sat upon the
sand confidingly by Kupule's side, with her long,
tapering extremity lying just dipped down into the
sea, swaying to and fro in the water in time with
her song; but as she warmed to her work, she
drew up her pliant fluke, and coiled it in a half
circle about her upon the sand.

Clinging to the small, soft hand of the Queen, Oluolu kept her large dark eyes fixed ever upon her companion's, as if eager to note the impression she was making with her song ; and Kupule took care to respond in a manner to reassure her little friend as best she could. She now observed that the charming Sea-girl could sit as erect upon the sand as her human sister. And could also stand upon her pliant tail until she reached up to the waist of Kupule, who, being larger, had to stoop to receive Oluolu's clinging arms about her neck ; for she had soon learned not only to acquiesce in the fond kisses of Kupule, but also to proffer her own timid osculation as something more than a mere symbol of girlish friendship between them.

While these two special types of the sister elements sat thus hand in hand, singing by the sea, the full-orbed moon had dipped down toward her western bourn, putting a new face upon the western aspect of mountain crag and forest gloom, having now compelled the boding shadows of midnight to seek out some new retreat.

So enthused had the young Queen become with the unearthly companionship she had found, that the changing hours and aspects of the night passed all unnoticed by her. Where a deep gloom had lain upon the western grove when she came to the shore, all was now robed in the priceless sheen of a tropic night, and a shimmering ray of silver was seen glinting down the long fronds of the tremulous palms above her.

Thus had the beetling shadow of Puawai been chased away by Luna; and in place of the black crag, rising from out the plain like a frowning warrior holding his shadow-shield over the town, there now lay a slumbering mountain, basking with bowed head in the moon-sheen; — as lies a brindled lion with half-shut eyes, drowsing in Afric's burning sun.

The interview between the maidens had been full of intensest interest to both. They had interchanged songs and salutatory greetings by osculation, — a new, sweet mystery easily acquired by Oluolu, — and indulged in abundant pantomimic prattle, and expressed admiration of each other by the orbal medium of their dark eyes. Meeting thus upon the verge of unknown elements of existence, they were a mystery and a revelation to each other; and no wonder that Kupule's gentle heart at length grew full of superstitious fears, lest Moa-alii, or other of the fierce sea-monsters, should come in search of their little Queen of the Sea.

As if her intuitive thoughts had given birth to her conceptions, there indeed were a gathering of dark objects now seen prowling about the bottom of the adjacent sea; dim, half-defined monsters, who curdle one's blood by the smallest glimpses of themselves, or their more hideous shadow shapes, when thus seen in the solitude of a midnight sea.

From behind the jutting coral rocks and shrubs there glowered fierce-eyed creatures, and flitted

black, unhallowed shapes, watching with furtive
glances like ambushed demons, as with concerted
intent to snatch the two Queens from shore. At
the moment Kupule discovered the gathering, a
score of great man-headed Eeries were arraying
themselves in a cordon about the maidens ; like an
invisible vanguard, only perceptible by their flimsy
outline of fish-shape, with the head and arms of
monstrous human giants. Not a ray of moonbeam
was obstructed from shining through body and arms
of the impalpable creatures, who now showed a
greater ghostliness than by sunlight.

But being upon the land, and that a tabued shore,
where it were deemed that neither gods nor men
could harm a Kapu Alii, Kupule's courage was
equal to the occasion, and she clung fast to Oluolu — whose back was to the sea — as if in defiance
of all the gathered clans of the nether world.

But the end was not yet come ; for there now
appeared a gigantic Octopus, large as a whale,
rearing up, out in mid-bay, standing on the water
upon his half-score of tentacles, until he lifted his
hideous body fifty feet into the air. Bellowing
louder than the spouting of an angry whale, the
vast monster began clawing his way toward the
beach where the maidens sat.

Here was a foe more terrible than all else in the
sea, for he could not only reach sixty feet out upon
the shore to snatch his prey, without leaving his
native element, but he could also run like a mammoth spider upon the land, outstripping the fleet-

est-footed, and devouring a man at a mouthful as
he ran.   Thus the safety of the Kanakas only lay
in the dislike of the savage Devil-fish for the land ;
and though he rarely left his element, evidently
here was a case which had enraged him to the utmost, and Kupule's peril was becoming imminent.

At that instant, when Kupule began to comprehend her danger, and was about to rise, there
came a soft and kitten-like purring upon her cheek,
like that previously made by Nani ere they parted.
Turning to look, there indeed was the little Elf-
queen tugging at her arm, and pointing, with a
look of entreaty, for Kupule to flee from the shore.

Kupule's evident uneasiness had communicated
itself to the Mermaid queen before the Octopus
roared far out in the bay, or little Nani showed
herself over Kupule's shoulder.   And now, after
an anxious glance at the menacing monsters in the
sea, and a look of greater apprehension as she beheld the rage of the gigantic Devil-fish, Oluolu
twined her plump little arms suddenly about her
companion for a moment, looked a last tender farewell into her eyes, and then plunged like a porpoise
down into the shimmering sea, and was gone in an
instant.

Down went the enraged Octopus, disappearing
instantly from view.   While the surly rear-guard
of unrevenged Eeries prowled angrily about the
beach, casting ravenous looks of fury at Kupule as
she stood defiantly upon the shore, like one strong
in her right of domain.   But at length, one by one

of the great monsters slunk furtively away, but
with many a backward look of lingering rage cast
upon the unterrified Queen, as they returned to
their ocean lairs.

During all this time the tiny little Elf-queen sat
trembling upon a banana-leaf near at hand, her
sweet little face expressing the utmost anxiety for
the safety of her new-found friend, who, because
of her just indignation against the intrusion of the
sea-gods, would not stir from the shore until every
hideous-shaped creature had retreated from her
view.

But when the last vestige of even the ugly
shadow shapes were gone, Kupule stepped to the
banana tree and took little Nani tenderly into her
arms ; the sweet Elf-girl seeming so rejoiced that
no harm had come out of the many-shaped perils ;
dangers that Kupule evidently did not fully esti-
mate, hence the vivid apprehension of the wise
little Elf-queen for her safety.

Bearing the charming Fairy in her arms, Kupule
took her way along the beach toward the palace.
The delighted Queen bestowed many endearments
upon her golden-haired pet as she walked, while
Nani purred back her pretty responses with equal
delight. When approaching quite near to the
palace, Manona was discovered through the trees,
sitting in the moonlight, anxiously awaiting the
return of her much-loved sovereign.

Nani at once showed extreme uneasiness at seeing the *puua hele* of the Queen, and expressed many

a pantomimic wish to depart. But as Kupule looked with earnest appeal into the little violet eyes, entreating for a longer stay, Nani tarried yet a moment more ; but as they passed close to a large Bele pua — the bell-shaped *Datura brugman-sia* — whose delicious fragrance greeted them as they approached it, with a swift fluttering of un-seen pinions, the tiny Elf-queen was gone ; escaping in spite of Kupule's firm effort to retain her.

Only the swinging motion of the Bele pua, as it swayed bell-like to and fro in the moonlit air, disclosed the possible retreat of the Fairy mite, who was nowhere to be seen, though Kupule searched with a grieved heart everywhere within the ken of her eye. From that moment this weird-leafed biennial and its trumpet-shaped flowers were tabued forever — forbidden to the touch of mortal under penalty of death.

Many a night thereafter, during her sad, brief reign, Kupule and little Nani met in the moonlit coco-grove, by the aromatic cluster of Bele pua, together with many another of the charming companions of the Fairy-queen ; a trysting-place that is held sacred as a Mecca shrine to this day. There the whole Elfin world met, seemingly in such sweet sympathy because of the sad fate impending over Kupule, which only their immortal eyes could see with a positive visibility. There they would gather about the beautiful young Queen, each eager to assert their friendliness, singing their witching chorus of Elfin songs, than which nothing in lyric melody can be so charming to the few — the very few human souls gifted to interpret them.

Sometimes they would all meet on the tabued shore in front of the Heiau, where Oluolu and her sister Mermaids would join them ; when even the tawny moon and the pensive stars would come hovering down very near above, — their orbal souls kindling into ecstasy in metrical accord with these nightly songs by the sea.

What an insight into supernatural life was lost with Kupule, for only the blind old Bard survived to tell the little we know of the many interesting meetings between the winsome Mermaids and the tiny Elfin immortals on the Waikiki shore.

WHEN Pele's priests a Tabu make,
   The throes of earth fill man with fear;
For all the gods a part must take,
And heaven and earth are made to quake!
   And awful groans invade the sphere:
The tallest mountains rend apart,
From crest of snow to hellish heart! *
Unmask their demon monsters there,
And lay their seething lavas bare!
When blood is sought for Pele's fane,
   The nearest victims sudden bleed;
Then vain is flight — to plead is vain —
   Enough there are to do the deed,
Who stay to count nor cost nor pain.

But kingly Lono less will suit;
This gentle god accepts your fruit:
And who cannot the fruits bestow
May launch their boats and fishing go.
Moa-alii's wrath is not in vain:
Vast oscillations seize the main;
The bellow'ng winds escape their caves,
And billows rise to mountain waves!

Ah! who would Pele's *Kapu* dare?
Meteoric tempests fill the air,
And god Ahea invades the sky;
Hurls down his iron-stone from high,
Till awful tumult reigneth there!

---

  * The writer has seen a mountain on Maui that had been thus rent by
volcanic action, torn from top to base into three unequal parts.

CHAPTER XVI.

ATE in the afternoon of the following day, the air was suddenly filled with shouts of rejoicing at the coming of the King, accompanied by his immense fleet of war-canoes. They came bowling down before the brisk trades under press of sails and paddles, bringing hundreds of wounded chiefs and an army much dispirited and broken by their many defeats. Though the Oahuans had fought with the utmost desperation, yet the fast growing power of Kamehameha, aided by Pele, and the numerous trained white men with their fire-arms, had ever turned the scale of victory in favor of the Hawaiians.

Such sanguinary battles had never been fought in all the history of the Islands. In witness of this assertion we have only to mention that fought in the deep and dismal "Vale of Iao" — the Yosemite of Maui — whose gigantic cliffs rose on either hand two thousand feet above the heads of the combatants, ever robed in freshest verdure from their high turret peaks, standing like hooded monks ambushed in green ferns and climbing *ie* vines, down to the rushing waters of the roaring Wailuku — "waters of destruction" — whose dark waters

were so obstructed, dammed up by the dead and
the dying, that it overflowed its banks red with the
gore of the fallen braves. Yet, whom the gods of
the Isles favor must continue to win, whatever the
resistance brought to bear; and this feeling had
gradually possessed the minds of the army, and dispirited even the great Chiefs and their heroic King.

Worn with the ever-present anxiety of his long
warfare and numerous misfortunes, Kalani was
well pleased to again dwell in the soothing presence of his darling Queen. Beautiful as an angel,
and wise as a seer, the witching and womanly
Kupule soon acquired a judicious and abiding influence over the dark, depressing moods of the
King, until the valiant warrior grew into almost
oblivion of his losses, and came at length to more
than reciprocate the boundless adoration of his
darling.

The royal pair soon became as inseparable as the
dove from his mate, or the tropic night from her
stars, being often together, except when the King's
attention was needed to devise methods for the
better security of the army, against the desperate
battle that must ensue when Kamehameha followed on to Oahu with his victorious forces, as he
was preparing to do.

But when the new army of Oahu was fully organized, and gathered into the intrenched camp of
Nuuanu, and all their other plans for defensive
warfare were perfected, then Kalani left the daily
drilling to Boki and Kaumualii, and his other great

chiefs, and for the first time in his life gave himself up to the luxury of his love and the idolatrous duties of his religion.

Together the royal lovers daily visited the army, to aid by their presence the growing enthusiasm slowly manifested among the new forces. And together they boated and fished within the reef and far out upon the sea; together climbed to the high peaks of Waolani, until their whole island world lay at their feet, a varying picture of tropical beauty.

And it was in these days of wandering that Kalani spent much time at the Pali, the scene of his last desperate struggle — the Thermopylæ of the Isles. It is a wild and romantic spot at the mountain terminus of the Nuuanu, associated with events of sad and tragic interest — the subjugation of a kingdom. Here the King and his heroic chiefs made their last stand, until slaughtered upon the heaps of dead Hawaiians they had piled breast-high in the narrow Pass. Here Kalani fell, beneath the eyes of his loved young Queen, who sat on the jutting crag above his head to see him die.

Here Oahu's panic-stricken soldiers, who had deserted earlier in the day, were driven at the spear-point by the Hawaiians over the ragged cliff of the dizzy Pali; an army of cowardly men leaping a thousand feet of unencumbered fall. Grand and beautiful lies the garden-land of Koolau below, and deeper the green, and more thrifty the foliage and flowers, where headlong fell those thousands of Oahu's spear-tossed Serfs.

20

From the entrance of this renowned Pass, where Kalani fell, upward to the terrible precipice of the Pali, there winds a deep and narrow gorge walled in on either hand by precipitous mountain crags, some of which overhang so as to threaten the intruder with peril as he passes.

Rough and rugged and romantic as is the Pali and its historic gorge, — so haunted by the dreadful remembrance of its two battle-scenes, — yet the matchless view from the Pali's dizzy precipice will repay whoever climbs to behold it, for it is conceded to be the most beautiful, unique, and picturesque scene to be found in a life of wandering.

Here our royal lovers would sit for hours enraptured, while overlooking Koolau's pastoral scenes below, lying in one glad picture at their feet. It is a scene too charming to be easily described, and one never to be obliterated from the mind of the beholder.

From where they sat, on the Pali's cliff, there sweeps to the right and left a vast semicircle of mountains, tall and grand, forming the concave aspect of the matchless scene below ; awakening our utmost sense of grandeur by their jagged peaks, precipitous cliffs, and wild ravines. From over the lofty cliffs leap down cascades and waterfalls, tumbling thousands of feet from the wooded heights ; so high that often the leaping streams lose their aqueous identity before reaching the ever-verdant fields below; dropping their cool mist upon the upturned face like some ghostly benediction of the spirits of the place.

While such is the western aspect of Koolau, two miles away to the eastward rolls the most gigantic surf of an ever-heaving Ocean, crashing in on a rock-bound windward coast; impressing one with its vast reach of blue sublimity, and its long line of unprecedented breakers, which begin to rear their snowy crests far out upon some hidden reef-bed which shows a tinge of green beneath the meridian sun. Such is the distant convex of the shore-line. Thus between the blue Ocean and its wild roaring breakers on the east, and the green crescent of lofty mountains on the west, lie the ever-green pastures and low rolling hills of Koolau's enchanting land.

Our kingly lovers loved to sit hand in hand, and gaze down from the Pali upon the thrifty groves of tropic fruits and singing-birds, the limpid lakes and tinkling streams, watering gardens of nutritious taro and mealy yams. The whole happy land clothed with perennial beauty, fragrant with ripening fruits and ever-blossoming flowers throughout the whole year round.

Yet was this Eden-land wholly inaccessible from the Pali for aught but winged birds and the spear-tossed deserters who were soon after flung from its toppling cliff by the Hawaiian Guard. What a place for panic-stricken men to cling, gloating with longing eyes over the paradisiacal scene below, while their ears were agonized with the din of battle which they knew must soon ingulf them.

By such daily wanderings and intimate associa-

tion with his brave and beautiful Kupule, the dis-
heartened young King came once more into possession of his noble and heroic self; and not only
gained heart to finish up the life-work allotted him
by Pele, but also acquired a heroic determination
to embellish his last battlefield with deeds the future would not willingly let die.

At Kupule's ever urgent entreaty, Kalani was
led to devote himself to daily worship at Pele's
Fountain in the tabued grove ; at which times the
young Queen was assiduous in her efforts to induce the dread Goddess of Kilauea to relent in
the severity of her awful malediction against her
darling — a curse so disproportioned to his one hour
of sinful derision against the feminine fickleness
of his woman god.

The day following the King's return from Maui,
Paao, the High Priest, suggested the necessity of a
thorough *Kapu Kane* to the gods ; a religious ceremony of an imposing nature being called for because of their terrible misfortunes, and to enable
the assembled Kapu Aliis to mollify the evident
displeasure of the gods, as well as to consult the
dread deities about future events which now
seemed so ominous and disheartening.

Kalani consented to a limited Tabu of five days'
duration, and such was proclaimed by the Lunapai
over all the land. Though the tabu was brief,
and but few human manes were furnished for sacrifice, yet it was made one of the strictest religious
covenants with the most arrogant god of the na-

tion. The King and all the great chiefs went
down to Waikiki, and dwelt for several days in or
about the great Heiau, the vast temple of Pele,
built centuries before in the valley of Manoa.

The grounds containing the Heiau were an
immense work for their day, enclosed by a compact wall of stone. Its dimensions were two hundred and twenty-four feet by one hundred feet
wide. The walls were twenty feet high, twelve
feet thick at the base, and six feet at the top,
where it was paved with broad smooth stones, and
used as a promenade in times of worship.

The interior of the Heiau was laid out in terraces,
one rising above another, the upper one being
paved with flat stones. There were several of
these in the enclosure. The central terrace contained the great altar of Pele, where human manes
were sacrificed to the awful Goddess. This altar
was enclosed in a court, and only the King, the
High Priest, and the Kapu Aliis of highest rank
were permitted to enter into this holy of holies. At
one end of this court was a tall pyramid of stone,
quadrangular in form, with an arched door leading
into the interior where *Pua*, the beautiful bird-
god of Kalani, was kept in sacred trust, to be used
in case of sickness, or upon great state occasions.

At the opposite end of this court was a tall, hollow obelisk made of open wicker-work, in which
Paao enclosed himself when seeking religious communications with Pele. While the priest was
thus laboring for an interview with the dread God-

dess, the King and numerous high chiefs stood listening without the obelisk, ready to join in a wail
of entreaty to Pele for an answer to their prayer,
which the priest was enjoined to present. At
length when a communication was received from
the Goddess, it was imparted to the chiefs upon
the great outer wall, who in turn announced it
to the heralds without, when it was proclaimed
throughout the neighboring villages, and to the
people hidden among the hills.

The supplicating struggles of Paao in obtaining
important communications with the most imperious
gods were sometimes exhaustive and prolonged.
We are told that the intermediate demons, which
hold dominion between gods and men, are always
jealous of the priests because of their direct influence with the divine rulers of heaven and earth.

During the continuance of these dread tabus, on
the high walls of the Heiau were stationed many
huge wooden idols, often hideous to behold; and
while the behests of the gods were being promulgated, many of these great idols became terribly
agitated, contorting their faces and gnashing their
teeth — a visible illustration to all those *without*
the temple of the irresistible power of godhead.

And yet there were sometimes bold, bad men
among the downtrodden people who ventured to
ridicule this viable quality of the wooden idols;
and to further insinuate that the communications
purporting to come from the gods were cunningly
coined for the purpose by the priests, as all the

divine bequests were ever in favor of the chiefs and contained new oppressions for the people. But, alas! such scoffers soon sickened and died.

Upon the consecration of this great Heiau of Waikiki, after it was built by the mighty Umi, eighty lusty human victims were sacrificed, besides hundreds of animals fatted purposely for the gods. This so pleased the several presiding deities of the islands that this Heiau had ever remained the most favored temple from which to appeal to the gods. But during this present tabu the priest was more considerate of his dear fellow-creatures, and but ten men were sacrificed to Pele, together with numerous hogs and dogs to Moa-alii.

From these seeming outrages there was no appeal. The priest must do the bidding of the gods. Who can resist the demands of the dread Pele, or the voracious sea-god, Moa-alii? None! No, not even the priest; thus the doomed *must die* without questioning the cruel mandate of the gods.

The Tabu of Polynesia is one of the most cunning creations of heathen priestcraft the world has seen. The devilish ingenuity shown in its conception is unequalled by any device of Loyola in the days of his greatest iniquity. A more fiendish element of religious despotism could not be devised. While it adapted itself to every wish and arbitrary requirement of the proud and arrogant chiefs, proving their most effective weapon of civil or religious government, on the other hand it became the most murderous instrument of diabolism

for the infliction of cruelty upon the common
class.

The unconquerable dread pervading all classes
below the rank of chiefs, when the awful *Kapu
Kane* was in force, was horrifying beyond our conception. Through their all-pervading fear of the
Tabu, the superstitious people would submit to
the most humiliating enactments and outrages
when perpetrated by priest or chief, though it took
the food from their mouths, the wives from their
bosoms, or demanded their own bodies for the
Kapu Kane.

Though this heathen ecclesiasticism applied with
such rigid intolerance to the people, yet the *Alii
Kapus* suffered little inconvenience from the numerous mythological tenets arising out of its poly-
theism.

* Let the Priest but proclaim a *Kapu Kane* upon
a great state occasion, as upon a king's death, or
previous to going to war, and in the eyes of the
terrified people it seemed as if heaven and earth
contributed to deepen the horror that spread over
the land.

Man flies and hides himself for days and weeks,
starving in mountain caves and forest depths, fleeing as from an unchained monster, whose breath
is death to whomsoever it encounters. Woman
secludes herself in her darkened habitation, speaking only in softest whispers to the trembling babe at
her breast, the infant imbibing a sense of fear with
its pap. For should her maternal lullaby chance

to invade the ear of the Tabu Priest, while at his awful incantations in the *Wahi Kapu*, alas! it is death to some loved male of that household. It is death even to the loving wife should her shadow fall across the path of her chief. Death to light a fire upon the domestic hearth during the dark tabu days — whether its malediction pervades days, or weeks, or months.

But, thank heaven, the allotted period of the cruel *Kapu Kane* passes at last. The hideous face-making idols are taken down from the walls of the Heiau, and disposed of in their minor temples; the countless small white *puwalus* (flags) of the Tabu are withdrawn from houses and trees and canoes; and the half-starved people are once more seen stealing out, with furtive looks and scared faces, from their hiding-places; their cowed hearts imbibing an uncertain sense of gladness at their release — like the water-logged gladness of a drowning man just snatched from the sea.

Many weeks now passed in busy preparation to resist the threatened invasion of Kamehameha. Oahu had been drained so often during the past wars among the Windward Islands, that now a brave soldiery were much needed to defend their homes against the drilled forces of Hawaii, the material out of which to make an army was not to be found.

When every available fighting-man upon Oahu was mustered by his district chief, and gathered into the intrenched camp of Nuuanu, their number did not much exceed five thousand soldiers and five hundred chiefs. The material of which the rank and file consisted was poor indeed, for the purposes of the desperate warfare that was expected to ensue. Many of the new recruits were too young and untrained, or too aged and decrepit to be available. And such was the dread that Kamehameha had created by his successive victories, that many a stalwart youth would not answer to the call of his local chief. These cravens were hunted like wild beasts; their ears were slit, and they were brought into camp with a rope about their necks, to be exhibited as cowards, men who had refused to fight for their homes. And there were too many young recruits with slit ears to augur well for future wars.

Yet more than an off-set against the incompetent soldiery, were the large and noble-looking chiefs of Oahu and Kauai; the entire body of which were the finest set of fighting-men known. The gigantic physique of no other hereditary aristocracy was ever so distinctly marked by nature. Six feet was but common stature with both sexes, and seven feet a not uncommon height among these lordly nobles, especially among the titanic chiefs of Oahu.

Though of such gigantic frames, and so normally proportioned, yet these herculean chiefs were more renowned for their great strength and cunning use of arms, than for great endurance. Recognizing their deficiency in this respect, they were now training themselves to the utmost by daily feats of arms, and by running and wrestling, with a resolute purpose of selling their lives dearly in the last coming battle with the giant Victor of Hawaii.

Three and four hundred pounds was not an unusual weight with these huge chiefs. Yet they were active in warfare, and sparkling with intelligence in counsel, in spite of their enormous size and undue adiposis. They were also men of remarkable symmetry, lofty carriage, and majestic mien, — qualities denoting innate pride of birth and conscious nobility, — and as a body of warriors had no peers among all the warlike tribes of the heathen world.

No one who has seen these titanic chiefs when contrasted with the medium-sized common people, but may think with reason that they were of a distinct race from the peasants. But this controversy involves a never-to-be forgotten lesson for the anthropologist. Sufficient cause may be found for the disproportioned physical superiority of the chiefs over the serfs, in the exalted mental condition of the one, and the abject moral degradation of the other.

Pampered pride, and the untrammelled freedom of our mental faculties, will always conduce to expansion of mind and a well-nourished body; and successive generations of such favoring conditions of mentality have resulted in the gigantic Chiefs of Polynesia. While, on the other hand, searching closely for retrograde metamorphosis, we learn that a life of mental and physical oppression, where fear in a thousand ghostly and depressing forms, following one like an invisible Eerie, can never fail to impair digestion, diminish nutrition, and retrograde growth. Moreover, wherever such conditions predominate, they end by unduly augmenting the animal propensities at the expense of the intellectual faculties — always the heaviest possible drag-weight by which to degrade man from his kinship with Godhead.

Nothing less than the invigorating atmosphere of their mountain Isles could have upheld the down-trodden classes of the Hawaiian Islands from degenerating into imbecility, with such an ever-pervading fear blighting their lives. Transfer them to a low Atoll island — where no land-wind is ever engendered — and the peasant would become an idiot in three generations. This transfusive decadence may be seen going on at the Penuryhns and many other Atoll islands.

The sublime grandeur of lofty mountains serves to ennoble the human mind when acting through the sense of seeing. But how much more beneficial is their influence of atmospheric qualities acting upon mental and physical nutrition, — imparting hematin and caloric to the life-current, and abundant electric aura to both animal and organic nerve-centres.

Few of us but have noticed how sensibly mountain influence inspires sublime thoughts, and none but have observed that the dominant races of elevated regions are always large-chested and

massive-browed ; while upon all low, flat islands
— even in the bland air of the Pacific — we have
ever observed the indigenes to have retreating fore-
heads, bagging abdomen, and spindling extremities.
Conditions arising out of an excess of saline atmosphere, together with an undue exclusion of the
phosphatic and calcareous earth-salts, so impera-
tively needed to induce normal mental and physical development.

As the intelligent and well-fed chiefs of Oahu
had for centuries done all the thinking for the
nation, so they necessarily grew in intellectual
capacity above their serfs; while the ever-pervading despotism of the *Kapu Kane* crushed the
spirits of the people until they became the mental
and physical pigmies that we describe.

With all their capacity for inflicting cruelty
upon the people, yet among the chiefs a high degree of courtesy and kindness prevailed, together
with a refinement of language and gentle demeanor that betokens conscious nobility and pride
of birth. Contact with the serfs was deemed so
contaminating, that, to more thoroughly exclude
the commonalty from any participation or understanding of what transpired in good society, a
court language was invented ; and if any of its
terms became known to the lower order, those
terms were immediately discarded, and new ones
substituted. Death was a frequent penalty inflicted upon the peasants for slight infringements
of etiquette required by custom toward the chiefs.

We have entered thus minutely into the different quality of fighting-material comprised in the army of Oahu, that subsequent events might be better comprehended, when, in the last great battle of the Nuuanu and the Pali, one part of the army showed such unaccountable cowardice, while a small minority — the heroic chiefs — fought with a degree of desperation that wins our esteem, and almost engenders oblivion of their previous cruelty to the soldier serf.

It was known for weeks that Kamehameha had been mustering a powerful army of nearly sixteen thousand men in Sandy Bay, the westernmost point of Molokai, over across the straits from Oahu. Daily the lookouts watched from the eastern mountains for the coming of the Hawaiian fleet. All but the islands of Oahu and Kauai were already in the hands of the giant invader, whose greater sagacity in enlisting numerous white men into his service, and wisdom in abiding by Vancouver's instructions, to drill and discipline his army after the manner of the Europeans, had been the means of out-generalling and out-numbering Kalani everywhere, until he was now driven to fight for his last kingdom — Oahu.

Kamehameha had sent numerous messages down from Molokai, proffering affluence and freedom to Kalani if he would surrender without further fighting. For the fierce old warrior could not but admire the heroic bravery of his boy antagonist; and he could not but remember that Kalani was not only his reputed brother, but was also wedded to his natural daughter — the charming Pelelulu —whom he loved with his inmost soul.

But never for a moment had Kalani swerved from his noble purpose of defending his kingdom with his life. Therefore, his replies to Kamehameha were ever in defiance ; bidding the gigantic conqueror come on and do his worst, declaring that his last battle would be witnessed by the gods, and should be his best.

Never did gentle woman's love fulfil its divine mission to better purpose than Kupule's, in her unceasing endeavor to rally her Keiki Moi from his moods of depression, whenever he suffered himself to contemplate the enormity of his loss. Never had Kalani lost a battle until after he had so thoughtlessly cast defiance upon Pele — the fiery Ignipotent of the Isles — because of her apparent apostasy from his cause. He who defies the gods bruises his own head by his blows. From that moment the indignant Goddess had doomed her once favorite warrior to fight on and lose his battles ; condescending to a final promise of earthly forgiveness, and subsequent redemption after death in the dim region of Po, provided his last battle was to her liking. And for this the young hero and his great chiefs were preparing.

Many weeks had passed in final preparations for a desperate struggle ; and now all began to be impatient for the last great test of arms ; a conflict with but the alternative of a well-won free-

dom or death. The morning was a bright one;
the sea was smooth, and the trades were strong,
when suddenly a small Hawaiian canoe shot
swiftly into sight from around Diamond Head, an
object of sufficient interest to centre all eyes upon
it. Though the canoe was evidently one of the
enemy's, and without doubt coming from their
camp, yet it showed no hesitation, and came
boldly on, impelled to the utmost speed under sail
and paddles, and flying at the upper angle of the
sail a small white *puwalu* of the Hawaiians.

Word was brought to Kalani at the palace of
Nuuanu, and together with Kaumualii and Boki
— who had recently been wedded to the brave
and beautiful Leleha — he went down the valley
to receive the war-message, for such it evidently
was, when the canoe landed at Honolulu. As the
small craft approached the beach, some of the
paddlers were recognized as men from their own
army, having been captured by the Hawaiians in
the last desperate battle in the vale of Iao. They
had been sent by Kaiaua, a noble uncle of Kalani's,
and young Kaumualii, and a brother of Keao,
whom Kalani had slain in his great battle with the
Kauaians. This proud and ambitious chief was
Kamehameha's head counsellor, and one of his
foremost generals. But becoming arrogant, and
too intrusive in his ambitious schemes, the King
had long since shown his distrust of this famous
warrior. For this he became a traitor, and now
sought to join forces with Kalani, upon the prom-

ise of having the kingdom of Hawaii if Kamehameha was beaten.

The messengers also brought word that the whole Hawaiian army would sail that afternoon, with intent to land at Koko Point, the eastern cape of Oahu, and would camp in Waialae Bay. The further plan was to break camp and march from Kona to Honolulu before daybreak, and be ready to give battle during the early part of the following day.

Kaiana proposed to sail later than the others, deserting with his whole army corps, and by sailing around Koko Point and Diamond Head, to avoid the army, and land at early dawn at Honolulu before Kamehameha could reach the town to resist his landing. This news made the day a busy one with the army of Oahu, though everything had been previously prepared.

21

Beneath the grove of orange trees,
  Where Pele's gushing fountain bubbles,
Kalani sat, to catch the breeze
That fragrant wafts among the trees,
  Pondering o'er his kingly troubles.
Beside the Fountain at his feet,
Near where the stream and flowers meet,
With upturned face Kupule sat;
  Soft gazing on her lover's face,
And, woman-like, with gentle chat,
  Strove on his lip a smile to place.
His hand between her own she presses,
  Soft rests her chin along his knee,
Recalling him by sweet caresses,
  Begs him awhile let sorrow be;
Begs him to leave his grief and gloom
Awhile in dead Titeere's tomb.

Somewhat of this Kalani felt,
  While printing on that face his kiss;
To fairer soul ne'er lover knelt
  To bind himself in bonds of bliss.
That hour one-half the slaughter bred
  Whose crimson dyed the Pali's dell,
Where his own red blade the carnage shed,
  And piled the dead on which he fell;
But not too high for Love to climb,
  And on his bleeding bosom die,
To catch his dying call in time,
  And heavenward with *his* Spirit fly.

CHAPTER XVII.

IT was the last night of earth-life allotted to Kalani of Oahu. the kingly youth, the matchless warrior of his time! The long list of sanguinary conflicts assigned to him by Pele — the ruthless Ignipotent of Kilauea — had been fought, and lost, as she predicted, on that dread night of her maranatha by the fountain. Now the last battlefield awaits the Keiki Moi on the morrow, the final act of an heroic drama of kingly strife and kingly love!

During the day everything had been perfected about the army by its officers; and Kalani had bid Boki and Kaumualii to take charge of their respective forces until the hour of conflict arrived, as he wished his final interview with the Queen to be uninterrupted by affairs of state or war.

The royal pair had spent the afternoon happily together at the palace, with only Manona in attendance; for Leleha had girded on sword and dagger and joined Boki, her wedded lord, in the camp. Now that the evening meal was over, and one by one the stars came sorrowfully out over the land, the King grew moody and thoughtful; and taking Kupule's hand tenderly in his own, he led her away

up to the Kiowai in the sacred orange grove. A
feeling of reverence for divine things, and tenderness for the dear ones who clung to his heart-
strings, possessed the kingly boy in that hour.
He wished to give one final hour's worship to
their barbaric Goddess in lonely solitude with his
Queen ; though both, in their inmost hearts, had
already given ear to the white man's God, but
dare not, as yet, confess it aloud, so trammelled
were they with the cunning superstitions of their
priest-ridden land.

It was a hushed and hallowed night over the
ever beautiful valley of Nuuanu ; and there were
gentle angel-faces haloed by every star that met
the sad gaze of the worshippers in the fountain,
as the tinkling spray fell like bell-music about their
ears.   A thousand inarticulate cadences melodized
everywhere, in sweet accord with human bereavement, and the sacred song-spirits of the night
whispered their prayerful melodies down the yellow harp-strings of the stars in solemn nocturne.

Even the camp-fires across the Nuuanu quelled
down their flickering blaze into slumbering embers, lest they glare too obtrusively upon these
last momentous hours before the battle.   There
comes a soft and reverent hum from the low-
voiced army, blending with the prayerful waterfall, and the ceaseless vesper-hymn from the murmuring sea.   Until, to the sad young worshippers
in the tabued grove, there seemed a universal benediction pervading the soft gray silence, as it knelt

like a bereaved Spirit over the slumbering valley and the sleeping sea.

It was a night to make all men prayerful and reverent, — whether their mood be one of gladness or of sadness, — for the spirit of Deity pervaded the heavens, and the hush of a thousand listening angels brooded everywhere abroad over all this terror-stricken land.

There is ever a pathos in last hours and last meetings ; an element of sublime sorrow that can never be portrayed by the most artful array of colored tints, or the fluent tracery of words. We may possibly depict the quivering lip and the tender eye, but the lofty spirit of a great inward grief can never be portrayed. The soft inflection imparted to loving words, where sorrowing hearts seek to impress their own pulsation in tremulous quaver upon another's, when exchanging last messages, can only be interpreted by linked hearts and loving ears when most divinely attuned to receive them.

Thus had the royal lovers spent their last hours in the sacred grove, interpreting their agonized heart-beats to each other. Their last night's worship at Pele's tabued shrine. Their last night's communion below the stars! But when loving words became too tremulous for interchanging their pent-up loves, and articulation became too choked to give utterance to the voiceless affection within; then the kingly lover could only fold his little Queen in his strong arms, and permit their blended hearts to beat in wild unison together.

But last hours fly on swifter wings than others. Orion is now reflecting his sword and belt in the spring beside the lovers. Aldebaran and the seven sorrowing sisters have given place to the Hunter, who now lifts his club to strike where gleams the blood-red star on the head of angry Taurus. It was a warlike symbol, reminding our warrior King that the midnight hour was upon them; and the new day, the *last day*, had come, that was to be made the most momentous in the history of the mountain Isle — the dear Oahu that should be his heritage no more!

And Kalani put the fair, sweet face from off his manly breast, and turned Kupule's sad eyes and wet cheeks to the stars — till Aldebaran orbed himself within her dark orbs — until he could once more peruse the inmost soul within the queenly face he loved. Long had Kalani found that the best inspiration for his battle-god was in the fair, fond face that now prompted him to those yet greater deeds of carnage for the morrow; deeds that have linked his name forever with Waolani's mountain Pass, wherein the kingly hero fell!

The King now bethought himself to ascend to the top of Punch Bowl, where he could still pass the night with the Queen, and at the same time could watch for any signal of the enemy's approach from Kona, should the Hawaiians chance to be early on the move.

But it was necessary to leave word at the palace where they were going, lest Boki might wish for

the King, and know not where to find him. Kupule offered to run down to the palace and leave
the desired message. In an instant more she was
lost to view, as she sped away through the bended
boughs of the fruit-laden, flower-clad trees of the
tabued orange grove; following the laughter-loving
brook down the hillside, which quickened its gliding pace to keep company with the maiden as she
ran.

Kalani was thus left alone in the starlit solitude
by the fountain; and his loneliness was soon thick
peopled with the sorrows that ever invade the last
hours of life. Unconsciously he groaned·aloud in
anguish of heart as he contemplated the wrecked
hopes of his young life. It was indeed a thankless
task to enter upon another great battle with Pele's
cruel prediction yet ringing in his ear: " Because
of your defiance, you shall fight only to lose ! Your
last battle shall be your best; then the gods will
await you in the realms of Po above !"

With his young life thus oppressed with the malediction of the gods, what wonder that he almost
lost heart, and bowed his kingly head in sadness
as he sat by the purling fountain's rim! When the
royal boy uttered his wrung cry of grief, there came
a universal hush over the night, bringing a quick
sense of relief to his heart, followed by a whir —
dim and indistinct — as from a gathering of countless invisible sympathies in the grove; together with
a gentle tumult agitating the starlit waters. And
there, indeed, appeared the tiny Elf-queen, rising

softly to the surface ; and while half hidden by the
falling spray, and a cluster of half-closed flowers
and long pendent leaves that drooped down over
the spring, little Nani sat with her baby-hands
clasped, watching the sorrowing King. Upon her
star-like face was a look of such grief as only the
immortals may wear. But Kalani sat with bowed
head and heard not the kindly gathering above and
about him, nor saw the sad blue eyes of the sorrowing Fairy, though her golden tresses rayed the
darkness like abundant star-beams.

Presently there came a soft rustling along the
brook-side ; a stir among the dewy grasses and the
night-folded flowers ; a gliding, stealthy footstep
just invaded Kalani's ears, — though light as when
summer winds awaken the slumbering leaves. Now
a nearer rustle led Kalani to lift his head from his
folded arms, when he was greeted by a softly cooing voice, and two fond arms were twined tenderly
about the neck of the brooding King ; and tones
softer than the music of the *O-o's* song filled his
ear with the melody of gentle love and tender endearments. What wonder that Kalani could not
long sorrow when thus intruded upon by such a
bewitching presence !

It was Kupule. The god-born Queen had hastened back with stealthy footsteps to snatch her
Keiki Moi from his terrible forebodings because of
the hateful Pele's neglect of her doomed young
warrior, in this, his greatest hour of need. A sweet,
magnetic face lies close to Kalani's, and dark, soft

eyes, luminous as stars, hang over him, appealing to all that is tender and noble in the heart of man, to arouse up in all his strength of soul, and once more become the grandest possibility in the warrior and the King!

When little Nani saw the effect of Kupule's endearments in restoring the King to himself again, she, and probably many another of the unseen sympathies, quietly returned to their several vocations once more; though neither the King nor the sharp-eyed Queen knew of the unspoken sympathy of that midnight hour, convoked in such abundance about the Kiowai o Pele. Yet was he sustained by their united prayers, though he knew not why.

"Come, Kupule! come, my darling!" And the King rose up like a roused lion, and lifted the loved Queen to his side. "Let us climb to the top of Puawai and look down upon the glorious beauty of the night. Kalani would indulge himself in once more looking down upon the star-gemmed sea, where in youngest days he loved to swim in the bay, and ride swift as a tempest upon the great surf; as Pele rides upon her lava-sea in Kilauea."

"Dear Kalani! why speak you so? Why says my Moi 'once more'?"

"There's that between us two, dear love, that prompts Kalani to speak the unhidden thoughts of his soul to-night. The hour approaches when my noble kingdom must become another's. One well may grow sad to part with this dear land; with it and you — the fairest wahine ever bestowed upon a king!"

"*Auwe! Auwe!* O my Kalani! Keep heart! Be brave! You who have always been a great warrior since your youngest childhood."

"Fear not, my noble Queen. The courage of Kalani bears a quality that never dies; a courage that ever yet has exalted itself to the utmost needs of the hour."

"Kupule has feared lest your great misfortunes should crush the brave heart that has borne you up so long."

"And still will it bear your Keiki Moi into the utmost front of battle. Bear him on, until the red plume in his proud crest goes down forever!"

"Then what means this lingering sadness, lowering like a cloud upon your kingly brow? — like the mist-veil yonder on Waolani's topmost peak?"

"It means, Kupule mine, that the world has grown wondrous fair to-night; that Kalani has come to prize existence in these last hours of life. It means that Oahu — the last Isle of my kingdom — has grown beautiful when seen in such soft repose, until Kalani's heart goes forth to her as to none else but thee — my Aloha Alii!"

"It is indeed a fair and thrifty land, engirt by blue, prolific seas. Worth the fighting for as never a *Koa Moi* — warrior king — put forth his might before."

"So will Kalani battle for his loved kingdom, and his fair young Queen. But because both are *so fair*, well may I grieve their loss. And yet, darling, you shall see Kalani fight his last, best battle, with intensest hate of war!"

" Here we are, upon the rocky battlement of frowning Puawai. What would you here, upon this grass-grown crater's rim ? "

" See ! Pele has already lit her torch of war upon far-off Loa's brow. How gleams the Hawaiian's blue throughout the red flame ! The cold and cruel Goddess has indeed forsaken Kalani — else would a red gleam pervade her volcanic flame."

" Is there word of Kamehameha's having come?"

" Ay ! there lies his fleet in Waialae Bay, countless as the screaming sea-birds along the shore. Look ! your bright eyes can see the flicker of their camp-fires among the thrifty groves of Kona. How flash their hateful gleams against the peaceful sky !"

" I see their countless fires, more numerous than the stars. How large is my father's army ? "

" Sixteen thousand : so report my spies. All trained and willing warriors, led on by many hateful *haöle* (foreigner), and commanded by an ever victorious King."

" What strength have we, spears, javelins, and slings ? "

" Not six thousand, of all arms. And many craven, unwilling curs among our ranks ; Kanakas whose nimble legs are more fleet than the mountain winds — to seek the rear."

" Is there no hope of Kaiana's yet joining our ranks ? "

" The dawn may bring his traitorous aid. But whether he come to join Oahu's army or Hawaii's, time alone can tell ; for such ambitious men poise

on too varying motives, ever changeful as the wind.
The trades blow fair from Molokai to-night, and
Kaiana's fleet must be a-wing, if ever."

" 'Tis not a noble element to trust to in such a
cause as ours. But, come or come he not, your
little Queen will take spear for Oahu, and battle
beside her King ! "

" A pretty mark for a foeman's spear! " And
with a smile of pride Kalani drew her tenderly
to his side.

" You know not how expert my maidens are with
spears. Hearing of your defeat to windward, Manona, Leleha, and I, and dozens more of our wahine Aliis, trained to great expertness."

" It would mar Kalani's battle to see thy dear
form fall bleeding at his side."

" But we have also drilled for many a day to
fence and parry, and swerve, warrior-like, from the
swiftest spear the coming foe may cast."

" Kalani's arm would palsy, fearing lest the
spear that missed himself, might sheathe itself in
thee. Ah, Love! there's something worse than
defeat — something worse than death. And my
darling Queen must not put me to the test in such
an hour as this."

" Kalani's word is ever the law of the land ; and
thy lightest wish shall rule Kupule to the end of
being. But bid me not too far away from my darling, lest my Keiki Moi go down and Kupule be
not there to see."

" Nay, not too far away; for Kalani could not

battle his best were not your loving eyes upon his deeds."

. " Where would you that I should flee, with my maidens, in that dread hour? "

" There is a woody crag bends threatening down over the narrow Pass in the Pali's gorge — as bends a lowering tempest-cloud, beetle-browed above the sea — 'tis Kalani's chosen spot to die. There shall you climb and sit to watch me fight, and — if Pele wills — to see me fall ! "

" Auwe, my Kalani ; it must be within call, lest you die and I be not there."

" So shall it be. Not where the Pali's frightful precipice overlooks the surf-lashed shore, and Koolau's flowery plain. But where the frowning mountains show a kindly wish to meet."

" It is a dismal, narrow gorge, where a few brave chiefs who dare to die, may crown themselves with glory for all coming time."

" There will our best and bravest plant their feet to fly no more. Watch from your crag and see us make our breastwork of the slaughtered foes; but when thy dear name is cried out upon the summer air, then seek Kalani, and seek him swiftly; for only when this strong arm that twines thee now shall fail me, would Kalani have you come to see him die."

" *Auwe! kuu Moi!* — Oh, my King ! — Must death then await to-morrow's battle ? "

" Death, or Victory ! "

" Poino ! poino ! (alas! alas!) O Pele ! How *can* Kupule thus give up her King ? "

" Would my brave Queen have her Warrior live to become the slave of another? "

" Rather would Kupule wail over the slaughtered manes of her Keiki Moi! "

" So be it. Our minds are one. 'Twill be no task for Oahu's warrior King to fight and die. Yet remember, that only he dies happy who looks his last aloha into the eyes he loves."

" My Moi! My Kalani! How can Kupule lose you so? "

" 'Tis best so. And look you: though I climb beyond the stars, where all is fiery splendor, yet the twin-soul of Kalani shall abide with you forever. Constant as the dawn, Kalani's dual spirit shall attend the footsteps of his darling."

" Dear Kalani! " And she twined fast about his neck with a quiver of agony, while thus contemplating her loss.

" When Kupule awakes, with the sun on Waolani, Kalani's spirit shall await her, sitting upon the mountain wrapped in the glory of the dawn. The sweet songs of the pretty *O-o* shall be as my loving voice, calling to greet thee."

" Auwe! Auwe! Must we part? "

" Hearken, dear one! thou shalt not miss the endearments of thy Kalani. Even in thy fond dreams he will pervade thy slumber; whispering his kingly love into thine ears in tones sweeter than the perfume of the wildwood flowers."

" Dear, my King! You wring Kupule's heart with anguish, picturing the dear joys so unfulfilled

with thee. And must your Queen live to look
upon the pale face of her warrior dying — dead!
slaughtered by his hated foes ? "

"So Pele has willed it. But will it not be glorious to look down from your mountain crag upon
the heaped-up dead, thick strewn about your warrior King ? "

" Would it were not so, dear Love ! Life were
so sweet with peace and plenty in this dear land
of constant summer; with thy fond love thus
wrapped about me, as wraps your golden mamo
about your darling."

" How has Kupule's love changed the whole
world to Kalani. Once thy Warrior thought
earthly happiness meant only war, war ! with no
joy so great as during the wild battle-shout, when
spears fell like hail, and sabres flashed like lightning sporting through the summer showers."

"And now you hate this war, and love your little Queen. May one not take a swift *waa* and fly
from what we hate? Is there not some remote isle
awaits us far down the blue sea in the sunset-land
of rainbows? — the dear isles where the sunset gon-
fanons will henceforth wave no more for Kalani?
Ah, let us fly ! "

" Tempt me not! Do the brave ever fly in the
face of danger? Are there not things more terrible than death to a warrior? And were we tempted
to fly, does not Pele's cruel malediction yet wave
like a banner of blood above me ? Rather help your
Koa Moi to die face to the foe, that his name shall
be linked to Oahu forever ! "

"The quick eyes of a warrior are swift to see the right. Hearts blended like ours can people what world they will with bliss. Such loves gladden all things about them, as perfumes exude from flowers to gladden the heart of Deity."

"Almost you make Kalani wish to live. Yet how to live without war has never been known in all the history of Oahu."

"True, our gods delight in war, and bloodshed is the merriest pastime of their lives. Yet the Haoles, from over the sea, tell us that their God is Aloha (Love); ever whispering to them 'Peace, peace!' all their lives long."

"What a land were Oahu — my dear, sunny Isle — with such an *Akua Nui* throned upon Waolani! A white-faced God ruling my lazy Kanakas with smiles! A gentle God crying 'Peace! eat poi and fish; eat cocoa-nut and bread-fruit, and be happy!' But it is all a dream; there is no such god as Aloha. For are not all things at war with each other? The fish war upon other fishes in the sea; the birds tear their brother birds with fierce talons; and the very gods, who rule over our land, war with each other, fighting like snarling curs before our doors."

"Can there be no truth in the *Haole's* story?"

"It cannot be; they are liars. Being white, makes men false to each other, and untruthful to Kanakas. Did not Cook — the god Lono — take many shiploads of our food for a gift, and then repay us by pulling down the sacred gods from our Temple of Lono, taking them away in his boats to burn in his mokus? (ships.) Did he not speak lies, and thus entrap the great King Kalaniopuu? Did he not kill our people because of that lie, and when they saw it they slew him?"

"See, Kalani! there glows a new light yonder, where the Hawaiian camp-fires burn. Is it a signal-light on Diamond Head?"

"No, my Queen; 'tis but a gleam of starlight close down to the ocean's rim. Pele has just flung it to the low-down sky, perhaps with a touch of lingering tenderness for Kalani."

"Would it were a token of her returning affection, then all were well with the coming day."

"Time was when the heart of your King would have gladdened to be thus remembered. But the blood-thirsty *wahine Akua*—woman god—of Kilauea has already done her worst for Kalani; though she should relent of her cruelty, it is too late. I'll no more of her fickle love this side of Po. Almost would Kalani rather love the white man's God than her."

"Hush! dear Kalani. There bursts an angry flame from far-off Loa, because of your impious taunts of the nation's god. Forbear, my King; there is no wisdom in rejecting the love of the gods — be they good or evil. We err, who scorn the love of any. Keep all resentful feelings deep buried in your heart — 'tis but for a day."

"*Poino! wahine Moi;* has it not compassed your woman's wisdom that Pele resents one's *thoughts* as well as one's word? In my deep heart I did

22

but think, ' If Pele but loved me as of old ; ' when, behold, she flung down the white-faced Astarte from her hand, in instant answer to my thoughts."

" And will you not love the Goddess for the deed ? "

" Not I. She flung the pretty star of Aloha disdainfully down from her mountain throne, as one flings a stale fish to a dog. Seeing how Kalani scorns her laggard love — now that she has reft him of his Windward Isles — behold, how she thrusts her baneful war-torch into the midnight sky ; urging the hateful Hawaiians on to combat."

" Dear Kalani, is it not rather a proffering of her love ; a signal to warn my King of to-morrow's approaching war, when my Keiki Moi shall fill the world with fame? Is this not kind in the good Pele ? "

" Nay, nay ! It is a signal for Kamehameha to quicken his march. See you not the hateful tinge of purple in the flame? Pele has not forgotten the red plume worn in Kalani's crest ; nor the red flame that erst lit her young warrior to battle, ere that dread night before we fought Keao."

" But, ah ! what more than mother's love to let you win that battle, and slay Keao. Who shall say but Pele loves you yet ? "

" Let her keep her loitering love, and bring on her hateful war. Love and war are the heritage of kings. Kalani grows impatient, waiting to fight his last battle. I have wrestled with it so often in my slumbers, that the shrieks of combat are ever ringing in my ears, as when the night winds howl on Loa's snow-clad mountain top."

"Auwe, Kalani! Has thy troubled sleep been thus invaded?"

"Ay. Kalani has planned his battle scheme so frequently, and died his coming death so often, that the ghost of Oahu's King invades his waking vision, as it pervades his dreams. Thus, while yet alive, Kalani has seen his own grim Shade stalking over the land, like yonder huge Shadow-dark flung down by Waolani's topmost peak."

"What is yon light, flashing up so hastily from Leahi's jagged crest?"

"'Tis the watchfire's warning. What it means I know not; for Hawaii's army would surely march with Pele's first signal from Mauna Loa."

"Is all in readiness to receive Kamehameha?"

"As ready as ever the few can be to receive the many; the weak to receive the strong. Yet there is the might of a thousand warriors in my own right arm to-night."

"You look a very hero in the starlight!"

"Kupule, watch from your high perch on Waolani with calm, remembering eyes, that when Kalani is gone, you can relate his warlike deeds in the Pali. I would not that Kamehameha should deem Oahu's warrior King had lost the art of war. In future tranquil times, dear love, whisper some of my great deeds into the willing ear of the Lonely One, for 'tis said his ugly heart ever gladdens at the recital of valiant deed."

"Never two loving eyes can watch as will Kupule's, that she may recount thy glorious battle to the world, and whisper of thy mighty deeds to Kamehameha. I know my giant father better than my King can do. He'll weep hot tears to see you dead. For beneath his rugged breast lies a massive heart, tender as a wahine's to the touch of sorrow."

"I would my cunning *pahi* might make a scabbard of it! 'Tis an ugly, hateful heart to me; robbing me of my kingdoms and my love; my liberty or my life. Kamehameha has stood between me and Pele since childhood's hour. His name withers upon my tongue, and curdles the hot blood in my veins. Kalani asks but life to lay him low; and failing that, to heap the mightest heap of dead Hawaiians the conqueror's eyes e'er looked upon!"

"*Auwe! Auwe!* Is not that the glitter of spears marching along Waikiki's shore?"

"It is, indeed! Their countless footsteps hasten on to battle. An hour more will flood Nuuanu's dear loved vale with fiercest fiends. But we will linger yet on Puawai to observe the Hawaiians to the last."

"Darling! what is yonder long black line just rounding the dark crag of Leahi, winging along the white surf like low-flying sea-birds?"

"Ha! There comes Kaiana's friendly fleet, hastening with laboring paddle and favoring sail down from Molokai. 'Tis a goodly sight to Kalani!"

"What force does he bring to our aid?"

"As near as this dim light permits, I count an hundred well-filled canoes — full three thousand Hawaiian warriors to aid Oahu's little band. This is indeed a proof of Pele's love that Kalani will die remembering."

"Kupule's heart is made glad to see her King thus relent toward Deity."

"Kupule, dear, sweet love! this glad sight unfolds a task for thee. Are you fleet of foot, and can you bear a war-message to noble Boki?"

"Swifter than the white-bellied albatross will Kupule fly to bear Kalani's word, and joy to do his kingly bidding!"

And the King took Kupule into his arms for a last strong embrace before he could reply; covered her winsome face with kisses, and almost losing heart to part with her. As one clings to the loved dying, so clung the noble King to his darling. But it must be done, and he gave her his message and sped her tearfully away.

"Brave, sweet Queen! You have been my sole comfort in these dark hours. You shall be my watchword through the battle; my latest watchword when I fall!"

"Dear Kalani! I am repaid for all my love by this your kingly preference. Love Pele, and die bravely; and I will watch to see thee die!"

"Darling Queen! Kalani's fiery heart heaves like an ocean-billow, so troubled to part with you this side the stars. But war will rend many

another heart besides our own to-day. Fly to the
camp across the valley. Tell noble Boki that
Kaiana speeds down Waikiki reef with an army
to aid us. Let him meet my uncle, — *call him not
Traitor to-day!* — meet him at Honolulu, and
assign the Hawaiians to the left wing ; the farthest
remove from the coming presence of their fierce
old King — lest they run like whipped curs with
fear of his ugly frown. Now fly, dear Love, with
Kalani's latest kiss on lip and brow ! "

" Oh, Kalani ! Love was not made for such
partings ! "

" Stay ! One more last kiss — another — away !
lest I fling my sword down the steep mountain,
and hide me in the forest wilds with very hate of
death and war. Aloha ! my wahine Moi ! "

" Aloha ! my Keiki Moi ! my darling ! "

And Kupule sped away like a fawn, sobbing
audibly as she ran through the starlit crater, leaving Kalani still watching the progress of the Hawaiian army from the top of Punch Bowl.

CHAPTER XVIII.

" Well, Chiefs! Kaiana 's joined the foe :
    Doth thus our kingly gifts repay.
But cheer, my Braves, let Traitors go,
    He shall not cause an hour's delay.
Who here on fair Oahu's shore
But hopes to win, or would our force were more ?
Who wills to fight — we show the way :
Who craven feels — here let him stay :
Now march ! this land is ours ere ends the day ! "

AMEHAMEHA did not delay an instant because of Kaiana's desertion from his army. But seeing that his arrogant and ambitious war-chief did not arrive in due time from the camp at Molokai, he marched upon the enemy all the earlier, in hopes to intercept the deserters ere they could land at Honolulu, and endeavor to prevent Kaiana's joining forces with the army of Oahu.

But they had seen the fleet of Kaiana pass them as they marched with swift strides up Waikiki beach. And when day dawned, and the Hawaiians were marching up the Nuuanu, it was discovered that the deserters were already blended with the army of Oahu, where they awaited

343

silently and sullenly the coming of their country-
men.

Leaving a guard to take possession of Kaiana's
fleet of canoes, Kamehameha marched his whole
army of thirteen thousand men up the valley. As
he approached quite near to the intrenched forces
of Oahu, he ordered a halt, and with the utmost
precision and celerity formed his centre into a
great phalanx, with the two wings of the army
formed in double lines on either hand.

Within the great hollow square were Kamehameha and his staff of chiefs, among them numerous
white men, trained to arms. Prominent among
the latter was John Young, the English boatswain,
and Isaac Davis, with their battery of four small
brass cannon, which had previously been the
means of winning several battles — naval and
land-fought — and subsequently became the turn-
ing-point, by breaching the ramparts, on this
terrible day.

In command of the centre, where were stationed
Kamehameha's regiment of giant guards, was the
gigantic Keeaumoku, noted for his immense
strength and prowess in war. This great warrior
bore the cognomen of the " Yellow-backed Crab,"
a name bestowed upon him after his cruel assassi-
nation of prince Keoua, and seven other brave
chiefs, who had laid down their arms and surrendered, after promise of safety from Kamehameha. As this foul deed upon so many great
chiefs was perpetrated in the presence of Kameha-

meha, it must ever remain a blot upon his usually
truthful and humane character. Keeaumoku had
from the first rendered his new King the most distinguished services of any of his great chiefs, and
was from that time forth the foremost general and
head councillor of Kamehameha, and also the
father of his favorite " Love Queen," the famous
Kaahumanu who proved the most remarkable
woman of her nation.

The right wing was commanded by Kalaimoku,
(Billy Pitt,) a relative of Kalani, and a brother of
Boki. But having been taken prisoner in one of
the long previous Hawaiian wars, Kamehameha
saved his life, which so won upon the grateful
warrior that he ever after adhered to his new
King. He was now second in rank to Keeaumoku,
and having a sagacious mind, and being a wise
statesman, as well as warrior, he was soon after
made prime minister in place of Kaiana — who
had just deserted — and also became Governor of
Oahu after the capture.

Kameeimoku, another formidable and ferocious
chief, presided over the left wing. It was this
savage giant who captured the " Fair American "
and threw Captain Metcalf and his crew over-
board to the sharks; young Isaac Davis being the
only one who was spared. To that vessel belonged
three of the cannon now in battery before the
ramparts.

In connection with this outrage it is due to
Kamehameha to say that he was highly indignant

with Kameeimoku, and shed tears while reproving
the fierce chief. But because of this maritime
outrage, the King himself detained John Young
that very day, lest the captain of the *Elenora*
should learn of the loss of his tender, and revenge
himself upon the town, as he had done with terrible effect upon a less occasion at Maui. After
firing guns off the bay for two days, and seeing
nothing of Young, the *Elenora* sailed away. From
that hour Young's history became closely inter-
woven with Kamehameha's, and he conduced
more to the conquest of the Islands than any of
the great chiefs.

When the army was thus formed in its great
central square, which was considered proof against
any attack that could be brought to bear, with its
double columns formed for attack upon the two
wings, Kamehameha ordered an advance close up
to the rampart wall of coral rock, behind which
Kalani, Kaumualii, and Kaiana had marshalled
their combined forces from the three Islands.

Calling a halt, Naihe, the smooth-tongued
orator and diplomatist of Hawaii, was sent forth to
offer peace, and agree upon terms of surrender.
In his hand he bore a large *ti* leaf, as a flag of
truce, and being seven feet in height and gracefully proportioned, he looked the suave and polite
courtier that he was.

Boki, the commander-in-chief under Kalani, was
sent forward to meet Naihe, and negotiate for the
surrender of the Windward Islands, if that could

be accomplished. The two chiefs met midway between the armies, both generals being unarmed.
Never were two diplomats more gracious and
persuasive in manner and mien than were these
mighty chiefs, though boiling over with hatred
against the opposing army.

Naihe argued that his great king had wept because of the rivers of blood already shed. Adding
that Kamehameha loved Kalani as a brother, and
was captivated by his heroism in battle ; and would
assign him honorable captivity should he surrender.

The Hawaiian entered into a lofty and weighty
argument against the possibility of Oahu's imper-
fect army winning against such great odds. Each
chief introducing himself as follows :

" Aloha ! kiekie Alii ! (Love to you, noble chief!)
I am Naihe, the great orator of Hawaii, and a councillor to my King. Kamehameha, the mighty king
of all the Windward Islands — by right of conquest — requests me to speak kindly to your young
King about a peaceful surrender of Oahu."

Boki bowed politely and replied : ";Aloha! Naihe,
ke kiekie Alii ! The warrior before you is Boki,
the commander-in-chief under the mighty King,
and a councillor of the nation. We esteem it a
duty to offer Kamehameha any courtesy he comes
to ask. If your noble King and his fine army have
come to visit Kalani, and return in peace, after receiving our recognition of your right by conquest
to the Windward Islands, we shall be glad to entertain you royally. But if you come to seek another

kingdom, you surprise us. If you come for war, you amaze us. For when did the ears of a Hawaiian ever hear of a chief of Oahu crying for peace, or declining the pleasure of a combat?"

"Most noble Boki, you are a great Orator; a man of wit. I admire you, I am sure we should be friends. This valley of Nuuanu is indeed a pleasant place, a fine place for a *Kauaawa* — bitter contest. With this pretty stream babbling through it, it must remind the great Boki of the Wailuku, in the terrible 'Vale of Iao;' where we dammed up the waters with your dead braves."

"Naihe has a fine eye for beauty. Your mountains of Hawaii are a trifle taller than ours; but such a Valley as this is not to be found. Nuuanu is indeed the place we most love; the place where our mighty warrior, the King, and his *Kapu Aliis* mean to live, and — by your leave — mean to die. Whoever comes to take the beautiful Nuuanu from us, will see a worse *Kapaniwai* than that in the dismal Vale of Iao, where, if our memory serves us right, there were more dead Hawaiians *Stopping the Waters*, than of our people."

"Noble Boki! how fleeting a thing is memory. Let me hope that the lost battle of Kohala, where we destroyed your whole fleet, has not been forgotten?"

"I believe some little misfortune did happen to us there, all from want of due preparation; and your having the Britannia and the three cannon which you stole from the haoles. But the event was of so trifling a nature that it has long been forgotten by our warriors. Strange you should still remember that slight affair ! "

" We have often inquired in our camp why the army of Oahu left Maui with such nimble legs after the last battle ? "

" Auwe ! Did it seem to you that we left with any degree of haste ? Ah, yes, there were matters of importance calling us to Oahu."

" We are to have a fine day for a little brush; and as you are at home, there will be nothing to call you hurriedly away from battle."

" Be sure, Naihe, we will entertain you well to-day."

" Confess your admiration of our powerful army ; and our having those terrible guns of the haole's must make you Oahuans tremble."

" It is indeed a fine army ; but Kaiana, who is on a little visit to us, has just told us that you have but little *okaoka* (powder) for your big yellow cannon, so they are like big yellow dogs with but very small barks — *what a pity !* "

" It would not be well for your king to take the word of a vile Traitor, in such matters. These cannon will make a fine frolic knocking down your flimsy wall. They would even knock a hole through the Waolani, if we wished it."

" Indeed, Naihe, we do all admire your big guns ; they are of the color of the mamos of kings, and make a sweet noise and a pretty dust when animated. But what a pity you have so little *okaoka* to make them howl in the air."

"But the morning is passing, and we must soon fight it out. Now what shall I say to my King about this matter?"

"Say to the mighty Kamehameha, that, rather than surrender more than you have already taken, we are prepared to die fighting for our fair Isle of Oahu."

"I regret to take back such a message to Kamehameha, for the wrath of the 'Lonely One' is terrible to look upon. But I think we shall have a fine day for a good battle. Aloha! Come and take a calabash of poi and a fine mullet with Naihe, if convenient after the battle."

"Aloha! kiekie Naihe.. And if *your wounds* are troublesome at the end of the fray, I'll see to it they are well dressed by doctor Koleamoko."

Politely bowing to each other, with many genial smiles, the two chiefs returned to their respective kings; and ere the sun went down that day the one great chief was lying dead in the Pali's gorge, and his Leleha dead by his side; and the other was badly wounded by a fearful sword-cut inflicted by his diplomatic brother of the morning.

When Naihe communicated to Kamehameha the untoward result of his mission, the savage old King frowned till his massive forehead fluted like the corrugated front of a volcano, and he roared forth his orders for battle in the voice of a maelstrom.

In an instant all was bustle and commotion among the Hawaiians. The front of this square was now opened by the guards deploying to the right and left, and assuming positions convenient for again quickly closing up the phalanx in case of a strong sortie from the fort. This movement discovered the battery to the Oahuans stationed along the ramparts, though the cannon had already been seen by Kalani and his chiefs from their elevation upon the hillside.

Kalani had assumed this position upon the rising ground to overlook the battle, and was now seen giving his last orders to Boki, Kaumualii, Kaiana, and Paoa. And while the two former hastened down to the ranks to assume their commands, the two latter remained with the King watching the Hawaiian preparations for attack.

Kalani was dressed in state on this occasion of opening the battle, as was his gigantic rival opposite upon the knoll. The young King had his golden mamo over his shoulders, and his helmet glittering with yellow feathers upon his head; from its crest waved a small crimson plume, composed of the red spike-feathers of the tropic birds' tails. He was personating the commander-in-chief to-day, presiding over the whole army, in imitation of a custom brought into use by Kamehameha.

Kamehameha wore a gay-colored calico shirt under his magnificent feather war-cloak, which, being larger and deeper, was more costly than Kalani's — as it had taken " nine generations of kings to fabricate this superb garment." The head of this monstrous man was surmounted by a

lofty helmet, elegantly composed of yellow feathers and decorated with the choicest seed-pearls —
the rarest gems their divers had gathered during a
thousand years.

The shirt was a present from Vancouver, who
also gave him his ponderous sword and costly
dagger, together with a British suit of scarlet
regimentals, ostentatiously trimmed with gold lace,
and the epaulets of a general. This the huge
King often wore upon state occasions.

But war was no child's play with Kamehameha,
he who subsequently aspired to capture Tahiti,
thousands of miles away over seas. Thus in time
of action, he was always dressed prepared to take
a leading hand in the forefront of battle, if it came
to the worst. It was but the work of a moment
to throw off his war-cloak, leaving him with nothing but his new-fangled shirt, and the usual malo
about the loins, worn by all men. In other days
he fought in a complete state of nature; but
having now assumed that the weapon of man
could never wound his body, the shirt was worn
to hide the wound received at the cannonading, at
the time of Cook's death — for he was an actor in
that scene, — also to hide the scar from a paddle-
blade made during a battle with Kiwalao. But
more than all, it was worn to hide the deadly
wound inflicted by young Kalani, when the Boy
King made his raid on Hilo Bay and left the old
King dead on his palace floor, from which death-
swoon none but the divine Pele could have recovered him.

Seen, as now, with his lofty helmet upon his head, and clothed in his great mamo, so large that it trailed upon the ground, no one could look upon this herculean King without a thrill of admiration, at beholding such fine symmetry in one so massive. Kamehameha seemed gifted with an intellect as capacious as his body. When unbent from command he seemed humane, and sagacious, and kind-hearted, and won instantly upon all who approached him in such hours. Titanic in stature as he was, yet the great King awed one more by the eagle glance of his dark piercing eyes, and by a certain awful majesty of presence, than by his stupendous proportions.

But seen as now, when his ire was lit up, till it flamed like that on Loa's brow, while he was receiving Naihe's version of Boki's saucy reply to the demand for surrender, especially when he listened to Boki's sarcastic taunts about their being short of powder for the cannon — as they really were — his vast figure towered loftier than ever. His coal-black eyes flashed fire with every imprecation he uttered, and his savage glances penetrated the boldest chief who approached him in that moment.

No wonder Naihe dreaded to take a saucy rebuff to his King, for his fury was fearful to look upon. His huge nostrils dilated, and rose and fell like a mettled charger's. And a savage, ruthless pride, and murderous meaning, was imparted to his every angry gesture. He belched forth his orders,

23

voiced like the mutterings of an earthquake, so
loud and hoarse and angry, that they echoed back
from the jutting crags overhanging the camp of
the foe, reverberating from cliff to cliff like remote
thunder. All this display of savage frenzy, in the
ferocious King, was seen to make a strong impression upon Kaiana and his Hawaiian deserters,
which boded no good for Oahu's cause.

But Kalani, being of a temperament incapable
of fear, was seen to enjoy the frightful mood of his
mammoth rival. Though the face of the Boy King
was flushed, and his nostrils were dilated almost
as much as were his foe's, yet it was the flush
and quickened respiration of a born warrior, impatient as a leashed hound for the coming clash of
arms.

Not in all those armies of heroic men was there
a figure so noble, a presence so elegant and com-
manding, a chief so calm and yet full of such concentrated heroism, as Kalani, the lineal descendant
of a long line of warrior kings. Descending
from the Spanish cavalier, wrecked on Pele Point
at Hawaii, centuries before Cook rediscovered the
Islands, his hair, like that of most of his ancestors,
had the wavy terminal curl of the noble Hidalgo
of long ago.

Boki, the next in rank to Kalani, was resolute,
and as full of fiery ardor as ever, in spite of the
preponderance of men and arms against them, yet
he knew nothing of the prophetic doom that hung
like an unseen pall over his beloved companion

and King. Kaumualii was as pale as his olive complexion would permit, for it was an open secret that the effeminate king of Kauai was no lover of war, and now seeing Kamehameha so savage — for it was Napoleonic in that age for great leaders to personify rage on such occasions — it had the effect to cause Kaumualii's nervous fingers to unconsciously pluck the rare *iiwi* feathers from his kingly mamo, as a rejected lover pilfers the petals from his recent rose-gift.

Kaiana stood sullen and savage beside Kalani, and being seven feet in height, had a little advantage of the King in that respect. The fiery chief was sumptuously arrayed in a rich red mamo; for though a great chief, a mighty warrior and brother of a king, yet he was not of sufficient rank to wear the royal yellow — a privilege only conferred upon kings.

No one can envy Kaiana his situation or his feelings as he stood there confronting his late lord and king; a traitor, and deserter, from one who had ever been a kind benefactor to him. Now his conscience was rebuking him, for his military sagacity must have convinced him that the Oahuans had a hopeless task, fighting against such great odds in numbers and discipline. He well knew that the battle must end in victory or death for him.

All being in readiness to open the battle by endeavoring to breach the ramparts, through which to assault the Oahuans, Kamehameha directed Young to open fire directly upon the coral wall, in

line with Kalani and his group of chiefs upon the
hill above. As the distance was short, and they
could fire a plunging shot, every discharge from the
battery told heavily upon the porous coral rock,
until stone by stone were knocked steadily away;
and a good-sized opening was fast being made.

Kamehameha now ordered up a column from
each wing, to be held in readiness to advance before the central column of assault, and draw the
fire of the Oahuans before the real attack was made.
Boki and Kaumualii were in command of the centre and right wing, awaiting to oppose the threatened onset. Kalani and numerous chiefs still kept
their position to overlook the coming assault.

Kamehameha now called Young to his side, leaving Davis and other foreigners to keep up the can-
nonade. Drawing his long two-edged sword, he
pointed with his ponderous blade where stood
Oahu's King and chiefs upon the hillside. History
records Kamehameha as saying :

" Young, my *Puua hele* (bosom-friend), see you
where yon beetle-browned Traitor stands ? "

" Ay! Sire. To the right of Oahu's gallant
King."

" I'm growing maddened, looking at the Villain!
Try your pretty guns on the Traitor, who stands
there frowning upon his King and benefactor. Kill
me the troublesome fellow! and you shall be made
an *Alii Kapu nui*, upon the spot."

" I'll try, my King ; but would you have me risk
harming the noble Kalani ? "

"Kill me the big Kauaian!" exclaimed the old king impetuously, "for I'm *huhu nui!* (much mad.)   And let the gods protect Kalani."

Returning to the battery, Young loaded his own favorite piece and elevated the gun to its utmost lift, high up over the rampart wall and the mass of heads and spears beyond, until it trained upon the high ledge where stood Kalani and the chiefs. Kneeling on the grass, Young trained his gun with the utmost precision upon the royal group, who, though witnessing all his doings, were far too proud and fearless to skulk behind the numerous sheltering rocks above and around them.

Rising from the ground, Young swung his portfire to impart more certain glow, freshened his priming and fired his gun.   As the torch was applied there came a flash, a double echo, and a crash resilient from crag to crag ; followed by a long-drawn reverberation converging back from the two mountain-walls of the valley.   So dissonant and deafening were the sounds, that all were impressed that something had been struck and shattered, creating a wild confusion among the Oahuans ; and causing a mournful, piteous wailing from their ranks, as if the King himself had been killed.

But as yet the results could only be guessed, for the sulphurous smoke of the gun rolled in a gyrating cloud over the scene — now swayed to the one side by the demoniacal shouts of the invaders, and now recoiling back from the grievous wail of the afflicted — rising at length slowly and majestically

over the rampart wall, over the glittering spear-
points of the soldiers, over the green grass plots
and gray lava rocks, until it became evident that
the ball had struck and splintered the rock whereon
stood the King and Kaiana; leaving the one untouched, while the other lay weltering in his gore
— dead on the day of his iniquity.   Not another
chief in all that dense group of nobles was harmed.

Wild and delirious were the shouts from ten
thousand Hawaiian warriors, made joyous by the
knowledge that Kaiana had fallen.   For there are
no public recreants more generally hated than a
traitor ! — a deservedly great soldier deserting his
general in the hour of battle.

Even Kamehameha flung up his gigantic arms
with grim delight; unbending for a moment from
his savage frown, until his ugly visage lighted up
with sardonic laughter — as a distant storm-cloud
may blush with fitful lightning in an hour of gathering wrath.

But not for a moment did the ferocious king forget the object of the hour, for instantly brandishing
his glittering sword in the morning sun, he gave
the preconcerted signal for the assault.   And while
yet the columns were hastening to the breach, the
grim devotee turned his flashing black eyes upon
the blue, volcanic flame on far-off Loa, and with
extended arms reverently thanked the good Pele
for her divine interposition in his favor, making his
oblation aloud, in the savage gladness of his heart.

Next to Pele, there was yet another to thank.

Flinging off his saffron-colored mamo upon the green-sward at his feet, and shaking his ponderous blade hungrily in the air — as if his murderous heart was famishing for battle — Kamehameha called lustily for Young. As he came from his battery the King bade him kneel to receive his knighthood, and title to the imperial rank of Kapu Alii — Tabu Chief.

As Young advanced, he exclaimed : " A Chiefdom ! Sire, I've laid the Traitor low ! "

" Ay ! my *Puua hele.* He lies half torn in two ; cleft well as our good blade could do. Good Pele sent the missile there, the beautiful Goddess of Kilauea. Kneel, *haole maikai* (good foreigner), though time be brief, we name you Keone Ana ! — Chief ! — a noble and a brave. Now up and batter down yon wall, for we begin to war-like feel, and would have at them if at all."

> From Ana's shoulder snatched his sword,
> That just had made him noble lord ;
> Rough shook its blade of pond'rous length
> As if he longed to try its strength.

Turning to the Chief of his central column, who yet waited the King's signal to advance, the elated old Monarch shouted :

"*E hele !* Hawaii! " (advance, Hawaii !) " Who wins yon breach the battle wins ! "

His hoarse voice rang loud above the utmost clang of battle, as a hundred lusty chiefs sprang to the front, and led their spears-men serf into the ragged opening through the rampart wall ; until a

thousand wolfish men were pressing on to enter
where not fifty could pass in line.

Such was the favorable opening for the Hawaiians, and the ominous dread thrown over the allied
armies of Oahu, that every serf belonging to Kaiana's deserters, followed by thousands from among
the Oahuans, broke ranks and fled over the far end
of the rampart, and up the Nuuanu to the Pali's
gorge; flying with a panic-stricken terror that
lent the utmost speed to their sudden flight.

Grief and uncontrollable indignation filled Kalani and his chiefs, to behold the paltry cowards
run so prematurely, before even a blow had been
struck to mar their ranks — except the death of
Kaiana. But around the breach the great chiefs
drew, gathering undismayed about their young
King who had led them to battle so often, and for
hours the clash of steel and the rattle of spears
rang high.

It mattered little how impetuously the disci[*]
plined Hawaiians flung themselves into the breach,
or attempted to scale the rampart wall ; they were
everywhere met with equal bravery and equal skill
for long hours of terrible conflict. The rude shelter behind which the Oahuans fought, made their
lesser numbers long able to resist the ceaseless onset of fresh Hawaiians, which Kamehameha continued to hurl with savage fury against the breach.

Thus the forenoon passed, and thousands lay
dead or wounded about the broken wall ; yet un-
glutted war still raged with unabated fury. Un-

daunted the trained Hawaiians sprang into the breach, and unweariedly were they hewn down by the great chiefs of the allied armies, who toward the last were compelled to take the front of battle.

By Boki's side his fair Leleha fought, serving her blows with skill, and defending herself and him she loved with a subtle cunning known to but few stalwart braves. The foe who doth her Chief assail is sure to feel Leleha's spite. And whoever in that fierce melee aimed an ungallant blow at Boki's spouse, feels Boki's avenging blow upon his undefended head, and falls to fight no more.

> So would the brindled Lion fight,
>   Should hounds try fierce his mate to tear;
> Thus show his whelpless mate her might
>   On all who dare invade their lair.

On high was heard Kalani's voice, checking or cheering his overwilling chiefs. His orders rang like bugle-notes, clear and shrill over the din of battle. Not often was his strong and skilful arm needed to take part in the varying fight. But when the valorous King did see a foeman worthy of his steel come slashing his murderous way though all who were opposing him, then Kalani's flashing mamo was from his shoulder cast, and wild and wicked were the deeds of daring our Keiki Moi accomplished.

With the breach free from such untoward pressure, Kalani would fall back to his place of observation and again direct the battle along the line; but with ever an impulse to spring forward again

whenever another great chief of unusual skill succeeded in breaking through the mad waves of
frenzied men and gleaming steel.

Resuming his mamo, which some chief had looked
after, and sheathing his dripping sword, the young
King would seek out some position to overlook
the defence, from which he could send reinforce-
ments here and there as need demanded.

Once Keone Ana and Kalani fought for a moment; Young, exulting with his new rank, having
hewn his way through the breach. But these
two most skilled swordsmen were soon forced
apart before either had half the fight they wished
in which to show their skill. For the surrounding
chiefs — each side fearful for their loved leader —
pressed forward in eager haste, compelling the
two cunning combatants to separate and fall back,
or seek some meaner foe. For it was not a time to
waste one's skill on special choice; but an hour in
which to lay your nearest neighbor low, and bide
your time to show your skill on some proud head
of more exalted breed.

It was soon after discovered that Keone Ana had
been recalled from the breach, and was planting
his battery against the extreme right wing of the
rampart. Keeaumoku being left to assail the
breach, while Kamehameha had himself gone to
make a new opening, having his body-guards in
reserve if needed. This precaution showed a real
meaning to break through the rampart instead of
being the feint it was thought to be.

Kaumualii was reinforced with all his Kauains, and left to meet the emergency as best he could, as it might prove to be only a feint to draw off some of the best troops from the main battle. An hour passed, and a new breach was opened. Then a furious assault was made by the guard, led on by Kamehameha himself, sweeping all before them in an instant.

Hark to the mad yells that fill the new-made breach! Hark to Kamehameha's giant tread! the hugest monster of all among his thousand guards. The " Lonely One " has come to teach the swiftest blow to heart and head. His very shout appalls! — bellowing hoarser than adjacent thunder — throwing a sudden palsy over the already defected Kauains, who fall confusedly back to the right hand and the left, crying out like cravens, " *Luka lua! Luka lua!* " — beaten, beaten! — and surrender with a cry for mercy.

Kaumualii, being slightly wounded in the attack, was taken prisoner by Kamehameha himself. This was a consummation more to the liking of the timid young King of Kauai than fighting such a tigerish foe, for which he had little constitutional taste at any time. Before night this feminine young King contrived to escape to Kauai, and lived to rule years over his Island Kingdom.*

* Years after Kamehameha gathered an army of seven thousand well-equipped men to take Kauai, but a contagious disease assailed them, and broke up the expedition. But fourteen years after the battle of Nuuanu, Kaumualii came voluntarily in

Thus the battle of Nuuanu was lost in an instant
through the feeble resistance of the Kauaians, commanded by their cowardly King. Kalani saw what
had happened, and well knowing that his decimated forces could not contend in open field with
the well-drilled Hawaiians, called Boki and Paao
to his side. It was at once decided to call off their
remaining warriors, and retreat steadily up the
valley to the Pali. This was the favorite gorge
which they had previously chosen, where the few
could meet the many, and where they could hold
out to the last man, yielding the inaccessible Pass
only with their lives.

When it was known among the worn and
wounded remnant of Oahu's army that Kamehameha had broken through their rampart, round the
hill to the right, and that he was leading his awful
guard of herculean warriors down upon their rear,
at least another thousand of Oahu's timid serfs
broke ranks and ran for their lives.

But there yet remained to Kalani four hundred
invincible chiefs who loved the clang of battle as
they loved their lives; these, with nearly a thousand acceptable warriors, were now called off from
defending the breach, and led by a mountain path
around the left wing of the rampart, leaving the

---

an American ship, and ceded his island to Kamehameha, who
reinstated him as King to rule in fiefdom. But Liholiho, Kamehameha II., afterward abducted Kaumualii, and married both
him and *his son* to his father's "Love Queen," Kaahumanu,
keeping him a state prisoner.

whole Hawaiian army to crowd through the deserted breach, and take possession of the camp.

By doing this the Hawaiians lost their only opportunity of heading off the retreat of the Oahuans to their stronghold in the Pali. But it was not supposed Kalani designed retreating up the valley, but rather over the mountain into the district of Waialua, and thence, perhaps, to Ewa Bay, where he might have had canoes stationed to take him and his army to Kauai. This plan was feasible, but that his plan had ever been from the first inception to retreat to the Pali, and there fight to the death, defending the last rood of his dear vanquished land.

"Hark ye, my braves!" — His dark eyes shone,
His voice was like a bugle-tone;
He looked to th' white man's God on high
For aid divine, yet knew not why;
But soft within his heathen heart
The voice of God was then impart.
He kissed his blade, all dun with gore,
As in the Pali's gorge he swore: —

"Hark ye, my braves! I swear to all
    On this red brand my father wore —
    This sword I oft have stained with gore —
Here will we fighting win or fall!
Who would not rather fight and die
Beneath some fond and loving eye,
Than make them blush to see us fly?"

He paused for breath: his chieftains cheer,
    And swear to die the death of braves;
Saw down the vale their foes appear,
    And sent the loved ones to their slaves.

"They come! my chiefs; hark! to their hateful call;
'Tis true our little band is small,
    And Hawaii's warriors strong and many;
But there 'll be less of us to fall,
    And few to tell the tale — if any!

Now let each blade to battle leap!
In foeman's heart each steel shall sleep!
Let every arm, with latest blow,
Pierce to the hilt some hated foe!"

CHAPTER XIX.

HEN the Hawaiians saw that Kalani had fairly withdrawn his forces along a narrow mountain path, where not more than three abreast could follow, they be-lieved he was fleeing not only from the camp, but was endeavoring to leave the Island. Thus Kamehameha sent on Keeaumoku with his division of two thousand strong, to harass the retreat and discover Kalani's destination.

The remaining part of the Hawaiian army were suffered to occupy the camp of Oahu, and partake of such food as could be found for famished men. But what was their surprise and annoyance to soon after observe Kalani's army leaving the western mountain side, and crossing over the Nuuanu in the direction of the Pali, which, it was at once surmised, had been fortified and provisioned for a siege.

The Hawaiians were at once called off from their half-eaten dinner, re-formed, and sent on in hasty pursuit, with orders to overtake and give battle to the fugitives, with a determined purpose to crush the little army before they could reach the mountain Pass. Kalani had debouched into the valley

367

through a narrow pass easily defended by his small
rear-guard in charge of Boki; thus Keeaumoku was
held in check while the main body crossed over the
Nuuanu on their way up to Waolani's sheltering
Pass.

Kamehameha, Keone Ana, and Hewahewa the
High Priest, remained behind with the Guard to
finish their dinner, for all believed the main fighting was over, and that Kalani's design was only to
secure a mountain covert from which he could make
better terms of surrender. Thus even the Hawaiian
King deemed the day was won, and remained leisurely behind, smoking, and relating valorous inci-
dents of the storming of the rampart, little dreaming that more than two thousand of his warriors
must yet fall before Oahu's heroic King was subdued in death.

When Kalani saw the Hawaiians leave the camp
on the double-quick, endeavoring to cut him off, he
feared for his rear-guard, which was holding Keeaumoku at bay. Halting in a strong position which
covered his retreat to the Pali, he sent back a swift
runner with orders for Boki to withdraw and fall
quickly back upon the main army which awaited
him; for he chose to risk a battle, rather than the
safety of his loved commander.

By a swift retreat Boki succeeded in reaching a
position within supporting distance of the King,
and then fell steadily back until the Oahuans were
all combined once more, and they might have fallen
quickly back into the protection of the Pali. But

because the now concentrated force of Hawaiians pressed on so heedlessly, as though following a rout of panic-stricken foes, Kalani manœuvred, and drew them into a position where he could hold both flanks with ambushed columns, and then brought to a stand and closed in upon the unsuspecting enemy — and terrible was the slaughter that followed.

Planting himself in the very fore-front of his central column of huge chiefs, — the finest fighters in the world, — Kalani sought not to spare himself in the least. Hewing his way into the thickest of the melee, he smote the foe who nearest pressed ; and as many a daring chief leaped from the Hawaiian ranks to cross swords with Oahu's gallant King, many a noble warrior went down in that hour before the resistless blows of him who was famed to be the finest fighter among their Isles.

Though it is evident that Kalani brought on the battle before reaching the Pass, with intent to make it his last fight, yet survivors tell us that never seemed the Boy King so cool and wary as in that awful slaughter. Like a row of monstrous Gladiators stood his great chiefs around him, striking no blows at random to waste their strength ; but where they smote, the leaping crimson ran, until the dead bodies of noble chieftains strewed the mountain path by which Kalani retreated.

Brave, worn, and wounded, Kalani and his chiefs withdrew at length from sheer exhaustion, so overpressed by numbers. Their footsteps dyed the green herbage and mountain flowers along the

24

path they climbed, still face to the foe ; their dripping wounds pooling their noble blood upon the
rocks wherever they stood at bay.

Thus they fought, and then retreated, until of
all their thousands arrayed in order of battle at
dawn, there were now but three hundred chiefs
remaining, though numbering their noblest and
their best, together with a few hundred wounded
warriors from the ranks, men already too sickened
to fight more, from loss of strength and loss of
courage.

At length in Waolani's rock-ribbed Pass they
stand a heroic band of large-limbed, large-hearted
braves. Though weary and wounded, and hopeless to win the day, yet still devoted to their young
King, with a barbaric love that surpasseth the wish
for life or the love of woman.

It was a sight to draw tears from the gray lava
rocks about them to see those gnarled old warriors
ever seeking to guard their Keiki Moi — the image
of their old king — throughout the sickening
slaughter of that memorable day. Without knowing that he was seeking death with every onset of
the battle, how they watched to guard him, their
only hope in battling now being to *save him* from
the covert harm that every foe aimed at his breast.

When once Kalani's little band was safely
within the deep, cool mountain Pass, with the
unassailable crags and jutting peaks of Waolani
towering above and behind them, where fifty men
could keep a thousand at bay, then the murderous

Hawaiians called a halt, and fell back to re-form and organize for a swift succession of the desperate assaults which Keeaumoku — who was in command — saw would be required to win the day. For well the Hawaiian leaders knew that their fierce old King would suffer them no rest until the last of the brave Oahuans were dead or routed beyond recall.

When Kalani had formed his little band of chiefs into a forlorn hope, consisting of six lines of fifty men each, and saw that the Hawaiians had fallen back out of view, after the touch of terrible slaughter they had encountered, he ordered his weary warriors to snatch what rest they could during the brief respite allowed them.

Turning his dark eyes upward to the rough crag that leaned with a savage friendliness out into the gloomy gorge above his head, he discovered his darling Queen among her maidens, together with thousands of other wahine wives, mothers, and daughters, clinging wherever a cliff or tree afforded shelter. And the King called to Kupule and her maidens to come down.

Instantly Kupule began the descent with a hundred other women who saw husbands or brothers below, bringing with them water and fruit from the cool forest, and fruit in abundance for the famished warriors. Not one that came but had loved friends among these battle-scarred heroes.

Setting the example for his chiefs by freeing himself from sword-belt and mamo, Kalani flung

himself wearily down upon the scanty herbage of
grass and flowers resting under the crisp shadow
of the beetling crag, with the strong trades yet
blowing merrily through the deep gorge which
opened out at the Pali high above the inrolling sea
a short distance beyond.

Soon the grief-stricken women, headed by Kupule, made their appearance in the ravine, and
sprang down among their dear wounded ones, dis-
tributing food and drink with deep solicitude in
every eye.

Kneeling in a pool of her royal lover's blood,
there among the frenzied warriors whose only
thoughts were of further murderous deeds, their
very faces grown wolfish with the terrible slaughter
of that day, Kupule supplied food to the King,
while Manona and Lelu bound the *ti* leaf upon his
gaping wounds, the loving Queen stripping up her
own tapa covering for her King and his chiefs to
bind upon their wounds.

It was a sight, never to be forgotten, to behold
that fair young creature so crushed by her speechless grief, murmured neither with lip nor eye, satisfied only to pressing her fond kisses upon the
dear hand that stroked her black tresses and patted
her pallid cheeks in passing token that he knew
her to be there. But too well she knew Kalani's
tongueless sorrow in that hour. Weary, haggard
smiles were the best the war-worn monarch could
bestow upon his darling, so weakened by his
wounds, and just then so exhausted by his superhuman efforts during the last hour's retreat.

Though Kalani gave no hopes of saving the land, yet he calmly spoke of the rivers of blood that must yet flow. But when he suffered his fond gaze to dwell too long upon the soft eyes and grief-stricken face before him, his thoughts of leaving his darling in such an hour choked his utterance, and made his olive cheeks ashy and wet with unseemly tears such as his kingly eyes had never wept before.

Soon a scout came running up the mountain path, reporting the Hawaiians coming up the Nuuanu in immense force, led on by Naihe, with Kamehameha and Keeaumoku following with the guards. On the instant Kalani was up with glowing cheeks and flashing eyes as full of undaunted valor as ever.

When Kupule had helped to buckle on his swordbelt, and put on his mamo; Kalani snatched a kiss and one brief look into her dear eyes — so human, yet so divine — and sent her away to her eyrie, there to watch the last act in the drama of conquest — the death-battle of her King!

Turning to his war-scarred Chiefs as they caught up their arms, and rose slowly from the ground — so stiffened by their wounds as to make them dispirited by the hopeless task before them — Kalani endeavored to instil something of his own enthusiasm into the grim old veterans of his father's day.

As he looked down the Nuuanu and saw the dense masses of freshly organized Hawaiians, eagerly advancing to the frivolous music of the bam-

boo fifes and the circubita drums, coming with the
fell purpose of crushing his little band at one mad
swoop, then his great heart beat wildly, and his
dark eyes lighted as with flames, at thought of the
opportunity now presenting to carve his kingly
name on the rock-hewn battlefield of the Pali,
where grand old Waolani should pinnacle his fame
unto the remotest ages.

Kindling with the uprising spirit of his own heroism, Kalani's dark eyes shone as with the sudden
frenzy of a madman; flashing at times with such
glances of leaping light as to awe the irresolute
ones about him, as with the awful mandate of a
god. It was thus he had often inspired those of
kindred mettle with a resolution as vaulting as his
own. As Kalani addressed his blood-stained chiefs
in that dark hour, it is asserted by those upon the
crags above — *for not one below lived to tell the tale*
— that his resonant voice rung through the gorge
like a war-bugle sounding to the charge !

And it is also said that, prompted by some sweet
impulse — yet an impulse so differently interpreted
— he suddenly turned his eyes heavenward, looking up through the mountain crags to the summer sky and the white man's God, as if reverently
appealing for divine aid in that terrible hour. Can
it be that he knew not to *whom* he appealed? that
he knew not *why* he sought another Deity than
Pele, in that awful moment of existence ? Who
will believe it ? Not I !

Let us rather believe that softly within his

heathen heart — so roused by the magnetic impulse of the hour — there breathed the *still small
voice* of the Almighty Father, that comes to us all
alike in the one supreme moment of prescience
during last hours of dissolution. It was noticed
that neither love nor fear of the heathen Goddess
of the nation found place in his soul after that
awful moment of battle-frenzy and religious fervor, as he thus addressed his savage and sullen
Chiefs :

"Hark ye, my Braves!" And his voice was
like a tempest's when storming along the sea.
"Here in this gorge let us swear to *win or die!* I,
upon this good brand my kingly father wore in all
his hundred battles with these same hated foes ;
given me to wear with honor, or render up with
heroic death, I swear it, by a new Deity you know
not of — my battle-GOD! and my KUPULE! —
You swear by your own loved ones yonder, clinging like maimed birds to the rocks and crags of
Waolani.

"Who of you would not rather fight and die beneath those fond eyes of our loved ones, than have
them blush to see us fly? Who will not joy with
me to here meet the foe, so walled in by friendly
cliffs they cannot pass ; for farther upward even we
cannot go, unless like yonder craven serfs we'd
leap — as many will — the dizzy Pali's steep!"

He paused for breath, and joyed to hear his savage Chieftains cheer, and swear alike on sword and
spear! — by Lono and by Pele! — to die with their

Boy King the gallant death of Braves! Looking
down the valley, round the curve of the ravine,
the front rank could behold the near approach of
the exultant Hawaiians; could see them handle
their long spears for sudden use; and watch them
draw their glimmering swords with a swaggering
leer, prompted by thoughts of easy conquest. Ob-
serving the small esteem in which the Hawaiians
held them, Kalani could not forbear yet one word
more to rouse his noble warriors:

"See! they come, my Chiefs. Hark, to their
insulting calls! 'Tis true our little band is small,
and Hawaii's fresh forces strong and many; but
there'll be less of us to fall, and few to tell the
tale — *if any!* Now let each blade to battle leap!
Let each strong arm with latest blow *pierce to the
hilt* some hated foe!"

And Kalani shook his ponderous blade in the
saddening sunlight, that hung low down in the
western sky, and raised his flashing eyes to the crag
above for one last look from Kupule; who, dear
soul, answered back with but a haggard smile,
though a low cheer came rippling down from her
chieftain maidens, ambushed among the shaggy
wood-growth of the cliff.

Whoever has seen a couchant tiger ambushed in
his native jungle, ready for a spring upon the approaching foe; seen his green eyes flashing with
demoniacal rage; his ruffled tail swaying to and
fro with nervous tension; his huge flexor muscles
working taut and vibrant as bowstrings; may con-

ceive something of the concentric hate and fiery
ardor of Oahu's outraged King, when thus driven
to the mountains by his powerful antagonist.

Kalani stood there at bay like a tawny gladiator
who accepts his fate, but who grows maddened —
insane with impatience — at the swaggering approach of his foe, and the tardy prolongation of
his doom. The withering curl of his kingly lips
was moulded in intenest scorn of all that vast array
of might and skill, coming pouring up the Nuuanu
to assail his haggard, wounded few. His dark eyes
flashed with electric gleams, raying the shadow-
gloom in which he stood with brighter than sun-
ray, where it glinted the mountain cataract above;
whose dismal roar dwelt in his ear in hoarse unison
with his rage! Standing thus, poised for battle,
ready to spring upon the first comer, in search of
the one only brainal alleviant — murder of his foe
— delay intensified his mania, and augmented his
muscles into countless drawn bows, intent to hurl
their impatient arrows of wrath!

As the enemy approached very near, Kalani
sprang one step in advance of his chiefs to give his
sword-arm better sweep, and show the hated Hawaiians with what kindling relish he awaited their
coming. Instantly six long spears were at him
flung, with an unerring aim that never missed their
mark. This furious assault made it earnest work
for Kalani to defend himself, until the contending
forces could come into the hand-to-hand conflict
that he sought.

The first spear Kalani caught in his left hand, and with *it* parried four others — careering them skyward — ever keeping his sword-hand fast on his weapon ready for instant use. Dropping the first spear, which had been flung by Naihe the commander, Kalani caught the sixth one, flung by a tall and swarthy chief, hideous in visage as Kamehameha himself. Turning the spear-point to the front, Kalani hurled it back with inconceivable swiftness, through and through the great savage who had cast it, who fell with a yell of pain; and he thus became the first corpse in the human foundation of that memorable rampart of slaughtered foes.

Then followed the fearful clash of arms, too confused and chaotic ever to be described, too horrible to depict by any other symbol of warfare than that of the two thousand dead, subsequently heaped up together in this never-to-be forgotten battle of the Pali. Then smote the kingly sword that struck for love and fame. Then struck many a noble chief, whose only thought in battling was to save their young Keiki Moi — loved better than life, and home, and friends.

Some fought in that hour for the dear loved ones who looked sorrowfully down with frenzied eyes from Waolani's jutting crags. Some battled for their loved homes in the dear enchanting valley below. Some fought because others fought around them; because it had been the pleasure and the pastime of their long barbaric lives; the

one murderous joy sufficiently brutal to reach
down into their strong hearts. With these callous-
hearted ones **there abided** no love of home, no
yearning need of friends sufficient **to awaken such**
exemplarious valor as they here displayed. They
played at battle as aimless women play at battle-
door, or gamesters play at chance. Their pride
of life lay in their cunning fence, and the murderous quality of their unerring blows. Good soldiers
these : but cautious men, who take admirable heed
of their own heads — not of the King's. Such
men were assigned to the flanks, and there they
fought, impervious as the rocky gorge they were
set to defend.

Not so with the chivalrous Boki and many
another large-hearted chief about the King, who,
failing with his swift defensive sword to ward off
two murderous slashes aimed at once upon his
King, flung up his bare left arm and took the
savage blow meant for his loved young Monarch's
head, and fought on from that hour with his left
arm lopped off at the wrist; while the wifely
Leleha thrust home her girlish rapier into the
bosom of him who thus maimed her dear loved
lord.

Thus with Paao, the aged warrior-Priest, who
in long past years had fought bravely for Titeere,
as he now fought with tender affection for his old
King's son. The life of the brave Kapu Alii was
perilled an hundred times that day striving to save
his loved Kalani. Twice was his aged breast

offered to shield the King's from random spears,
flung by some of the rear ranks over the heads of
those fighting before them.

What a sight of horror was all this when seen
by fond mothers from the mountain above; what
a cold thrill crept over the heart of the young
wife who witnessed her maimed husband totter
and stagger and fall, to be trampled upon by
friend and foe alike, in the brutal haste to glut
their inhuman lust for blood. One scents the
fresh flowing gore in sickening odor reeking up
from the gorge as a thousand cruel heart-stabs
gloat the mountain air, as when a furious wind-
demon sweeps bellowing over the sea, tattering
the frothy wave-crests into sibilant spray, and
filling the landsman's nostril with a saline flavor
that awes his timid soul with the storm!

Ah! who can portray such a murderous encounter? Who fill your ear with the confusive
dins of such awful revelry? What pen so graphic
as to possess your mind with the possible *charm* of
such warfare; the wild, delirious joy of thus
battling on the toppling border of death! fighting
for the loved ones — for freedom — for the dear
native land! when thus assailed by a hated Invader? And yet many of these Hawaiians, who lead
the assault, fall and give place to other as eager
assailants; yet they fight for none of these senti-
ments. War is their vocation, and they fight as
eagerly as hungry curs fight for possession of a
bone.

Hark! to the shouts of Oahu's banded chiefs; shouts duplicated by a thousand answering spirits of the place, as the wild echoes call back from cliffs and crags and caverned dens in the mountain wilds. Yell and echo alike being carried, wind-blown, by the rush of trades through the gorge down upon the mad sea of upturned faces below.

The low-lying sun — the last to Kalani — bathes his hot face with its farewell glory, lighting the ponderous blows of his swift- falling sabre as it flashes over his head and falls crashing into his naked foes. Still the enemy press eagerly up over their dead companions, infatuated with the cruel wish to slay the King; this Boy-Monarch who thus stands fighting for his liberty and his life; the new-found God, and *She* dearer than all else! — the darling of his heart!

Not always did Kalani wait for the over-eager Hawaiians to climb over the dead heap and reach his lines. But as some huge war-chief of great renown came staggering up over his slaughtered companions, savage for revenge, while yet he raised his ponderous arm to cast his spear, tottering with unsteady foothold on the dead, Kalani would spring up over the rampart of dead foes with the bound of a leopard, ward off the chief's clumsily managed barb, and lunge his hungry steel, with a lightning plunge, into his unsteady foe! springing back unharmed to his place in the ranks again.

How wild were the friendly shouts at such heroic exploits as these, not only from his own surrounding chiefs, but from thousands of women and aged men perched among the rocks above. So swift at times fell the sabre-blows of the chiefs, that they glowed in the torrid sunlight continuous gleams of lightning-flashes, often bathing the gray rocks of Waolani in seeming flames of leaping firelight. But, alas, what availed the scores and hundreds of dead Hawaiians that fell, where other eager hundreds continued to rush up in an unbroken wave of glittering spears and savage shark-swords ?

Well were there need for the multitude of prayers said for Kalani by the horror-stricken women on the cliffs above; for where one spear was cast at any other chief in the ranks, there were ten thrown at the naked breast of the Boy King. But with the one-armed Boki on the one side, aided by the keen-eyed Leleha and a dozen more; and with Paao, Kahiko, and Owaiee on the other, all eager not only to defend *him* with their weapons, but also ready to thrust even their own bodies between their Boy King and danger, — together their affectionate watchfulness had saved him from all but flesh-wounds until now.

But in other ways was Kalani reminded of the love of his people. Once he lost his foothold, and fell on the topmost pile of fallen dead, having just stricken down the leading chief. Instantly a wild wail of agony rang out over the Pali from all the thousand voices on Waolani; rolling down the

Nuuanu to Kamehameha's ear like an avalanche of sorrow. Hearing this, it was deemed by all that the day was won by the fall of the King.

But before Boki and Kahiko could spring to his aid, Kalani was up again; slaying two great chiefs who were rushing up to impale him where he lay, killing each with a single blow by two lightning sweeps of his sword. This act showed to his sorrowing people that their young King was unharmed.

Then rose the counter-shouts of joy in utmost *tempo*, rending the blood-smeared air with deafening applause; rising like a billow of lark-songs into the summer sky! How full of blended reverence for Pele and Lono, and all the mythological deities were those shouts! — so brim with that magnetic acclamation for heroism which ever wells up with unmistakable spontaneity from the hearts of the loved ones! Kamehameha had no need to ask what meant this sudden revocation of their grief; his remark to Keone Ana covered the whole ground as interpreted to a distant ear: "Kalani had but fallen; but has risen again. The fools, to make such an outcry!"

Hark, now, to the mad yells of the on-rushing Hawaiians, so frenzied by these joy-shouts that meant not only joy for the rescued King, but a scornful derision of his enemies, who had as yet proved so futile in their utmost efforts. How press the invaders to the front, every chief cognizant of the black rage of their old king as the

derisive shouts of the Oahuans reach his ear!
Listen to the whir and hum of their blood-thirsty
spears, flung whistling through the air by the frenzied arms of savage men!

Alas! alas! what power can save Oahu's little
band from such clouds of flying barbs? If but one
spear strikes its human mark, so that the cool eye
of the Oahuan Chief becomes less wary for an instant, failing to duck and dip and dodge with the
swiftness of thought, — heavens! how fast follow
a score of other spears into his naked breast, until
he falls, bristling with spear-staffs! Still the ranks
of the Oahuans are not broken for an instant, for
as one chief falls or tires, another springs with mad
haste to the front, filling the gap eagerly as a blood-
hound for the fray.

But so narrow is the entrance to the Pass, only
permitting ten assailants to fight abreast, while fifty
Oahuans can serve on the defensive, owing to the
sudden widening of the gorge, that the advantage
is greatly with the defenders. Thus they stand
like a wall of rock against the inrolling wave of
fresh foemen. But the red blood trickles down
the muscular sides of their naked bodies as they
occasionally miss a spear and receive a flesh-wound
therefrom. But not one wound nor many can induce the brave chiefs to leave their places until
the fatal wound pierces them, and they fall in their
tracks, content to die the death they have fought
for.

Some there were who fought until they could no

longer keep their places in the ranks, but rather than pass to the rear, and die by inches, with yet undying hatred of the foe they would creep snake-like upon the heap of dead foes, draw their long daggers, and await with eyes blurred with death to stab whomsoever came within reach of their dying hands; thus fighting upon the dead heap until the fast-falling enemy buried them in a living tomb.

At length there came a pause in the ceaseless battle, caused by the demoralized Hawaiians being called off to prepare for some more concentrated effort to save the day. Thus Kalani and his few remaining chiefs were left to stanch their wounds and refresh themselves for a brief half hour, though momentarily expecting the reappearance of the enemy.

Could another such three hundred heroes be now put into the Pass, it is possible that the Hawaiians would have been unable to complete their conquest of the Island. But that could not be, for there were not another such three hundred among all the group, much less could any suitable material be found among the panic-stricken army hidden away in the Pali beyond.

25

THE flowers bloom in the tropic sun
   Where fell the King in that awful hour;
Perfume and die, as they grieve for one
   Who died that day in his pride and pow'r!

The birds flit out from the Pali's dell,
   Their whole lives long they have sung his praise;
As they sing the charms of the Queen, who fell
   Heart-broken with grief where her lover lays.

So sings the sea, with its sad refrain,
   Where rolls its surf on the Koolau shore:
But never a song for the cowards slain,
   Spear-tost by the Guards, from the cliff flung o'er.

Though grass is green, and the flowers bright,
   Where died the Serfs who desert that day;
Yet grim are the ghosts who invade the night
   To curse the spot where the cowards lay.

386

CHAPTER XX.

HE day was now fast drawing to a close, as the last assaulting force of Hawaiians were seen pressing on up the Nuuanu, led by the gallant Englishman, Keone Ana. He was coming at the head of Kamehameha's own personal guard of gigantic warriors. This new attacking column consisted of a fresh body of Hawaii's bravest and most expert spearsmen. They pressed on in silence, with long, eager strides, wearing a look of sullen, savage determination in their dark faces, that was foreboding and dreadful to look upon.

Not a tap of the drum, nor a note of the fife, awoke the surly echoes of frowning crag or mountain forest. Only the heavy measured tread of a thousand large, fierce men, who had never yet failed to break through or override any force they had been sent against. They were all men chosen for their previous deeds of courage and carnage, of enormous strength and monstrous proportions; many of them being petty chiefs, and having the prowess of three common men in a hand-to-hand conflict; a chosen body of heroes, who needed not the cheap accessary of martial music to whet their courage for battle.

On came this famous Guard, more like famished wolves hungering for a feast of blood, than human combatants. A cruel, brutal set of savages as a whole, with nothing in life so gladdening their blood-thirsty hearts as battling to the death with few or many of their kind.

Yet why Young was sent in command of such a column of murderous savages, instead of Keeaumoku, their general, none could tell. Keone Ana was a man of mercy, a kind-hearted, gallant foe. It was surmised that Young came with the Guard with an offer of peace; but, alas, peace offered at the spear-spoint — " Accept it, or die ! "

As the Guard came nearer, Kalani rose up and assumed command again, weakened by loss of blood and stiffened by his wounds, as were all others of his band. Together they cleared the Pass of its dead, by heaping up their ghastly rampart breast-high. They had, hours since, been deprived of their first and most favorable position, by the constant encroachment of the dead, which crowded them back up the gorge, until now there was a width permitting the enemy to approach fifty abreast; a great disadvantage for Kalani's few remaining braves.

Though haggard and worn from his previous herculean efforts, and bleeding from many ghastly wounds, yet Kalani was still full of courage and eager to fight it out to the last. His few remaining chiefs gathered cheerfully about him, with an expression of anxious love for their King, such as no other act in life could test like this. Not the remotest thought of escape or surrender entered the hearts of any.

It was a cheering thought to think what they had accomplished. One by one they had resisted and cut down the numerous forces of the foe; but now their position was less favorable, their numbers few, and their strength ebbing fast away. All knew the character of the invincible giants now sent against them, yet all were eager for a personal test of the fighting quality of this renowned Guard of chosen warriors. ·

As Kalani assumed his former position in front, and stood awaiting the coming Hawaiians, leaning wearily upon his long sword, whose point pressed upon the naked breast of a huge chief of his killing, he turned his dark eyes tenderly upward upon Kupule among her group of maidens, sitting upon the overhanging crag thirty feet above his head. The hiding-place of the Queen had been in the rear when the fight began, but now, owing to the encroaching dead, the Queen sat in front of the line of battle just formed across the Pass.

With a gleam of gladness Kupule's fond eyes answered back to Kalani's loving gaze; but oh, how sad were those gentle eyes, how pinched with agony of inward grief was the winsome face of his darling, as she pressed her small clenched hands upon her beating heart with futile endeavor to still the wild upheaval of her garmentless bosom! For too well Kupule knew the inevitable result impending, now that her father's ferocious Guard was sent to finish up the day.

When the Hawaiians had approached very near, Young took a side position and bade the Guard, "*E hele!* Hawaii!" (advance, Hawaii!) And while the savage monsters were yet mounting over the wide rampart of dead, Kalani looked up to Kupule with his last look, and called out his last farewell:

"Aloha! Kupule." And he too pressed his sword-hilt upon his upheaving heart, striving with hilt and hands to keep down the strong agony within.

"Aloha! Kalani," was her reply; adding, "Let me come down to you, my darling? We who love so should *die together!*"

But the King had only time to wave her a negative reply with his sword, as the front ranks of the Guard came thundering into action with the onset of a tempest; pressing back the whole line of Oahuans at first with the very preponderance of their strength and weight and concerted action.

How echoed the caverned places of Waolani with the demoniacal yells of those gigantic monsters! Hoarser than the crescendo of an earthquake were the awful maledictions of those thousand unearthly voices, blended in hellish concert of madness; louder than the frightful bellowing of a tempest—less destructive than they. But once settled to their work, the Guard did their fighting silently and sullenly, as their severe discipline demanded.

How rang the contending steel of Oahu's noble Chieftains in that hour, though many of the foremost line went down in that first terrible onset. And how the Boy King escaped in that fray, the angels alone can tell, unless, as many supposed, the Guards were ordered to take him alive. After the first terrific shock the banded chiefs could not be moved by all the fury of successive assaults, and gradually struck down the foremost comers and gained their late position near the rampart of dead.

It was a moment full of such glory as imparts superhuman strength to heroic hearts when moulded to receive it, — a moment of exultant, delirious joy, to those brave defenders, grown battle-mad as they witnessed the successive failure of each new onset of their gigantic foe, who never since their formation had been so held in check before.

Those who witnessed these last frenzied hours of Kalani's battle, shudder with newly awakened horror while they relate the awful carnage witnessed among their loved ones ; though often their blear old eyes brighten at thought of many a knightly deed accomplished by that fast falling band of heroes, as they dropped one by one riddled with spears, about their King.

And it is ever with a wail of woe, and a furtive look of fear, that they depict the fall of one venerable white-head, the great Tabu-Priest of the

land. For at length Paao, the finest swordsman
about his King, went mad with desperation, fighting so fiercely with the hot sun upon his over-
wrought brain. Standing in the front rank beside
Kalani, where, because of his exalted priesthood
many a superstitious warrior dare not assail him,
suddenly Paao ceased all efforts at defence, and
sprang forward from the ranks, staring with glazed
eyes upon the foe, with a look of vacant mania in
his blood-shotten eyes.

Instantly some unhallowed hand cast the first
spear, crashing into his chest, followed quickly by
others, until a dozen great spears stood bristling in
the aged breast of the noble Priest, who fell forward with a thud and a groan upon his dead foes,
heaped up waist-high before him.

When Paao fell, Leleha's superstitious fears were
so awakened for the moment, that while her attention was thus briefly withdrawn from her own defence, she too received two cruel spears into her
bridal breast; and a brave and noble chieftess
went down, wringing a cry of grief from gallant
Boki, and, alas! with none left to fill the places
of these fast falling ones.

There now came to be a gap necessarily left open
on the right wing, between the north cliff and the
Oahuans, into which the wolfish foe wedged in on
the instant, and soon flanked Kalani with a semicircle of bristling steel. There were now but
forty able-bodied chiefs left about the King, and
it needed sixty to span the Pass; and all were be-

coming too much wounded and too weary to resist much longer.

Seeing the grim circle of Hawaiians thus close in about his wing, and thinking to close up the scene, or drive the intruders back again, Kalani called out his battle-cry, and wheeled his front to assail them. The impulse was so sudden, and the assault so furious and well pressed, that Kalani and those about him cut their way through the line of guards, and turning upon those up the gorge, slaughtered them to a man. Among those who fell by Kalani's ponderous blows were several great chiefs, officers in the Guard.

As if satisfied with the work of the moment, or utterly exhausted with his furious effort, Kalani fell back under the sheltering crag with but ten remaining chiefs; and together they set their backs against the rock, standing on the defensive to re-cover their breath. A huge spear was seen hang-ing in the thigh of Kalani as he retreated, its long staff dragging after him as he pressed back to the cliff, rankling terribly in the wound. But, alas! every other chief was more seriously wounded than their King; and none dared stoop down to free the wound of its weapon; but Kalani raised his leg and broke the staff, and tore the cruel spear from his thigh.

But it was now noticed that the look of impend-ing death mantled quickly over the face of Kalani; he paled to an ashy hue with the agony from his lacerated wound. At that moment the piteous cry of Kupule was heard from above, crying out: "Oh, Kalani! Oh, my King! Let me come down to you ere you die !·"

That cry from his darling brought back the leaping life-blood to his kingly face once more. Then the tottering, half-blinded King suddenly found strength to weakly wave his dripping sword to the dear one on the crag, in heroic token of his undying love for this brightest and best in the land.

Glancing gratefully up to Kupule, while yet his pale lips moved without power to articulate, so speechless with his agony, Kalani stood tottering there in the clotted puddles of his own blood, leaning wearily against the cold damp rock to rally himself, while with superhuman effort he kissed his reeking sword-blade with heart-touching reverence to his darling. O Pele! cruel deity, to suffer such a wrong!

Heavens! who can guess what transpires above and around one during such acts of heroism and devotion as these? Who can interpret the whispered sympathies of the Unseen, ever hovering anent the dying hour of such great souls? Even the savage Guard now stood with suspended weapons, every organ of sense agape, while they reverently watched to see the great King drop down and die. What wonder that even these brutal men were awed by such heroism, and the piteous, pleading cry of the weeping Queen — the god-born daughter of their own great King.

Suddenly a furious whir of *unseen* wings was

heard invading the dusky gorge, appalling every
heart with thought of some ghostly Presence in
their midst.   And there stood a dim, vast *Shadow-
shape* hovering between the dying Kalani and the
strong light of the setting sun.   This sudden shad-
ow-gloom was vividly impressed upon all ; but was
made most visible to the dying King in the gorge,
and the weeping Queen on the crag.   From the
pale lips of both, there fell the same glad expressions of joy ; the same outcry seemingly addressed
to Deity ; as if both the one and the other were
speaking face to face with the Divine One they
called upon.

Kupule's tears gave place to grateful smiles in
an instant ; and Kalani ceased to grope about as if
blinded, and ceased to sway and totter against the
damp cliff, like one about to fall.   His blanched
face grew calm, as when a fierce tempest is suddenly stilled by a mandate ; and he stood reverently up with bowed head, like one who had been
regenerated in a moment — one tardily forgiven of
his long regretted sins.

What really had transpired was only known to a
few divinely exalted souls at that time.   As the
vast figure of *Shadow-dark* passed from before the
face of the sun, there soon after appeared to the
witnessing eyes of thousands, a thin, feathery mist-
cloud, full of awful mystery and meaning, gathered
about the topmost peak of Waolani.   A rough and
rocky peak, high up above the gorge, where only
the mountain eagle soars ; and below which the

cawing tropic birds wheel and scream in countless numbers about their nests.

Weird and demoralizing was the mystery that possessed the gorge in that awful moment, and which subsequently gathered about the seeming mist-cloud like a divine Shechinah upon the peak, wearing a look of soft and silky texture that was not born of the usual trade-cloud that had now ceased to invade the gorge for the day. It had more the aspect of those thin gray mists of the morning, when touched by the sun; those half visible vagrant exhalations of the ghostly night-airs that come stealing out with perfumed footsteps from every dell in the valley, and every wooded gorge in the mountain wilds.

Yet this flame-illumined mist was none of these. For look at it as they would, it seemed so haloed about with sadness as to awaken human tears. A dim, uncertain vapory something haunted with the half definable figure of a woman; but woman too massive to be earthly, and too sorrowing to be heavenly — for tears are not the heritage of the blessed.

To those who watched with keenest gaze and deepest introspective vision, there appeared at times the unmistakable contour of a sweet, sad face, more beautiful than a thousand stars. But in an instant the divine conception was snatched from view, hidden by the ever gyrating vapor, which often seemed rayed through and through as by the yellowest masses of moonbeam. But this

proved to be but the typical gold-locks of all
divine ones — long and wavy tresses — like the
shimmering moonlight on a rippling sea.

Watching closely there was often outlined sweet
glimpses of large milk-white pinions, white as the
sheeny wings of the tropic-birds careering below,
though a thousand times larger. Sometimes these
snowy wings seemed half extended, as when
dawning thoughts of sudden flight transpire. Sometimes the pinions seemed folded tranquilly at rest,
but oftenest they hung with a limp and sorrowing
droop, restless and fluttering, like the palpitant
heart-motion of one bereaved by an unspeakable
sorrow.

When the restless, rolling vapor gathered most
densely about the divine head and comely figure,
then there could be distinguished the voluptuous
outline of large and shapely limbs — though
twenty times the size of life — altogether com-
prising a womanly outline of most unearthly
beauty. When only the limbs of the divine one
were visible, the one flexed knee well comported
with the bowed head and drooping pinions of a
grief-stricken Spirit of another world than this.

Thus the whole divine figure subsequently became unmistakably outlined from these frequent
glimpses in detail, until all were possessed of its
divine origin. " 'Tis Pele ! " whispered the thousand heathen hearts who beheld the mystic revelation through their tears. " 'Tis the ANGEL of
GOD!" whispered the few apostate ones who

were secretly inspired with the white man's revelation of a being *higher* and *holier* than all their
heathen deities.

Great was the surprise of all to see Kalani thus
rally and throw off his deathly faint; but just
what the inspiration had been to thus snatch him
from death, but few could tell.   It was a mystery
that had inspired the Guard with awe, and had
kept their murderous hands in check till now, that
they saw Kalani arouse and prepare to fight again.

As the brave King recovered from his swoon of
death, he remembered the thousand loving eyes
that were watching his every act from Waolani,
intent to report his battle-deeds to posterity.   Ah,
how a brave heart may rally when thus inspired
by such a thought; and how may he fight again
with renewed valor, when battling before such an
audience of loving eyes!

Knowing that his power of defence was fast
weakening, Kalani now caught up his feather
mantle from a cleft in the rock, and wound the
costly mamo round his left arm to serve as shield.
The remainder of his red plume, already cleft in
two by a keen sabre-cut that had left its trace
upon his cheek, still hung from his clotted hair,
where it had been secured by Kupule after the loss
of his helmet.   Wounded as he was, the great
soul of the young monarch yet illumined his noble
face brightly as ever.   But there was now observed a set and savage resolution settling down
over his pallid countenance.   His usually full, red

lips, had lost their arched voluptuous bows, and were now set firm and hard, and thin and pale, expressing an undying resolution that was not wholly linked with the battle — as we learn from his swift, *irreverent* glances, flung at the occupant of the mist-cloud on the mountain peak.

The usually broad open brow of the King was now severely knitted into frowns, furrowing his face with an appearance of having aged within an hour. But whether the frowns and flutings upon his stern young face were the effect of mental or physical pain, — a withering scorn of his confronting foes, — or his newly awakened apostasy to Pele, is a matter still in dispute among the few survivers who recorded his appearance.

The ten remaining Chiefs stood grasping their bloody sword-hilts as they leaned panting and bleeding against the rocky wall of the gorge; every countenance worn and haggard, but still radiant with an inward expression of undying love for their heroic King that was very touching to behold. There was that in every menacing eye that promised, unasked, to die gloriously by his side. Their pale lips curled with scorn at the general expressions of pity seen in the sinister faces gathering in strong battle array around them — wounded men, who dare not leave the support of the cliff lest they fall from weakness.

But the Guard had tasted the terrible might of these men of Oahu, and their experience taught them that they must be cut down before they

would yield, and as they prepared to accomplish
this piece of noble butchery, there was indeed an
expression of truest pity upon their faces, that so
gallant a King, and Chiefs so brave, should have to
be hewn down like common foes.

" Would Kalani but surrender — he who has
won such undying fame ! " — became such a universal wish, not only of the Guard, but of the
thousands upon the mountain side, until the very
air became pervaded with the sentiment that
Kalani should not thus die. And it was perhaps
in interpretation of this sentiment — implied or
expressed — that led Keone Ana to now spring
forward and strike down the levelled spear-points
just in act to spring, ten to one, upon the wounded
chiefs, while he called for Kalani's surrender in
the name of Kamehameha :

" Yield, noble King ! Oahu is lost ! Kamehameha would save his kingly foe."

" Ha ! English Young. Have at thee too. Why
lags behind my bastard brother ? Kalani asks but
life to lay him low."

" Stay, Kalani ! I've come to save you, with
the promise of all honors my great King can bestow."

" Nay, fool ! The wish for life is past. Invaders
come to glut with blood, not parley with a kingly
foe. Come on ! brave *haole*. Kalani would rather
fall by thee than any."

" Ha ! Smite you so ? To parley thus were
death to me."

And Young now put in his own swift, strong blows, with something more then defensive might.

" Ah ! Young : that bit the flesh. Your blade is keen ; your arm is fresh."

The flesh wound inflicted by Keone Ana, so nettled Kalani, that he sprang madly forward, and for the moment rained down his blows upon the brave English sailor ; pressing him steadily back through his own ranks of wondering Guards, who opened to the right and left to let them pass, until fifty ferocious warriors stood there with bristling spears on either side of the two combatants.

Five of Oahu's chiefs fell during this onset, and the noble Boki was the last to fall. This Kalani saw, even in the midst of his own furious attack upon Young ; and as the great Hawaiian who had killed Boki, stooped down to snatch a valued trophy from his neck, Kalani swerved one of his downward blows — first meant for Young — and cleft the great Chief's head from off his body, and again resumed his work with Young as though un-interrupted.

As by common consent, not a spear was now raised against the heroic King, or his five chiefs ; but a hundred gigantic Hawaiians circled-about the two combatants, with a view to witnessing the desperate sword-fight between two skilful con-testants, such as none of them had ever witnessed before.

Step by step Young had been compelled to give way, falling back from one side of the rocky gorge
26

to the other, keeping mostly to the defensive, leaving Kalani to spend his furious forces, as soon as
he must. When the brave King's blows began to
slacken, and he breathed heavily and staggered
from exhaustion ; then Young took to the offen-
sive, and steadily pressed Kalani back to the opposite cliff, with but five haggard chiefs tottering
about him, with madly menacing faces as they retreated.

It was now believed by all that Kalani would
surrender ; for he was so weak that but for the
rocks at his back he would have fallen to the
ground ; and with this intent Young kept back
the Guàrd and gave the breathless, tottering King
time to recover a moment.

When Kalani had rallied from the previous
swoon of death at the interposition of the supernatural agency of — *of something* — we know not
what ; the sad, uncertain mist-cloud then lay motionless and impenetrable ; rimmed half-about with
the sad sunset's liquid gold fringing the western
disk of the vapory sphere with a crescent of beauty.

But now that Kalani again tottered to his fall,
the mist-cloud was startled from its previous repose ; its vapory veil swayed wildly in unequal
rifts, like wind-blown smoke, — but such smoke as
serves only to smother a furious flame. Now a
negligent mood of sorrow seemed to possess the
awful power within that flame-cloud, again permitting a partial disclosure of the divine mystery
to wondering human eyes. The ghostly Spirit now

became so visible as to cast its shadow-shape darkly upon the gray rocks below and the sea beyond, dense even as Waolani's lengthening shadow falls upon the far eastern sea.

What has thus disturbed the divine incumbent of that awful mist-cloud? What but Young's loud-ringing steel, falling furious and fast upon Kalani's parrying sword; or burying itself deep into the yellow mamo shielding the young King's arm. How heaves the billowy cloud with such agony as only the immortals know, glowing with a fiery radiance as if incandescent within! It rocks verily like the tumultuous rise and fall of a human bosom tempestuous with sorrow.

Why will the Divine One — if such it be — not stay the battle and save the heroic King? Certainly it is not from lack of more than maternal love for the invincible hero of the battle ; for see, how tenderly the bereaved Spirit leans out over the gorge, intent upon the ghastly slaughter below. If it *were* Pele — though reputed to so love the fierce contentions of men — even *She* should now be palled by the awful massacre in the Pali, and stoop down with divine condescension to save her *once loving* devotee ; though now, alas for him ! become a Christian apostate from his heathen Goddess. Ah! when has ever a scorned divinity of her sex — whether human or divine — been known to revoke her unjust maledictions against a defected worshipper? Were it not so, the vocation of ambient angels were no more needed in this world of sorrow.

As Kalani recovered breath sufficient for Young
to renew the negotiation for surrender — though
apparently by no help from the sorrowing Deity in
the mist-cloud — the English chief again appealed
to him in kindest words to cease the useless battling :

"Yield, brave King! Why fight in vain, and
fall at last? Surrender! and end the battle."

"Never! — Would you *enslave* a King? Up,
my brand, and smite the *haole Alii* for the thought!"

And with a sudden influx of momentary strength
— the last mortal impulse of a spent soul — Kalani
slashed furiously at the English general as he approached to take his sword, following up his blows
with the infuriated rage of a madman, wounding
Keone Ana severely on face and shoulder. Seeing
one of them *must* go down, Young now struck
home with his utmost cunning, and soon put in the
final blow.

"*Kaha! Haole Alii!*" (Ha! White Chief!)
"Well struck! You've ... done ... for ... Kalani. 'Tis .... best .... so."

And with a superhuman effort, the last act of his
life, he raised his reeking sword to Kupule — high
as his dying arm would permit — and let fall the
weighty weapon with a heavy clang upon the lava
rocks; exclaiming, as the frothy blood bubbled
from his lips, and he fell beside his sword :

"Kupule! Kupule! — *Auhea ... na ... Ku-pu-
le ?*" (Where — is — Ku-pu-le ?) "*E ko-ku-a
... none ...* Young." (Be-friend — her — Young.)

" Befriend . . . my . . . Dar-ling ! — *Hoi . . . ma-hope !* . . . *Hoi . . . ma-hop-e !* " (Too — late ! — Too — la-t-e !)

And thus Oahu was bereft of her King ! He had raised his ponderous weapon too high in battling with so cunning a foe, in the vain endeavor to acquire strength for a downward blow — too high for guard — for Young thrust his sword to the hilt into Kalani's exposed breast ; withdrawing the cruel weapon to see him reel — cry out to his Darling — and fall to the earth to rise no more !

The mist-cloud on Waolani flashed with angry lightning when fell the King, and the rain poured down in torrents upon all below where it hung. The earth rocked and reeled as if the Pali's gorge was about to be closed up upon all its combatants forever. The very mountain-peak leaned savagely out over the gorge with the dreadful inclination that portends a fall. But only for a moment was sorrowing nature thus convulsed, for soon all became quiet upon the mountain, and tranquil in the gorge.

When Kupule saw Kalani fall ; saw his last appealing look as he raised his dying eyes to her sorrowing face ; heard his broken outcry — half choked by his own heart-blood — as he called feebly for his darling, — she sprang up with a cry of pain, a shriek of wild horror at the cruel deed she had seen perpetrated upon a wounded King !

Flinging off the restraining hands of her sorrowing maidens, who sought to withhold their frenzied

Queen from rushing into that savage tussle of
maddened men below — for the Guard were still
slaughtering the remaining Chiefs — Kupule rose
madly up from the stunted foliage that had served
to shelter her from the Invaders. Springing down
with the wild bound of a hunter-scared antelope
from off the overhanging crag where she had
watched the inhuman battle rage, she stood half
stunned by the shock in the gorge below.

The shriek of thousands of agonized women
rang out upon the mountain wilds, followed by a
moment's wailing of five thousand voices — wild,
anguished, and awful — smiting upon the deepening gloom of the twilight gorge with a universal
sorrow. Then all was still as the hush of death,
awaiting the result of the Queen's leap from the
crag. Appalling indeed is the simultaneous hush
following the multitudinous cry of a sorrowing
people. It was like the ghostly, chilling stillness
of impending death; as when we stand by the
bedside of the dearest and the best, and see the
taper of life put out in spite of our appeals.

But the immaculate soul of Kupule was possessed by a divine instinct in that hour, — an instinct inherent to all, when the chill shadow of
our own impending death approaches, for it is
then that the alert Spirit immortal asserts precedence over the crumbling clay. Thus the young
Queen was but essaying her embryo pinions in
that leap; impennate pinions, yet soon to be called
upon to wing her ethereal element to the skies —

heavenward to its new-found God! If this were not so, why was not Oahu's tender Queen crushed on the instant by that perilous leap? falling upon the slippery, blood-stained rocks below!

One bound over the intervening rocks — over the heaped-up dead friends and dead foes lying thick strewn about her dying King — *her dear loved one! her dear lost one!* — and Kupule flung herself upon the heaving bosom of Kalani, with the frantic bound of an ocean-billow leaping upon the long-sought shore! rousing him from the death-swoon that had already possessed him, by the warm pressure of her fresh young lips to his, so blood-stained with the oozing heart-current of a truly noble soul.

"Ku-pu-le!" — vocalized itself feebly upon the latest expiration of the dying King. He breathed no more! It was all the dying hero found voice to utter, while the quick, quivering shudder of death was even then visibly struggling through his manly form. It was the last superhuman effort of one already moribund, recalled by the sweet spirit of Aloha, for one last farewell utterance to his darling, whom he loved so well!

"Auwe! Kalani. *Auwe, Kuu make Moi!*" — Oh, Kalani! O my *dead* King!

And she covered his face with her kisses, and listened for another dying *aloha;* exclaiming in her agony of sorrow as she listened in vain for yet one more dear message from his dead lips!

"*E Kali! — E Kali! — Makou oia aloha like,*

pono make pu!" — Wait! wait! — We who love
so, *must* die together!

But the Boy King of Oahu was already dead!
He could not "wait" for his darling, his beautiful
Kupule; although he loved her more than his
kingdom and better than his life!

When Kalani's dead arms had relaxed their tender clasp about the neck of Kupule, after clinging
intelligently to her throughout the whole death-
struggle; and it had fully dawned upon the half-
dazed brain of the Queen that he was indeed dead
— gone from her forever! — then a low heart-
broken wail escaped her, so piteous that it called
Death's ministering angel down. A stifling struggle seemed to gain the mastery over the young
creature for a moment; then burst the red heart-
blood in torrents from her small, sweet mouth —
covering Kalani's dead face with the life-blood of
his darling — and *she too* lay dead upon the bosom
of her dearly loved King.

The soft and lambent gleam of two gifted souls
lit up the Pali's gorge as with a flambeau of glory,
and departed heavenward in that moment; winging Godward with a swift transition-flush of eager
happiness, so joyed that earthly sorrows were
passed, to be renewed no more forever and forever!

> Mourn! O ye mountain Waolani!
>   Sing soft! ye trade-winds in good weather:
> The Boy King lies dead in your Pali;
> The Keiki Moi, and his fair Wahine Alii:
>   Fond souls! dying blissfully together!

Slow falls the daylight down the western sky; for the long tropic day of slaughter — the battle-day is done. The approaching twilight purples the sea and hangs a dying glory on the mountain-peak; from which the awful mist-cloud of the grief-stricken Pele has departed, with a vow that war shall be *no more* forever in the land ! Though the Goddess had forgiven Kalani, as she had promised, to do, in the death-hour, and had lovingly snatched him from dissolution, and would have gladly redeemed him to his late kingly possessions again; but the now Christian King rejected her tardy revocation of his trivial sin — coming at such an unseemly hour — and in proud defiance fought on to the death, dying in happy belief of another God than the dread PELE of KILAUEA !

Thus the cruel deed of conquest is over, and every homestead in the land is bereaved of its master; and the women of all the fair Island will be given as baubles to whomsoever may demand. Only the God in heaven knows how such national crimes are balanced in the ponderous scrolls of Time, or how compensated for in the crystal records of Eternity !

The low rhythmic wailing upon the mountain grew deeper and louder, with this new accession of a nation's woe, multiplying timidly with the approach of twilight gloom, and the oft recurring

---

* The Afterthought, or the Sequel-thought.

mist-like mirage of the many departing souls, hastening skyward to their bourn.

Though the dread day of battling for a kingdom
is over, what horrors are still being perpetrated
by the murderous Guard at the Pali's precipice
above ; and what holocausts of human sacrifices
yet remain to complete the conquest of this fair
Isle of Oahu — where Liberty and Love lie dead,
rather than live to be *enslaved* by the Invader !

The blood-red sun — a true emblem of this day
of slaughter — has already set beyond the far Island of Kauai — the only free land remaining of all
the Eight Isles — where the mailed foot of the
ruthless Conqueror never shall tread, neither he
nor his invincible legions of war, for Pele has said
it, in sorrow and in wrath !

To the sad eyes of the dying warriors on the
mountain side, the sunset now discloses the fair
" Isles of the Blessed," awaiting them in a gorgeous sea of purple and ruby and gold. There the
brave and the noble will tarry in intermediate bliss,
to receive the *visé* to their passports, whether they
be doomed to go down to the dread *Gehena* of the
ungodly, or merit to wing joyously upward, on tire-
less pinions, to the glorious *Ouli* beyond the stars,
where the *Akua nui* awaits the just, and dispenses
His glory to the righteous.

Aside from the frightful groans of the wounded,
and the soft murmur of inarticulate bereavement
that hangs like a funeral pall over the mountain
crags, where the lurking fear of death pervades all

who chance to wail too loudly for dead friends, there now broods a thickly peopled silence over all the land — a tearful, timorous silence, engendered by Oahu's unspeakable woe!

Well may the strong, cool trades of this grievous battle-day now soften down their merry windbugles into the tenderest minstrelsy of sorrow, reverently folding their bronze wings for the night, and hushing their rhythmic cooings among the tutui trees of the mountain, and the drooping palm-fronds along the shore.

As the twilight deepens into darkness throughout the gorge, all visions become sombre, and all sounds grow sad; harmonious accessories awakened by the universal bereavement over the much-loved dead. How strange it is that maternal Nature should thus sadden with our sorrows, assuming a funeral aspect to comport in tenderest sympathy with the momentous achievements of man! How subdued has become the great Ocean surf on the Koolau shore! how tuneful the mountain waterfall!

Now only the coy, soft breezes of a tropic night venture languidly out from Waolani's wooded dells, blowing too lazily to ruffle the feathery bamboo foliage, or jangle the golden bell-flowers on the tall *hau* trees; airs too timorous to fly swiftly, and too sorrowing to sing loudly, while thus dispensing their elegiac perfumes from forest wild-fruits and untutored flowers; coming, like ministering angels from Valhalla, to proffer their floral tributes to the

dying, and scatter their holy incense over the dead.
How broods the weeping Silence and the dusky
Night — twin Niobes — in deepening sorrow over
the dead chiefs and their *homeless* friends! Hush
your timid heart-beats, lest they jar upon the sepulchral air. Awaken eye and ear to their utmost
tension, and watch intuitively for what transpires
around. See you not that this duskiness is not
wholly the encroaching *shadow-dark*, stalking forth
from its accustomed haunts, but rather the rustling
of sepulchral Ghouls and benign Spirits invading
the Pali's dismal gorge!

Look into the sky! Observe how the sorrowing
star-beams are frequently shut out, for one swift
instant, from the gaze! What mystic wing-mo-
tions are these, fanning cold and dank upon the
evening air? Ah! what indeed, but an awful
gathering of the numberless *Unseen*, ever called
forth upon the ghostly missions of the dying!

Noiseless as the bronze-footed *Makani-ao* (trade-
clouds) flit down the benign Spirits from the bending skies, hastening, on wings lighter than thistle-
down, as they bear their messages of peace to whom
peace is due, wherever a dying warrior utters his
righteous call.

Well might the soaring night-eagle wheel on
uneasy wings high above the starlit peaks of Waolani, having scented the battle-blood from afar,
and come to gorge upon the festering dead as his
due; yet now holding aloof from his prey, so awed
by the muffled voices of multitudinous wailing, and
the ghostly incumbents of the Pali!

There are those still living on these sunny Isles of the sea * — though grown wondrous old and gray — who claim to have witnessed with their young eyes, from Waolani, all we have here depicted of this frightful battle, and its awful sequel. Shrivelled old gray-beards, who vouch for having seen the *two cherished Souls* redeemed from their dead clay by the Christian's God — a new Deity in that day — saw their spirits winging heavenward to eternal glory.

It was then that the weeping Pele flashed her volcanic flame angrily from the Mist-cloud, shattering the rocky mountain-top — as we can witness to this day — as she spurned it, and tore away like a thunderbolt through the evening air, swift-winged for Loa's flaming crater.

Be that as it may, we do know there *are* watchful spirits in the Pali, still lingering through all the changeful century, guarding the hallowed spot where fell the brave and died the fair! Whoever wanders here, in rapt communion with these benignant Shades, may invoke sights and scenes — natural and supernatural, visible and invisible — whose weird and witching beauty will henceforth hang its cherished pictures on memory's shrines forever.

Who can stand on the Heights of Abraham and not awaken to new emotions when reading, "Here died Wolf — Victorious!" And who, I ask, can

---

* The first draft of this work was written on the spot, thirty years ago.

stand here in this historic Pali without lifting a floodgate of rapture, whose visions shall sculpture into marble, and limn themselves in tablets of beauty when remembering, Here fell Kalani, who died for his *new* God, and his darling!

Here we leave our KEIKI MOI and his noble Queen, so beautiful even in death! — leave them in the loving hands of Him they found at last; the God who blessed them with an heroic courage and the wisdom to cherish their young affections! — leave them to the mournful requiems that nightly sing their vesper-hymns over the Pali's gorge; piteous, intrusive Spirits, ever wondering with ourselves over a wrong *so* great, where sweet Love and noble Liberty were thus suffered to die!

HOPE, ALOHA MELE.*

Our Tale is done : one brief Adieu!
And friends, we'll mount our steed, and leave you.

Here — in this gorge — the Heroes fell!
   Their ashes strew the craggy Pass;
Where ran their gore adown the dell
   Blooms vigorous the verdant grass.

The flowers wave their leafy plumes,
   Yet weeping hangs each pensive head;
Perpetual, each constant blooms,
   Perennial mourners o'er the dead.

How lovingly their perfumes cling!
   Their fragrant·task is one of love;
From dust of Liberty they spring;
   Who would such sacred buds remove?

Ye Shades of Heroes! forgive these tears,
   My heart your woe — your glory weeps;
I love to trace your hopes and fears;
   Your valor — fond remembrance keeps!

Song-borne I hear your battle-shout!
   Your voices down the distance sound;
Such tones old Time ne'er blotteth out,
   For aye — respond these cliffs around.

At times the Keiki Moi appears,
   And acts the awful past anew;
Down through the Pali's gloom he peers
   And doth his warrior Shades review.

Hark! hear them wing the vast profound!
   Their rustling plumes thrill through the air;
Their whisper'd breathings plaintive sound,
   Anguished with earth's last hours despair!

---

* Final Farewell song; or, final Love song.

www.ingramcontent.com/pod-product-compliance
Lightning Source LLC
Chambersburg PA
CBHW030818110726
47900CB00006B/1655